By day, **Maggie Wells** is bu̶̶̶̶
she pens tales of intrigue
sheets. She has a weakness
endings. She is the product ̶̶̶̶̶̶̶̶̶̶ ̶̶̶̶̶̶̶̶̶̶ ̶̶̶rogue and a
shameless flirt, and you only have to scratch the surface
of this mild-mannered married lady to find a naughty
streak a mile wide.

Amber Leigh Williams is an author, wife, mother of
two and dog mum. She has been writing sexy small-town
romance with memorable characters since 2006. Her
Mills & Boon romance series is set in her charming
hometown of Fairhope, Alabama. She lives on the
Alabama Gulf Coast, where she loves being outdoors
with her family and a good book. Visit her on the web at
amberleighwilliams.com

SHADOWING HER STALKER

MAGGIE WELLS

COLTON'S LAST RESORT

AMBER LEIGH WILLIAMS

MILLS & BOON

First Published in Great Britain 2024
by Mills & Boon, an imprint of HarperCollins*Publishers* Ltd
1 London Bridge Street, London, SE1 9GF

www.harpercollins.co.uk

HarperCollins*Publishers*
Macken House, 39/40 Mayor Street Upper,
Dublin 1, D01 C9W8, Ireland

Special thanks and acknowledgment are given to Amber Leigh Williams for her contribution to *The Coltons of Arizona* series.

ISBN: 978-0-263-39696-6

0125

MIX
Paper | Supporting
responsible forestry
FSC™ C007454

This book contains FSC™ certified paper and other controlled sources to ensure responsible forest management.

For more information visit: www.harpercollins.co.uk/green

Printed and Bound in the UK using 100% Renewable Electricity at CPI Group (UK) Ltd, Croydon, CR0 4YY

SHADOWING HER STALKER

MAGGIE WELLS

To my adopted home state and all the Arkansans who have made me one of their own—even if I still sound like I'm 'not from around here.' Thank you for sharing the beauty of the Natural State with me.

Chapter One

Most of her life Cara Beckett dreamed of being one of those
actors who had to wear a disguise to get through an airport
undetected. Yet, here she was—rich, famous in a way she
never imagined and completely incognito as she walked
through Little Rock's Bill and Hillary Clinton National Airport dressed in soft, faded jeans and a flowing white tunic.

When she booked her flight, it hadn't even registered
she'd be traveling on October 31. She'd been too wrapped
up in thoughts of getting out of California to notice anything
different at LAX. Then, when she changed planes in Dallas,
a woman who was either dressed as a witch or channeling
her inner sorceress sat down across the aisle from her in the
first-class cabin. As the other passengers boarded, she noted
at least three men dressed as a high-profile European soccer
coach, a couple teenagers in full pop star mode and multiple women wearing sweaters or appliquéd sweatshirts with
pumpkin or fall motifs. She'd forgotten all about Halloween.

For the first time in a week, she breathed easy. She was
definitely not in LA anymore.

The young woman working the rental counter was wearing a wedding dress with strategically placed rips and tears
and a smattering of bright red paint Cara supposed was
meant to be blood. Her heart lodged in her throat as she

inched closer to the counter. She was glad the girl didn't know actual blood was darker. Thicker. And definitely didn't smell like craft paint.

One week ago, Cara found out her personal information— full name, address and mobile phone number—had been posted on a forum favored by self-proclaimed tech wizards. Not being a techie herself, she'd never heard of the message board, nor had she thought the breach of privacy would turn out to be a real threat. She'd thought the doxing was puzzling. At first, she was annoyed. She couldn't figure out why anyone would care who she was or where she lived. She wasn't truly a big shot in the tech sector.

But her lack of industry credibility was exactly what angered the people coming after her. And in the last week they'd gone beyond angry to terrifying.

Someone attacked her neighbor Nancy as she walked her dog two nights ago. Nancy had paused to let her Pomeranian, Buster, use the tiny patch of meticulously maintained lawn in front of Cara's Los Feliz property as his toilet, though Cara had expressly asked her not to. Cara found Nancy sprawled on the grass bleeding from stab wounds to her abdomen and side with her ever-faithful Buster barking his head off.

Nancy would recover, thank goodness, but the incident had left Cara shaken. She didn't become truly terrified until detectives looking into the stabbing showed up at Cara's door the night before asking if she had reason to believe someone would wish to harm her. They believed she had been the intended target. According to Nancy's statements to the police, her assailant had called the name "Cara" when he jumped from the passenger seat of a nondescript gray sedan. He'd also repeatedly said, "Breathe in life," while stabbing poor Nancy.

"Now, go out there and breathe in LYYF," was the tagline

Cara said at the end of each lesson or meditation offered by the app she'd helped create.

To some in the tech world, she was an actress who lucked into doing free voice-over work. They believed Chris Sharpe and Tom Wasinski were the geniuses behind LYYF, the lifestyle and social application downloaded on over seven hundred million mobile devices each year. She was simply the face. And the voice. Few would call her the key to the app's success, though the truth was, the business hadn't been going anywhere until she'd stepped in.

At times she wished she never had.

Curling her lips in, she bit down, breathing deep and evenly through her nose. She needed to keep her anxiety at bay for now. In ninety minutes, give or take, she'd be safe at home with her parents. All she had to do was get in a car and drive. Soon she'd be about as far from Los Angeles as a person could be—mentally, if not geographically. Far from a world where people measured every success against their own failures. In a place where internet and cellular service were both still spotty and the residents had more important things to worry about than whether they had Wi-Fi available 24-7.

Ahead of her, a man argued with the rental agent. Apparently the largest vehicle available was a midsize sedan and they'd reserved an SUV. She glanced over and saw a harried woman trying to keep track of three kids under the age of ten. Cara smiled sympathetically. It was clear both mother and father were fighting a losing battle.

When he finally stepped aside, resigned to shoehorning his family into the available Hyundai, she took her place at the counter with a wan smile. Holding up her phone so the agent could scan her reservation, she said, "I'll take whatever you have."

The young woman pulled up the reservation, asked Cara

to answer the rental agreement questions on the tablet mounted to the counter and, with a relieved smile, offered her a map of the area.

Cara waved it away. "No, thank you. I know where I'm headed."

"You can choose whichever car you like from section 104," the agent said as she slipped a printed ticket into a sleeve and wrote "104" across the front in black marker. "Thank you and Happy Halloween."

Cara took the paperwork from her. "Thanks," she replied tiredly.

Making sure her massive leather tote was still riding securely atop her roller bag, she wheeled out of the line. The man behind her stepped up, peering closely at his phone, thumb scrolling frantically. "Hang on," she heard him say to the clerk. "I can't find my reservation email."

Should have used the app, Cara thought as she strode toward the exit.

She spotted a ladies' room and decided to stop. She had a long drive ahead and too much coffee in her system. After washing her hands, she flicked a few drops of cold water at her face in hopes of freshening up. By the time she exited, she saw a brown-haired man dressed in the Midwestern male uniform of khaki pants and a polo shirt making a beeline for section 104. There were only two cars parked there—identical silver subcompacts.

She smiled as he slowed to a halt behind her. "Should we flip a coin?" she asked.

He shook his head, but barely glanced in her direction as he held out a hand. "Ladies first."

"Thanks."

Too worn out to do anything but keep moving, Cara approached the vehicle on the left. Not bothering with the trunk, she stowed her roller bag in the back seat, then tossed her tote into the wheel well on the passenger side. The fob for the ignition was in the cup holder. She put her foot on the brake and pressed the button and the engine purred to life.

She saw the man move to the driver's side of the rental beside hers as she pulled her door shut. Mentally mapping her route out of Little Rock, she was fastening her seat belt when the passenger door opened and the khaki-clad man dropped into the seat beside her.

"Don't scream, no one's around anyhow," he said in a gruff whisper.

Wide-eyed, she stared at the gleaming weapon pointed at her. *Gunmetal gray,* her brain supplied unhelpfully. She looked up to find her new passenger had pulled a safety-orange balaclava down over his head and topped it with a leaf-and-twig-printed cap.

A flash of a long-forgotten trip to the feed store with her father came to mind. Home from California for Thanksgiving, she'd been about the only person in town not dressed in forest browns and bright orange. Her father had cracked himself up musing about how camouflage was never more effective than in the fall in Arkansas.

It was true. Too true.

"What do you want?" She pointed a trembling finger at the tote half-crushed under his feet. "There's cash in my wallet. Take it. Take what you need."

The man gave a derisive snort. "I am taking what I need. Now drive, or I'll shoot you right here."

In the moment, the notion of being left for dead in a subcompact rental parked in section 104 of a nearly deserted parking deck sounded like the worst possible fate. So she shifted into gear, and pulled out of the space.

"Where do you want me to go?"

"Get us out of here," he ordered.

She chanced a glance at her passenger as she pointed the

car toward the exit. No, she hadn't imagined the gun. Or the khakis. Or the polo shirt. But even if she could describe them down to the weave of the cotton of his shirt, the police would still be looking for a needle in a haystack.

There was absolutely nothing notable about the man beside her.

Cara eased out of the parking deck and into the lane leading to the airport exit. There'd be a gate to clear. Someone would see them. She'd be able to get help.

Consoling herself with the knowledge they were in a well-populated area, she headed for the parking attendant. But as they rolled to a stop behind another car, she saw none of the white booths with their sliding glass windows were manned.

To her horror, she saw the velvet-cloaked arm of the wizard family patriarch wave his rental agreement at a scanner attached to the side of the booth. The electronic gate lifted, and the overstuffed sedan rolled away.

When Cara pulled up to the booth, she gazed up into its emptiness in bewilderment. The man beside her bumped her elbow. She jumped and looked down. Had he nudged her with the gun? No. His hand. He shoved the rental envelope she'd tucked into her tote at her.

"Stop messing around," he growled.

She blinked back a hot rush of frustrated tears as she took the sleeve bearing the printed barcode and held it up to the scanner.

The barrier lifted, but she couldn't seem to take her foot off the brake.

"Drive," her abductor ordered.

"Drive where?"

He turned in his seat to square up with her, the gun clutched in his right hand. "Go. Now."

He uttered the commands through clenched teeth, and Cara's brain engaged. She hit the gas and the small car lurched forward, engine revving. The road leading away from the single-terminal airport was nearly deserted. As she approached the entrance to the major arteries surrounding the capital city, she instinctively lifted her foot from the gas.

"Take the ramp," he ordered.

She put on her signal, but took the right turn at a high rate of speed. Cara chanced a glance at her passenger. He gripped the console between the seats to keep his equilibrium, but kept his weapon pointed in her direction.

The bypass ended a few miles from the airport, one lane leading to downtown Little Rock and Interstate 40. She gravitated toward it, intent on following the route to her parents' ranch in a snug valley of the Ozark Mountains, but the man beside her had a different plan.

"Stay in the middle lane," he instructed.

"But—" she began to protest.

"Middle lane," he repeated, cutting her off as an eighteen-wheeler forced its way out of the merge lane, neatly boxing her in.

She followed the flow of traffic onto Interstate 30 South. The other lane circled the south side of the city on its way to Texas. Cara's mind raced across the miles ahead. She wasn't overly familiar with the southwest corner of the state. She'd never been to Texarkana or any of the other towns between Little Rock and Dallas. And the only times she'd been to Dallas, she'd flown.

"Where are we going?" she asked, speaking only to fill the silence. Perhaps, if she got him talking—

"We're going to drive until I tell you to stop."

She gripped the steering wheel tighter, her knuckles glowing white against her skin. "You can take the car. I don't care," she offered. "Take it."

"I am," he said, a note of smug amusement in his tone. "And I'm taking you with it."

His insouciance annoyed her, but she kept her eyes glued to the traffic ahead of her. The last thing she needed was to tick off the man with the gun. Traffic was light as they raced past the small bedroom communities flanking the highway on the other side of the county line.

They flew past strip malls and chain restaurants, budget hotels and car dealerships. Logic told her the thriving commercial areas denoted miles of civilization beyond. They were driving through what passed for urban sprawl in a sparsely populated state. But it wouldn't last long. Soon, there wouldn't be anything but large tracts of forest dotted with tiny towns. Sleepy, slightly run-down communities with a post office, possibly a diner or barbecue joint and, if they were lucky, a gas station.

Sure enough, shopping centers gave way to a few edge-of-town motels. A billboard advertised a travel plaza at the next exit. Green highway signs listed the mileage to Hot Springs, Arkadelphia and Texarkana.

As the highway narrowed to two lanes in each direction, Cara forced herself to take three deep, deliberate breaths, counting in her head as she cycled through each one.

"There you go, breathe in life," the man beside her said, his voice faintly mocking.

Cara's blood ran ice-cold.

Breathe in life. Breathe in LYYF. She'd ended every recording she'd ever done for the LYYF app with those soothing words.

Now they terrified her.

The guy who'd pointed a gun at her in an airport parking deck had twisted them. Taunted her with words meant to reassure. He knew who she was. This wasn't some random carjacking. Had he been waiting for her. Why? This could not be happening.

Clutching the steering wheel, she turned to look at him, wide-eyed. "What did you say?"

"You heard me," he answered, waving her disbelief away.

"You know who I am?"

She cringed as the words came out of her mouth, but her brain was blown and she wasn't feeling up to playing cat and mouse. What was the use when the cat was holding her at gunpoint.

"Do you buy into all the woo-woo meditation stuff, or do you do it because they pay you to say it?"

He sat there pointing a gun at her and he expected her to answer questions about her job?

She clenched her jaw as one of the three semis boxing her in decided he wanted to work his way into the right lane. She slowed to avoid being clipped as the big rig edged over. A sign advertising a gas station with a fast-food franchise flashed past her window. The truck ahead of her slowed. Cara looked to her right and spotted the brightly lit station.

The driver ahead of her sped up as they approached the ramp. Cara accelerated too, but when she checked her mirror, she saw the semi on her rear bumper was signaling his intent to exit.

They were almost past the ramp when Cara jerked the wheel hard to the right, throwing her passenger against the door.

The tires kicked up loose gravel from the shoulder.

The man beside her cursed a blue streak.

The driver behind them indicated his displeasure by blowing his horn at her.

A trailer hauling wood chips sat stationary at the bottom of the ramp, right turn signal flashing. Cross traffic on the county road at the bottom of the ramp did not let up.

"What do you think you're doing?" the man holding the gun yelled, reaching across to grab the steering wheel.

Cara jammed on the brakes, her arms locked against the steering wheel to counteract the laws of physics. Her passenger boomeranged into the dash. Behind them, brakes screamed in protest and the driver laid on his horn.

The moment they jerked to a halt, she thrust the gearshift into Park, popped the latch on her seat belt and rolled out the driver's door onto the gritty berm.

The man shouted, but she didn't look back.

She ran.

Cara ran flat out, streaking down along the side of the trailer filled with fragrant wood shavings. Oblivious to the drama playing out behind him, the driver let off his brakes enough to make the hydraulics sigh with anticipation. Cara skidded into the ditch running alongside the ramp, thanking the stars above she'd had sense enough to wear sneakers for the plane ride.

She watched as the truck crept forward a few feet, then jerked to a stop again. Glancing behind her, she saw a battered pickup hurtling down the county road. She heard another shout, followed by a terrifying pop.

Cara didn't wait for the man to get a second round off. Using the pickup as cover, she darted across the ramp in front of the semi, praying the driver wasn't tempted to inch any farther into the intersection.

Breathless, she slid down the slope on the other side of the ramp. Peeking over tall grass, she saw her passenger sliding behind the wheel.

Flattening herself in the damp grass, she held her breath as she heard the rev of engines. Another blast of impatient honking told her the driver stuck behind her abandoned rental had had enough shenanigans for one day. Seconds later, she heard the rumble and sigh of air brakes again.

Cara raised her head enough to peer over the edge of the culvert. Beyond the beams of a tractor hauling a flatbed filled with spooled steel, she saw the taillights of a silver subcompact flash as it sped up the entrance ramp on the opposite side of the country road.

He was taking off without her.

Relief pulsed through her veins.

He was gone.

Panting, Cara lowered her head to rest on the backs of her trembling hands. Cold dampness seeped into the knees of her jeans. Her palms throbbed. She had no doubt she'd find them speckled with glass and gravel from her dive for safety, but she didn't care.

He was gone.

She was alive.

She was safe.

"Breathe in life," she murmured. And she did. She drank in the cool, damp air until her lungs were full to bursting, and held it there.

Then, a pair of battered boots tramped down the grass right in front of her. Every oxygen molecule she'd ingested exploded out of her when a man spoke.

"Do you have some kind of death wish or something, lady?"

Chapter Two

Wyatt Dawson didn't mind working late. Truthfully, he preferred the office after hours. Because they were a small team, most of the members of the cybercrime division took work home with them, but he liked the time in the office alone. He wasn't antisocial, though some would say he was; it was more that he liked the idea of keeping his work at work.

And he was so close to zeroing in on a solid lead.

Sitting at his desk with his feet up, he was scanning lines of data, looking for the IP address needed to confirm his suspicions. If he could connect the dots, all the extra hours would pay off. The spot on the multiagency task force investigating the sale and movement of illegally produced distilled spirits through northwest Arkansas would be his. He was close. He could taste it. So close he was tempted to ignore the ringing desk phone.

But he couldn't. The cybercrime division was still in its infancy. He and his tiny group of talented colleagues were on a mission to prove their worth to the Department of Public Safety. And because they were worthy, he would take the call. Even though it was after hours.

Even though it meant shifting mental gears at the precise moment he needed them locked on target.

He frowned as the desk phone continued to pester him.

The short two-tone ring indicated an intraoffice phone call. The last thing he needed was for someone on the inside to insinuate they weren't pulling their weight. Dropping his feet to the floor, he reached for the receiver of the desk phone and wedged it between his ear and shoulder.

"CCD, Dawson here," he said as he typed a note into his spreadsheet to mark where he'd left off.

"Agent Dawson? This is Trooper Chad Masterson," the caller said with brisk efficiency. "I have a sort of unusual circumstance unfolding here, and I'm wondering if you might be able to help me."

Wyatt shook his mouse to keep the computer from transitioning into sleep mode then sat up straighter in his chair and took hold of the receiver. "Happy to. How can I help?"

"Have you ever heard of a woman called Cara Beckett?" the trooper asked.

Scowling, Wyatt picked up a pen and jotted the name on a pad of sticky notes he kept beside the phone. The name did ring a bell, but he found the man's coy approach annoying. He wasn't a big fan of fishing expeditions whether they employed a line and hook, or clumsily delivered yes or no questions.

"I'm gonna need a little more than a name," he informed his colleague.

"Cara Beckett," the trooper repeated. "Says she works for a company called LYYF. Spelled with two *Y*'s. *L-Y-Y-F*." Masterson was unable to mask the disdain in his voice as he spelled out the company name. "I believe it's some kind of phone application."

Wyatt sighed. The number of electronic troglodytes he encountered within the ranks of law enforcement never failed to amaze him. Sure, they were all for DNA matches and advanced ballistics, but tie a computer, tablet or smartphone to a crime and they bragged about how they were still using

AOL as their email provider. Or pretended they hadn't heard of one of the tech world's biggest sensations.

"Yes, I'm familiar with the application," he said briskly.

Truthfully, he was more than familiar. He was a daily user. He reached for his own phone and swiped through a couple of screens, stopping when he spotted the bright orange icon with the stylized *L* at its center. The home page loaded and he stared at the photo of a woman seated in the lotus position, her eyes closed and her lips curved into a serene smile.

All the puzzle pieces fell into place.

"Cara Beckett is one of the founding partners of LYYF. It's a lifestyle and wellness application." He tapped his pen on the desk a couple of times then opened the app, anxious to put the name and face together. "You probably have it on your phone too," he informed Trooper Masterson. "Our health insurance provider gave everybody a free subscription to the service for a year as part of our benefits package a couple years ago."

"Hmm, I'm not familiar," Masterson said, unable to mask the hint of derision in his tone. "I'll have to ask my wife if she tried it. She likes all those lifestyle things." He guffawed. "I pay for the whole dang cable package, but all she ever watches is the home-makeover channel. If I come home to one more set of paint swatches I'm going to spit."

Wyatt clenched his jaw. He had to take one of the calming breaths he learned from using LYYF before posing the obvious question. "Why are you asking me about Cara Beckett?"

"From what I gather, she's some kind of celebrity."

Wyatt frowned at the descriptor. Celebrity? Maybe in some circles, but not in the way Masterson would recognize.

"Not a Hollywood celebrity, but in other circles, yeah, maybe," he conceded. "Again, why do you ask?"

"Because I got her sitting in an office down here. A

trucker said she practically leaped out of a moving vehicle to get away from the guy she was ridin' with.'"

"Leaped out of a moving car?"

"Says she was abducted. Man with a gun jacked her rental car at the airport. The woman is pretty shaken up. No purse or phone or ID of any kind. No money. The guy who found her took her up to the truck stop and waited with her until a patrolman arrived. They brought her back here and dropped her at my desk, but I'm not quite sure what to make of her story."

"Is there a reason why you don't believe her story?" Wyatt asked.

"No particular reason," Masterson replied cautiously. "It's not something that happens around here very often."

"Oh, I'd say we see our fair share of carjackings." Wyatt himself had a friend who was lured from her car at a fast-food restaurant and left standing by as her vehicle sped away. She'd been one of the lucky ones.

"She keeps talking about somebody docking her and I'm not sure what she means." Wyatt could hear the guy scratching his head. "She seems to think there's some connection between the docking and what happened to her today. Keeps saying it can't be a coincidence."

"Docking?" Wyatt scowled as he watched the progress bar at the bottom of his screen creep toward completion. He glanced down at the name he'd scrawled on the sticky note, then zeroed in on the blinking cursor as if it might give up the answer to what was nagging him.

"What is Cara Beckett doing in Arkansas?" he whispered, talking to himself.

But Masterson answered. "Says she's from here. Folks own a place up in Searcy County. Ranchers."

"Searcy County? That's north, isn't it? They were heading south," Wyatt noted.

"I don't think this guy with the gun was hoping to meet the folks," Masterson said dryly.

Wyatt turned the information he'd been given over in his head. "Docking? I don't know what she means."

"Makes two of us. I tried to get a better answer out of her but she kept goin' on about her home address and phone number being leaked and someone called Nancy gettin' attacked outside her house. Frankly, she's a bit...overwrought," Masterson drawled.

Wyatt sat up straighter partly because he was annoyed by the trooper's supercilious attitude but mostly because he was catching on to exactly what Cara Beckett was trying to tell them.

"Do you mean doxing?" he demanded, his tone sharp.

"Excuse me?"

"Doxing." But saying the word louder didn't help it penetrate the trooper's skull. "Doxing is when somebody on the internet, usually a hacker or some kind of troll, unearths someone's personal information and publishes it for the world to see."

He paused to let the explanation sink in, but Trooper Masterson remained quiet.

"It's slang for dropping the documents on someone."

"But why? Who is she?"

"She's a partner in a tech company."

"So shouldn't she be able to stop this, uh, doxing thing?"

Wyatt rolled his eyes at the man's naivete. "Picture some internet users as a pack of rabid dogs. There are always a few who will chase after a person at the slightest provocation."

"You think this Cara Beckett person provoked this threat against her?"

"I'm not saying anything of the sort. She could simply be guilty of nothing more than breathing oxygen on a daily basis. It doesn't take much to get a few disgruntled users to go after a high profile target."

"You think her profile is high enough people would, uh, dox her? Kidnap her?" The other man sounded dubious. "I've never even heard of her."

"You follow tech trends pretty closely, Masterson?"

"I know who Jeff Bezos and Elon Musk are," he countered.

"Congratulations," Wyatt said dryly. "Listen, the lady you have sitting in an office down there might not be Bezos or Musk, but she's far wealthier than you or I can ever dream of being." He thought back to the article he'd read about the masterminds behind LYYF. "They're about to take the company public. Soon Cara Beckett's net worth will be stratospheric."

"She doesn't look like a millionaire right now," Masterson grumbled.

"Billionaire," Wyatt interjected.

"She's wearin' jeans and a plain white shirt. All muddy and stuff from rolling in the ditch. And the trucker gave her twenty dollars because she didn't have any walking-around money." Masterson added the last bit as if it was conclusive evidence against Wyatt's claims. "She's down here right now making some calls to see if she can round up a hotel or place to stay the night using a police report as ID."

Wyatt swiped at his cell until his internet browser popped up. A quick query yielded the article he had read a few days before. In it, a slim smiling young woman with chic, close-cropped blond hair and wide blue eyes beamed out at him. She stood a half step in front of the men she claimed were her two best friends from college.

There were plenty of people who thought an out-of-work actress didn't deserve the 33-percent partnership the creators of LYYF offered her in exchange for voice-over work when they were prestart-up. But they made a deal, and Cara Beckett become the voice and later, when their popular video sessions were added, the face of LYYF.

The trolls and tech bros liked to grumble about the equal partnership Chris Sharpe and Tom Wasinski had traded for her services at the beginning of their venture. But no one could deny Cara Beckett was as much a part of LYYF's success as their clever coding and attractive graphics. No amount of superior interface could have made the app a phenomenon. Her face and voice were key. As was her willingness to step out from behind the curtain and become the public spokesperson her collaborators never wanted to be.

He scrolled through the profile he'd skimmed the week before. In the article, her cofounders weren't shy about giving her the respect she deserved. Without Cara Beckett's easy, open smile and welcoming demeanor, the application wouldn't have been half the hit it was.

Glancing back at the desk phone, he noted the extension Masterson was using and rose from his chair. "Hang tight. I'll be there in a few minutes to talk to her. If even a little bit of what you say she says happened to her is true, at best we're dealing with the situation straddling multiple jurisdictions."

"And worst-case scenario?"

"The media finds out," Wyatt said grimly.

"Exactly what I'm afraid of." Masterson heaved a sigh. "Come on down. She's got nowhere else to go and no way to get there anyhow."

MASTERSON WAS EVERYTHING Wyatt expected from their conversation. Tall and not quite barrel-chested, he wore his dark hair in a high and tight buzz cut. As he drew closer and the two shook hands, Wyatt could see short strands of silver intensified the effect of the trooper's white-walled haircut. Deep creases furrowed the man's brow, and squint lines radiated from cool blue eyes. Wyatt couldn't blame the man for his natural skepticism. No doubt, the man had seen some strange things in his years of service.

Cara Beckett sat in one of the small offices on the perimeter of the bullpen. The door was closed, but the miniblinds covering the office window were drawn up. She looked different in person. It wasn't the grass-stained clothes or the smudge of mud dried on her jawline. Her hair looked softer. It was an inch or two longer than in the photos on the app, and the color was more a honey gold than beachy white-blond streaks.

She looked tired. Small. And though he knew from her yoga videos she was strong and almost rubber-band flexible, under the fluorescent lights of the Arkansas State Police Headquarters, she came across as almost unspeakably fragile.

"Have you gotten anything more from her?" Wyatt asked.

Masterson shook his head. "She just got off the phone."

Wyatt nodded, then gestured to the door. "Do you mind if I have a chat?"

Sweeping an arm toward the door, Masterson said, "Have at it. I have a call in to the rental company to try to get the information on the stolen vehicle."

With a nod, Wyatt started for the office door. He gave it a couple raps with the knuckle of his index finger, then cracked it open. Cara Beckett looked up with wide, frightened eyes.

He kept the opening to little more than a crack, but made sure to smile to show her he meant no harm. "Hello. Ms. Beckett?" She nodded, but he made no move to enter the small office. "I'm Special Agent Wyatt Dawson. I'm a member of our cybercrimes division. Trooper Masterson called me. May I speak with you for a few minutes?"

She eyed him warily. "Cybercrimes division? They have one of those here?"

He pushed the door open a few inches more, and allowed his smile to widen as well. "Anywhere the internet goes, so go the scammers."

"And the trolls," she said, bitterness edging her tone. "And the out-and-out criminals."

"May I come in?" He pointed to the chair opposite the small desk where she'd sat to use the telephone.

She inclined her head, and he caught the light bounce off the diamond studs she wore in her ears. They weren't ostentatious, but were certainly more than mere chips. As he settled in the chair he took in the gold bangles on her wrist. A delicate chain holding a pendant with a large multicolored stone encircled her throat. She wore rings on multiple fingers and one thumb, but the third finger on her left hand was bare. He filed the information away as he leaned back in the chair, assuming a pose more in line with casual conversation than interrogation.

"You don't believe the man who abducted you intended to rob you." He made it a statement, knowing it would draw more of an answer from her than a question.

She shook her head. "No. I offered him my wallet, the car, anything he wanted. He said he wanted me."

Wyatt pursed his lips, letting the words hang in the air for a minute as he formulated his next question. But before he could ask it, she shook her head.

"No, not wanted. Needed. I told him to take what he needed, and he said he was, then ordered me to drive."

Nodding, Wyatt resisted the urge to lean forward in his chair. He didn't want to come across as aggressive. He wanted her comfortable enough to tell her story her way. To remember things as they actually happened without framing them through the lens of hindsight.

"He wasn't familiar to you at all." Again, a statement, not a question.

"It's been a long time since I've lived in Arkansas, Special Agent Daw—"

"Wyatt," he interrupted.

"Wyatt," she repeated with a nod, a small smile tugging at the corners of her mouth.

"Something funny," he asked.

"I don't run into too many Wyatts in LA."

He smirked. "Maybe not." Since she felt comfortable enough to mock him, he leaned forward, planting his elbows on his knees and clasping his hands. "May I call you Cara?"

"Yes."

"Cara, tell me about the doxing incident," he said, driving straight to his main point of interest. "Do you know what precipitated it? What fallout have you experienced? Did you feel you were in danger in California?"

She gaped at him for a moment, seemingly stunned by the abrupt shift in conversation. "I, uh, I don't know why," she managed to stammer. "I mean, there have always been, um, detractors, but no. I have no idea why someone decided to make my personal information public. And I don't know why anyone would be interested. I'm not a celebrity or anything." She opened her hands in a helpless shrug. "I'm not even an influencer."

Wyatt huffed, charmed by her naive assessment of her standing in the virtual community. "Aren't you?"

He pulled out his own phone and woke the screen. The welcome page of the LYYF app appeared, and front and center was a close-up video of Cara asking, "Are you ready to get the most from your LYYF?"

She didn't respond, but her expression hardened. "As for fallout. My address and phone were posted on a number of message boards. If you're at all familiar with the internet, you know there are some users who aren't always pleasant."

"Harassment?"

She nodded. "Mostly in-app and social media messages at first, but then they hacked my company email and things spiraled even more from there. The LAPD have been on the case. I can give you the information of the..." She paused, grimaced, then shook her head. "I had contact information in my phone, but now—"

Her phone was gone.

He watched her swallow hard and hoped she was gulping down her fear. It was hard to outrun internet harassment. Life outside of the app would be better if she gathered her resolve and found a way to stand her ground. Then again, the woman had jumped out of a car in the middle of nowhere when a man was holding a gun on her. If knowing when to bail wasn't the biggest part of taking control of one's life, he didn't know what was.

"You've never seen the man who abducted you?" he asked, shifting into lightning-round mode.

"No."

"Did he mention LYYF, or give any indication he knew who you were?"

She started to shake her head, then stopped. "Not directly. He only said the part about taking what he needed then ordered me to drive."

"But you believe the implication was you were what he was after," he concluded.

"Yes."

Wyatt nodded, then pressed on. "Did he make any sexual advances? Insinuations? Touch you in any way construed as intimate?"

"No. He didn't touch me at all." She let out a whoosh of breath. "No. Nothing, uh, sexual."

"So let's assume for now robbery and sexual assault weren't his motive." He sat up straight in the chair again, holding her gaze. "If he wasn't someone you knew or recognized, we might also shelve personal agenda."

"Personal agenda?"

"Old boyfriend, spurned lover, the guy who wanted to take you to the homecoming dance but never worked up the nerve to ask you," he said with an offhanded wave. "You tick anyone off on the plane?"

The question coaxed a short huff of a laugh out of her. "I don't think I talked to anyone."

"Hog the armrest?"

She shook her head. "Dozed most of the way here. I haven't been sleeping well."

"Who knew you were coming to Arkansas?"

She shook her head. "My assistant. I think she told my partners. The neighbor who shares my cat."

Lifting a brow, he asked, "You share a cat?"

"She's a stray. Huge commitment issues. The McNeils and I both feed her. Why settle, right?"

He gave her a wry smile. "Smart cat." Nodding to the desk phone, he asked, "Did you call your folks?"

She shook her head, but when she spoke her voice was barely more than a whisper. "No."

"No?"

She raised one shoulder in a shrug, and the ruined white shirt she wore nearly slid off her shoulder. She wore some sort of spaghetti strap tank top thing under it. Her skin was tanned to a shade lighter than a golden glow. He wondered if the color came from the sun or a booth. Or maybe she had one of those spray-on jobs done. Either way, it was definitely more California tan than the blistering burns the Arkansas sun doled out.

She tipped her chin up. "My parents didn't know I was coming. And now... I don't want my mom to worry."

Wyatt sensed there was more to the story there, but he didn't press. Shifting gears, he hooked an arm over the back of the chair. "There are some nice hotels downtown. New ones, or you could go with a classic and stay at the Capital Hotel." He bit the inside of his cheek. "Were you able to contact anyone who can help?"

She nodded. "Trooper Masterson let me call my assistant, Zarah. Thank goodness she had contact information on her website. She's having a phone delivered from the TechMobile store and overnighting my passport, so I have official ID, and a credit card. I have a copy of my driver's license in cloud storage as well. I assume I can use it along with the police report, if needed." He nodded and she went on. "She also rented a condo here in town for a couple of nights. I'll get a rideshare from here once I get the phone and pick up a new rental tomorrow."

Wyatt pressed his lips together to keep from letting out a low whistle. "She sounds very efficient." It never ceased to amaze him how money could pave right over the biggest potholes in life. Still, he wasn't sure she'd thought her plan through. "Did she set the phone up from your previous account?"

Cara blinked twice. "I assume so. Why?"

He did his best to hide his grimace. With a single-word question, she'd proved the tech bros right about her lack of technological savvy. "You said you've been receiving messages from strangers either through apps or email?"

"Yes."

"Texts as well?"

"Yes."

Her eyes widened as she turned toward the window. Trooper Masterson approached the office, his expression sour as he raised his hand for them to see. A plastic bag imprinted with the TechMobile logo dangled from the tip of his index finger. The man was clearly peeved to be reduced to the role of delivery boy.

Wyatt stood and opened the door. "Thank you," he said as he relieved the older man of the parcel. "If you want to finish up with Ms. Beckett's statement, I'll get this set up for her to use."

"You don't need—" she started to say as she rose from the chair, but she stopped when Wyatt looked over to her for permission to pull the familiar box from the bag. She nodded her assent.

"I'm happy to set this up to forward any communications coming in to your number to a dummy we'll set up here. Once I'm finished, I'll talk you through how best to use it without giving too much information about your location away," he interrupted. "Then, if you'd like, I can drop you off at your rental." When she seemed taken aback by the offer, he rushed to put her at ease. "Or we can get a patrol car to take you. Rideshare apps rely on cellular signals and GPS to triangulate location. We want to avoid anyone getting a read on where you are if we can."

"You think someone will use my phone to track me?" She appeared both incredulous and horrified by the notion.

"It's the fastest way. With all the apps we rely on and location-based services, we make it too easy," Wyatt said with a grim scowl. "But I can help you. Let me help you."

Cara Beckett scooted out from behind the desk to join Trooper Masterson in the doorway. She eyed the uniformed man for a long moment, then turned to Wyatt, taking in his flat-front khakis and checked button-down shirt.

"Thank you," she said quietly, then slipped past the trooper to head back to his desk.

Wyatt and Masterson exchanged a nod-shrug combo before the older man turned away.

The second they were gone, he unboxed the phone and powered it up. The greeting screen appeared, and a smirk twisted his lips as he zipped through the multistep setup, denying the palm-sized supercomputer access to any of Cara Beckett's information. As he continued to delete applications, deny access and ignore dire warnings, he murmured a steady stream of mumbles. "No. Nope. Bye now. Can't accept. Decline. Nope. Nuh-uh," he muttered to himself.

Once he'd pared the smartphone down to its minimal functions, he sat back, satisfied with his work. Reaching for his own phone, he dialed the number displayed in the settings. Cara's phone sprang to life. He declined the call, then saved his contact information in her empty contact list.

He'd have to go over a list of dos, don'ts, and never-evers with her. Surely she'd see the reasoning behind it all. She had to. He'd make her see. Somehow, he had to make Cara Beckett understand if she wanted to get her life back, she'd have to do so without the help of the LYYF app in the short term.

Chapter Three

Cara sat on the rock-hard sofa of the condo Zarah had secured for her and stared down at the phone Special Agent Wyatt Dawson had programmed for her. She couldn't recall the last time she'd held a device set up to have so little function in the modern world. Cara took him up on his offer to drive her to the short-term rental. She was still reeling from the events of the day and found she was more than willing to let someone else take over.

As if defying the man with the gun and taking a leap toward freedom had depleted all her decision-making capabilities.

Agent Dawson, Wyatt, had insisted on walking her to the door. He actually groaned when he spotted the bags waiting for her on the unit's welcome mat. "Who is this Zarah person?" he'd asked as he helped her carry the haul inside.

"Zarah Parvich is my assistant. Virtual assistant. She works out of her home in the San Fernando Valley."

"She's definitely on the ball."

"I'd be lost without her."

Wyatt set the bags on the condo's kitchen island, then launched into a lengthy spiel on smartphone safety. Then he proceeded to check and double-check the settings on her new device. By the time he was finished, she was looking at a phone she could only use as, well, a phone.

"I programmed my number in as well as the numbers for Masterson and the CCD extension," he said as she continued to stare at the unadorned wallpaper on the screen. "I've also set it to decline any unknown callers. I'd recommend you refrain from adding more contacts. Any call coming to this new number will go straight to voicemail."

No apps. No email. No turning the cellular signal on unless she intended to make a call, and then she was to remember to switch it off the minute she hung up. She had a new phone number, one she'd have to use to call Zarah and communicate verbally if she was getting the gist of Agent Dawson's instructions.

"Assume everything is compromised," he told her. "For the time being, write things down."

He gestured to the spiral-bound notebook Zarah had shipped with the bags of food, toiletries and a wardrobe of leggings, T-shirts and zippered hoodies. Zarah knew Cara well enough to include a journal. Cara was a big fan of journaling and often encouraged others to dump their concerns onto the page.

She tried not to think about the notebook tucked into her carry-on bag. All her innermost thoughts and worries were riding around with a kidnapper. Possibly fodder for ongoing stalking.

"Do you think it would be okay to connect to the Wi-Fi here?" Wyatt nodded slowly, and Cara could practically feel the tug of his reluctance. "What?"

"I downloaded a more secure browser. It's the one with the fireball icon. Use it instead of the default." He went on, rambling about how Wi-Fi connections in public spaces where log-in was not required would be best from a security standpoint. He mentioned fast-food restaurants, coffee shops or stores, but cautioned her against attempting to log into any of her social media accounts. "Oh, and be sure to clear your cache when you're done."

She nodded. "Thank you. I will."

Wyatt clapped his hands together, then rubbed his palms. "Okay, then. You'll be all right here?"

His obvious reluctance to leave her alone in this strange place touched her. "I will be."

He walked to the window and peered down into the complex's parking area. "It's a weeknight, so there shouldn't be much trouble."

"I'll call if there are any issues." Wyatt scraped his palms down his pants as he turned back. He looked…nervous. "Is there something you're not telling me?"

"Nothing. Uh—" he flashed a weak smile "—I, um, I wanted to say… You should know…"

When he petered out without actually saying a damn thing, she set the stripped-down phone aside and rose to her feet. "I should know what?"

He shook his head, holding up his hands in futile surrender. "Nothing bad. I was only… I use your app."

The words came out in such a rush it took Cara a moment to process them. "Wha— Oh. Oh… You do?"

"Yes." He wet his lips, then gave a vigorous nod. "Actually, I know a few people who do. They made a free trial part of our healthcare package a couple years ago, and well, I'm a fan." He tossed the last off with a dismissive little laugh. "Ponied up for my own subscription."

But Cara wasn't inclined to dismiss anyone who appreciated her work. "Wow. I'm flattered. And so gratified you find it helpful."

"Very helpful."

She wanted to ask what he liked best. Wanted to know if he was in it for the finance or life coaching, like most men claimed, or if he stuck around because he found some benefit in the wellness practices. Or had he—as the fouler emails and messages she'd received implied—found a more prurient solace while watching her videos or listening to her voice?

She didn't want to know.

Not only was he a competent, attractive man who looked good in his buttoned-up clothes, but also because, like the truck driver who'd coaxed her out of the ditch and made sure she was delivered into safe hands, Wyatt Dawson seemed inherently decent. He didn't seem to be infected with the sort of Southern-fried misogyny Trooper Masterson and so many of the young men she'd known growing up were steeped in. He hadn't once condescended to her, or made her feel like a nuisance. Quite the opposite. He was warm, easygoing and seemingly determined to put her mind at ease.

Fixing her most serene smile in place, she rose and offered him her hand to shake. "Thank you… Wyatt. I appreciate both your diligence and your kind words."

He bobbed his head, then backed away. "I'll get out of your hair. If I hear anything, I'll call."

"Thank you again," she said.

He stepped into the hall, but made no move toward the building's entrance.

"Is there something else?" she asked.

He didn't bother to hide his sheepish smile. "I guess I don't need to remind you to lock up."

"No, but you can stand there and listen as I do." She flashed a quick, shaky smile. "Good night, Special Agent Dawson."

He inclined his head and mimicked touching the brim of a hat. "Good night, Ms. Beckett."

She closed the heavy door between them, then made a racket of engaging the locks before moving to the electronic alarm panel. It was set up differently from the one at her home, so she took a moment to scan the printed instructions the unit's owner had framed beside it.

"Don't forget there's an alarm," he called from the other side of the door.

"I'm doing it now," she called back. "Jeez. Give a person a minute."

"Sorry."

The buttons beeped and she pressed them in the preset sequence. Three short bleats signaled her success. She glanced down to where a slit of light from the hall crept into the unit. She could see his shadow.

Cara was about to call out to him. She wanted to chastise him for hovering, but his presence was disturbingly comforting. A childish part of her wanted to chase him off for that reason alone. She could accuse him of acting like a creeper. Say he was—

"Good night." His voice seeped through the door, quiet, calm and deep. "Try to rest tonight. Tomorrow is as good a day as any to start fresh."

She listened to his footsteps as he walked down the hall. The outer door latched with a loud *ka-thunk*. Stepping back into the unit, Cara placed her hands on her hips and let her head fall forward. She drew two breaths before releasing her hands and shaking her arms until they went noodle limp.

Once she'd released some of the tension in her neck and shoulders, she made her way into the small galley-style kitchen to sort through the bags Zarah had had delivered. As she unpacked each item, she made herself pause for a moment of gratitude.

She was alive.

She was well.

She had everything she needed.

Cara truly believed her life was better than a fairy tale. She got to build a company from the ground up with her two best friends at her side. Every day, she got to do work she loved. She brought people comfort in times of anxiety and solace in moments of sadness, and helped them find peace in the beats between each breath.

On the day Chris and Tom asked her to do the voice-over work on the new application they'd created as part of their final project before graduation, she'd planned to audition for a shampoo commercial. But they were desperate, and she didn't want to let them down. She'd been so naive when they met in their freshman dormitory at the University of California, Los Angeles. Like thousands of other transplants, she planned to be a star. Chris and Tom wanted to be the next Jobs and Wozniak.

They'd been the first friends she'd made in California, and for a lonesome girl from a small town in Arkansas, their friendship meant more than the possibility of commercial residuals.

She reached into another bag and her hand closed around a tube. She pulled it out and saw Zarah had thought to buy her favorite brand of deodorant. Tears filled her eyes as she offered up heartfelt gratitude for her young assistant.

Cara knew she had people who loved and supported her. People who knew her and understood her better than her own family.

Her folks thought the whole acting thing was a phase. They didn't mind her going out to California for college because she'd sailed out on a flotilla of scholarships and financial aid programs. Cara knew they had not so secretly hoped when she got out to LA and realized how mercurial Hollywood could be, she'd settle into a more practical degree program. They hadn't counted on her loving every bit of the hustle and grind.

They never imagined she wouldn't come home and take over the land three generations of Becketts had toiled over. A sharp pang of guilt twanged through her as she glanced over at the phone she'd abandoned on the coffee table. Should she call them? Maybe not get into the details of what happened, but let them know she was coming to stay for a little while?

Her heart rate ramped up at the very thought, but the next thing she knew, she was palming the phone. Her thumb hovered over the keypad as she checked the time. They'd be getting ready for bed. Things had been strained between her and her parents for so long. They weren't estranged, exactly, but her refusal to come home after graduation had cracked the foundation of their relationship.

Biting her lip, she punched out a 424 area code rather than the 870 attached to the landline her parents insisted on keeping.

Zarah picked up on the second ring. "Hello?"

"It's me," Cara informed her.

Her assistant let out a long breath. "Are you okay?"

"Yes. Yes, I'm fine." Cara nodded, even though she knew the younger woman couldn't see her. Maybe she was trying to reassure herself.

"Did you get the stuff I ordered? Is the place okay?" the younger woman asked, breathless. "I can't believe this happened to you. In Arkansas! I mean, I expect to hear about bad stuff out here, but I didn't know you had anything more than, uh, farmland in Arkansas."

"You're not far off. Actually, rice is the biggest crop here," Cara said, doodling the words "rice is nice" on the first page of her new notebook.

Zarah's spongelike ability to absorb random bits of information was one of her most charming quirks. The quickest way to talk her down was to load her up with tasty tidbits of trivia she could whip out at a moment's notice.

"Really?" The younger woman hummed as she filed the information away in her mind palace. "I had no idea."

"Facts are fun," Cara said, forcing a bright note into her tone. "Were you able to get into my place without any trouble?"

"Oh, yeah. No problem. I grabbed your passport for ID and found the credit card right where you said it would be. I raided petty cash for a couple hundred and put it in the envelope in case. I overnighted it all to you in care of Special Agent Dawson at the Arkansas State Police. It should arrive before 8:00 a.m."

Cara fought the urge to roll her eyes. When Wyatt Dawson found out Zarah had sent supplies from one of the superstores to the condo, he insisted she call her assistant back and route any future shipments through him. Cara thought it was overkill, but she'd been too tired to fight him on it.

"Thank you so much for all you've done."

"Oh, jeez, no problem," Zarah said, allowing her native Minnesotan to show through for a second. "I'm so relieved you're okay. So scary, you know?"

Smiling her first genuine smile of the night, Cara said, "I know."

"Are you calling me from the new phone?"

"Yes, but don't give the number to anyone yet. The police are cloning my old number. Anything sent to it will show on this one too. They're monitoring both numbers, so they can capture any calls or texts."

"Oh. Cool." She gave a little laugh. "It sounds like they're pretty cyber savvy there in Arkansas."

Cara frowned, both mildly offended on behalf of her home state and bemused by the younger woman's blunt assessment. "Yes, they are. But that also means the guy who has my phone might be checking it too, if he can get past my security code. I'm not putting anything past anyone these days."

"I totally hear you," Zarah said.

Tired, and not prepared to answer questions, Cara shifted

into business mode. "Hey, so I need some contact information. If I send you a list, will you email them back to me?"

"Email? Can't I text them?"

Zarah sounded perplexed by the notion of using such antiquated means of communication. Smirking at the notebook where she started jotting names, Cara wondered if Zarah would find Special Agent Dawson nearly as cute if she passed on his suggestion regarding the pen and paper.

"We're trying to go low-tech on this," Cara informed her. "I'm staying off apps, and texts are not secure. We know my work email has been hacked, but I have an old address I use as a spam catcher. I was thinking maybe if you don't mind me sending a list to your personal email?"

"Oh! Yeah. Totally makes sense."

Zarah rattled off an email address. They ended the call and Cara tapped her pen against the pad as she racked her brain for any other contacts she wanted to add to her list. Then she opened the secure browser and attempted to access the email account she never used. It took three attempts before she recalled the correct password, and even then she had to run the gauntlet of selecting security images of cacti and bicycles before the server demanded access to send a one-time code to her phone.

Gnawing her bottom lip, she weighed the risk of exposure before typing in her digits. She figured her detractors would have to be pretty darn dedicated to watch her every move all the time. Besides, she'd done all of her travel correspondence through her work email. The odds of anyone tracking down the handle she'd barely used since college had to be slim.

She fired off the list of names along with her heartfelt thanks for going above and beyond, and the reassurance there was no hurry to reply because she'd be logging out and heading straight for the shower then bed. The message whooshed its way to California. Her inbox was full of un-opened newsletters, discount codes and special offers she'd relegated to limbo. With a couple taps, she sent them all to the trash bin.

She logged out of the email server, then backed out of the secure browser, sure to wait until flames rolled up the screen as an indication the connection had been torched. Satisfied she'd done all she could to cover her tracks, she stowed the last of the food items before grabbing the clothes and toiletries and heading for the bathroom. The sooner she got to sleep, the sooner morning would come.

Standing under the hot spray, she did her level best to tap into the gratitude and positivity she touted on the app, but her mind continued to whirl. Then her ankles gave out.

Sitting on the floor of a strange tub with her legs drawn close and her head pressed to her knees, she let the tears flow. They ran down her cheeks hot and salty as the cooling water pummeled her shoulders and back. Shivering, she told herself everything would be better in the morning.

It had to be.

Because if things could get worse than being abducted at gunpoint, she didn't want to know how.

HEAVY POUNDING WOKE her from a fitful sleep. She wasn't quite ready to surface, but the dream of someone sawing her in half was every bit as disturbing as the persistent thumps. Cracking an eyelid, Cara found herself staring at sunlight streaming through unfamiliar curtains. Another round of demanding knocks came, and the phone she'd clutched until she fell asleep buzzed insistently from under her pillow.

She sat up, her eyes gritty from too many tears and too little sleep.

Someone was calling her name through the door. She ran

a hand over her hair. It was flat on one side and sticking up on the other. She'd fallen asleep while it was still damp.

"Cara? If you don't answer in the next thirty seconds, I'm busting down this door."

The person issuing the threat was a man. But it didn't sound like a threat. It sounded like a warning. Yanking the phone from its nesting spot, she swung her legs over the side of the bed as she read the name on the screen. Swiping with her thumb, she said, "Agent Dawson?"

"Why aren't you answering your door?" he demanded. His tone was edgy and sharp.

"I was sleeping," she grumbled, staggering across the living room to the door.

She started disengaging the locks, but his gravelly bark stopped her. "Peephole."

"I know it's you," she argued. "I can hear you through the door and the phone."

"Check anyway," he growled.

She obliged him with a huff. Sure enough, Special Agent Wyatt Dawson stood in the hall holding an overnight envelope and wearing a shearling-lined denim jacket. "Nice jacket," she said, matching him grump for grump. "You headed out to rope some steers this morning?"

"Disarm the alarm."

She wanted to tell him where he could get off, but she was hoping the envelope contained the cash, cards and passport Zarah had shipped.

"Sir, yes, sir," she replied, turning away from the door. She disabled the alarm system, then twisted the locks. Stepping back to allow him entry, she muttered, "You're eager to get a jump on the day."

He stepped over the threshold, then quickly closed the door behind him. Once he had her locked in again, he turned and thrust the envelope at her. "Do you have a Webmail address?"

"What?"

"Do you have a Webmail email account?" he demanded.

"Yes, but I don't use—"

"Did you send an email to someone last night?"

Cara pushed her hand through her hair, her anger rising even as her stomach sank. "What if I did?" she challenged.

"If you did, you exposed your account and someone got hold of it," he shot back.

"How? I was barely on there for two minutes," she cried, incredulous.

"Doesn't take long if someone is tracking your every move. Did you do some kind of password recovery or two-step verification?"

She squeezed her eyes shut and blew out a long breath. Apparently, Wyatt Dawson knew a confession when he heard one, because he pressed on.

"We got a call from a sergeant with Company E this morning. A woman claiming to be Elizabeth Beckett contacted them about an email she received concerning her daughter," he said, watching her closely.

"Elizabeth Beckett? My mom?"

His lips flattened into a thin line. "I suppose so." Wyatt pulled out his phone and started tapping. Once he got what he was after, he turned his phone over to her. It was a photo of a computer screen. On the screen was an email from the account she'd used to contact Zarah the night before, but this one was addressed to her parents' email address.

It was a ransom letter from a man who claimed to have taken her from the parking deck at Clinton National Airport in Little Rock. The amount he was asking for to secure her release was absurd. Her parents were ranchers. Even if they sold every head of cattle and every acre of land, they couldn't have come up with the outrageous figure demanded.

She looked at the time stamp on the email. It was sent

less than an hour after she emailed Zarah the list of contact names. "Oh, my God," she whispered. She swiped at the phone screen, desperate to make the message disappear. "I need to call them."

"They know you're okay," Wyatt assured her, gently removing his phone from her grasp. "I spoke to your mother. Your father too. I gave them a brief rundown on what's happening, but I think we should vacate in case this location is compromised."

"Compromised?" she repeated, willing her brain to catch up.

"They obviously have a thumb on your correspondence. Probably phished your work email to identify your personal accounts. I'm going to need details on everything since you were first aware someone had your information." He blew out a breath, his hands braced on his hips as he scanned the condo. "Gather your stuff. You can call your folks once we're out of here."

Her stuff? She looked down at the package he'd thrust at her. Pulling the tear strip, she peered into the envelope. An envelope she assumed held the cash Zarah had mentioned, two credit cards—though who knew if they'd be any good to her—and her passport.

"What do you mean *we*?"

"Apparently, Mrs. Elizabeth Beckett knows people," he said with a wry smile. "You related to Paul Stanton? An uncle or something?"

"Paul Stanton?" she repeated blankly. "I, uh, I don't have an uncle. There's my aunt CeCe, but she never married."

"Nope. The name doesn't ring any bells? Lieutenant Governor Paul Stanton," he repeated.

She squeezed her eyes shut as she tried to recall the bits and pieces of hometown news her mother relayed whenever they spoke. Finally, the light bulb came on. "Oh, Paul Stanton. He's not actually my uncle. A family friend. Or friend of my mother's, I should say. He and my mom went to prom together and kept in touch. My dad hates him, but I remember her telling me he's some kind of big shot now."

"Well, your mama called him, and good old Uncle Paul made a couple calls, and it looks like you've got yourself your very own special agent," he said, holding his arms out wide.

"What?"

"Come on." He made his way to the kitchen and began bagging the supplies she'd unpacked the night before. When she didn't move, he motioned to the bedroom. "I'll fill you in on the way."

"On the way to where?" she asked, standing her ground.

He dropped a box of her favorite cheese crackers into the delivery bag and looked up at her, one dark brow raised. "I am to escort you home, Ms. Beckett."

"Home?" Dread pooled in the pit of her stomach when she pictured poor Nancy bandaged up in her hospital bed. "To California?"

"Oh, no, ma'am. I'm under strict instruction to deliver you into the hands of Mrs. Elizabeth Beckett ASAP."

"My mama?"

He looked her straight in the eye. "We're headin' to Snowball. Hope you have a jacket. It can be chilly up in the hills this time of year."

Chapter Four

Forty-five minutes later, he had Cara Beckett and her meager belongings packed into a state-issued SUV heading north on US 65. They were quiet as they exited the busy metro area north of Conway and headed up into the foothills of the Ozark Mountains. The moment she'd sat down in the car, she called her mother from his phone, having surrendered the new mobile to him by way of tossing it at the condo's sofa.

Wyatt didn't call her out on her decidedly less-than-Zen attitude. Her life had been ripped out from under her feet in the past week or so. And with the LYYF company's public offering about to take off, things were only going to get more hectic.

He'd offered her coffee and a fast-food breakfast, but she'd refused, keeping her arms crossed tight over her chest. He ordered a bottle of water along with his morning dose of caffeine.

Caught by a red light in Greenbrier, Wyatt cast a sidelong glance at his passenger. She sat stoically staring through the windshield when he offered her the bottle of water. "Single-use containers are poisoning our air and killing our oceans," she said stiffly.

He stared back at her, keeping his expression neutral

though he could feel his ears heating. "How did you sleep last night?"

"I didn't," she retorted.

He waggled the evil water bottle in front of her. "A lack of proper rest can lead to dehydration. Right now, my mission is to keep you alive. We'll worry about the planet tomorrow."

"Exactly the sort of attitude responsible for our current climate change crisis."

"I'm not covering the planet today. I'm tasked with taking care of you. Drink the water," he ordered, tossing the bottle into her lap as the light changed.

He accelerated, trying to swallow back his exasperation. She wasn't sulking, per se, but she was not thrilled about the arrangement. And she wasn't drinking the water. He added stubborn to his mental list of things he knew about Cara Beckett. A list not nearly long enough if he was going to be any help in figuring out who was behind the cyber and real-world attacks against her.

"So, you grew up in Snowball?"

She shook her head. "Snowball is the closest dot on the map."

"Your parents own a ranch?"

"A little over six hundred acres. My dad keeps anywhere between fifty and seventy-five head of Black Angus cattle."

Her tone was flat, but he picked up a hint of pride in her delivery. "Wow. Sounds like a lot. Is it a lot?" he asked, glancing over at her for confirmation.

She shrugged. "I'd say about average for a family ranch." Her monotone response faded into a faintly mocking tone. "Let me guess, you're a city boy? Grew up in Little Rock?"

He shook his head, his lips twitching into a smirk meant to show her exactly how wrong she was about him. "Nope. Born and raised in Stuttgart, home of Ricebirds."

He felt her appraising stare. "Were you a farm kid?"

Unable to keep up the ruse, he allowed the smirk to take over as he shook his head. "Nah. My dad sold insurance."

"Ah."

Awkward silence descended like a thick fog. Grasping for information and a conversational straw, he asked, "You get along with your parents?"

She shot him a sidelong glance. "Do you?"

"Yeah," he replied without hesitation.

"I do too, but you know what they say…"

"What?"

This time, she couldn't repress the smile. "You think you're enlightened, spend a week with your family."

He chuckled. "I get you."

They drove in silence for a while. Finally, he prompted her to tell him her version of the story. "Start at the beginning. What was the first odd thing you noticed?"

Cara's fingers curled around the edge of the console between them. She was quiet, and for a minute, he thought perhaps she would not answer. He couldn't blame her for wanting to play things close to the chest. Her personal information had been scattered across multiple forums. He'd seen at least a half-dozen entries himself. And the threats came standard with this kind of cyberattack. People talked tough when tucked safely behind a keyboard. But somebody, or some people, had taken a giant step out of the shadow of internet anonymity.

Hopefully, it would make them easier to find.

"It's hard to say," she murmured, her face turned toward the scenery whizzing past.

The fall foliage was near peak color as October gave way to November. It seemed wrong to spoil such beautiful scenery with talk of ugliness.

"There have always been messages. Even before the app took off. You know, the usual online slime. People trying to slide into my inbox. Once LYYF started gaining traction, I got hit up for money more often than I was hit on," she said, a wry smile twisting her lips. "Tom likes to say he knew we'd made it when guys starting fishing for my account numbers rather than my phone number."

"Tom is Tom Wasinski," he clarified, shooting her a glance.

"Yes. Tom Wasinski."

"He and Chris Sharpe are your partners in LYYF," he stated.

"Yes."

"And you knew them from…college," he prompted, hoping to get her talking.

"Yes. We were suite mates our freshman year. Stayed friends through school and after."

"You did the voice-over work for them from the beginning?"

When she didn't add anything more to the story, he stole a peek at her. She stared stone-faced through the windshield, and he winced. "Sorry. I didn't mean to trample all over your story."

"Not my story," she said in a clipped tone. "But you seem pretty well-versed in the lore of LYYF, so who am I to spoil it for you?"

Biting the inside of his cheek to keep from groaning his frustration with himself, Wyatt tightened his grip on the steering wheel. "You're right. I'm sorry. I think I was trying to impress you with how much I know." He offered her a wan smile as they slowed to pass through one of the myriad small towns along the route. "I want you to feel comfortable talking to me. Safe. I'm here to help."

She shifted in her seat, turning to face him more fully. "If you want me to feel comfortable telling my story, you might try listening. I don't need you to recite the press clippings to me."

Chastened, he ducked his head to acknowledge the point scored. "I'm sorry," he repeated. The tires hummed as silence overtook them once again. He waited, but when she didn't volunteer anything more, he pressed his lips together and nodded, owning his ignorance. "Would you tell me what happened?"

She blew out a long breath, letting her head fall back against the seat. The woman beside him didn't look anything like the glossy, glowing guru on his app. She looked haunted. Hunted. When she spoke, her voice was hoarse.

"Everyone latches on to the voice work like all I did was show up and read a few cue cards one day."

For once in his life, he had sense enough to keep his lips zipped.

"They were working on a finance app." She gave a dry little laugh. "It wasn't much more than a bookkeeping tool. Like one of those account trackers my mom used to use to record each check or ATM withdrawal. You know, the little booklet with three years' worth of calendars printed on there?"

"Checkbook register," he said with a nod.

"Exactly. Anyway, they were developing it all through school. It changed and evolved as we did. People weren't tracking checks and more banks had apps where you could see your transactions real-time, so they started retooling it to be more of a finance guide for kids our age." She waved a hand dismissively. "Simple stuff. Interest calculators, a stock market widget and some how-to guides one of the business majors a couple years older than us wrote up as part of their thesis project."

"Interesting."

She scoffed. "It wasn't. It was boring. But by the time we

graduated, almost everyone we knew had made some sort of contribution." She gave him a smirk. "I recorded a few videos with tips and tricks for acing job interviews."

"And this was under the LYYF banner?"

"At the time it was Life. *L-I-F-E*. We even had some cheesy tagline about it being the only tool a person needed to win at the game of life."

"Catchy."

"Anyhow, the concept grew and evolved, and as Tom and Chris became better programmers, the possibilities kept expanding."

She propped her elbow on the door and pressed her thumb into her temple as if talking about the past gave her a headache. But he didn't give her an out. He couldn't. Her life was on the line.

"How did LYYF as we know it come about?"

She gazed out at the passing scenery. "Sometime in my sophomore year, I'd gone on a commercial audition where I met a woman who was into Transcendental Meditation. We got to talking, she told me about a retreat happening near campus. It was free, I was…searching…"

The last word trailed away, and he let it go for a few minutes. He knew sifting through memories was sometimes like reading lines of data—whatever you were looking for usually popped out the moment you let your focus go a bit fuzzy.

They were navigating one of the steep downhill stretches before she spoke again.

"Anyhow. I got into meditation and yoga as a way to deal with the constant rejection," she said quietly.

"And all this time you were in school?"

She nodded. "I booked a few local ads, but never a national campaign. I was too generic for most casting directors."

He blinked, taken aback. The woman had to know she

was a knockout, but her unflinchingly harsh assessment of her looks sounded too clinical to be false modesty.

"You're hardly a generic anything."

The words he intended as a compliment came out awkward, stilted by his desire not to cross any professional boundaries. When he chanced a peek at her, he found her wearing the serene half smile she wore on the app's welcome screen.

"Not only is he a protector, but also he's a poet," she mocked, eyes crinkling with humor.

Heat prickled his neck. Determined to brazen out his embarrassment, he shot her a quelling look. "You know what I mean."

"I do. And thank you," she said, sounding thoroughly amused. "But pretty enough by Arkansas standards means I wasn't even in the ballpark in LA." Before he could argue the point further, she continued. "I was telling Tom all about this breathing technique I was using to help deal with nerves, and he said something about how it wasn't only actors who needed coping skills. The next thing I knew, I was cooking up a short script about how I got into meditation and the practical applications." She shrugged. "We purposefully omitted as much of the new-age terminology as possible and replaced it with some of the corporate catchphrases we were hearing all around us. Soon, we had about ten sessions written up, each focusing on a particular stressor or coping technique we thought would be helpful. I recorded them on my phone sitting in my closet using an earphone mic. And now you know the real LYYF origin story."

"Why were you sitting in a closet?" he asked, perplexed by this odd little detail.

"Sound absorption," she explained. "It had this nasty beige carpet left over from the nineties. We hung blankets on the walls and pushed most of the clothes back so they wouldn't be too close around me, but yeah. It worked."

"I guess so," he said, impressed.

"By the time we graduated, the guys were off and running with the life management idea. I was still making the rounds, doing auditions and waiting tables."

"Where were they getting their money?"

"Chris had money. Trust fund kid. Tom's parents supported him too. His dad was a surgeon and did well enough, but it wasn't inherited money like the Sharpes'. But Tom's parents were the competitive type. They wanted to keep up with the Sharpes, so they pretty much gave him an unlimited line of credit."

"And your folks…" he trailed off.

"Are rich in land and not much more. You know how it is," she said with a shrug.

And he did. There were plenty of families like hers around Stuttgart. Rice farmers with large stretches of valuable farmland who scrimped, saved and relied on government subsidies to keep from selling parcels off as the modern world closed in around them.

Cara continued her story. "When those first ten sessions started getting more clicks than some of the other sessions, they asked if I wanted to do more." She shrugged. "I wrote another ten and people seemed to like those too."

"And eventually, they asked if you wanted to be their partner?"

Pressing the tip of her tongue to her upper lip, she shook her head hard. "Uh, no," she said with a sharp little laugh. "They asked me to write and record more. I had two waitressing jobs, was pulling some temp hours doing reception work and still trying to land a part, any part. I told them I didn't have time."

"I see."

"A couple weeks passed, then Chris called me back saying they would pay me."

"Did they?"

She nodded. "A thousand bucks for another ten sessions. It doesn't sound like much now, and in context, but at the time it was the difference between making rent or buying a plane ticket home." She sighed, twisting her fingers together in her lap. "But, naturally, they were always more focused on the technology than the content. When the new sessions dropped and users started asking for more, they didn't want to spend time and money on developing content to be delivered regularly. Chris was the one who suggested they cut me in as a partner."

"Sounds like a big leap. For all of you," he added.

"It was a great deal for them. Particularly if the app didn't find traction. I was responsible for writing, producing and performing all consumer-facing wellness and lifestyle content. Research, scripting, recording…everything. We used to like to joke about how they made the widgets, I made the rest."

He let out a low whistle. "I had no idea."

"Most people don't." She gave a short laugh. "At the time, I was still auditioning for my big Hollywood career, so I was happy to let them handle what little press we got for LYYF. Since the only exposure we got in the early days was on tech blogs and forums, the narrative developed from there."

"Chris and Tom went on to become tech stars and you were cast as the wannabe actress who finagled her way into a very lucrative partnership."

She nodded, but her smile was self-deprecating. "I can't complain. It's been the most celebrated role of my entire acting career."

"Made you famous."

"It made me known in certain circles," she corrected.

"Anyway, my point is, there have always been people who believed I didn't deserve what I had. They let their feelings be known on forums and chat rooms, then when the app itself became geared more toward interaction, direct messages. So, you see, it's hard to pinpoint a time when the harassment started, because it's been happening all along."

Wyatt hummed his understanding. The tech world was still disproportionately male, and some quarters were openly hostile to female interlopers. "What was your first hint it was going beyond the usual?"

"I started getting more direct messages on the app and on social media."

"What kind of DMs?"

"The usual. Name-calling. People saying I'm nothing but a parasite. No talent. Ugly. Commentary on my body, my voice, the way I breathe," she said tiredly.

"The way you breathe is a lifesaver for some people." The words were out of his mouth before he could vet them. Mortified, he kept his gaze locked on the series of curves ahead of them.

"I tell myself it is," she said quietly. "But some days it's easier to believe the bad over the good."

He knew the feeling too well. "I understand."

"I didn't start to get worried until the texts began."

"I imagine those were more of the same?"

"Yes," she confirmed. "But coming directly to my phone, they felt more...menacing."

"What did you do?"

"I sent them to Tom. He's always up for solving a mystery. In this case it wasn't much of a challenge for him. A simple search showed my name popping up in various forums. The next thing I knew, we found my cell number along with my home address, as well as several personal email addresses posted." He sensed her looking at him and turned. "The one I used last night was not one of them."

"So someone is actively monitoring your internet usage," he concluded, meeting her gaze.

She heaved a weary sigh as she smoothed her eyebrows with her thumb and middle finger. "I need to text Zarah and tell her I've checked out of the rental."

He nodded. "Use my phone." As if on cue, his phone rang. The display showed the caller to be Trooper Masterson. He hesitated for a moment before answering, but at Cara's questioning look, accepted the call.

"This is Dawson. We're hands-free," he announced, wanting to give the other man fair warning.

"Dawson. Is Ms. Beckett with you?" Masterson asked.

"Yes," Wyatt said.

"I'm here," Cara answered at the same time.

"Ms. Beckett, I wanted to let you know your rental car has been recovered," the trooper informed her.

"It has?"

"Where?" Wyatt asked, stepping over her words in turn.

"It was found in section 104 of the parking deck at the airport," the older man replied.

"Section 104," Cara murmured.

"Anything recovered?" Wyatt pressed.

"We have a team going over it now, but it appears most of your belongings were left intact. There was a large leather bag with your wallet, phone and other personal items on the front floorboard, and a travel bag in the back seat."

He let off the gas and coasted toward the shoulder of the road, tires crunching on loose gravel as he slowed to a stop. A car whizzed past. Seconds passed before a speeding tanker truck left them rocking in its wake. He and Cara shared a glance.

"Any cash or credit cards in the wallet?" Wyatt asked.

"My officer on scene checked. Says it doesn't look like your passenger took anything."

Wyatt did his best to keep his expression impassive. She was searching his face for clues, and he didn't have one to give. "So no theft," he said, his tone flat.

"Other than the vehicle," Masterson supplied.

"Which was found in the exact spot where Ms. Beckett found it," Wyatt supplied.

"But I... He..." she spluttered. "This wasn't some fantasy abduction I made up to scare people," she insisted, voice rising in agitation. "The truck driver. Eustace. Mr. Stubbs. He saw us. He saw me jump out of the car. He saw a man take off with the rental car."

"We do have Mr. Stubbs, the driver who picked you up. He gave a statement and as much of a description as he could," Masterson said in a patronizingly soothing tone. "And we may get lucky with some hair or other fibers."

But it didn't sound like he was expecting much. And even if they did come up with forensic evidence, the perpetrator would have to be somewhere in the system for there to be a match.

"Okay," Wyatt said, hoping to redirect the conversation. "Let me know what the forensics team finds. I have Emma Parker with the CCD working on some data tracking for us too. I'll have her loop you in if she uncovers anything helpful to the case."

"Appreciate it," Masterson said gruffly. "I'll keep you updated."

Wyatt thanked the man, then ended the call.

A logging truck rumbled past. Two minivans and an SUV zipped along close behind it. All three of the drivers jockeyed to be in position to overtake the larger vehicle, all too aware once they got past Clinton and started climbing into the hills, the highway would narrow to a single lane in each direction. When they hit the switchbacks, there would only be the occasional passing lane made available for traffic relief. He'd be stuck behind them all.

He was already so far behind.

Who was hacking into Cara Beckett's accounts? Who disliked a woman who swore by gratitude journals and daily meditation enough to terrorize her? Chase her from her home? Kidnap her in broad daylight?

"Why would he leave everything?"

Her tremulous question broke into his thoughts. He turned to face her, but when his eyes met hers, he could see she already knew the answer. Robbery was never the intent.

This time, she spoke in little more than a whisper. "Why does someone want to hurt me?"

"I don't know," he answered honestly. "But I promise I'm going to do my best to figure out who it is and stop them."

Understanding arced like an electric current between them. But she didn't reach for his phone. Instead, she held his gaze so long he had to jerk his attention back to the road.

"Do you mind if we stop and get a coffee before we head for my parents' house?" she asked. "I'd like a moment to… collect my thoughts."

Wyatt nodded and checked their location against the GPS. "I know exactly the place." Hitting his blinker, he craned his neck to check traffic. A rooster tail of grit and dust rose behind them as he steered the SUV back onto the highway.

Chapter Five

Cara clutched the paper cup holding her coffee close as a breeze with a biting edge to it whipped her hair from her forehead. The view from the scenic overlook touted on a billboard outside of Marshall did not disappoint. The valley stretched below them like a patchwork quilt sewn from scraps of vibrant autumn colors. Red, orange and gold specimens shone bright against a backdrop of dark evergreens and leaves already dried to crisp golden brown.

"The cemetery where my mother's grandparents are buried sits on top of a hill covered in these huge red maple trees," she murmured when Wyatt approached. "Every fall, they turn the most incredible red-gold color I've ever seen. I bet it's spectacular about now."

"We can go there if you like. It's not like we'll have to hide out in your parents' basement."

"Good to hear," she said. He half turned and flashed a wry smile. "Because they don't have a basement. Nothing but a nasty old storm cellar filled with ancient canning jars and spiders." She glanced back at the SUV where he'd been making and taking calls while she ruminated. "Anything new?"

"We have an IP address from where the email was sent. It gave us a trail to follow. There's a forum user from Hot Springs we suspect may have been your, uh, passenger."

Cara whirled to face him. She swiped at her hair ineffectually. "Is it so easy to find people?"

"If you know how and where to look. Special Agent Parker has a talent for tracking these things down. Probably because when she was younger, she used the same talent to cover her own tracks."

"What do you mean?"

He smirked. "A member of our team was once a teenage hacker."

"Like Tom." The words slipped past her lips. She raised her hand to cover her mouth, but it was too late. She could tell by his expression he'd caught them. When he didn't express any surprise or press her for additional information, her eyes narrowed. "Did you know?"

He shrugged. "It's one of those open secret things. The truth is, a lot of people who go into programming or security started out trying to break into things. It's not much different from kids who grow up to be mechanics or engineers taking stuff apart to see how it's put back together again."

"Except it's illegal."

"Right. But most don't do anything truly harmful like hack into NORAD."

She blinked twice. "Right," she echoed. Then, shaking her head in disbelief, she turned back to the view. She cradled her coffee in the crook of her arm and pulled the cuffs of her sweater down over her hands. "So, they're looking into this lead?"

He nodded. "She'll call me as soon as they can get something solid."

She drew on her bottom lip, biting down to quell the swirl of anxiety and anticipation pooling in her belly. Letting her gaze go soft and unfocused, she imagined pulling the lovely patchwork blanket of fall foliage up around her shoulders.

The visualization helped a little but not enough. She needed to let Wyatt know what he was in for on this trip.

"You should know my parents and I have a...shaky relationship."

She felt his glance but could tell by the shift in his posture he'd gone back to staring out over the vista. "Okay."

"We don't fight or anything," she felt compelled to add, waving her coffee cup in a dismissive circle. "I'm an only child and let's say we wanted different things—for me—and leave it there."

"I understand."

He shifted his weight, and Cara got the feeling he actually did.

"My dad wanted me to take over his insurance agency. They only had me and my older sister. Shelby went off to school at Ole Miss, met my brother-in-law there and never came home. When I was up at the U of A, I majored in computer science. I told my dad I could use everything I learned to bring the agency up to date, automate everything, you know..."

When he let the story trail off, she turned to face him again. "But you never went to work for him."

Wyatt shook his head. "I met a guy who worked for the Department of Public Safety. They were recruiting on campus. Looking for people with tech skills to join the state police. I imagined myself as the guy who figured out who was sneaking around the dark web and what they were doing and stopped it all before things got too out of hand," he said dryly.

"So you and Agent... Parker, was it?" He nodded. "You come at things from different angles."

He shrugged, his hands buried deep in the pockets of his jeans. "I suppose you can say we do. But we work well together. Balance each other out."

"That's nice. Balance is good." She sighed. "I suppose we should get moving." Turning on her heel, she walked off in the direction of the car. She settled her coffee into the cup holder and waited for Wyatt to join her.

He took another moment to drink in the view. Which gave her the same opportunity with him. He was tall by Hollywood standards, probably just over six foot. He was lean, but not skinny. The Henley he wore with his jeans showed off broad shoulders and toned arms, but he didn't appear to be pumped up like a gym rat. All in all, he suited the scenery. Natural and unaffected.

He dropped into the seat with a soft "Oof," and she jumped.

"Sorry," she said, laughing at her own skittishness.

"No worries," he assured her.

"I just need to take a breath," she murmured. When she inhaled deeply, he did the same.

"Okay, now let it go," he said, parroting the words she used so often in her meditations as he started the car. "Now breathe in. Breathe in LYYF."

His eyes crinkled as he said the last bit, and a laugh burbled out of her. She reached over and gave his arm a friendly swat. "Don't mock me."

"Mock you?" he repeated through a laugh. "You? The guru? Never."

They'd strapped into their seats when the phone she'd left in the console vibrated. Beside her, Wyatt tensed. They both eyed the device warily.

"Text message," he grumbled, giving the notification the stink eye. "Know the number?"

She shrugged. "Not off the top of my head, but I don't memorize many numbers anymore."

"We've been forwarding all calls from unknown numbers

to headquarters. You should only be getting messages from people who have the new number."

"I gave it to Zarah. She may have passed it along to Tom or Chris," she speculated.

He nodded, but neither of them reached for the phone despite another insistent buzz.

"I suppose you should check it," he said at last.

A chill of apprehension ran down her spine as she leaned over to grab the phone. The screen sprang to life, and Cara sucked in a sharp breath when she saw the number in the little red circle. Seven. Someone had sent seven text messages to her phone. She opened the first.

856-784-4544: Have you missed us, Cara?

773-238-5795: Did you think we wouldn't be able to tell you rerouted us?

413-648-7993: I don't think she wants to talk to us anymore. I'm hurt.

630-721-9173: Hear she's run away to Arkansas, of all places.

325-545-1899: Arkansas sounds…like Arkansas. I bet Cara has ditched her shoes, cut off her jeans, and is kissin' a cousin right now.

213-566-5487: I can't believe some hick from a flyover state thinks she can cash in on Chris and Tom's genius because she slept with one or both of them back in the day. Where is Arkansas, anyway?

565-982-1167: You breathing LYYF in, Cara? Does the air taste better in Ar-Kansas?

"Oh, my God," she whispered.

"What?" Wyatt leaned over to get a look at the screen.

"They're texting this number," she said, jerking her gaze up to meet his.

"What?"

"They know we were forwarding calls and messages," she said, eyes wide. "They must have somehow traced the forwarding back to this number."

The phone in her hand vibrated again, and she jerked so violently she squeezed it from her grip. Bobbling the device, she let out a gusty whoosh of breath when Wyatt caught and held it still in his steady hand. Then, Cara read the latest entry.

228-798-1163: It's nice here, isn't it, Cara. Warm days and cool nights. Isn't sweater weather the best?

She began to shake. "Oh, no," she murmured, shaking her head. It started out a slow denial but grew more adamant with each swing. "No. No. No. They can't come here." She turned pleading eyes on Wyatt, unable to hide behind a mask of cool any longer. "We can't go to my parents' house."

"We're going to your parents' house," he replied, pressing the button to power down the phone.

"But we can't. I can't." Her voice grew sharper with agitation. "I can't bring all this to their doorstep. They didn't want me to be a part of this from the very start. I can't show up with a passel of stalkers hot on my tail."

"Understood," he said in an annoyingly calm tone. "But there isn't a passel of stalkers following you."

"Didn't you read what they said? It is sweater weather. They know where we are going."

"They do not. Those texts were all sent through an autodialer. The phone numbers were too random. Someone may know you flew into Little Rock, and they may figure you know people here, but it doesn't mean they know where you were heading."

"They emailed my mother a ransom demand," she practically shouted at him.

"Because they found someone with the name Beckett in your address book on an ancient email account," he countered. "They got lucky."

"No one gets that lucky," she argued.

"Either way, it doesn't matter. When I spoke to your mother, she said the first thing she did was pick up the phone and call her friend the lieutenant governor's office. From a landline," he added. "She didn't reply to the email or forward it to anyone from her account."

"Paul Stanton," was all she could manage to mutter.

"Your mother didn't do anything but open the message. They have no way of knowing they hit a bull's-eye."

He tossed the phone back into the console. Cara wanted to snatch it back and toss it out the window. But she knew she couldn't. They would need every scrap of evidence they could gather.

He swiveled in his seat to look her straight in the eye. "All the sender could possibly know is someone opened it. They're fishing, Cara," he said, reaching over and wrapping his fingers around her forearm. "I wouldn't take you anywhere near there if I didn't believe we could keep you all safe."

The gesture surprised her. From the moment they'd met, he'd kept a respectable distance between them. But this touch didn't feel like a boundary crossed. The size of his hand was reassuring. The warmth of it, a balm. He held her gaze, sure and steady. And she believed him. He would do as he said. He'd keep her safe.

"Fishing," she repeated.

"Or phishing, with a *p-h*, if you would," he said with a self-deprecating smirk. "Don't freak out, Cara. We're on top of this, you have my word."

"I don't know you. Your word may not be good for much," she muttered sourly.

One side of his mouth kicked up. "Let me put it this way. I value my career too much to take a celebrity who has been the victim of a crime, and has friends in high places, into a situation I believe to be dangerous to her or the people around her."

She choked on a laugh. "Celebrity? Hardly. And my mother is the one with the friends in high places. I haven't lived here since I was eighteen. I doubt I could pick the actual governor out of a lineup, much less the guy my mom went to the Marshall High prom with in 1978."

"I guess we should consider you an unreliable witness, then," he teased, reversing out of the parking spot. "For all we know, good old Uncle Paul Stanton might have been the one tryin' to hitch a ride with you at the airport."

"Ha ha."

He glanced over at her before accelerating onto the highway again. "I wouldn't put you or your parents in danger. I don't want to be in danger," he added with a laugh. "I know the title special agent sounds cool and all, but I'm a desk jockey. A computer nerd, remember?"

She huffed a laugh. "I've spent most of my adult life surrounded by computer nerds. Trust me, you carry the special agent thing off much better."

His lips curved into a sly smile. "I think there may have been a compliment wrapped up in there somewhere."

"Only an observation," she disputed, willing herself not to blush. Focusing on the curving road winding its way down into the valley carved by the Buffalo National River, she steered the conversation back to the investigation. "Tell me what's happening behind the scenes. Maybe I'll feel better about everything if I know what's going on behind the curtain."

Wyatt nodded. "I get you." He paused. His mouth puckered as he considered his words. "Okay, so we start with what we know. Someone has hacked into your accounts. They likely found their way in through one of your personal accounts rather than something attached to LYYF. Corporate security, particularly in tech firms, tends to be tight. Corporate espionage and so forth."

"I think everyone at LYYF knows I'm not the one who will be swiping critical codes," she said dryly.

"Perhaps not, but I'd wager most people inside and outside the company would assume you have access to critical information."

He lifted his foot off the gas and signaled for the left turn onto AR-74. Leaving the highway behind, they crossed Bear Creek and headed deep into the rolling hills and lush valleys of Searcy County.

"I'm guessing it was through a social media platform. They tend to be the most vulnerable, and some barely even try to make it hard to cage user information. From there, they likely gained access to other platforms, and possibly your company accounts." He paused for a moment, mulling something over. "Did you receive emails at your LYYF address as well as your personal accounts?"

"Yes, but they started with PicturSpam messages. I think you're right, they messaged on various other accounts, including LYYF, before the emails started."

"And I assume you were getting direct messages and emails long before they leaked your information and the texts started."

"I wouldn't say long before," she hedged.

"In internet terms, long can mean hours or days," he clarified. "Think wildfire speed."

The Californian in her shuddered at the comparison, but she nodded. "Right. It was probably no more than a day or so. It seemed like everything happened at once."

"I can take a good guess at what most of the messages said, but tell me someone said something to make you hop on a plane less than two weeks before your company goes public and you become a multimillionaire."

Cara stared out at the scenery, wishing she could jump out and hide behind one of the huge round bales of hay dotting an autumn-browned pasture. Heck, it wouldn't be the first time she'd leaped from a vehicle this week. But Wyatt was sailing down the county highway at a steady clip, and she knew there was no way she could outrun the madness infiltrating her life. The only way out would be through, she reminded herself sternly.

"It wasn't what they said, it was what they did," she said, unable to look directly at him.

"Okay," he replied, the very soul of patience. "What did they do?"

"Well, let's see…" Pausing to gulp down the fear clawing at her throat, she focused on her hands clasped in her lap. "There was the petty vandalism. Nasty words spray-painted on my garage door, crude graffiti on my driveway. I've gone through three mailboxes in two weeks. All this in addition to the barrage of written and verbal harassment."

"Death threats?"

He asked the question as casually as if he was curious about her favorite color. So she answered in the same off-handed way. "Of course. Who gets doxed and doesn't get their fair share of death threats?"

Wyatt cast a quelling look in her direction. "Any the police were particularly interested in?"

"I'd like to believe they found all of them interesting, but there were a couple with, uh, specifics."

"You gonna tell me, or do I need to wait until the records we requested from California come through?"

She drew a deep breath, then let it out to the count of six. "One…person…said they liked my dog, and they'd be sure to take good care of it when I died."

He glanced over at her, his brow knit. "Your dog? I thought you said you have a cat."

"Half a cat," she corrected. "JuJu is a time-share."

"A stray you and the neighbor both feed," he recalled.

"My neighbor had a dog, though. Has. She has a dog. They are both alive and well, thank God."

Wyatt shifted in his seat, and she knew he was catching on, but she wasn't quite ready to say more. Instead, she pointed to a large metal building ahead of them. "Go past the Bakers' barn, you'll want to take a right on County Road 36. The road is barely more than one lane, and Mr. Baker likes to make a point out of farm equipment having the right of way around here, so look out for cranky old men on tractors."

"Got it."

Wyatt flipped on the turn signal even though there was no other car in sight. Cara smiled. He must have been telling the truth about growing up in farm country. Only city dwellers waited until the last second to signal their intention to turn. Out in the country, one never knew who or what might be coming up behind or poking along around a bend.

The tires scrambled for purchase on the crumbling concrete roadbed. Cara was pleased to note he'd heeded her caution and accelerated at a sedate pace. He let a good mile or so pass before he asked, "What happened to your neighbor?"

"She was out walking her dog. A car pulled up and a guy jumped out and grabbed her. He had a knife," she said, her words ending in a whisper.

"He stabbed her?"

Knowing he was watching her out of the corner of his eye, she simply nodded.

"But she wasn't fatally wounded," he confirmed.

"No."

"And the dog wasn't hurt."

Cara couldn't help but release a tense little laugh. He sounded so falsely encouraging it was ridiculous. She didn't know Wyatt Dawson well at all, but she felt safe in assuming optimism didn't come naturally to him. Why would it? He was a cop. He spent his days up to his elbows in all the worst things people did to one another.

"Buster is fine. Has a new little harness with LAPD printed on the back." She nodded to a crossroad ahead of them. "Keep going, but our turn will be coming up on the left."

"Got it. So Buster is an official K-9 officer now?"

"I wouldn't say official, but he was tough enough to get one of the officers to say every department should train a pack of Pomeranians. They may not be able to take a bad guy down, but they can sure wake the neighborhood." She pointed to a narrow driveway marked with three blue reflectors on their left. "Here we are. Home sweet home."

Chapter Six

When they pulled to a stop in front of the single-story ranch house at the end of a very long lane, a lazy yellow Labrador retriever bestirred itself enough to let out a single warning bark, then lay back down. Apparently, he felt he said enough. No one would ever accuse the big yellow dog of being a Pomeranian.

Wyatt barely switched off the engine before a tall, slender woman with long gray-blond hair woven into a thick braid burst through the screen door and bounded down the stairs.

"You're here," she cried, arms flung wide.

Cara fell out of the passenger seat and into the woman's embrace. "We're here," she replied, her voice muffled by an exuberant hug.

Wyatt watched them, arrested by the sight of the two women wound tight around one another. He nearly laughed out loud when he spotted a man wearing a shearling-lined denim jacket just like his and an Arkansas Razorbacks ball cap speeding toward them on an all-terrain utility vehicle. Her father abandoned the battered old gator before it came to a complete stop and hopped the low fence separating yard from pasture.

Wyatt noted the older couple were both strikingly attractive. Looking at them, it was no stretch to see into Cara's future.

"Hey, there," Cara's father said gruffly, pulling his daughter from her mother's arms and into his own. Like his wife and daughter, he was tall, but James Beckett was anything but willowy. Barrel-chested and burly, the man was more akin to a sprawling live oak tree.

"Hi, Daddy," she murmured as he crushed her to him.

"Hi, Sugar," her father grumbled into the top of her head. Without releasing his hold on Cara, he extended a hand toward Wyatt. "You're with the state police?"

"Yes, sir. Wyatt Dawson." He supplied his name as he shook the man's hand.

"I'm Betsy and this is Jim, and in case you haven't figured it out, we're Cara's mama and daddy."

"I put the pieces together," he said as he shook hands with Elizabeth. "Pleased to meet you both. Wish it were under better circumstances."

"Oh, my stars, I know." Elizabeth Beckett threaded her hand through his arm and propelled him in the direction of the porch. "I can't even believe this is happening." She whirled and pinned Cara with an incredulous glare. "Why is this happening?"

"Because the world is a crazy place, Mama," Cara said with exasperated patience.

By the time they reached the porch the dog had roused itself enough to stand at attention. "Hello, Roscoe," Cara cooed. "Who's a very good boy?"

Betsy snorted. "Good for nothing but warming the floorboards," she said, herding them all up the steps. "Come in. Come in. I have some stew on the stove and a pan of corn bread if you're ready for lunch. I know Jim's probably ready to eat his hat."

Cara's father pulled the battered Razorbacks hat from his head the moment he crossed the threshold. "I am hungry."

Wyatt stole a glance at his watch. It was early afternoon,

but the Becketts had been hard at work long before the call from his commanding officer woke him. The scent of richly spiced beef stew filled the entry. He tipped his head back appreciatively and Cara's father chuckled.

"Come on in and have a bowl while you get us all caught up," he said, gesturing for Wyatt to follow his nose.

Betsy turned to Cara, her forehead crumpled with worry. "Now, I know you don't eat meat, but I forget whether cheese is okay or not."

"I, uh, yeah, it's fine, Mama," Cara said, her cheeks turning pink. "Don't worry about me. I can sort out whatever I need."

"Born to raise beef cattle, but the minute she stepped foot in California she turned vegan on us," Jim Beckett blustered.

"It didn't happen the minute I moved to California," Cara shot back. "Like every other red-blooded college kid out there, I lived on pepperoni pizza and pad Thai for the better part of four years."

She turned toward Wyatt and rolled her eyes dramatically. He couldn't help but wonder if he was there to protect her or act as referee.

"But I'm not vegan anymore. I love dairy too much."

"I should ship you off to the Bakers. They can keep you in milk and cheese if my beef isn't good enough for you," her father grumbled as he pulled out a kitchen chair. "Have a seat, Officer Dawson. Tell me what you plan to do to catch the jerk who sent that email," he ordered.

Wyatt fought back a smirk. Jim Beckett was clearly a very focused man. He wondered what Cara and her father would say if he attributed her ability to maintain balance and stay centered to him. Before he could get himself settled, Cara jumped in, acting as his self-appointed public relations representative.

"Actually, it's Special Agent Dawson, Daddy. Wyatt is a member of the Cybercrimes Division."

"Cybercrimes?" Betsy repeated as she ladled up bowls of stew. "Sounds fascinating."

"Betsy loves watching those crime shows. The ones with all the DNA testing," Jim said with a nod. "It is amazing what they can figure out with nothin' more than a few hairs or a drop of blood."

"You like them too," his wife shot back.

"Yes, uh, technology has helped in some incredible ways." He cast a glance at Cara and found her reaching into a high cabinet to pull down a jar of peanut butter. Her sweatshirt rose as she stretched, exposing a couple centimeters of skin, and Wyatt felt compelled to shift his gaze back to her father. "I deal more with the ways it hasn't helped," he admitted with a wry smile and apologetic shrug.

"Like the email," Betsy said, juice flying from her ladle as she pointed it at him.

"Exactly." Wyatt surreptitiously wiped the droplet of scalding stew from his cheek as he debated what information to divulge. He didn't want to panic the Becketts, but he also needed them to be on their guard. "And you did exactly the right thing by not replying to or forwarding the email, Mrs. Beckett."

"Pssht. Call me Betsy," Cara's mother said as she plunked a bowl down in front of him. With a quick intake of breath she drew back as if she'd burned her hand, a worried frown bisecting her brows. "I didn't ask. Do you eat meat, Special Agent Dawson?"

"It's Wyatt, and yes, ma'am. I love stew."

"Oh, good," she gushed, clearly relieved. "I poured tea for everyone, but if you want something different—"

"Tea's great. Thank you."

He picked up the spoon Betsy placed on a paper napkin,

but waited until Cara and her mother joined them at the table to dig in. Cara darted a glance in her father's direction and rolled her eyes. James had already depleted half his bowl. By his daughter's bemused expression, he gathered this was the norm in the Beckett household.

"Help yourself to some corn bread," Betsy invited, gesturing to a napkin-lined basket she'd placed at the center of the table.

Cara raised an eyebrow, smirking at the basket of warm corn bread as she slathered peanut butter on a saltine. Apparently the presentation of the corn bread was not a part of the norm. He smiled as he helped himself to a wedge of the warm bread, then crumbled some into his stew.

"Thank you. It all smells delicious."

"If you ask me, everything smells fishy," James declared, not looking up from the depths of his bowl. "Why don't you tell us what the heck is goin' on here?"

"Jim, let them eat their lunch in peace," Betsy admonished.

Wyatt met Cara's eyes across the table. She swallowed the cracker she'd been chewing, then washed the crumbs down with a gulp of sweet iced tea. When she was ready, she folded her hands in front of her and angled her body to look her father directly in the eye.

"I'm not sure if you're aware, but my partners and I have decided to take our company public. We'll make a number of shares available for the public to buy on the stock market," she began.

"I know what goin' public means," James growled. "I'm not uneducated, and no matter what you think of this place, your mother and I don't live under a rock."

"I know, Daddy," Cara said with the wary patience of a person who has covered this ground before. "Okay, so I guess you know it means I'll make a lot of money when it happens. On paper, at least."

"I told you from the beginning, this whole thing is like a house of cards," James started. "Monopoly money. It's all paper printed up in New York City and assigned a value by some…guru who pretends to know the value of air."

Cara tensed and Betsy cringed. This obviously wasn't the first time they'd heard his opinion on Cara's business.

James waved his hand in the air like he was wielding a magic wand. "How can you build anything real without hard assets? Land, buildings, equipment, cattle—"

"Cattle you take to market and sell at a price set by demand on the commodities market," Cara interjected. "A made-up number conjured by the beef oracle of the sale barn."

"Actually, companies like LYYF and other web-based businesses do have real assets. Intellectual property, patents, trademarks and copyrighted catalog are all tangible and valuable assets," Wyatt interjected smoothly. "There's also licensing, subscription and franchising." James opened his mouth to argue, but Wyatt shook his head. "But we're not here to debate the valuation of Cara's company. We're here because your daughter has become the target of some very real threats."

Cara's father's jaw snapped shut and a hush fell over the room. Wyatt nodded to Cara. "Go on. Tell them."

"I started getting messages online. Which, to be honest, is not unusual. Women are not particularly revered in technology circles. There's a small, but vocal, faction of people out there who don't believe I should be a full partner in LYYF because I didn't contribute to the technological side of its development."

"But it's your face out there," Betsy countered. "Your voice people want to hear."

"Thank you, Mama."

Cara sighed and reached for another saltine even though the rest of them had stopped eating. She smeared creamy peanut butter onto cracker after cracker, setting them out in a row as she detailed the threats she'd been receiving, the attack on her neighbor and finally her flight to Little Rock and the events of the past twenty-four hours.

"Oh, my Lord, Cara," Betsy said, pressing one horrified hand to her chest and covering her mouth with the other.

James Beckett sat with his fist clenched tight and his head bowed. Silent. Unmoving. And seething.

"You can rest assured we have our best people working on the case," Wyatt said, speaking up for the first time since Cara started her recitation.

"Your best people?" James lifted his head, his jaw set and his eyes alight with the need to take action. "What about the FBI? Shouldn't they be working on this? She was kidnapped, for the love of everything holy," he cried, shoving his chair back and jumping to his feet.

Wyatt didn't move. If he were to get up too, it would only stoke Cara's father's ire. What they needed now was de-escalation. Calm. Sanctuary.

In other words, they all needed to take a deep breath.

"We are liaising with agents in the FBI field office, but since Ms. Beckett has been recovered unharmed and no one crossed state lines, they are deferring to the state police as lead on the investigation. Of course, we have full access to any resources they have when it comes to the identification and apprehension of the man who abducted her."

"I have every faith in Special Agent Dawson and his associates," Cara announced.

Wyatt did his best to mask the surprise and pleasure he took from her endorsement. Still, it was good to hear.

"And I promise you, we have been taking the case quite

seriously." Wyatt glanced over at Betsy and flashed his most winning smile. "Even without the nudge from the lieutenant governor's office."

"Lieuten—" James started then stopped on a grunt, shooting his wife a sidelong glare. "Naturally, you called your old pal Paul for help."

"I told you I called him," Betsy said, rising from the table. She picked up her own barely touched bowl, then snatched James's nearly empty one from his place.

"You think I couldn't have called someone?" James demanded. "Dewey Roarke is a senator, for crying out loud, and we've been buddies since we were seven. We could have called him."

"Dewey is a state senator, and he's *your* buddy," Betsy countered, dropping the bowls into the sink with a clatter. "You were out at the barn when I saw the email, and I called who I knew to call."

"Good old Paul Stanton, always ready to ride in on his white Cadillac."

"I called you first," she shot back. "It took you forty-five minutes to get back to the house."

"I was in the middle of feeding—"

"Hey," Cara shouted, cutting through their bickering like a hot knife through butter. "It doesn't matter who called who. I didn't need anybody to ride in to rescue me. I'd already rescued myself."

Mr. and Mrs. Beckett both fell silent. Betsy turned toward the sink, gripping its edges for support. James slumped, his broad shoulders sagging and his hands falling limp to his lap.

"You must think we're awful," Betsy whispered, shaking her head side to side.

An awkward beat passed, then Cara asked, "Me or Wyatt?"

A watery laugh escaped Betsy Beckett. "Both."

"Oh, Mama." Cara slid out of her chair and went to wrap

her arm around her mother. Betsy's shoulders shook until Cara pressed her cheek against her mother's back. "I love you even when you're awful. It must be nice to know Daddy's still a bit worked up over the guy who took you to a dance back when you all still had a feathered hairdo."

Betsy choked out a laugh, and James moved to them as if they were magnetized. Soon, both women were engulfed in the larger man's arms again. "I hate he drives a nicer car than me," he grumbled into his daughter's hair.

"I'd buy you whatever car you want," Cara said, her voice muffled. Gradually, their family knot loosened, and Cara swiped at her cheek. "I'd even shell out for one of those enormous pickup trucks killing the planet."

"You know I have no use for a truck too pretty to haul hay," her father answered gruffly. "Let's sit down. I need to hear more about what started all this."

Before they could resume their places, Wyatt's phone rang. He checked the caller ID and saw it was Emma Parker. She was calling instead of sending a message. He could only guess something big was happening. "Excuse me for a moment, please," he said, scooting his chair back. "I need to take this."

Wyatt didn't wait to see if the Becketts were put off by his abrupt departure from their table. Nor did he look back. "Dawson," he said in a low voice, hurrying back through the living room toward the front door. The screen door didn't squeak when he pushed it open, and old Roscoe didn't stir from the patch of sun on the porch. "What's happening?" he asked as he ran down the shallow steps.

"We know who the guy is," Emma informed him without preamble.

"What? How?" Wyatt pushed a hand through his hair, all too aware he was firing questions faster than she could field them, but unable to stop. "Are you sure it's him?"

"We got latent prints off the steering wheel and gearshift, but those could have been anyone's since it was a rental car. But we had two different prints match with some we lifted from her phone."

"Is he in the system?"

"He is. Permitted for concealed carry," she informed him.

"Seems like everyone is these days," he grumbled. "This joker have a name?"

"Yes. Gerald Griffin. Thirty-eight. Residence Garland County, outside Hot Springs."

"Okay." Wyatt gave the back of his neck a squeeze, then let his hand fall as he turned back to take in the scope of the Becketts' ranch. "I guess we need to start looking for good old Gerry."

"Found him," Parker informed him, her tone grim.

Wyatt froze, his gaze locked on the overfed dog napping on the porch. "You answered fast enough to make a guy say *uh-oh*."

"I traced a debit card Mr. Griffin used to buy gas at a station near the airport."

An incredulous laugh burst out of him. "He topped off the rental before he returned it? What kind of a criminal is this guy?"

"A dead one," Emma said bluntly. "I'm thinking he filled up his own vehicle. It was parked outside his double-wide when the sheriff's deputies got there a little while ago. They identified themselves when they knocked. Mr. Griffin responded with a single gunshot."

Grimacing, Wyatt tore his gaze from Roscoe's sweet face and focused instead on the mud-splattered utility vehicle James Beckett had left parked on the other side of the fence. "He shot himself."

It was neither a question nor a statement, so Emma's only response was to expel a long breath.

"Notice anything unusual when you were poking around in his financials?"

"Depends. If you consider a series of deposits under ten K apiece made over the past few days unusual, then yes."

"I take it Griffin hadn't been getting regular direct deposits before?" he asked, knowing the question was a mere formality.

"Only his unemployment draw," Agent Parker responded tiredly.

"So we're assuming someone paid him to take her." Wyatt nodded as he allowed the pieces of information gathered to settle into place. "Safe to assume the payments came from encrypted accounts?"

"Yep. Offshore and numbered."

"And you're digging into his online activity?"

"Yeah. Nothing directly tying him to Cara Beckett, but ugh, the dude totally suffered from main character syndrome."

She scoffed in such a derisive way, Wyatt ached to refrain from asking her meaning. He already felt like he was aging out in the cyber world as it was, but he needed to know. "Main character syndrome?"

"Thinks he's the main character in every story, you know? Reading his posts you'd never guess he was driving a rusty compact and living in a run-down trailer out in the middle of nowhere."

"Delusional?"

"I'd say more aspirational," Emma hazarded. "From what I can see, grabbing Cara at the airport wasn't the only odd job he's picked up."

"Other abductions?" Wyatt pressed the heel of his hand to his forehead, wondering if this Griffin guy was some sort of kidnapper for hire.

"Nothing I can find. Lots of other things, but nothing this

big. Skimming ATM cards, robbery—both commercial and residential—random credit card scams, pretty much a jack-of-all-trades."

Behind him the screen door opened, and the dog let out a low snuffling sound. He didn't need to look to know Cara was standing on the porch waiting for him. He could feel her stare.

"Okay, well, keep digging. Thanks for the intel."

He ended the call, then did a quick search for the term *main character syndrome* on his go-to slang database. A quick scan of various entries made him wonder when they'd stopped calling people plain old narcissists. He turned and found Cara sitting on the top step, feeding the dog bits of her peanut butter crackers as he gazed at her adoringly.

"News?"

The knowing trepidation in her tone told him she'd seen or heard enough to be wary. "Yeah. We identified the man who carjacked you." He crossed back to the porch, but stopped when his foot came to rest on the bottom step. "Unfortunately, when officers went to his home to speak to him, he, uh…" He hesitated for a moment, then decided there was no good way to break the news. "He killed himself before he could be questioned."

She dropped the sandwich, and her hand flew to her mouth. Her eyes squeezed shut as she murmured, "No no no no no," against her fingertips.

Wyatt scooped up the remains of the sandwich before old Roscoe could get his paws under him, then took a seat on the step beside her. "You know it is not your fault," he said, pitching his voice low.

"I know," she whispered. But it was clear from the rigid set of her shoulders she didn't truly believe what she was saying.

"I'm not even going to go into all the ways this man's

choices were not your responsibility," he continued, steam-rollering whatever internal meltdown she was currently experiencing. "You need to get there yourself."

"I know," she repeated, sounding the slightest bit steadier. "Who was he?"

"A guy out of Garland County named Gerald Griffin. Sound familiar?"

She shook her head. "I'm not even sure where Garland County is."

"Hot Springs," he answered, giving her a geographic touchstone.

She shook her head some more. "No. I don't know anyone from Hot Springs. I went right from here to California for college. We only went to Little Rock to shop or catch a flight. If we vacationed, we went north to the Buffalo or sometimes Branson or Lake of the Ozarks in Missouri."

"We have to fill your parents in."

"No." The word was little more than a croak, but the stubborn set of her chin reminded him of the spat he'd witnessed at the kitchen dining table. The Becketts were fighters, it was clear. And they were tough. Resilient. Like their daughter.

"They need to know. You can't keep them in the dark. Not only is it not fair, but also it could be dangerous. For you *and* them."

Her eyes flew open. "What do you mean?"

"Someone paid this man to take you, Cara." Gripping her upper arms, he bent until he looked her straight in the eyes. "He was paid to take you and do what with you...? We don't know."

"You think someone will come for me again," she concluded.

"We have to assume they will. And until we have the instigator in custody, I think we have to believe they are not going to be satisfied with a job half done."

Chapter Seven

Her parents' reactions to the news about the man named Gerald Griffin came as no shock to Cara, but she could tell by Wyatt's stunned expression he expected more questions than he received.

Once it was made clear the man who'd taken her was no longer a threat, her father had slapped his knees and pushed himself out of his chair, promising to be back from the south pasture before dark. Her mother murmured an insincere "Lord have mercy on his soul" before retreating to her kitchen to clear away the remnants of lunch and start preparing dinner.

For her part, she'd shown Wyatt to the guest room, told him he was welcome to set up his laptop in the seldom-used dining room and provided him with the network and password information for the Wi-Fi. Physically and emotionally drained, she retreated to her childhood bedroom, hoping some time alone would allow her to rest her mind and perhaps gain some desperately needed calm.

Gerald Griffin.

Stretched out on the twin bed she'd slept in as a girl, she tried to conjure a mental image of the man who'd turned her world upside down, and failed. How many nights had she lain in this very bed dreaming of a man sweeping her off her feet? Too many. Then, when one actually did, he turned out to be a mercenary with a gun instead of a knight on a white horse.

Had she taken a good look at him? All she had were bits and pieces cobbled together into a jumbled composite of good and evil. Brown hair? She thought so. Polo shirt. Khaki pants. Camouflage. Safety orange.

He'd seemed so harmless. Boring. An average guy renting a boring car at a middling airport in a medium-sized city in the middle of a state most non-natives would never deign to visit.

Then he'd jumped into her car, and he was the personification of a threat, complete with a handgun and masked face. The irony of it was, he was probably less remarkable without the disguise. Maybe the addition of the disconcertingly bright safety orange made him seem more menacing.

"Breathe in," she coached herself in a whisper.

She counted to four as she inhaled, waited four more seconds, then exhaled slowly. But three rounds of box breathing later, her heart still jackhammered against her breastbone. How was it possible she managed to escape a gun-wielding maniac, but found it impossible to relax in the room where she'd spent nearly half her life?

For a moment, she missed her phone with an almost physical ache. She wished she could open up the LYYF app and disappear into dissecting and critiquing her own meditations. Or tap into someone else's reserve of Zen for a bit. She'd even go for a podcast, or a particularly juicy audiobook.

Better yet, a boring one.

A book with a narrator so monotone it lulled her to sleep.

Inspired, she rolled over to gaze at the shelves above the desk where she completed hundreds of homework assignments. She spotted the cracked spines of a teen detective series she'd devoured as a girl. On impulse, she hopped up and pulled one down. Smiling, she drank in the horrendously dated cover art as she carried it back to the bed.

Less than thirty pages in, she was sound asleep with the book spread over her chest.

A TAP ON her bedroom door startled her. She sat up, pressing her hand to her startled heart. "Come in."

The door opened a crack, but rather than her mother, Wyatt Dawson peeked in. "Sorry," he said gruffly. "I hate to disturb you, but your mother says it's almost time to eat."

Cara glanced at her watch. It was nearly six o'clock. "Wow. I sacked out."

"You needed it."

She swung her legs over the side of the bed, but before she could rise, he held up a hand to stop her. She raised surprised eyebrows as he stepped into her bedroom and closed the door. She suppressed a wholly inappropriate giggle. She'd never been allowed to have a person of the opposite sex in this room. Part of her couldn't help wondering if her mother was on the other side of the house having a complete meltdown.

"I've been on the phone with the office most of the afternoon. Listen, I'm sure you want to call your partners, but I wanted to talk to you before you speak to them."

"Okay," she prompted cautiously.

"First, I want you to return any calls from your new mobile or even mine. I don't want to take the chance of anyone tracing your parents' phone number or mine through theirs."

"Sounds reasonable."

"Second, I'd like you to, uh, obfuscate a bit about your exact location."

He looked awkward and uncomfortable, and she couldn't help wondering if it was due to his word choice or the action he was asking of her.

"Obfuscate," she repeated. "I can...but why? I assume Chris and Tom know what's happening. Zarah said she would reach out to them."

"I'm only asking you to keep things vague. How much do they know about your hometown, anyway?"

She shrugged. "They know I grew up in a rural area of a state they like to poke fun at."

He pressed. "Would they know the name of your hometown if asked?"

"No, but I've mentioned it in interviews, I'm sure. It's never been a secret. As a matter of fact, I'm sure I've referred to the peace and tranquility I've found in the Ozarks in more than a few recordings."

He bobbed his head. "You have. I guess what I'm asking is how much your partners in particular know about your folks and where they live."

She stood, suspicion blossoming into incredulity. "You suspect Chris and Tom of having a hand in this?" she asked, offended for her partners. They may not be as close as they were before success pulled them in different directions, but Cara still regarded the men as two of her closest friends.

"I have to consider it," Wyatt replied, his tone even and reasonable. "They have means and a strong motive." She must have looked as horrified as she felt because he rushed to soothe her. "I sincerely hope I am wrong because I have admired them both for some time, but as an investigator, I have to take a long, hard look in their direction. They have both the money to pay someone to terrorize you and enough followers to whip into a frenzy."

"A strong motive?" She gaped at him. "What motive? We've been friends since we were eighteen, and now all of a sudden they want to get rid of me? Have me kidnapped?"

"Someone did," he interjected. "Someone paid thousands of dollars to a guy you've never met or heard of but happens to live in your home state to grab you at the airport. Some-one who knows you well enough to know your schedule. Your movements."

"They didn't know where I was going."

"As far as you know," he shot back.

He crossed his arms over his chest, straining the shoulder seams of his shirt. Cara looked away. She knew he was speaking the truth, but for the first time in her life she was learning that the old cliché about how the truth could hurt underplayed the sensation. *Hurt* was not a harsh enough word for the searing pain a few stark facts inflicted.

"Your abduction wasn't random. It wasn't a crime of opportunity motivated by robbery, like most carjackings. Gerald Griffin was waiting for you. He took you. You said it yourself. You offered him money and the car, told him to take what he wanted. He said you were what he needed. Why? What did a man you've never met need from you?"

"I don't need you to remind me," she snapped.

"No, but you do need me to help figure out who's behind all this and make them stop," he responded.

She closed her mouth so hard her teeth clacked. Cringing, she crossed her arms over her chest and leaned her head against the door frame. "I know, but I—"

She took another big gulp of air to center herself, then did exactly what she encouraged people who used their app to do. She asked for exactly what she needed.

"Can we not tonight?" Her voice trembled, but she squared her shoulders and let her hands fall to her sides, standing her ground. "I understand time is of the essence, but for tonight, one night, can we eat my mom's pot roast and talk cows with my dad? My brain is tired. I'm on anxiety overload. I need to…be for a few hours." His broad shoulders rose as he inhaled. She rushed into the breach. "I promise we can start fresh in the morning."

Wyatt allowed his cheeks to fill before he let the oxygen seep out between parted lips. "Okay. We can wait until morning."

"Thank you," she said, clasping her hands over her heart.

He started to turn away but froze as if remembering something important. "Wait. You don't eat pot roast."

Cara inclined her head in acknowledgment. "Nor will I eat the potatoes and carrots cooked with it."

"You're going to starve here," he grumbled.

She smirked, both tickled and touched by his grudging concern. "I won't, I promise. We live in the middle of nowhere. Mom keeps the pantry well stocked and I'm sure the freezer in the cellar is filled with good stuff put up from her summer garden. I'll throw something together."

He gave another one of those slow, thoughtful nods. "I won't grill you any more tonight, but tomorrow, I need everything you can give me."

"Deal," she said with a brisk nod. "Were you able to get set up okay?"

"The connection out here must be bouncing off a satellite launched during the Ice Age."

"Slow, huh?"

"Glacial. But steady so far." He held up his crossed fingers. "I'm getting surprisingly good reception on my phone, though."

She nodded, then reached past him to open the bedroom door. "Yeah. Much faster to build cell towers than to run fiber-optic cable up here."

"If I need to speed things along, I may run into town to get a wireless router," he said as he followed her down the hall to the living area.

"I hope you realize running into town from here will likely mean going back to Conway or heading up to Harrison," she warned. "Maybe Clinton, but I doubt it."

"I figured. But I haven't reached the level of frustration where I feel the need to shop," he said with a chuckle.

Cara smiled at the attempt at levity. "Well, if the urge does overcome you, the router's on me. I keep offering to upgrade things for them, but Mom insists she only uses the computer to place supply orders and check email."

"She told me she plays a mean game of online mah-jongg," he informed her as they passed through to the kitchen.

"Does she now?"

Cara raised her eyebrows when she spotted the woman in question transferring a hunk of cooked beef onto a serving platter usually reserved for Thanksgiving. Biting back any commentary about houseware choices, she crossed to the counter and pressed a kiss to her mother's cheek. "I'm sorry I fell asleep. You should have given me a shake. I would have helped."

Her mother's mouth curved into a pleased smile and Cara stayed where she was, inhaling the familiar scents of home cooking mixed with Chanel she bought for her mother each Christmas.

"You needed rest," her mother said in her usual no-non-sense tone. "I made you a sort of stir-fry." She jerked her chin at the sauté pan brimming with a jumble of colorful garden vegetables. "Used a bit of oil, some soy sauce and some all-purpose seasoning. I also have some rice. It's the boil-in-a-bag kind, not the fancy stuff," she warned.

"Sounds great, Mama," Cara said, then gave her mother another impulsive peck on the cheek. "And I don't need rice, regular or fancy. But thank you."

Cara wasn't sure if these unexpected concessions to her dietary choices were because Wyatt was here or if her mother was simply glad some strange man hadn't made off with her only child. Nor did it matter. She appreciated the effort.

"Your father is getting washed up," Betsy informed her.

"If you'll get Wyatt whatever he'd like to drink with supper, I'll get this to the table."

"Here. Let me," Wyatt said, stepping up and extending his hands to take the platter.

To Cara's surprise, her mother acquiesced without even a token protest.

"Sweet tea okay for everyone?" she asked, turning to the fridge. It was a rhetorical question as far as she and her parents were concerned, but she didn't know Wyatt well enough to presume.

"We also have milk, water and what appears to be a life-time supply of fruit-flavored carbonated water," she called.

"It was on special at the store. Buy two, get one free," her mother said with a sniff.

"Tea is fine for me, but—"

Wyatt trailed off as Cara pulled a pitcher filled with sweet tea from the fridge. But when she turned, she found him standing beside the round kitchen table where they'd eaten lunch looking perplexed. She quickly ascertained the cause for his concern. The table she and her parents had used for most meals had always been big enough for the three of them, but now, with the addition of a place setting for Wyatt, there was no room for the serving platter.

"I'm sorry I've taken over your dining table." He turned to her mother, a deep furrow of consternation bisecting his brows. "If you'll give me a minute, I can get things cleared—"

"Oh, for heaven's sake," Betsy interrupted, then pushed past him to remove the wooden napkin holder with its nested salt and pepper shakers to make room. "There." She gave him a brisk nod. "We never eat in there anyway." She pulled Cara's plate from her usual spot. "You can fill your plate at the stove, can't you, Sweets?"

"I can."

Cara was pouring tea over crackling cubes of ice when her father appeared, freshly showered and changed into clean clothes. With his damp hair combed and the remnants of his summer tan offsetting his blue eyes, Cara caught a glimpse of the handsome young man who'd wooed and won the heart of Elizabeth Watts. Her parents were an attractive couple. One day in an LA spa and they could easily shave twenty years off the birth dates shown on their driver's licenses.

She listened with half an ear as she filled her plate at the stove. Their conversation was so casual, so normal, it made her hands tremble. This time the day before, she'd been diving out of a moving vehicle. Now her father was naming off random items he wanted her mother to add to their supply list. Yesterday, a strange man named Gerald Griffin had been alive and well and pointing a gun at her. Today, he was dead, and her mother was pushing food on a handsome special agent from the state police.

Staring down at the kaleidoscope of vegetables on her plate, Cara focused on the vibrancy of their colors. Rounds of bright orange carrots, red pepper and yellow squash were offset by dark green zucchini and pale chunks of cauliflower. She was safe. She was home. Her mother had made this gorgeous stir-fry for her, and she was grateful. More grateful than she could say. Wetting her lips, she grasped the plate hard enough to mask her terror as she turned to join them at the table.

She wouldn't let whoever was doing this steal these precious moments from her. She would pass the few hours in peace, then tomorrow morning she and Wyatt would put their heads together and start figuring things out.

Forcing a smile, she placed her plate on the table and dropped into her chair. When she was sure she had the shaking under control, she reached for her glass and gulped the sugary sweet tea. As the cool liquid soothed her parched throat, she couldn't help thinking about how horrified her friends back in La-La Land would be if they knew she was sucking down tea brewed with leaves trapped in bags with little tags and sweetened with no less than two cups of refined white sugar.

Wyatt's phone rang and they went still.

"I'm sorry," Wyatt murmured, but they all knew the apology was both reflexive and performative. Of course he would take the call.

"It's almost as if people are aiming for our mealtimes. Go on," her mother encouraged, but her smile was nervous and forced. "We want to know everything we need to know."

But do we? Cara thought as Wyatt rose, swinging his leg over the sturdy wooden chair and pulling his phone from his pocket in a fluid motion now familiar to her. She placed her cutlery across the edge of her barely touched plate. She stared down at the brightly colored dish her mother had gone to the trouble of preparing for her, knowing she wouldn't manage another bite. Her stomach was too sour. Her throat bone-dry.

Betsy reached over and covered Cara's hand with hers. "Try to eat something. You need your strength."

Across the table, her father sat with his knife and fork clutched in each hand. "What do these people want?"

"Honestly? I don't know," Cara confessed.

"Is it money?" he persisted, jabbing his fork into his slice of roast a mite too forcefully. "They asked for ten million dollars in the email." He snorted. "Who could possibly come up with so much money?"

Cara bit her bottom lip. She didn't know how to tell her father she could. If she were to sell her portion of LYYF to Chris and Tom now, she'd be able to cover the ransom demand and still have money left over. And if she waited until after the company went public…well, according to Chris, ten million would be little more than pocket change.

As if reading her mind, her mother zeroed in on her. "Do you have that kind of money?"

Uncomfortable with the topic of money in general and feeling cornered, Cara squirmed in her seat. "I, uh," she started. Her father stopped chewing and stared at her as if he'd never laid eyes on her before. Caught in his steady blue gaze, she confessed, as always. "Not, um, you know, liquid."

Her dad gently lowered his silverware to his plate and pulled his napkin from his lap, never breaking eye contact. "But you have access to large amounts of money?"

Cara cringed inside. She'd spent most of her adult years downplaying the perceived extravagance of her California lifestyle. Particularly in the three years since the app went stratospheric. She'd sent them photos of her charming little house on Sunset Drive, but she never told them she'd paid nearly two million dollars for fifteen hundred square feet of space. It wasn't the kind of math people who clip coupons and pride themselves on canning homegrown vegetables and preserves would understand.

"I do," she replied, but added nothing more. Thankfully, Wyatt reappeared and the subject was dropped. "What's happening?"

"Not a lot. I guess Chris Sharpe has left for New York. Something about meetings with some fund managers before the stock offering. Emma says she spoke briefly with Tom Wasinski, and he says he'd like you to call him."

"Nothing more on tracing the money?" she asked as he reclaimed his seat.

Wyatt settled his napkin into his lap. "No, we've hit a dead end on the numbered accounts, but Emma is monitoring chatter on a couple forums she thinks Griffin was active

on, and I have some other angles I want to track after dinner."
He picked up his fork again. "I'm sorry for the interruption."

The rest of dinner passed in fits and spurts of congenial small talk. After they were through, Cara helped her mother with the dishes while her father saw to Roscoe's evening kibble and Wyatt retreated to his laptop. She was settled in the den with her parents watching a police procedural when he reappeared, looking rumpled and worried.

"Anything?" she asked, motioning for him to join them.

He skirted Roscoe's enormous orthopedic pet bed as he stepped into the room. The dog gave him a cursory snort as he passed. "Nothing we didn't already know. Countersurveillance on your accounts is running as it should," he reported, taking a seat on the opposite end of the sofa. "Nothing has popped yet."

The detective in the television show started rattling off a list of supposedly damning physical evidence they'd collected during a cursory search of the victim's sister's bedroom, and Wyatt let out a disdainful scoff.

Cara and her mother looked over at him, surprised by the interruption, but her father was the keeper of the remote. The moment the scene cut to a commercial, he muted the volume and shifted in his recliner to look directly at Wyatt.

"I take it things don't tie up so neatly in the real world," he said with a nod to the television.

"Most of the testing they mentioned doesn't exist. Or, if it does, it either produces results too unreliable to use as evidence or is so expensive most municipalities couldn't afford to implement it," Wyatt explained. "Good physical evidence is much harder to come by than fictional."

"I can't believe you dare to sit here and spoil one of our favorite shows," Cara accused.

Wyatt raised his hands in surrender. "Not another word," he promised, a smile playing at the corners of his mouth.

"I think it's far more interesting to know what's real and what isn't," her father interjected.

"Jim is hooked on those true crime documentaries they show on CineFlix." Betsy shuddered. "I prefer my crime scenes off camera and the bad guys rounded up at the end of an episode." She gave him a wan half smile. "I don't suppose it happens very often in the real world."

Cara shot him a look, hoping he'd tread carefully. Given the circumstances of their visit, the last thing she wanted to do was add to her mother's worry by piling on depressing crime statistics.

"You'd be surprised," Wyatt said, crooking his arm on the back of the sofa and angling his body in the direction of her parents' matching leather recliners. "In most cases, things are so obvious they wouldn't make for good television."

They finished out the hour and by unspoken agreement segued right into the next episode. "Tell us where they get things wrong," her father prompted as they joined the investigators on the scene of yet another grisly murder.

"I have to tell you, I've been to relatively few crime scenes," Wyatt warned. "I'm more the guy back in the office pulling the background reports or analyzing data."

"Fake it," Cara said out of the corner of her mouth. "I promise we won't know the difference."

So he did, and for the next hour, the three Becketts peppered poor Wyatt with all manner of questions, doubts and pie-in-the-sky theories as to the unraveling of the crime. By the time the case was resolved, the four of them were exhausted from poking holes in each other's theories. And Cara was able to forget she was the subject of an ongoing investigation.

For a few hours, at least.

Chapter Eight

Cara awoke to five young men dressed in an assortment of leather pants and jackets gazing down at her, each one smoldering harder than the next. She rubbed the sleep from her eyes, then rolled them as she recalled Wyatt's smirk when he saw the old poster tacked to the wall of her childhood bedroom. Fixing her gaze on her longtime favorite, she whispered, "Don't worry, guys. He's jealous of our love."

It was early. The light coming through the partially open blinds was the dusky rose of dawn. Reaching out, she switched on the milk glass lamp on her bedside table. Gold incandescent light flooded the room, and idly, Cara wondered when her parents changed the bulb. Probably not long after she'd stopped gazing longingly at her teenage crush each night before she drifted off to sleep, she figured.

Lifting her arms over her head, she indulged in an extravagant stretch. It felt so good, she laced her fingers together and pressed her open palms toward the ceiling. The next thing she knew, she'd fallen into a rhythmic four-count breathing pattern, her gaze fixed on the blooming sunrise.

She heard her parents moving around the house. The rumble of an ATV engine signaled her father's imminent departure. When it faded into the distance, she closed her eyes and listened hard for any clue as to whether her mother had gone with him to the barn. The clank of cast iron against the stovetop grate rang out with the promise of breakfast.

Cara smiled as she sank into the moment, feeling more centered than she had in weeks. It always felt good to come home, even if she hated admitting it.

The sky morphed from peachy pink to pale violet. Memories of running through the back door of a simple clapboard farmhouse that used to stand less than a quarter mile up the lane came flooding back. The slap of the screen door. The scent of fresh-baked bread. Sheets snapping in the stiff breeze whistling around the tree-covered mountains and through the valley.

She loved her grandparents' house. The old house, as it was called. There was always a pan of leftover biscuits on the stove. Whatever wasn't eaten at breakfast would be gobbled up with whatever Grandma tossed together for lunch. Or dinner, as she'd called it.

After Granddad died, Grandma moved up to the new house with Cara's parents. Her dad claimed the old house was falling down around her ears, but Cara didn't see it. When you're a kid, you don't think about drafty windows, rotting floorboards on the porch or dripping pipes.

Grandma June brought little more than her cast-iron skillet and her love of all things Hollywood with her to the new house. She slept in the room Wyatt currently occupied until the day she passed. They watched old movies together well after her parents had turned in. When she was small, Grandma June happily paid a shiny quarter for a ticket to whatever living room production Cara cooked up in her head. She'd helped Cara run lines for every school play or drama club soliloquy.

Her grandmother was the one who'd dipped into her life savings to cover Cara's airfare to California. Her gran was the first person she'd called when she'd thought she'd blown an audition or got a callback for a second look. When she passed, Cara'd spent the entire flight home sobbing into a wad of paper napkins a kindly flight attendant had provided while the businessman next to her pretended not to notice.

In her absence the old house had fallen into even more disrepair. Sitting empty, there was water damage. Rot. Termites. Black mold. When it was demolished, Cara was hurt beyond reason. She accused her parents of tearing down the best parts of her childhood. Trips home became less frequent. Phone calls were kept brief and perfunctory.

She opened her eyes, a fresh surge of anger and betrayal coursing through her veins. If they had only waited a few more years, she could have had the old house restored. But she knew such wishful thinking was fruitless. Her parents would still have been saddled with the upkeep on a house she'd visit once, maybe twice a year. She shook her head, dismissing the thought and the rush of emotion it rode in on.

Her father had done what he needed to do.

Resolved to make the most out of this unexpected time with her parents, she swung her legs over the side of the bed. The floorboards were cool underfoot. She reached for the hooded sweatshirt she'd hung on a bedpost and pulled it on over the T-shirt she'd slept in. By the time she shimmied into yoga pants and some socks, the tantalizing scent of bacon drifted down the hall.

She closed her eyes and drew from the well of inner strength, hoping it would allow her to withstand temptation. Of all the foods she'd eschewed when adopting a vegetarian diet, bacon had been the hardest habit to break. Turning the doorknob, she stepped into the hall, promising herself an enormous bowl of old-fashioned oatmeal topped with brown sugar and pecans.

The guest room door opened, and Wyatt poked his head into the corridor. She smiled when she saw one side of his hair was still artfully rumpled, while the other appeared to be suffering a near terminal case of bedhead.

"Do I smell bacon?" he asked, darting a hopeful look in her direction.

"Undoubtedly," she replied. "Dad usually only has a cup of coffee first thing. He'll come back in for breakfast once the cows are fed and turned out."

He pointed to the bathroom door. "Do I have time to shower?"

She nodded. "Yeah. I'll go help Mama and take mine after we eat."

He gave a quick nod then ducked back into the bedroom. Shoving her hands into the pockets of her sweatshirt, she shuffled through the house, her shoulders hunched against the autumn chill.

Cara found her mother fishing strips of crisp bacon from Grandma June's skillet and smiled as she listened to her hum an old Beatles song. Not for the first time, Cara thanked the heavens she'd inherited her father's ear for music. Her mother couldn't carry a tune in a paper bag.

"Mornin', Mama," she said, falling back into the easy vernacular of her youth. "Can I help?"

"Morning, Sweets," her mother said, turning from the stove with a wide, guileless smile. "I've got bacon, eggs and toast." Her smile faded and she cast a worried glance in the direction of the bedrooms. "I hope that'll be okay with Wyatt."

"I'm sure it will be," Cara assured her. She moved to the cupboard where the coffee cups were kept and pulled down the biggest one she could find. "He smelled the bacon."

Her mother wiped her hand on the crumpled dishcloth beside the stove and nodded. "I won't start the eggs until your daddy comes in, but what am I gonna feed you?"

Cara bit her bottom lip and refrained from shaking her

head. Every meal, the same despairing question. "I was hoping for some oatmeal," she said as she poured the rich, black coffee into her mug. "And maybe a handful of pecans if you have some stashed somewhere?"

Her mother gave an indelicate little snort. "You can have more than a handful. Those trees your granddad planted dropped enough to feed an army of squirrels this winter."

"Then I definitely won't starve." Cara cradled the mug in both hands and took a cautious sip of the steaming brew.

Thirty minutes later, the sun was up, Wyatt had emerged fully dressed, her father had returned from the first of his morning chores and Cara was doctoring a steaming bowl of cereal. She could feel her father's gaze on her as she swirled a liberal sprinkling of brown sugar and cinnamon into the oats before dropping chopped nuts into the mixture.

"Would you like some of my oatmeal, Daddy?" she asked without looking up. Her father hated hot cereal. Always had, always would, he'd proclaimed on more than one occasion.

He picked a strip of bacon cooked shy of burnt off his plate and held it out to her. "Wanna bite, baby girl?" he taunted, his voice morning gruff.

Cara smiled. "No, thank you," she replied sweetly, looking up in time to see a puzzled expression cross Wyatt's face. "It's a thing we do," she explained.

Their customary exchange complete, her father pierced the orange-yellow yolk of his perfectly fried egg with the corner of a piece of toast, then pinned Wyatt with a stare. "So tell me, what is it you do exactly?"

She wanted to object to the blunt question, but Wyatt's quiet chuckle assured her there was no offense taken. On the contrary, he seemed bemused.

"Do you want the big picture version or the dreary details?"

Her father took his time chewing his toast before answering. "I want to know how whatever it is you're doing applies to keeping my daughter safe. I want to know how you're going to catch whoever's doing this to her."

Wyatt paused, giving the question serious consideration. Idly, he broke off the end of a strip of bacon, popped it into his mouth and chewed, his gaze never leaving her father's face. "Do you remember me telling you the tracing technology had far exceeded what you see on the television police procedurals?"

"Yessir," her father replied, sopping up some more of the runny yolk with his toast. "Why I'm askin'. It seems like you should be getting more answers than you have."

"We do have answers. We simply don't know how they fit together yet. We know what's happening. We know how they're surveilling her. We know what's being said online and by whom in many cases. We even know where some of the communications have originated."

Her mother spoke up. "If you know who and where they are, why aren't you going after them?"

"Because most people don't use landlines anymore. We can ping whichever towers a cellular call is coming from, or trace the IP address of a message, but the technology is mobile now." He shrugged. "And even if whoever is posting these things is sitting in the parking lot of a police station, the most we can do is question them. What they say is protected under their First Amendment rights."

Wyatt said the last with an edge of rancor, but her parents responded with true outrage.

"People can't go around publicly threatening people," Betsy argued. "Isn't it some form of terrorism?"

Her father dropped his fork with a clatter. "What if there's evidence those threats are credible? Someone abducted her at gunpoint."

"We have no evidence connecting Gerald Griffin to any

of the threats against Cara. From everything we've uncovered, he was hired help."

"Hired help," her mother repeated. "What a world we're living in."

Cara reached over and gave her hand a gentle squeeze. "The world is wonderful. There are some bad people in it, but there always have been." She gave them a sad smile. "The only difference is, now they have more ways to spread ugliness."

"Exactly," Wyatt said with a decisive nod. "Most online chatter is nothing more than someone using a keyboard to make themselves feel heard. They can say whatever they like about somebody, and no one can stop them. Makes the powerless feel powerful."

They fell silent for a moment, their cutlery still as they digested this unsavory bit of reality.

"I don't know about y'all, but I'm feeling pretty powerless right about now," Betsy admitted.

"Me too, Mama," Cara said softly. Then she thought about those desperate people sitting at their keyboards grasping for any opportunity to feel heard. She looked from her father to her mother, then across at Wyatt, then she smiled. "But at least we aren't alone."

CARA WAS PARKED at the dining room table pretending to write scripts for upcoming recordings, but it was hard to come across as calm and centered when her life was skidding out of control. Catching her bottom lip between her teeth, she stole another glance at Wyatt. He'd been alternating between feverish typing, glaring at his screen and muttering soft oaths under his breath for the past hour. She'd tried to engage him in conversation a couple times, but his curt answers and unwillingness to look up for more than a second telegraphed his unwillingness to engage in her procrastination efforts.

Thankfully, her phone rang.

Wyatt frowned at the name on the screen, then slid it across the table to her. "Zarah."

"Hey, Z," she said into the phone. "Hang on, let me go in the other room."

She slipped from her seat to move to the other room, but Wyatt caught her wrist as she passed, shaking his head and mouthing, "Stay."

Everything in her rebelled against his high-handed order. But the man was here because of her. He'd packed a bag, picked her up and taken up residence in her parents' house all to keep her safe. She needed to stop fighting for control. The sooner she gave herself over to the situation she was in, the sooner she'd find her way through it. Struck by her own moment of clarity, she moved back to her notebook, anxious to capture the thought. She scribbled the words "give over to get through" on the paper, then reclaimed her seat with a grin.

"What's up? Aside from you," she added, glancing at her watch. It wasn't even seven Pacific time. "You're usually still unconscious until at least nine."

"I got a call from the short-term-rental company," her assistant began, and Cara sucked in a sharp breath.

She'd completely forgotten to text Zarah to let her know she'd left the condo. "Oh! The condo." Her gaze flew to Wyatt. He widened his eyes, then grimaced. He'd clearly forgotten about checking out of the place too.

"Are you okay? What happened?" Zarah demanded. "Where are you?"

The level of panic in the younger woman's voice set alarm bells off in her head. Cara pulled the phone away from her ear, pressed a finger to her lips to indicate Wyatt should keep quiet, then put the call on speaker. "What's going on?"

"You tell me," Zarah demanded. "They called this morning saying the place was torn up and informing me they were charging the entire security deposit. Not the unit owner, but the actual company. The app," she babbled. "Little Rock police got a noise complaint. Neighbors said it sounded like there was a big fight going on. Anyway, they called the owner, but they live in Oregon. They asked the cops to check it out, and when they did, they found the door wide open and no one there. It was trashed."

She and Wyatt exchanged wide-eyed stares. Cara wet her lips, then forced a word past her suddenly dry throat. "Trashed?"

"The police sent pictures. The unit looks like someone was totally raging."

Without a word, Wyatt reached for his own phone and started typing a text.

"I left early yesterday morning and everything was fine," Cara said in a rush. "I meant to text you so you could check out, but I forgot. I'm so sorry. I didn't trash the place. You know I would never. But I packed up my stuff and left. I'm sure I locked the door after me." She darted a glance at Wyatt for confirmation. He thought for a moment, then nodded his agreement. "When did they get the noise complaint?"

"They said yesterday morning," Zarah replied. "I guess it took some time for it to get from the police back to the owner to the rental company. I freaked when I heard. I thought maybe the kidnapper was coming after you again."

"No. No one came after me," Cara said, her mind awhirl.

"Where are you?" Zarah asked again.

She opened her mouth to speak, but clamped it shut again when she caught sight of Wyatt wagging his head hard. "I, uh, I'm staying with a friend. I didn't like being alone after, um, what happened."

"What friend? Where?"

"Listen, Z, I want you to go ahead and reach out to the company and the owner and assure them I did not do this. Also let them know I'm happy to cover any damages, though. I should have let them know I was out of the unit. You have access to my cards and accounts. Do what you need to do to make this right."

"But you're okay? You're safe?" the other woman prodded.

"I'm safe."

"When are you coming home? Do you need me to book a flight for you?" Zarah persisted.

"Not yet. I'm still…decompressing. Catching up with my friend. But I'll call you as soon as I'm ready," she promised. "Would you please take care of the condo for me? I feel horrible. Maybe I didn't lock the door properly after all. Either way, at the very least, I should have let them know I was out so they could set the alarm." Wyatt made a motion for her to wrap it up. "I'll call you back later, I promise."

She ended the call before Zarah could wedge another question in and looked up at Wyatt aghast. "Someone broke in yesterday. It must have been right after we left."

His mouth pulled into a grim line. He nodded as he raised his phone to his ear. "I have a friend with the LRPD. I'm going to see what I can find out from them."

"Do you think it was this Griffin guy? I mean, could it have been?" She moved her chair a few inches closer to his, shaken and needing to feel his proximity.

"It could have," he murmured. "Need to see if the timeline fits." He held up a finger for her to hold the thought. "Yeah, this is Wyatt Dawson from the state police. Is Mark Jones in, please?" He must have been put on hold because he lowered his finger and resumed their conversation without missing a beat. "Does he return the car, gas up his truck, then go looking for you? No." He shook his head, dismissing the chain of events. "He'd go looking for you in the rental. Wouldn't want to risk anyone ID'ing his vehi— Hey, Mark," he said, his tone shifting from speculative to professional in the space of a syllable. "Wyatt Dawson. How are things?"

He listened for a minute, nodding. "I hear you. Yeah, we'll have to do that. Listen, I won't keep you, but do you think you can find out who's handling a break-in and property damage case for me? I think it's connected to an active investigation." He rattled off the address of the condo, tapping his pen against the side of his laptop. "Yeah, give them my number. Appreciate you."

Cara couldn't suppress her bemused smile.

When he looked over at her, the crease between his brows deepened. "What?"

She shook her head and wiped the smile from her face. "Nothing. I was— It's funny, is all."

"What is?"

"The weird kind of conversational shorthand guys have. If I'm interpreting your two-minute conversation correctly, you commiserated about the job, asked for what you needed, confirmed the urgency and need for response, and made some vague plan to get together—"

"Which we never will," he interrupted.

"Exactly. All wrapped up in a neat little package." She skimmed her palms together as if drying them off. "I wasn't criticizing. In fact, I was admiring your skill."

He dropped the pen to the table and leaned in to look at her. "It would have to be a wildly tight timeline for it to be Griffin," he mumbled.

She watched as he snatched up his phone and started to fire off another text.

Narrowing her eyes, she asked, "How do you know your

messages are safe?" His head popped up, and for a moment he looked affronted. "I'm only asking. I mean, are they regular texts or do you have some sort of secure channel like on TV?"

"We have an encrypted network, but it's not foolproof. Some people love to crack codes," he muttered, finishing his message.

She inclined her head. "People like you and Agent Parker," she said quietly.

He studied his screen, a smile tugging at his lips as he jabbed at the trackpad. "Exactly." Then he scowled at his laptop. "I don't know how your folks can stand service this slow. Thank goodness they weren't trying to use a computer while watching CineFlix—it would crash the bandwidth. It'd get hung up right in the middle of the big forensics reveal."

His phone dinged and he glanced down at it. "Eight fifty-three a.m.," he reported. "If he trashed the place, he wouldn't have been too far behind us."

"What time did we leave?"

"Somewhere around there. I got the package with your stuff and came right to you."

"So he was doing all this in broad daylight," she murmured.

"Sometimes it's easier. People notice a commotion in the night. We're actually pretty lucky someone was home to hear it. Most people would have left for work already."

"Yeah, we're so lucky," she said with an edge of sarcasm.

He fixed her with a stern stare. "We are. We were already gone. Now, Emma's emailing a copy of the receipt for the file." He checked his computer, then grabbed his phone. "I'm going to switch to my phone's cellular hot spot. This is driving me crazy."

A few seconds later the email with the scanned transaction from the gas station came through. He sent off two more emails before switching off his hotspot and settling back in his chair, fingers poised over the keys. "You up for running through this all again?"

Cara nodded, sitting up straighter in her chair. She spoke low and steady, keeping her breathing even as he typed a bullet-point timeline of events starting with the day she noticed an uptick in hostile messages and brought them to the attention of her partners. When they got to the attack on her neighbor Nancy and her decision to fly home to Arkansas, he slowed her down, asking her to get more granular as he added incident after incident. Her voice cracked when she recounted her decision to jump from the car, still not quite able to believe she'd done it. She hadn't realized how high and tight her voice had become until Wyatt stopped typing and reached over to cover her hand with his.

"Breathe," he encouraged. "It's okay. I've got the rest."

She nodded, dragging in a deep but shaky breath. "Okay. Okay."

"I've got you," he assured her, giving her hand a quick squeeze before releasing it to resume his typing.

Cara sagged in her seat, exhaling slow and low and feeling more confident than she had in weeks. "Yeah. We've got this," she whispered.

Chapter Nine

The rest of the day passed with agonizing slowness—on all fronts. Wyatt tried his best to refrain from grumbling about the antiquated internet service running to the house, but programs and scans he could run at high speed in Little Rock seemed to be caught in some old sci-fi movie's vision of a wormhole. Whenever he could, he switched to using his phone as a hot spot. It seemed counterintuitive to be able to get better mobile reception than satellite internet. When he mentioned as much to James Beckett on their afternoon ride around the property, the older man simply pointed to the flashing beacon on a tower poised atop the nearest hill and muttered something about Betsy's boyfriend opting for improved cell service instead.

When they returned to the house in time for Jim to fire up his propane grill, they found the fridge restocked and the two women sitting on the back deck sipping white wine.

Betsy Beckett countered her husband's raised eyebrow with a smug smirk. "I thought pork tenderloin would be nice for a change. Cara has some vegetables in there she'd like you to grill too. Oh, and I bought you boys some beer."

"Sounds good," Jim said. He leaned down and kissed his wife's cheek on his way to the door. "You pick up ice cream for dessert?"

Her lips curved into a serene smile. "You know I did."

"Perfect. I'll get things ready, then be out to get things fired up."

"I chopped and seasoned some veggies and threw them in the grill basket. Would you cook them up for me, Daddy? You're so good at grilling," Cara called after him.

Her father simply raised a hand in acknowledgment of her shameless flattery. Wyatt smiled at Cara. She looked a thousand times more relaxed than she had when he left with her father after lunch. Whether it was the wine or the nap she'd planned to take while he was out, he wasn't sure. Either way, it looked good on her. An afternoon in the fresh air had done him a world of good. Wyatt decided he was going to do his best to be sure the rest of the evening remained mellow. They all needed a bit of a breather.

"All quiet on my end," he assured her. "I'm gonna go help your dad."

She toasted him with her wine. "We expect great things from you," she called as he followed her dad into the house.

In the kitchen he found Cara's father rooting around in the back of the refrigerator. When he surfaced, he held up a package of microwavable mashed potatoes and fixed him with a challenging stare. "Life lesson—there's no need to peel, chop, boil and mash when you can have these hot and tasty in less than five minutes. Don't judge me."

"I grew up eating instant rice."

"We both believe in working smarter," Jim said with a conspiratorial nod. "Let's get this going. I'm starved."

When they sat down to dinner, her mother picked up the platter of sliced tenderloin and offered it to Wyatt as she addressed the table in general.

"Did I tell you I ran into Delia Raitt in town?" He helped himself to a piece of the meat, but before anyone could answer, she pushed the platter back at him. "Take two. Y'all look famished and you know Cara isn't going to have any."

His attention caught on how Cara stiffened at the name, he did as she asked with a murmured "Thank you," then relinquished the fork. When no one commented on Betsy's conversational gambit, he asked, "Delia Raitt? Is she someone you went to school with?"

"Mrs. Raitt was the principal's secretary when I was in school," Cara answered stiffly. "Liked to stick her nose in everyone's business."

"Well, the school district has consolidated and she's working for the superintendent now. The school system is all different now, but Delia is the same."

Jim Beckett ate steadily, oblivious to his daughter's unease. "Still nosy."

Betsy didn't seem to notice Cara's discomfiture, because she continued on without further encouragement.

"So nosy I'm surprised she doesn't trip over the end of it," Betsy said with a tinkling laugh. "Anyhoo, Dee said they've been getting calls about you."

"What kind of calls?" Wyatt asked, working to keep his tone neutral.

"Reporters, mainly. She said people have been calling and asking about your big business deal in New York," she reported, blasting Cara with a wide, proud smile. "I didn't say anything before because I wanted your daddy to hear too, but she said they're all real proud of you around there. Apparently, all sorts of fancy technological magazines have been calling and asking whether you'd come home to talk to the kids about working in big tech and what it's like to build a business from the ground up and all." She waved her fork in an all-encompassing circle before using it to stab a hunk of grilled squash.

Jim Beckett dropped his fork and stared at his wife with

the open disbelief Wyatt wished he could show. "Are you kiddin' me with this?"

Betsy blinked, her smile slipping as she cast a glance at Cara, then back to her husband. "No, I'm not kidding. I told her we were proud of her too." She reached over and gave Cara's hand an encouraging pat. "And we are. Even if we don't understand it all. Aren't we, James?"

Cara's father blinked, then stared at her with such naked incredulity Wyatt cringed inwardly. "Were you drinking before you went to town?" he demanded.

"What?" Betsy asked on a sharp inhale. "No. Of course not."

"Don't you get it?" Jim shook his head. "The people callin' the school might not be reporters. They could be the people behind this whole mess." He threw his hands in the air. "Criminy, Elizabeth, we're not supposed to let anyone know she's here."

"I didn't tell anyone she's here," she retorted, shoving her chair away from the table. "I'm not a fool, and I won't be spoken to like one in my own home."

"Okay, okay," Cara interjected. "Let's all…take a breath."

Her father rolled his eyes. "Take a breath," he muttered under his. "Same mumbo jumbo for the folks willin' to pay for it."

"Fine," Cara snapped. "Let's all calm down and talk rationally," she demanded, sounding about as far from calm and rational as a modern-day guru could. "Do you think we can manage to get through one meal without bickering or picking at each other?"

Wyatt held his tongue as the older man nodded then ducked his head, reapplying himself to his plate. "I'm sorry. I didn't mean to be a jerk," Jim said quietly.

"You were a jerk, but your apology is accepted," his wife responded, punctuating her largesse with a prim sniff.

"People are calling the local school asking questions about Cara?" Wyatt asked, rephrasing the gist of the conversation.

"Yes," Betsy said, her tone markedly more subdued. She twiddled her fork, routing out a divot in the mashed potatoes he'd so painstakingly nuked. "I didn't think it sounded threatening. At least, Delia Raitt didn't make it come across like it was. She was goin' on about what a big deal Cara was now, and how proud we must be, and how she never thought little Cara Beckett would turn out to be a fancy big shot." She turned to look at her daughter. "Her words, not mine."

"Did she happen to name any of the publications they said they were calling from? Did you recognize any of them?"

Betsy shrugged, then shook her head, her smile turning rueful. "She said a couple of names, but they sounded computer-y to me." Jim snorted and her eyes lit with fire. "Like you know any better, James Beckett. You tell me the name of one of those tech blog thingies," she challenged.

"Doesn't hafta be one of those. It's been all over *Forbes*, the *Wall Street Journal*, the *New York Times*," Jim said quietly. When they all turned to look at him, he glanced up from under lowered eyebrows. "What? I don't live under a rock."

Cara ducked her head, and Wyatt couldn't help but stare as a peach-pink flush crept up her neck to her cheeks. The woman practically glowed with pleasure at this small concession from a man Wyatt himself had reclassified from remote and disinterested to quiet and observant over the course of an afternoon in his company.

"There are dozens of legitimate publications interested in profiling your daughter," Wyatt said, gently breaking the spell. "I know to those of us back here at home it may seem like she has put herself out there with LYYF, but in truth, Cara is kind of an enigma in tech circles. Aside from her work published on the app and the social media connected to it, she has stayed out of the media. If there are interviews to be given, it's usually one of her partners in the spotlight."

"Usually Chris," her mother said with a nod. "He loves to be the one doing the talking. Always was the slick one. I remember from the time we came out there to visit."

"Chris is a talker," Cara conceded.

Wyatt jumped back in before they strayed too far off track. "From everything I can find, and believe me I have looked through all accounts connected to her, Cara doesn't put much of herself out there. Which is why she found it such a shock to have people on the internet taking such an, uh, intense interest in her personal life."

"I don't even take pictures of my food," she said with a wry smile.

"And here I thought all people put on those sites were pictures of their plates," her father said gruffly.

Cara flashed him a grateful smile and Wyatt felt his shoulders drop as the tension in the room dissipated.

"I can't," Cara said, her tone turning serious again. "I learned early on. The second I post something, a yummy dinner or a pretty blue sky, people crawl all over themselves trying to interpret the hidden meaning behind my post."

"Some people can't accept the appreciation of a pretty blue sky at face value," Wyatt said, nodding his understanding.

"Exactly. People say I'm making a statement about climate change, or take the opportunity to lecture other community members about the proper use of sunscreen. I have to be very careful about everything I post online. You never know how people will interpret it, and there's always someone waiting to pounce."

Her father shook his head in disgust. "People have nothing better to do."

"Everyone has to share their opinion," Wyatt commiserated.

"My daddy used to say opinions were like belly buttons—everyone has one, but you don't need to go around flaunting it," Betsy chimed in.

"I heard it using a different body part," her husband said under his breath.

Betsy frowned. "What body part?"

Wyatt chuckled at their byplay but refused to further the conversation. Instead, he turned to Cara. "I'm assuming the company has a publicist or PR firm they work with?"

She nodded. "All official media requests are supposed to go through a woman named Amanda Pierce. She has a boutique firm out of Palo Alto. It's called APPR," she added. "But it's not unusual for people to try to work around the process. We all get requests. Zarah fields them for me every day."

"But the bigger outlets will go through the publicist," he asserted. "I can see individual vloggers trying to get around the gatekeeper, but there'd be no reason for the *Times* or the *Journal* to do an end-around. Publications like *WIRED*, *TechCrunch*, *CNET*...they'd want everything on the record, and they'd want to be able to follow up on anything newsworthy."

"You think these people calling the school district were only pretending to be reporters?" Betsy asked, fear warring with incredulity in her voice.

Wyatt flashed an apologetic smile. "It's possible. You're sure you didn't give any hint of Cara being here?"

A deep crease of concern appeared between Betsy's brows, and she bit her lip as she closed her eyes, no doubt scouring her memory for any innocuous little comment. "I'm sure," she said at last. "She asked when we were going to California to visit again, and I said something vague about maybe over the holidays."

She flashed a wince of a smile, and Cara reached over to

squeeze her hand. "You know I'd love to have you out any-time you can get away."

Both women looked at Jim, who'd remained laser focused on his food through this whole exchange. Without looking up from his plate, he mumbled, "I did like fresh-squeezed orange juice in the mornings."

Judging from the radiant smiles breaking across the women's faces, his confession was as good as a promise. "My lemon tree has started producing too," Cara informed him.

"No need to gild the lily, sweetheart," Betsy admonished softly. "We'll make arrangements for one of the Ford boys to come look after things while we're gone."

The ladies spent the rest of the meal extolling the many virtues of California living, only requiring the occasional "Huh" from him and grunts of affirmation from Jim. By the time Cara jumped up to retrieve the ice cream and bowls, the mood was considerably lighter. But the supercomputer in Wyatt's head hadn't stopped running probabilities and turning over possibilities.

After they were through eating, Jim said something about needing to make some calls. Wyatt escaped to the dining room and his laptop. A few quick queries gave him the low-down on the newly consolidated school district and its administration. If he'd grown up anywhere else, he might have marveled at the odds of a cold caller actually connecting with a person who knew Cara and her family, but he was an Arkansan. He knew better. People born and raised in the Natural State either stuck close to home or ran far away.

He'd stuck close.

Cara had gone about as far as she could go, shy of buying a boat.

Grabbing his phone, he fired off a quick text to Emma to let her know about the calls to the school administrator's office. It wasn't critical information, but at this stage they were massing every bit of data they could and sifting through them like the tourists who spent days sieving dirt at Crater of Diamonds State Park. At this point they were hoping one of the bits of nothing they unearthed turned out to be a precious gem.

Next, he ran a general search on Cara's name. Scrolling past results for her website, links to LYYF, a Wikipedia entry and optimized entries for some of the more popular pages on the LYYF website and blog, he found an article in a respected tech journal about the company's upcoming stock option and the buzz surrounding one of the world's most popular apps. He skimmed nearly halfway through it before he realized her name had not appeared in the text. He hit the Control and F keys and typed "Beckett" into the pop-up search box.

One result returned.

Holding the arrow-down key, he scanned the screen until he found the highlighted name.

When he spotted it, he stared at his screen in disbelief. Cara, the face and voice of the LYYF app, and her 33 per-cent ownership, didn't garner a single mention in the body of the post. He'd found her tagged in the article's keywords, but nowhere in the lengthy, and somewhat fawning, narra-tive about the company's inception and astounding growth.

Skipping back to the top of the article, he checked the by-line. The author was someone named Nate Astor.

He searched the site for other articles by the same author and discovered Astor was one of their main contributors. Scrolling through his previous articles, he found two more related to LYYF.

One was a one-on-one interview with Chris Sharpe pub-lished the previous spring, and the other was an opinion piece in which he debated the value of creation versus con-tent. About two-thirds of the way through the article, he spotted Cara's name. Biting the inside of his cheek, he read and reread the man's hot take. Wyatt found it ironic the reporter, whose job it was to create content for an online magazine, dared to question Cara's contribution to the LYYF app's success.

"So much for solidarity, huh, Nate?" he muttered, clicking back to look through more of the man's work.

Not surprisingly, he found more than one post concerning GamerGate. He grimaced. He'd been in school when a band of misogynist jerks claimed to be on a quest to fight "political correctness" in the online gaming world by harassing, doxing and threatening female media critics and game developers with bodily harm.

"Finding anything good?"

He jumped, reflexively tipping the cover of his laptop down to shield her from his discoveries.

Cara blinked, then let out a bitter huff of a laugh. "Wow. I was kidding, but I guess you did. Was it about me, or were you looking at X-rated websites in front of my mother's Precious Moments?"

"What?" He glanced over his shoulder when she gestured to the collection of figurines on display in a corner curio cabinet. "Oh. No. You startled me is all."

"Reading something good?" She sank into the chair adjacent to his, her stare unflinching.

"Went down the GamerGate rabbit hole," he confessed.

She made an exaggeratedly horrified face. "I didn't peg you for a misogynist, so you must lean toward masochist."

"The guy who wrote the article has also done a couple on LYYF," he explained. Then, angling to face her, he asked, "Does it bother you when they leave you out of the press coverage?"

She opened her mouth, then closed it. He could almost see her swallowing whatever flip answer she kept on hand for this type of question. Rolling her shoulders back, she met his eyes directly. "Yes."

"Do you ever say anything about it to them?"

"No." She shook her head. "Not anymore."

"Why?"

She pointed to his laptop. "Ironically enough, Gamer-Gate." Folding her hands in front of her, she let her gaze slide down to the computer. "Whenever Chris or Tom even mentioned my name in connection to the business end of things, the trolls came swarming out. So we stopped." She dropped her eyes to her clasped hands, a rueful smile curving her lips. "I contented myself with the idea of being the face of LYYF, and for the most part, I like it better this way too. I get to be the star without the freaky hero worship Tom hides from, or the constant pandering Chris loves and loathes."

"But in serious publications where they're discussing the future of the business..." He trailed off, unsure he wanted to push too hard on a point that was glaringly obvious to him but may not have occurred to her.

"The lack of attribution may make people think my contributions have not been commensurate with full partnership," she concluded.

"Or give the impression your partners feel they are not," he said, fixing her with a pointed stare.

Cara unwound her tightly knotted fingers, splaying her hands open wide and flat on the tabletop to stretch them. "At first, I was happy to have what I thought would be a shield from the vitriol," she said, nodding toward the laptop again. "But after things took off there were times I felt credit wasn't being given where credit was due."

"Did you speak to them about it?" he prompted again.

"I did. On more than a few occasions," she said flatly. "To be fair, most of the requests for interviews have been fielded by Chris. He enjoys the spotlight more than Tom."

"Enjoys it to the point of hogging it. In most of the articles I read, Tom is relegated to nothing more than a couple lines. Even then, he's spoken of as some kind of tech wizard hiding behind the green velvet curtain. You're barely mentioned at all."

"None of us got into this to be famous," she pointed out.

"But I have to assume the guys, at least, got into it to get rich," he retorted. "It was basically a run-of-the-mill personal finance app until your posts started taking off." He tapped on his phone to wake it, then opened the application. Within seconds, the Cara Beckett who'd calmed his anxieties and gently lulled him to sleep appeared. He turned the phone to face her. "You made this app what it is. Everything they built…it's all scaffolding for your genius, not theirs." He leaned in, his stare searching. "Are you trying to tell me it doesn't bother them?" When she didn't answer, he gentled his tone. "Why haven't they called, Cara?"

She shook her head. "You don't get it. Things are complicated—"

"No, I don't get it." He interrupted whatever excuse she was planning to employ to excuse the shortcomings of the men she still called friends. "And I don't see it as complicated. If my friend was being attacked from all sides, I'd be there. If my friend had been abducted at gunpoint, I'd do more than text her assistant for updates. But then, my friends aren't about to increase their wealth exponentially by taking a share of the money I may or may not believe to be rightfully mine."

"Now, wait a minute—" she began, but he held up a hand to halt her protest.

"I won't say anything more. They are your friends and your partners. You know them a thousand times better than I do," he conceded.

"I do."

"But I want you to know, as far as I am concerned, no one is above suspicion. Because you and I both know there's no enemy with better ammunition than a person's best friends."

"I understand."

"And you mentioned something about Zarah having access to your accounts. Do you mind if I do a deeper dive into your financials?" He didn't need to ask, really. He could probably hack his way into every account she'd ever opened without any trouble, but she was starting to trust him, and he didn't want to risk compromising her trust.

"My financials?"

"I only want to be certain there are no...anomalies. If people have accessed everything else, it wouldn't be much of a stretch."

"Oh, wow. I never thought." She cocked her head. "I hardly ever even look at bills or account balances anymore. Zarah has everything covered."

"Just a cursory glance," he assured her.

She nodded and looked to be about to say more when Betsy appeared in the dining room doorway.

"Come on, you two. Enough work for one day. Jim has time for one episode before he hits the hay and I want to see if you can solve the case before Detective Pemberton figures it out." She made a shooing motion, then declared, "I'm making popcorn."

With a sigh, Wyatt powered down his laptop and closed the lid. Cara showed no inclination to move. Placing his hands on the edge of the table, he pushed his chair back. "Come on. Your mom is right. We've done enough for one day."

Wordlessly, Cara followed him into the family room, where her father had an episode of a murder mystery cued up and ready to go.

Wyatt smirked when he saw the show they'd selected. "You remember I'm not a homicide detective, right?"

"Neither am I," Jim answered gruffly.

"But I bet you have a friend who's one," Cara said, petulance lacing her tone.

"I do, as a matter of fact." He turned to look at her, but she stared straight at the screen. He'd hit a tender spot in questioning the quality of her friendships with her partners, but he couldn't say he regretted doing so. If she spent even a few minutes thinking deep thoughts about her relationship with the men she's helped make rich, maybe she'd reach the same conclusion he had.

Internet bullies were thick on the ground, for certain. But no one had better motive for wanting her out of the picture than Chris Sharpe and Tom Wasinski. Everything she'd told him about her life and the lives of the two men would suggest their friendship had become distant. A relationship bearing a label bestowed by nostalgia, but in truth boiled down to a business arrangement forged by people who were little more than kids.

But it wasn't a real friendship.

"Hurry up. I have to be up in seven and a half hours," Jim called to his wife.

"Hold your heifers," she retorted as she bustled back into the room. She distributed bowls of microwaved popcorn to each of them.

"Isn't it supposed to be 'Hold your horses'?" Wyatt asked Cara, hoping to break the ice, but she remained silent.

"Not on a cattle ranch," her parents replied in unison.

Jim pointed the remote at the screen as Betsy claimed her seat beside him. The opening theme music played and he darted another glance at Cara. She sat stone-faced, her jaw tight as she glared at the television screen. In the dim light, he thought he caught the faint shimmer of tears in her eyes and looked away.

They were less than five minutes into the show before he and Jim pointed to a slick-looking charmer on the screen and declared, "That one," in unison.

"Oh, honestly," Betsy muttered as she rolled her eyes. "My grandma could have seen him coming." With a huff, she grabbed the remote away from her husband and clicked through the menu. "Go to bed, spoilsport."

Chuckling, Jim kicked the footrest of his recliner back into place and rose with a groan. "Maybe I should become a homicide detective. What time do y'all have to be at work most days?"

"Long after you are," Wyatt replied with a sympathetic smile.

"Night, all," Jim called as he dumped the remainder of his popcorn into Betsy's bowl. "Wire to stretch in the morning."

"I'll be along in a bit," his wife promised as she scrolled through the options. She paused on one featuring characters in elaborate costumes. "Oooh. Wyatt, do you like *Pride and Prejudice*? Cara and I love this one, don't we, hon?"

Wyatt smiled and nodded, stuffing his cheeks with popcorn to avoid having to say more. If watching people who carried parasols and walking sticks was what it took to get back on Cara Beckett's good side, he could take it. At least, he hoped he could.

Chapter Ten

Cara jerked out of a dream where she was hurling herself from a car being attacked by birds. Why she thought she'd be safer outside when they were pecking viciously at the glass, her conscious mind could not fathom, but there—

The tapping came again. Pushing up to her elbows, she glanced at the window first. No. Someone was pecking at her door. She blinked into the darkness, then figuring it was one of her parents coming to tell her they were off on their predawn errands, she croaked, "Come in."

The bedroom door swung inward, but Wyatt stayed firmly on the other side of the threshold, his phone pressed to his ear. She sat up in her single bed, the covers drawn up to her chin, waving him in. The last thing she wanted to do was wake her parents.

"Emma Parker," he mouthed to her, indicating the other agent was on the opposite end of the call as he stepped into her room. He glanced at the door and raised a brow. She nodded and he closed it behind him, sealing them both into the small bedroom. She hit the switch, and the glare of the ceiling light set them both blinking.

"You said someone called Cara's phone? Which one?"

Cara threw back the covers and sprang from the bed.

The display on her ancient clock radio showed it to be approaching 2:00 a.m.

"And what did they say, exactly?" he persisted. Cara scowled and tugged on his arm, but he held firm, his lips thinning as he listened. "I see. Any confirmation of damage?"

She tugged again, and he pulled away, then motioned for her to remain patient.

"What is happening?" Cara hissed between clenched teeth. She grabbed hold of his free wrist and squeezed. "Damage to what? Where? The condo?"

"Ah, okay. I see." He nodded, then gently removed her hand. "I'll let her know and call you back when we've had a chance to figure out next steps."

He ended the call, then lowered the phone, his brow furrowed with worry. "What? What is it?"

"A little after midnight Emma had a call come through to your original mobile number from the new one and thought it was odd, so she picked up."

Cara frowned. "After midnight? Is she working twenty-four-hour shifts?"

He shrugged. "We're a small department and most of our work can be done off-site. We often take our work home."

"You said something about damages. What happened?"

"The caller claimed there was a fire at your residence, then hung up. Emma checked the voice mailboxes for both numbers and found one where the caller said something along the lines of 'accidents happen when you play with fire.'"

"Play with fire?"

"Emma put in calls to the LAPD and fire departments, and was able to confirm an emergency services call to your address, but they wouldn't give any additional information and the detective assigned to your case has not returned her calls as of yet."

She let out a breathy snort. "Yeah, I can believe it. I know they have their plates full, but…yeah." She pushed a hand through her hair, and the corn-silk strands fell right back over her eye. "So what do we do?"

"Do you have anyone you can call who lives nearby? Zarah?"

Shivering, she tugged at the hem of her top, wishing she had long sleeves and pajama bottoms rather than the cotton T-shirt and sleep shorts Zarah had procured. Shifting to place one cold foot atop the other, she shook her head. "Zarah lives out in the Valley. We do most of our work virtually."

"A neighbor? Your cat people?"

Color flooded her cheeks. "We, uh… I don't have their phone numbers. Any of them," she added, looking down at her hands clasped in her lap in bewilderment. "It's not Arkansas. I've only lived there a few years and…"

He tried to pretend he understood, but the idea of not knowing at least some of his neighbors must have been almost incomprehensible to him. Little Rock was a good-sized city, but in many ways it was still as interconnected as a small town. The truth was, there were few degrees of separation between most Arkansans, and even the city folk tended to look out for their neighbors.

He cleared his throat, and plowed ahead. "Em has been on the forums." He gave her a sympathetic wince. "The scuttlebutt online is it wasn't an accident and the damage is pretty bad."

"You think someone set fire to my house?" She blinked up at him, not quite certain they were speaking the same language.

He reached past her, plucked a hoodie from the bedpost where she'd hung it and handed it to her. "I'm telling you there was possibly a fire at your residence in Los Angeles, and we have heard rumors it may have been the result of arson, and the damage is extensive. Nothing is confirmed, and no one has tried to reach out to you. Not the local officials, not Zarah or any neighbors. For all we know, this is a hoax."

Cara shrugged into the sweatshirt. "Someone is saying they set fire to my house," she repeated flatly.

He nodded slowly. "Yes."

"They said they'd burn it all down," she murmured as she huddled into the fleece-lined warmth.

"Who did?" he prompted, his brow furrowed. "Who said 'burn it all down'?"

Cara shook her head, her bewilderment turning to helpless fury. "They did." She practically spit the words. "The people sending me nasty messages and scaring my poor mother half to death. Whoever paid Gerald Griffin to pull a gun on me in an airport parking garage." She threw her arms out wide, as if gesturing to the wide array of invisible threats closing in on her. "They are doing this. Whoever *they* are."

"Until we can get confirmation from a trusted source, we need to assume these are simply rumors." He held her phone out to her. "Emma sent the number for the person she spoke to with LAFD. You need to be the one to call." She reached for the cell phone with a sticky note affixed to the glass, but he held firm for a beat too long. "It's possible they won't give you any information over the phone."

"They'll give me the information. If being a semipublic figure is good for anything, it's being recognized." She yanked the phone from his grasp.

She stared down at the name scrawled below a number with the familiar area code. Investigator Shanna Gleason. The moment the call connected, she introduced herself and, reading from the sticky note he'd handed her, asked to speak to Investigator Gleason.

A moment later a woman picked up. "ACTS, Gleason here."

"Um, hello. Yes," Cara stammered, her gaze darting to Wyatt. "Am I calling the Los Angeles Fire Department?"

"Yes, ma'am."

A huff of self-conscious laughter escaped her. "Sorry. I guess I expected you to say LAFD when you answered, but you said something else and I wasn't sure," she rambled.

"Who's calling?" the other woman asked.

"Oh, right. This is Cara Beckett. I'm calling about reports of a fire at my house on Sunset Drive in Los Feliz," she said, focusing on the facts. "I believe you were contacted by Special Agent Emma Parker with the Arkansas State Police trying to confirm there was a fire?" Again, her gaze found Wyatt's, and he nodded encouragingly.

"Yes, ma'am, I spoke with Agent Parker," the investigator on the other end confirmed.

When she said nothing more, Cara gestured her frustration at Wyatt. "Ask to put her on speaker," he whispered.

"Ms., uh, Investigator Gleason, I'm here with Special Agent Wyatt Dawson of the Arkansas State Police. Do you mind if we put you on speaker?"

There was a moment of hesitation on the other end, then a curt response. "Sure."

Cara pressed the speaker button, then nodded at Wyatt. "Investigator Gleason, this is Agent Dawson. I work with Agent Parker and am currently with Ms. Beckett. What can you tell us about these reports of a fire at her property?"

"Are you currently in police custody, Ms. Beckett?" Investigator Gleason asked. "Isn't it the middle of the night in, uh, Arkansas?"

"It is, but I am not," Cara answered, stiffening at the implication. "Agents Dawson and Parker are working on a case in which I was the victim."

"I see," the other woman answered in a cautious tone.

"Ms. Beckett has been the target of several credible threats to her safety," Wyatt informed her. "One of those threats turned into a reality when she landed in Little Rock. I am here with her now as both an investigative and protective partner." He caught her eye and held her gaze. "Tell me, what does ACTS stand for?"

"Arson Counter-Terrorism Section," she replied crisply.

"I see," he replied.

Cara only whispered, "Arson."

"You believe someone set the fire intentionally," Wyatt prodded.

"I'm afraid so. I'm happy to hear you were not in the structure at the time, Ms. Beckett. Can you confirm whether anyone else should have been on the premises in your absence? House or pet sitter? Guests?"

"No. No one."

Cara pressed her fingertips to her chin to keep it from trembling. She loved her house. It was the one extravagant purchase she'd made since the app took off, and she'd spent countless hours making it her sanctuary. Now, because some jerk hacker decided to post her address for all the trolls to see, someone had violated her sanctuary. Again.

"How bad is the damage?"

"Looks worse than it is," the woman on the other end assured her. "You'll need to contact your insurance company and get someone out there to start restoration. It may take a while, but in my estimation, the house should be habitable again."

"I'm assuming you found evidence the fire was set intentionally?" Wyatt asked.

"We didn't have to look very hard. They left gas cans

in the yard. And before you ask, no, we weren't able to get any physical evidence from them. I'm assuming our firebug wore gloves."

"I see." At a loss for how to proceed from here, Cara sought Wyatt's steady reassurance again.

He nodded to her cell phone. "We'll ask Ms. Beckett's assistant to help with the insurance and getting the place secured. Has Agent Parker shared any information with you on the case we're working here?"

"Only to route all attempts to contact Ms. Beckett through your office for the time being."

"Thank you. I do have some information I can share. I think it may be helpful to you. If you would send me your email address, I will send you a link to the files. I warn you, it'll be encrypted and will ask for about everything but your blood type and the guarantee of your firstborn son."

He said the last in a lighter tone, but Cara couldn't even muster the weakest smile.

The other woman chuckled. "My son is acting every minute of his fifteen years these days, so if you want him, you are welcome to him." She paused to take a breath. "I'm curious to see what you have in your file, Agent Dawson. As long as it doesn't have one of those 'click on pictures of bridges' things," she added. "And Ms. Beckett?"

"Yes?" Cara responded in a reedy voice.

"I'm very good at catching firebugs," Shanna Gleason assured her.

Cara straightened her spine and inhaled through her nose as if taking in the other woman's confidence. "I'm sure you are. Thank you," she added, a small smile tugging at the corners of her mouth.

She ended the call but didn't relinquish the phone.

Wyatt looked down at her and sighed, his expression troubled. "Maybe I shouldn't have told you until I knew more."

"No." She sat down on the edge of the bed. "Don't shut me out. What I don't know *can* hurt me, Wyatt. It can hurt me badly. I don't want you withholding information from me."

He inclined his head. "I agree. So now you know." He stepped back, groping for the doorknob. "It's unlikely we're going to get more information at this hour."

"I guess not," she conceded.

Then she heard a muffled cough from down the hall. Her parents. Biting her lip, she looked up at Wyatt, her expression pleading. "Listen, can we keep this quiet for now? I don't want to worry my parents any more than I already have."

He nodded solemnly. "What happens in California stays in California." Wyatt held out his hand. "I'd like to hang on to the phone. Emma and I are still checking incoming messages and voicemails regularly."

She placed the device in his hand without protest. She was discovering how pleasant it could be to have a buffer between her and bad news. "Take it."

He ran a hand through his hair. "Try to get some rest. There's nothing we can do from here. We can come at this fresh in the morning."

She sank back onto her heels and smirked. "Are you going to sleep?"

"I'm going to try." He gave her a lopsided smile. "I know things start earlier around here than they do in Little Rock."

She glanced at the ancient clock radio on the bedside table. "My dad will be up and out in a few hours."

"Try to sleep. There's nothing we can do right now. Your house can be fixed, and we know you're safe here." He started to back out of the room. "We'll go after them again tomorrow."

"Right," she said, though she couldn't imagine how he planned to go after anyone. She felt like Don Quixote, fighting off imaginary foes. "We'll go after them again tomorrow."

"Good night, Cara." He pointed to the poster on her wall, then hit the light switch as he backed into the hall. "Try to get some sleep. Dream about boy bands," he added in a loud whisper.

Cara snorted and wondered why her mother had left the poster tacked to the wall for all these years. "Good night."

The door clicked shut behind him, and Cara climbed back into bed. Pulling the sheet and quilt up over her legs, she leaned back against the pillows, the hood of her sweatshirt pushing up against her ears. She yanked it up over her head and sank into it.

Trolling, threats, doxing, attempted assault, thwarted kidnapping and now arson. Uncrossing her arms, she stretched them wide before drawing them into her sides. The ceiling stared back at her. Closing her eyes, she reached deep into her bag of tricks.

It took three rounds of deep sleep meditation before she landed on a course of action. Decision made, her mind quieted and she finally drifted off.

WYATT WAS UP a while longer. Grumbling about the slow internet connection, he attempted to comb through the hundreds of direct messages, forum entries, social media posts and emails sent to Cara within the past month. Sure enough, he found some reference using the phrase "burn it all down" in every mode of communication. Bone tired, he created a folder titled "Fire" and added screenshots of each one to it.

When he was finished, he powered down his laptop and set it aside in favor of pen and paper. But rather than making case notes, he reached into the bag of tricks he'd picked up from the LYYF app in an attempt to clear his mind. Pen in hand, he numbered a blank page in the battered composition notebook he carried with him with numerals one through ten. Then he did his best to distill everything nagging him into a list of no more than ten bullet points to be addressed the following day.

Thoughts, hunches and random observations. He listed them all in no particular order. Everything from his suspicions about Cara's business partners to the need to talk to Jim about getting better locks installed on his doors. He noted the guest room was decorated in a trendy farmhouse scheme, but Betsy Beckett had left a poster of a boy band taped to the wall of Cara's old bedroom. He started an entry about her blue eyes, but caught himself in time to change it to a more businesslike inquiry regarding whether she wore prescription eyeglasses. Then, annoyed with himself, he recopied the list of IP addresses he'd isolated and wanted to run the next day as punishment for getting too personal.

In the end it was a mishmash of to-do items, reminders and worries a desk jockey like himself was in over his head on a protection detail. He was forgetting something. What was it?

Tapping the end of his pen against the paper, he gnawed his lip until he tasted blood. When was the last time he'd been to the shooting range? He'd been raised in duck-hunting country and firing weapons since he was big enough to hold a pellet gun, but being responsible for the safety of a living, breathing woman was a far cry from shutting down phishing schemes and heading off malware attacks.

He set the notebook aside and rolled out of bed and padded down the hall to check the door locks. If nothing else, he could cross number three off his list straight off the bat. Satisfied they were as secure as the flimsy lock sets would allow, he returned to the guest room. The notebook teetered on the nightstand. The inside of the waistband holster he preferred took up much of the free space. He'd found an outlet for his phone charger behind the headboard. It sat charging and silent since the call from Agent Parker. He could only assume everyone was in bed. As he should be.

But his mind would not slow.

On impulse, he grabbed his phone and scrolled through his contacts until he found the number for a guy who'd graduated from the academy not long before him. For most of his career with the Arkansas State Police, Ryan Hastings had provided personal security for politicians, visiting dignitaries, sports figures and, most recently, a very high-profile heiress before retiring to start his own agency.

Having done all he could do for now, he toed off his shoes as he tapped out a quick message for Ryan to contact him at his earliest convenience, then stretched out on the bed without bothering to undress or pull back the duvet.

Wyatt stared at the ceiling for a full fifteen minutes before his flighty thoughts landed on the thing he'd forgotten. Grabbing his pen and paper, he scrawled, "Follow the money," on his list of things to do, before tossing the pad and pen on the unused pillow.

He was asleep in seconds.

Chapter Eleven

He awakened to a light knock on the door. Wyatt cracked an eyelid and was surprised to find bright autumn sunlight streaming through the window. Judging by the angle, he guessed it was early by city standards, and likely midday in ranch time.

"Come in," he croaked.

The door opened and Cara poked her head in. "Hey. I tried to let you sleep, but I couldn't wait any longer."

He sat up and swung his legs over the side of the bed. Feet planted firmly on the floor, he scrubbed the sleep from his face with his palm. "No. I should be up." He checked the time on his phone. Seven thirty. He'd slept for a few hours, but it still didn't feel adequate. "You get any sleep?"

She smirked and shrugged. "Some here, some there. Restless."

"Fretting," he corrected.

"I think I'm entitled."

Her retort was sharp enough to jolt him fully awake. "Of course you are."

"Sorry." She glanced over her shoulder, then returned her temple to its resting spot on the door frame. "My mother always says I get snappy when I haven't had a good night's rest." She paused long enough to roll her eyes. "I hate it when she's right about me."

"Parents. They think they know everything." He pushed to his feet and stretched. "I suppose yours have been hard at work for hours?"

She nodded. "Dad said if you want, he'd take you out again later."

Wyatt nodded and scratched his stubbly cheek. "I'd like that."

"They left biscuits and sausage gravy for you."

"Great." Then he caught her wording and paused. "Left? Did your mom leave?"

Cara's eyebrows shot up. "Was she under house arrest?"

"No, I thought…" He trailed off, his ears burning.

"You thought she stayed here all day making stew and doing the mending?" she teased.

"No. I mean, I know she handles the paperwork and such, I didn't know she did, uh, work out there." He hooked a thumb over his shoulder. He clamped his mouth shut. He was digging himself deeper with every single word. "I need coffee."

Cara took mercy on him. "I'll pour you a mug. Mama went to pick up some wire fencing they need for repairs. She'll be back by noon, but I warn you it's Daddy's day to cook, so it'll be cold cuts for lunch and something grilled for supper."

Wyatt inclined his head to indicate her message was received. The Beckett Ranch was an equal opportunity operation. "I'm going to take a quick shower. Clear the cobwebs."

"Go for it," she said, pushing away from the doorjamb. "I only wanted to get my phone."

"Your phone?"

"My cellular device?" she prompted. "I don't want to take the chance of anyone tracing the landline, remember?"

"Right, but who are you going to call?"

This time, only one brow rose. "Do I have to clear it with you?"

The icy edge in the question had him straightening his shoulders. "No, but it would help things if you kept me in the loop."

"I'd like to call my assistant, if you don't mind," she returned with a sniff.

As if on cue, the phone sang out its generic ringtone. Cara raised an eyebrow at him, then let her gaze trail over to the phone lit up atop the dresser. The display showed Zarah's number. "Speak of the devil. It's Zarah," she informed him, swiping to accept the call.

"Put it on speaker?" He did his best to phrase it as a request rather than a demand, but it could have gone either way. Thankfully, Cara complied.

"Hey, Z. You're on speaker and my pal Wyatt is here," she said, darting a glance at him. They'd agreed to play their relationship to one another off as friendship in case someone was listening in.

"Cara! I can't believe it," Zarah said in a rush. "Is it true it's a total loss? Your beautiful house. It was so adorable. I'm heartbroken."

Cara's eyes darted to his and Wyatt scowled. He tapped the mute button then said, "We need to think for a minute about how much you should say to people. Can you tell her you'll call her back? Let me get a cup of coffee and kick-start my brain."

She nodded, the tip of her tongue pressed against her top lip as she blinked rapidly, clearly trying to get her emotions under control before she spoke. He squeezed her shoulder, then stepped away, giving her space. "Hey, yeah, we're actually on another call. Can I call you back? I'll fill you in as soon as I can."

"Of course. Call me if there's anything you need me to do. I don't mind driving down there," Zarah offered.

"I appreciate the offer. I'll let you know when I've wrapped my head around it all."

Wyatt waved his arm to get her attention and when she looked over at him, he mouthed, "How did she know?"

"Yeah, um, Z? Did someone call you or something? I mean, how did you find out?"

She darted a glance at Wyatt and he gave an exaggerated nod. She'd hit exactly the right note of vague but focused calm. It wasn't until he saw her take a slow, deep inhale that he realized it was because she was using the same voice she used for meditations on the app.

"Find out? The news. It's all over the news," she cried. Then she caught herself. "Oh, wait. It's probably not making the local news there, is it?"

Cara pulled a face, then shook her head as she wrapped up the conversation with promises to call back.

Wyatt pulled up the browser on his phone and typed "Cara Beckett house fire" into the search engine. Within seconds he had all the information he needed. Without a word, she took the phone from his hand, her lips parting in shock as she took in the photos of what used to be her picture-perfect home.

Wyatt stared too. Though he had been the one to deem the posts a credible threat, he hadn't truly believed someone had done the deed. But they had. Whoever they were. They set fire to her house. The house he'd looked up on a popular real estate site the night before. To a guy from the mid-South, the California cottage looked high-end. Sleek, clean lines. Solid surfaces. It looked like it was built to withstand anything Mother Nature could throw at it.

Too bad there was no way to guard against the darker side of human nature.

Beside him Cara emitted a guttural groan.

"I'm sorry," he murmured, knowing the words to be wholly inadequate.

"I have to..." She fumbled with her phone. "I'm calling Zarah back."

He reached for her hand, but he wasn't sure if he was trying to stop her or steady her. "Hang on a second."

"I can't. I can't hang on," she insisted, her voice rising with agitation. "I have to get back." Zarah must have answered because Cara snapped into planning mode. "I have to get back. Can you book me a flight?"

Wyatt had no idea what Zarah's response was, but he started shaking his head. "No. You can't."

"I'm a couple hours from Little Rock, so I'd need a flight tonight," she continued, undeterred.

"Not a good idea," Wyatt insisted. He reached for her elbow, but she spun out of his grasp.

"Maybe look at flights out of Springfield, Missouri. Or the regional airport in northwest Arkansas?" she persisted. "Or even Memphis."

"Cara, it's not safe for you to go home right now," he said, raising his voice in a vain attempt to break through her stubborn streak.

She spun on him, her eyes bright with fear and fire. "It's not safe here, either."

He stepped closer to her, hoping to force her to back off from a bad plan. "You know it's better here than there. No one knows where to find you here. And even if they did, they'd have to go through me to get to you."

Their gazes clashed and locked. She lowered the phone from her ear, and for a split second he thought maybe he'd gotten through to her. But rather than pressing the button to end the call, she switched the audio to speaker.

"I can get you out of Little Rock after seven tonight. You'd connect through Dallas and get into LAX a bit after midnight," Zarah reported.

Cara continued to drill holes into him with her laser-like focus. For a hot second, he fooled himself into thinking she was coming around to seeing things his way.

Lifting the phone close to her lips, she looked him dead in the eye and said, "Book it."

She ended the call, then stepped calmly around him and stalked back to her room.

"Cara," he called, whirling on his heel. "I know those photos are awful, but you have to think this through."

But he was speaking to an empty hallway. He skidded to a halt in his sock feet, gripping the frame of her bedroom door to slow his momentum. She was riffling through one of the plastic bags of clothes.

"You can't go to California."

"I'm not going to California," she replied in a tone so placid he wondered if he'd imagined the whole phone call.

"But you—"

"I asked Zarah to buy an airline ticket," she interrupted. She pulled a pink hooded sweatshirt from the bag and snapped the tag off with a vicious yank. "I didn't say I'd be on the plane."

He blinked twice. "You're not going?"

"I'm not a fool," she said, shrugging into the hoodie.

Narrowing his eyes, he assessed the woman in front of him. "I would never mistake you for one, but do you care to clue me in on your plan?"

She started pacing the room, phone clutched in her hand and movements jerky with pent-up frustration. "I don't have a plan. All I know is some joker posted my private information for all to see, and my neighbor got attacked in front of my house. I try to get out of town for a few days, and a random guy I've never laid eyes on tries to kidnap me. I get away from him, but then, said random guy ends up dead. Meanwhile, back on the coast, someone set fire to my house, Wyatt. I don't know if they thought I was in it, or if they even cared—"

"They know you weren't in it," he interjected.

She whirled. "How do you know?"

"We're monitoring the chatter online." He pressed the heels of his hands to his eye sockets in a vain attempt to quell the throb building in his brain. "Can I please take a shower and have some coffee before we play twenty questions? We need to talk, and I can't think," he said, exasperated.

"Fine." She waved a hand at his rumpled clothes. "Go take your shower. I'll go brew a fresh pot."

"Thank you." He exhaled the words in a gust, then turned and trudged down the hall to gather his stuff. If they were going to go multiple rounds on how best to handle this fire situation, he needed to be as clearheaded as possible.

CARA POURED STEAMING coffee into two mugs as she waited for Wyatt to shower and change. The scent of her mother's fluffy biscuits still filled the kitchen. She lifted one corner of the tea towel covering the ancient iron skillet. Her stomach rumbled like distant artillery as a battle of will raged inside her. Cara knew the heavy pan had been greased liberally with the bacon drippings collected in the can on the counter. But the biscuits themselves were made from the same self-rising flour her grandmother had used, and fresh butter and buttermilk from a neighboring farm.

Nostalgia made her chest ache. The sight of those golden brown biscuits made her mouth water. Her stomach gurgled again, and she abandoned her principles.

"Desperate times," she murmured as she pulled one from the still-warm pan.

She split the biscuit, slathered it with butter and drizzled fresh honey on top before taking an enormous bite. Closing her eyes, she hummed her appreciation as she chewed. It was a taste of her childhood. A bite of a time when things were simpler. Safer.

Absently, she licked at a drip of buttery honey oozing down the side of her hand.

Cara popped the last bit into her mouth, chewing slowly as she doctored the other half. This time, she nibbled at the edge of the biscuit, letting the butter and honey flow onto her tongue as she peered out the window over the sink. The land where the old house once stood had long since been reclaimed by Mother Nature, but it was still vivid in her mind's eye.

"What's your plan?"

She jumped at the sound of Wyatt's voice, and the remains of the biscuit crumbled in her hand. Butter and honey oozed between her fingers. She'd been so deep in her thoughts, she hadn't heard him approach. Her face flamed with embarrassment and a touch of shame as she shook the clumpy mess off into the sink.

"Sorry," he said as he approached. "I thought you'd have heard me talking to Roscoe."

"No, I was…" She turned on the tap and cool water rushed out, coagulating the goo coating her hand. She closed her eyes and drew a steadying breath as she waited for the water to warm. "I was in another world."

One filled with biscuits baked in grease-coated cast iron and dusty memories. A world where she envisioned herself being the next Meryl Streep rather than an internet-famous—or infamous—voice-over artist being terrorized by internet trolls.

He lifted the corner of the towel and eyed the leftover biscuits still nestled in the pan. "These look great. My MaMaw used to make biscuits in a cast-iron skillet too. Refused to eat the kind out of a can."

His use of the pet name for his grandmother triggered an involuntary smile. "Mine too. This was her pan."

Wyatt eyed the pan covetously. "I buy the frozen ones once in a while. They're better, but not like this."

"They're okay, but so full of preservatives."

"Californian," he muttered.

Cara chuckled as she wiped her hand on the dishcloth hanging beside the sink. "Plates are in the cupboard in front of you. Gravy is in the microwave."

She scooped the remains of her sodden biscuit from the sink with a paper napkin and deposited the wad in the trash. Then, taking one of the coffee mugs, she retreated to the kitchen table. Settling into a chair, she warmed her hands on the ceramic mug as she watched Wyatt move easily around the kitchen. His dark hair was still damp from his shower, curling slightly at his nape. He had the lean build of someone who runs, and overall, he seemed fit. She remembered him mentioning a float trip on the Buffalo River, and wondered if he was a hiker. He looked outdoorsy.

He turned toward the table, plate and mug in hand, and caught her staring. "What?"

Rather than giving in to embarrassment again, she switched into interrogation mode. "Are you the outdoorsy type?"

Wyatt eyed her warily as he took the seat across from her. "Why? You planning on dropping me out in the woods with nothing but a compass and a water bottle?" He pointed the tines of his fork at her. "I have to warn you now, I don't go anywhere without a laptop and a hot spot."

She shook her head, though the image of him trudging through the woods using his phone as a compass and with his laptop bag strapped across his chest was amusing. "I was curious. You mentioned floating the Buffalo."

"Oh." He turned his attention and his fork on the plate of food in front of him. "Yeah, sure, I like floating. I prefer a canoe to a kayak, even though I know kayaks are cooler right now. I hike the trails at Pinnacle Mountain a couple times a year, but mainly because it's so close to Little Rock and sometimes I need to get out of the office and out of my head, you know?"

"I get you," she said before taking a sip of her coffee.

Using the side of his fork, he cut the gravy-smothered biscuit into bite-size chunks. "I'm not big on camping," he said with a shrug and sheepish smile. "I'm fond of electricity."

"Me too," she assured him. "I mean, me neither." She gave a short laugh then summed it all up. "I don't camp."

"So, why are you asking if I'm 'outdoorsy' when I ask what your plan is?"

"Oh, I wasn't planning…" She laughed at the roundabout of non sequiturs they'd been riding. "Two separate trains of thought converged. Sorry."

"Ah, okay." He shoveled a bite into his mouth and chewed, closing his eyes appreciatively. After washing it down with a sip of coffee, he pulled a pained face. "I'm never going to be able to eat another frozen biscuit again."

"Ruined, huh?"

He stabbed another gravy-slathered bite but met her eyes when he answered. "Completely and utterly."

"My mama's biscuits can have an effect on a man," she cooed in an exaggerated drawl.

Wyatt only smirked as he chewed. She watched as he demolished half the plate before she spoke. "My plan is to stay here with you. Hunker down. Does your department have enough sway with Homeland Security to make it look like I boarded a flight?"

"We have sway, and we have, uh, other ways," he answered without looking up. "You want it to look like you're headed back."

"I figure it will buy us at least a day or so, and maybe a little breathing room." She wrinkled her nose. "What do you think?"

"Sounds solid. I'll loop Emma in on the plan, she'll let the others know."

"I'm going to use my phone to make a hotel reservation."

His approving expression morphed into a frown. "A hotel reservation?"

Wrapping her hands around the mug, she leaned in. "I need to make it look like I'm coming back to take care of the fire stuff. I can't stay at my house, so a hotel reservation makes sense."

"But they'll charge you for it."

Cara caught sight of the red flush creeping up his neck and opted to make light of his needless commentary. She might have money now, but it didn't mean she lost the practical frugality of a born and bred Arkansan. "I know, but I think it's important to sell whoever's watching on the notion of my imminent arrival."

He bobbed his head, but focused on his plate. "Right. Right. Good thinking."

She watched as he methodically demolished the rest of his breakfast. The moment he placed his fork on the gravy-streaked plate, she spoke up again. "There's more."

"I figured the wheels were turning." He wiped his mouth with a paper napkin, a wary gleam in his eye as he sat back. "Hit me."

"I'm going to call Chris and Tom today." Abandoning her grip on the coffee cup, she sat up straighter. She waited as he slotted the puzzle pieces into place.

"Okay."

She inclined her head. "I know Zarah sent texts letting them know I'm okay, but I need to talk to them. We have a lot happening in the next couple weeks and I need to be in the loop."

He studied her closely, biting the inside of his cheek as he weighed her plan. The morning light streaming through the window brought out hints of gold in dark eyes fringed by unfairly thick, dark lashes. The intensity of his stare should have made her uncomfortable. But it didn't. She felt safe with him. She could trust him. And, more important, he seemed to trust her.

"What do you plan to tell them?"

"Nothing in particular," she hedged. "I want to get their thoughts on what's been happening. They're far more involved in the tech community. Chris with the investors and entrepreneurs, and Tom with the people on the tech side of things."

Wyatt raised his arms and laced his fingers behind his head. She could see the temptation to rock her mother's kitchen chair back on two legs. Watching him wrestle it into submission was amusing and more than a little endearing. She wondered if he got away with tipping his own mother's chairs back. Something told her he didn't.

"What's their response been when you've had issues before?"

She shrugged. "Obviously, we've never had anything near what's happening now. Until now all I got was the usual mix of sour grapes and good old-fashioned misogyny." Thinking back on their cavalier dismissal of the vitriol slung at her day after day made her wonder if she shouldn't have been slotting them in with the chauvinists.

As if reading her mind, he asked, "Did they take it seriously?"

"No."

The answer slipped out of her before she could give the question more than a moment's thought. But it was the truth. They didn't take the chat room slurs and vaguely threatening messages posted by anonymous commenters to heart.

But now she couldn't stop shaking all over. Someone had tried to make good on those threats. It was time for Cara to insist her partners take her contribution to the company and the threats to her safety more seriously.

"Which is why I need to talk to them now."

Chapter Twelve

Cara pulled her phone from the pocket of her hoodie and placed it on the table between them. Wyatt glanced down at the blank screen then up at her, a question in his eyes. "You want me to listen in?"

A lump rose in her throat. Unable to trust her voice, Cara simply nodded.

He eyed the phone askance. "Do they know where you are?"

She shrugged. "Maybe." When his brows drew down, she knew the time had finally come to explain how complicated her dealings with her business partners had become. "My relationship with Chris and Tom has grown…distant over the past year or so."

"Distant as in contentious?"

She shook her head, dismissing the notion a smidge too quickly. "No, I wouldn't say so," she hedged. Wyatt lowered his arms and crossed them over his chest. He didn't speak. A tactic which proved more compelling than she cared to admit. "We've grown up. Grown apart. There hasn't been a fight or anything."

What she didn't tell him was she was almost one hundred percent certain the lack of friction could be attributed to her unwillingness to engage. The truth of the matter was, she wasn't as involved in the day-to-day running of LYYF as either Chris or Tom. Until this latest onslaught of abuse, she'd simply considered their arrangement a convenient division of labor. She handled the content. Chris kept them in capital and worked publicity like a pro. And the whole house of cards was built on a platform Tom created. The collaborative efforts of the company's early days were long gone. Now, instead of pizza, beers and brainstorms, they had conference calls.

"Tell me about them," he prompted.

She raised a shoulder and let it fall. "You've probably already read most of it."

"Give it to me from your perspective."

"Chris handles the money matters. Always has. He likes wheeling and dealing. Being in the middle of the action. He bought a place in Palo Alto the minute money started coming in and moved up there to be in the center of it all. Tom stayed down in LA for a while longer, but he hated the congestion. The only things he needs to be happy are surfing, solitude and a keyboard, so he bought himself a multimillion-dollar shack near Big Sur. I stayed put."

"You never wanted to live anywhere else?"

She gave him a rueful smile. "I was still chasing fame in Hollywood, remember?"

"Then it found you on the web," Wyatt concluded. "So the three of you live and work in completely separate areas?"

She nodded. "Yes. In both the company and geographically. Which isn't an issue. We're a digital company. There's no need for us to share office space." She shrugged. "We have operations offices for the tech side of things in Mountain View, and my content team has a small production studio near me in Silver Lake."

Wyatt took a moment to process the information. His

gaze dropped to the phone again, then he asked, "Do you like your partners?"

She should have been startled by his bluntness, but Cara was becoming adept at cop speak. He was trying to catch her off guard. He didn't realize she had no reason to have her guard up. Not here. And not with him.

"I do."

The answer was simple and mostly true. Chris had grown more than a little pompous, but he'd never been lacking in the self-esteem department. Tom was surlier and more reticent with her these days, but she'd chalked it up to a natural drift. Plus, the run-up to the stock offering was forcing him out of his happy place behind a keyboard and into the spotlight. A part of her hoped they'd both revert to the easy-going guys she'd met on dormitory move-in day, but she knew it wasn't likely. She wasn't the same starry-eyed young dreamer she'd been then, either.

"Have you ever...?" he started, then stopped. She looked up at him, all too aware of what his next question would be. She'd been asked dozens of times. Still, for some reason, it nettled to know it would be coming from Wyatt. But when he spoke, his surety surprised her. "You've never been romantically involved with either of them."

She shook her head. "No. I mean, Chris hit on me once. He'd come home from a party drunk our freshman year. I didn't take it personally, though. The minute I said no, he turned his attention to another girl on our floor." She gave him a weak smile. "As far as I know, he hasn't changed much. Chris's focus has always been money. The business. Women come and they go," she explained with a dismissive wave. "I've never known him to be serious about anyone."

"And Tom?"

"Tom was as focused as Chris, but more on the nuts and bolts. We, uh, he liked what I was doing with the meditation stuff. Tom was the one who convinced Chris to put it out there. They were light on content, and as I told you before, I was working for takeout in the early days."

"And your relationship with him never…crossed any lines?"

Her cheeks heated, but she held his gaze as she dismissed the notion. "No. I think… There was a time when I thought maybe he had feelings for me," she admitted. Gritting her teeth to ward off the blush threatening, she pushed through. "But I didn't, um, encourage him, and he never…pushed." She looked down at her hands, then chanced a peek at him from under her lashes. "I think his feelings sort of…fizzled. You know how it is. Nothing more than a crush."

"Who do you want to call first?" he prompted.

"Tom," she answered without hesitation.

Wyatt made a sort of there-it-is motion to the phone, and Cara couldn't help feeling she'd given her growing discomfiture away. Curling her lips in, she bit down gently as she took up the phone and dialed the number she'd jotted in her spiral-bound notebook. The call went directly to voicemail. When the tone sounded, she swallowed hard and did her best to keep her tone chipper. Upbeat.

"Hey, Tom. It's me. I guess Zarah has been keeping you guys up to date with what's happening with me. I, um, well, I was only checking in. Give me a call when you can," she finished, then jabbed at the red button to end the call.

"Well. Okay. Strange," she muttered under her breath.

Wyatt tapped a finger on the table to prompt her to look up at him. "Why strange?"

She exhaled long and low, her lips curving in a sad smile. "I can't remember the last time he didn't take my call."

"It's an unknown number."

She allowed her smile to grow and the blush to come. "Right. Makes sense. Logically. Feels strange though."

"Do you want to try Chris, or wait until after Tom calls you back?"

Cara caught the corner of her lip between her teeth. Staring down at the phone with its generic background and out-of-the-box ringtone, she tried to smother the unease she felt with Wyatt's confidence the call would be returned.

"I'll call him now," she said, grabbing the phone before she lost her nerve.

Once again, her call went to voicemail. She could feel Wyatt's all-consuming stare taking in every word and each morsel of nuance as she spoke. Drawing on all her years of training, Cara left the same chipper message for him, careful to say nothing more or less than she had to Tom.

When she hung up, a heavy blanket of silence fell over the room. Unable to sit still and wait, she pushed out of her chair. "More coffee?"

Wyatt declined with a shake of his head. "Your eyeballs are going to start spinning."

"I'm going to grab some water."

When she returned with two glasses filled with tinkling ice cubes, he was speaking into his own phone.

"No, I appreciate you calling me back, man," he said to the mystery caller. Mouthing an apology, he got up from the table as she reclaimed her seat, motioning his intention to take the call outside.

Cara sat at the dining table, studying the porcelain figurines her grandmother had collected for as long as Cara could remember. Her mother had helped Cara pick a new one for every birthday and Christmas Grandma June had celebrated. She'd displayed them on nearly every open surface at the old house. Now they stayed locked in a glass case, waiting for someone to take notice of them.

At times she felt like one of those Precious Moments dolls. There were days she felt her contributions to LYYF captured something innately human and essential. Other days, she wondered if she was purely decorative. She picked up her silent phone and scowled at it. The dark screen of her phone bounced her reflection back at her and she quickly altered her expression. There had been a time when she'd spent hours looking into mirrors, trying to nail the emotions with a simple shift in facial features. She could, when necessary, inject deep feeling into her tone.

Tom and Chris used to love it when she drew on her theatrical training to place their delivery or drive-through orders. "Tacos!" she'd exclaim into the speaker, breathless with desperation. "I need six tacos and a bean burrito or they'll kill me!" But LA servers were often actors or wannabe actors themselves. They rarely rose to the bait, even when she gave a performance her best friends declared Oscar-worthy.

"I called a guy I knew from the academy," Wyatt said as he strode back into the room, jolting her from her memories.

"Yeah?" she managed.

"Ryan Hastings," he said with a nod. "Worked for years on protection duty. He left the force last year to start his own security and protection firm up in Bentonville."

"Ryan Hastings," she repeated. "Why does his name sound familiar?"

"He was involved in a pretty high-profile case last year. Some big-shot attorney and his son were killed. Ryan was assigned to protect the widow. Turns out the guy's brother, a US senator, was involved."

"Yes, I remember hearing about it." She mustered a self-effacing smile. "Probably from my mother. I'm not big on absorbing the news of the world."

"It can do a number on you." Wyatt nodded. "I limit how much I take in too and try to get information from a cross section of sources."

"Wise," she affirmed.

The default ringtone on the mobile phone in front of her rang out. Cara glanced at the screen and drew in a deep breath. "It's Tom." Without looking to him for direction, she swiped to accept the call, then activated the speaker. When Wyatt sank back in his seat, she understood he meant to listen in unnoticed.

"Tom." She exhaled her old friend's name.

"Cara, are you okay? I heard about your house," he told her, sounding genuinely upset.

"Wow. It made regional coverage?" She shot Wyatt raised eyebrows. "I wouldn't have figured more than a mention on *LA Today*."

There was a moment of hesitation on Tom's end. "Zarah sent me a link."

"Ah. Okay. Makes sense."

"She said you weren't home?"

"I wasn't."

"Any word on the damages?"

"I haven't made it back to see for myself yet, but I'm told it's all fixable."

"Thank goodness." Tom released a gusty sigh. "Where are you? Are you coming back before New York?"

When she met Wyatt's gaze, he gave an imperceptible shake of his head, but shrugged as if to say it was her call as to what to tell him.

"Zarah has booked me a flight home." Her tongue tangled on the last word. LA had been her home for years, but now it may as well have been a million miles away. An awkward beat passed in which no one spoke.

"Yeah, uh, I think she said something about you coming back when she sent the news. Sorry. You know how distracted I get."

"I do. Anyway, I should get in late tonight." Feeling disheartened by the ever-widening distance between them, she grasped for conversational straws. "When are you heading east?"

"Day after tomorrow." The dullness in his tone told her he wasn't looking forward to making the trip, even if it meant he returned to the West Coast a billionaire. "I got the files you sent for the bedtime meditation series. Good stuff."

This was about as effusive as Tom ever was about the content she provided. Usually his persona of a disengaged, flighty genius amused her, but she found she was not in the mood to be dismissed. "Should be good for another ten million or so downloads," she said, affecting the same off-handed tone.

"What?" Tom coughed, then chuckled. "Oh, yeah. At least."

Irked by the stilted conversation, she decided to introduce a whole new topic. "Hey, did you also hear some guy tried to kidnap me at gunpoint?" she asked in a mockingly bright tone. "With a real gun and everything. Guess you can believe some of the stuff you read on the forums after all."

"Cara, I'm so sorry about what happened," he said in a rush of words. "I mean, you know I'm happy you're okay. I'd hate for you to get hurt—"

His verbal stumbling and bumbling only angered her more. He'd never been the most socially adroit guy, but this was beyond ridiculous.

"Can't kill the cash cow." She smiled as she said it, but a cold knot formed in her belly. Needing to end this torture, she leaned in, her face close to the phone. "I'll see you in New York, Tom. Safe travels." She ended the call with an angry jab of her forefinger.

When she looked up, she found Wyatt staring at her, brows raised. "And he's the one you're closer to?"

"He's… Tom. His mind is always miles down the road, you know?" She took a steadying breath. "I'm mostly used to it, but sometimes it would be nice if he could at least try living in the present."

Wyatt nodded. "There's this great meditation app I use…"

She gave an appreciative chuckle. "When he said the files I sent for the new series are good, I can guarantee he was talking about the audio quality, not the content." The corner of her mouth kicked up in a smirk. "Tom considers sleep a waste of productive hours."

"But Chris has to know content is king," Wyatt argued. "I mean, he's the guy out there pushing for investors and users, right?"

"Oh, yeah. Chris likes to say I'm the best impulse buy he's ever made."

"Whoa." Wyatt blinked and fell back in his chair. "Please tell me he's joking."

"I'd say it's about eighty-five percent joke," she conceded.

His brows drew down. "Do you ever think about leaving? Selling out and going off to do whatever you want to do?"

"Sure, I think about it." She shrugged. "The question is, what would I do? Actresses have a much narrower window when it comes to breaking into the business. Mine's pretty much closed. There's off-screen work, but there my success with LYYF may work against me."

"How?"

"Well, my voice is fairly recognizable now." She gave him a wan smile. "Having a familiar voice can be an advantage for men—look at Matthew McConaughey, Morgan Freeman or James Earl Jones. But women doing voice-over work? Sure, you get the occasional celebrities pushing perfume at Christmastime, or splash-washing their fully made-up faces for some beauty brand, but they're mainly hired for the on-camera work, not to be the voice of the product."

"And you're already inherently entwined with another brand," he said with grim understanding.

"Exactly."

She was saved from further discussion of her personal and professional choices by the buzzing of her phone. A peek at the display showed Chris's number. She smiled grimly and stretched a hand out to accept the call. "And now contestant number two."

She swiped the screen and called out, "Hey, Chris," before Wyatt even straightened in his chair.

"Cara, holy cripes," her longtime business partner gushed. "I'm so glad you called. I've been worried sick ever since Zarah told me what happened."

"What happened a couple days ago, or what happened last night?" Cara prodded.

"Last night? What happened last night?"

She looked up and met Wyatt's eyes. Chris sounded truly perplexed.

"Someone set my house on fire."

"The house where you're staying in Alabama?" he asked, sounding genuinely aghast.

She and Wyatt shared an amused smirk. "Arkansas. And no. I meant my house in LA," she corrected.

"No way! The little place in Los Feliz?"

"Yes." She leaned in closer. "You hadn't heard? I thought maybe Zarah—"

"Oh, she may have," he interrupted. "I've been running all over New York taking meeting after meeting," he said in a rush. "But you weren't there, right? You're in, uh, Arkansas?"

"Zarah booked me on a flight to LAX this evening." She held Wyatt's stare but said no more.

"Hey, Cara, you think you might consider hiring some security," Chris suggested. "At least until all this stuff blows over. I think we may have been a bit…"

In her mind, Cara filled the empty air space with a few choice adjectives: *condescending…dismissive*?

"I mean, you never know when to take the trolls seriously. Am I right?"

"Right," she replied flatly.

She stared at the phone screen, wishing they were on a video call. It was hard to get a read on this version of Chris. She'd grown so used to thinking of him as little more than her business partner. She'd almost forgotten they were once good friends.

"So, yeah, maybe it's time for us to be more proactive about security. For you, and maybe all three of us?"

Cara couldn't remember the last time Chris's innate confidence had seemed so shaken. Now she wished she could have her old cavalier Chris back. His obvious worry made her feel all the more exposed. Picking up the pen Wyatt abandoned, she twirled it through her fingers like a baton.

"Maybe. I'll look into it," she promised, her gaze darting back up to Wyatt.

"Let me know how things are when you get back to LA," Chris insisted. "When are you coming east?"

Not wanting to be pinned down to anything resembling a schedule, she kept her answer as vague as possible. "I'll be there a day or two before to do any media you want me to handle and will probably beat a path out of there right after. You know I'm not a New York girl."

"Some actor you are," he teased, echoing an old refrain. "Aren't you all supposed to claim to want to have a serious stage career?"

"Not me," she answered, trying to muster some of her old bravado as she tossed out the line he expected from her. "I never said I wanted to be an actress. I want to be a star."

"You are a star," Chris replied. "The investors love you. We all do. Be careful and I'll see you next week."

Three long beeps sounded to indicate the end of the call. She pressed her lips together to stave off an unexpected rush of emotion. Dropping the pen to the table with a clatter, she pushed back and escaped the dining room before Wyatt could get a word out. She didn't know what to say anymore. Everything seemed to be the opposite of what it should be.

Roscoe lifted his big, square head and let out a soft woof when she pushed through the screen door onto the porch. She stood at the rail, her arms crossed tight across her chest, staring out at the spot where the old house once stood. Her jaw clenched tight, she shivered when the crisp autumn breeze cut through the cotton sweatshirt she wore. Tugging the sleeves down over her hands, she scowled down at the discount store athletic wear. Why hadn't Zarah included some regular clothes? Did she think Cara would be practicing sun salutations and Savasana while on the run from her tormentors?

Cara clamped down on her uncharitable thoughts, her fingers biting into the thin cotton fabric as she hugged herself again. Zarah had done her best. She'd found clothing and other necessities at a store with delivery while sitting in her snug home office over a thousand miles away. She should be grateful for the ease and comfort of the clothing. For her safety. She should be happy there were other people who were glad she was alive. And she was.

"Cara?"

The quiet, husky timbre of Wyatt's voice sent a different sort of shiver through her. Roscoe, who'd settled back in his customary repose, did little more than open an eye. Her cheeks flamed as she heard the hinges on the screen door squeak. She didn't dare turn to look at him.

"You want me to grab one of your mom's jackets?"

"I'm okay."

She clearly wasn't. Cara could almost feel him struggling

to suppress the urge to argue the point. But to his credit, he retreated, the hinges creaking again. "How about I put on a fresh pot of coffee?"

A sob rose in her throat. Cara bludgeoned the knot of emotion with a short, sharp laugh. "I thought you were worried about spinning eyeballs."

"I'm a cop. I'm trained to withstand torturous levels of overcaffeination. I was worried about your eyeballs."

She turned to look at him, hoping he'd assume the color in her cheeks came courtesy of the wind. "Thank you. I wasn't quite up to my eyeballs yet, but didn't want you to feel emasculated."

"I appreciate your concern," he intoned gravely. He reached out to the side, pulled a fleece-lined denim jacket from the hall tree and popped the screen door open wide enough to thrust it at her. "I'll be in the kitchen when you're ready to talk."

She gave herself no more than five minutes to stew, sulk and otherwise sort through the swirl of conflicting emotions before she headed back into the house. Roscoe opted to relinquish his sunny spot in favor of shelter as well. She shrugged out of the jacket and hung it on its customary hook before following the old dog to the kitchen.

Wyatt was measuring grounds into the basket when she entered the room. Rather than jumping in to help him, Cara stopped at the table and watched. His movements were economical, but fluid. Almost graceful. He was comfortable moving around her parents' kitchen. She'd never pictured herself bringing a man home. Not that she'd brought him there in any sort of romantic way. But she'd never pictured it at all.

She'd never invited Chris or Tom to accompany her on trips home. Like most people from the coast, they considered anyplace west of Philadelphia akin to traveling to the outback. Tom had been offered an obscene amount of money to speak at a prestigious convention in Chicago and refused. To her partners, the middle of the country was an unappealing wilderness filled with dangerous creatures and backward people.

As Wyatt poured water into the coffee maker's reservoir, she felt an unexpected twist of sympathy for them. They would never know the pleasure of waking to the scent of strong black coffee and fresh-baked biscuits. They'd never know what a relief it was to have conversations with people who spoke slowly, choosing their words with thought and ending their sentences declaratively, rather than as questions. And there was no doubt in her mind which rock they needed to kick over next.

She gripped the back of her father's chair. "I think you're right. We need to take a closer look at Chris and Tom."

Wyatt stilled for a moment, then reached for the dishcloth hanging beside the sink to wipe his hands. When he turned to face her, his eyes were full of sympathy and a familiar resolve. "Ryan Hastings said the same thing. He says the threat almost always stems from a source close to the vic— uh, person of interest."

She gave him a wan smirk. "Thanks for not calling me a victim."

"You aren't one." He pulled a coffee mug closer. "Maybe we need to look at Zarah too."

Cara shrugged. "She doesn't have anything to gain from getting rid of me, though."

"True." He hit the button to start the coffee brewing, then gestured to the kitchen table. "But she seems to be in the middle of everything."

Cara conceded the point. It seemed more and more of her communication with her partners ran through Zarah these days.

Wyatt nodded. "We'll start with a brain dump of everything you can come up with concerning your partners." He hung the towel back on the hook, then fixed her with a look. "I asked Emma to rebook your flight for morning. If anyone asks, you can say you couldn't make the drive to Little Rock on time. Either way, it'll buy us a little more time on the going-to-California story."

"Good call." She nodded, impressed.

"I'd have handled it myself, but I couldn't be sure the connection would be there. I've crashed and burned more since we've been here than any time since I was in high school," he said with a grimace.

Cara laughed. "I'm sorry. And I have to say, I doubt you crashed and burned much in high school or since."

"Thanks, but either way, tomorrow we're driving into town to get a 5G gateway. I can't rough it with this faulty connection any longer."

Cara hid her smile as she moved to pull a fresh mug from the cupboard. Apparently, even the most down-to-earth men needed their creature comforts. "Sounds good." And it did. As good as it was to feel safe and secure on the ranch, she was starting to feel restless. It would be good to get out for a little while.

Chapter Thirteen

The following morning, the two of them drove north in search of a more reliable source of internet access. It was clear that if Wyatt was going to dig into the financials of three tech titans, he was going to need more speed than the spotty satellite could provide.

They rode in companionable silence, sipping coffee as they wound their way into Boone County. Wyatt glanced over at Cara as they approached the outskirts of Harrison, the next town of any size along the highway. "I should be able to get what I need at any cellular store, but if they don't have one in stock, we may need to head up to Branson or Springfield."

She shrugged. "Fine with me. My calendar is open all day."

"We can pick up anything else you might need while we're here," he offered.

She plucked at the front of her hoodie. Leaning against the door, she turned toward him. "My mom used to take me into Harrison to do my school clothes shopping. I didn't realize people bought clothes anywhere but JCPenney until I was about eleven and discovered the joys of a store called Goody's. They had all the cool stuff."

"My mom liked to drive up to North Little Rock so she could wander around the mall."

"Lucky you, shopping in the big city."

He rolled his eyes.

They crested one of the rolling hills and Cara's phone sprang to life with a series of texts from Zarah coming through in rapid succession.

Zarah: I went to pick you up and you weren't on the plane.

Zarah: Checked and saw you rebooked for AM. Hope all is okay.

Zarah: You're not answering my messages. Hot cop got your phone?

Her cheeks flamed as she read the last one, knowing at some point Wyatt would see it and know there'd been speculation about him. She was trying to formulate a response when a new message appeared.

Zarah: I'm picking you up at the airport. Hope you made your flight. Text when you land.

"Oh, crud," Cara muttered.

"What's the matter?"

"Zarah's waiting for my flight at LAX," she reported. She typed a response, then quickly deleted it. "You said Emma could do something to make it look like I got on the flight, right?"

Wyatt frowned. "Yeah. Why?"

"Zarah never picks me up from the airport. She lives on the other end of the earth," she mumbled, scowling at her phone.

"Hang tight." Eyeing a gas station ahead on the highway,

Wyatt signaled his intention to pull over. Once he'd pulled into a parking spot outside a bustling mini-mart, he turned to look at Cara. "Tell me all about Zarah."

Her eyebrows shot up. "All about Zarah?" she repeated, punctuating the request with an incredulous scoff. "Where do I begin?"

"How did you meet her?" he prompted.

"Well, I hired her long before I actually met her," she said slowly. "It was at the start of the pandemic lockdown, and we couldn't turn out content fast enough."

Wyatt unhooked his seat belt and turned to look at her. "So your relationship has always been remote?"

"Yes. I mean, we've met since then, obviously," she said with a helpless wave of her hand. "But we've never shared office space. A lot of LYYF's staff works remotely."

"How did she come to work for you?"

"One of the programmers," she said with a frown. "They are cousins or something?" She brushed the fuzzy details aside. "Anyway, she was doing some travel booking for Tom, and then Chris. When we opened the offices in Mountain View, Chris and Tom took offices there and they have someone on-site. Being based in Southern California, it only made sense for Zarah to focus more on me."

"But she doesn't do stuff for you in person," he clarified.

"No. She didn't even want a desk at the production studio." She shrugged. "Like I said, she lives out in the Valley. It doesn't seem like a long way away when you look at a map, but when you factor in LA traffic…"

"And the airport?" Wyatt asked, making a winding gesture with his hand.

"Is even farther."

"Can you try to find out why she's picking you up? You know, subtly?" he asked, looking troubled. "Without giving away anything about where you are?"

She rolled her eyes. "Gee, I don't know," she drawled,

settling into her seat. She typed out a message with her thumbs but before she hit Send, she turned the screen to him for approval.

CB: You're sweet, but it's too far away. Don't worry about me.

"Perfect," Wyatt said with a nod.

She sent the message and let out a long sigh.

The silence stretched taut between them. Finally, he broke it. "What are you thinking?"

She mustered a small, sad smile. "I'm thinking maybe I should give them all what they want."

"Who? And what?" he asked cautiously.

"Everyone. No one thinks I deserve my thirty-three-and-a-third of LYYF. Maybe I should sell out and go do something new. I mean, it's not like I wouldn't have options. I'd certainly have the money to coast for a while."

"Wait until after next week and you'd probably have the money to coast forever," he pointed out.

"Ah, but they don't think I've earned a big payday. People aren't assaulting innocent neighbors and burning down my house because they're hoping I sell after the stock offering. They want me out now. And what does it matter? Either way, I'll have more money than I need."

"What if selling isn't enough? From what I've seen and read, some people think you should be paying LYYF for the pleasure of putting together their award-winning content." He gave a little snort. "No. Don't sell out because they—whoever they are—want you to. If you want out, make sure you leave on your terms."

Her phone buzzed and she looked down. Another message from Zarah had arrived.

Zarah: It's no problem. See you soon.

"I have a feeling she knows I'm not on the plane," Cara said, her tone morose.

"Okay, so tell her." He gestured to the phone. "Let her know you talked to the LAFD and they said there was no reason to hurry back so you changed your mind."

"Tell her I stayed in Arkansas?" she asked, her forehead knit with concern. "What if someone's reading our texts?"

"You can make it sound like you decided to head to New York early. Might be the better idea," he added. "Let them try to find the needle in the haystack there."

Cara set her jaw. At last, she nodded and began to type.

CB: So sorry. Spoke to LAFD and they said no need to hurry back. Canceled flight. I'll deal with the house after the IPO. Probably head to NYC early. Go home. I appreciate the thought!

Then she turned the phone off and tossed it into the console. She caught his quizzical look and pulled a face.

"I'm starting to think all this technology is more trouble than it's worth." He chuckled and her expression brightened. "We could blow off getting your hot spot thingy. You know those phone places like to keep you trapped all day, and I know a place with the best onion rings you've ever tasted."

He let out a guffaw as he pulled his seat belt across his body and clicked it into place. "It's nine thirty and we finished breakfast less than an hour ago."

"I fail to see the conflict," she replied, straight-faced.

"How does this sound? I grab the gateway—it won't take long, the state has a contract with the carrier and it's all set up at the store." He sneaked a glance at her as he maneuvered out of the cramped parking lot. *Skeptical* wasn't a strong enough word for the look she gave him. "Seriously.

All I have to do is show my ID and pick it up." She shot him a doubtful glance as he pulled back onto the highway.

"Fine," she conceded ungraciously.

"Then we can see what we can do about finding you some different clothes. You brought the cash Zarah sent?" She nodded and gave an affirmative hmm. "Good." He smiled as they picked up speed, hurtling toward the small city nestled in the Ozark Mountains. "Then we'll replenish with those onion rings, but I have to warn you, I've had some good rings in my time."

"In your time," she echoed with a snort.

He drummed his fingers on the steering wheel, smiling as he glanced over at her. "So tell me, who is this hot cop Zarah asked you about?"

THE PICKUP AT the mobile phone store didn't go as quickly or smoothly as Wyatt had hoped. When all was said and done, it ate through a full hour of their morning and layers of his patience.

"Come on, we'll get a ridiculously decadent cup of coffee, then I'll let you sit and watch the world go by while I try on jeans and pick up a few sweaters." She treated him to a wide, winning smile. "I've lived in Southern California for so long I've forgotten how great sweater weather actually is."

As they waited at the window to pick up overpriced coffees, Cara leaned across him to ask the young woman at the register for shopping recommendations. When he ruled out a trip to the Branson outlets, she insisted he drive her to the town square. Wyatt eyed the area skeptically. Like most small towns, Harrison had dried up when the highway bypass was built and commerce flowed away from the business district.

"There it is." Cara pointed to one of the run-down storefronts. "Sassafras," she announced, repeating the name of the boutique the woman at the coffee shop said had "real cute stuff" but was "kinda spendy."

The display window featured a single mannequin sporting a pair of slim black pants and an animal-print sweater with an enormous collar pulled down around its sculpted shoulders. Wyatt tried to picture Cara wearing such an outlandishly gaudy print but found he could imagine the tempting hollows of her collarbones all too easily.

"Maybe we should go up to Branson," he said gruffly.

She let out a tinkling burst of laughter. "Maybe, but I'll take a peek in here first."

When she reached for the handle, he placed a hand on her forearm to stop her. "Hang on. Let me go in and check it out first."

Raising a single brow, she asked, "You think whoever is stalking me somehow got wind of a random conversation I had with a barista through a drive-up window?"

"No," he admitted slowly. "But I'm, uh, responsible for, you know, keeping you safe."

The other brow shot up to match its twin. "Well, come on, Captain Responsible, we're going shopping. You can hold my keeper pile."

She bailed out of the SUV without another word and Wyatt cringed at the thought. He could have handled a trip to a mall. Department stores usually had chairs for people to wait in, at least. But this place looked to be about the size of a postage stamp and, from what he could see through the plate-glass door, was stuffed to the gills with glitter, fringe and frills. When Cara stopped on the sidewalk, crossed her arms over her chest and tapped her foot, he made a shooing motion before opening his own door.

"Go on. I'm getting claustrophobic lookin' through the window," he called to her.

Cara's triumphant grin lit her face. "I won't be long," she called, then sailed into the store without a backward glance.

He heard the jingle of the bell above the store's door as he climbed out of the car himself. Carrying his coffee, he strolled along the sidewalk, peering around the edges of brown-craft-papered windows into vacant spaces, and stopping to admire the neon marquee of the historic Lyric Theater. Not wanting to stray too far, he settled on a wooden park bench across from Sassafras. He'd responded to three work emails and was sipping the dregs of his coffee when she backed out of the store, shopping bags pulling on both arms.

The yoga pants, T-shirt and sweatshirt she'd been wearing were nowhere to be found. Instead, she wore wide-legged bleached denim jeans with a preppy-looking sweater. She still wore the thick-soled canvas sneakers Zarah had sent with the other supplies, but he could see the distinct shape of a shoebox in one of the bulging bags. Tossing his cup into a nearby trash bin, he hustled to the car to help her stow her haul.

"Wow. I guess this worked for you?" he asked with a laugh.

"Such cute stuff. Fun but functional. They have a whole section of jeans called 'sassy pants,'" she informed him as he pried the handles of the shoppers from her fingers.

"I would expect nothing less," he said soberly.

"I'm going to tell my mom about this place. She'd love it too," she called as she headed for the passenger seat.

Wyatt had a hard time imagining practical, efficient Betsy Beckett shopping anywhere with so much sass, but he refrained from saying so. When he climbed back into the driver's seat, he could practically feel the buzz emanating from her. Her excitement was so infectious, he had to smile.

"I guess you needed some retail therapy?"

"I needed to make some of my own choices," she countered without missing a beat. She looked over at him. "I've been wearing clothes someone else picked out, sleeping in a bed I haven't felt comfortable in since I was seventeen, riding around in a car I don't own, with a guy I barely know, and eating random vegetables scrounged from the depths of my parents' deep freeze." She flashed a shaky smile. "I'm pretty sure there are jars of pickles in the cellar older than I am."

Wyatt blew out a breath, his shoulders drooping as he took in her words. "Man, Cara, I'm sorry—"

"No." She held up a hand, cutting him off. "I'm grateful. For all of it. Grateful I got away from Gerald Griffin, grateful to have friends and financial wherewithal to do this. Not everyone has a soft place to land…a place to call home no matter how long they've been away. I'm so lucky and I know it," she said earnestly. "But today, I needed a few minutes to just be me, you know?"

"I get it."

"It feels like all I've been doing for the past few weeks is reacting." She looked him directly in the eye. "Honestly, I don't know how much longer I can do this. I can't live my life according to rules other people make up for me."

"I understand."

And he did. Wyatt knew he'd be champing at the bit if he were in her shoes. Shock and sheer terror had carried her for days. She'd bounced from one blow to the next like a boxer pinned against the ropes.

But now she was coming around.

This punch-drunk powerhouse outfitted in her brand-new sassy pants would soon be ready to come out swinging, and he was going to be the guy to hold whoever was responsible for terrorizing her up for her to pummel.

She reached for her abandoned cup of coffee and took a healthy slug. She wrinkled her nose as she dropped it back into the cup holder. "Not so tempting when it's tepid."

"We can get a fresh one for the ride home," he offered, reversing out of the parking space.

"Nah, I promised you lunch, remember?"

"I rarely forget about onion rings," he intoned gravely.

She jiggled her knee, clearly still hyped up on her taste of freedom. "Excellent. Head out to Highway 7 South. There's a dairy bar down the road a piece."

"I love a good dairy bar." He hit his turn signal and headed in the direction she indicated.

A few miles outside town, Cara contented herself with an order of hand-battered onion rings while he wolfed down a ridiculously sloppy barbecue bacon burger the woman at the order window claimed was the best thing on the chalkboard menu.

Cara crunched into a ring the circumference of a softball and hummed her appreciation as she chewed, her gaze fixed on a point in the middle distance.

"Everything okay?" It was a ridiculous question, given their circumstances, but he was dying to know where her mind was.

"Do you mind if we stop by a grocery store on our way back through town?"

The request jarred a laugh from him. "Worried about your next meal already?"

"Always," she replied without missing a beat. "I was thinking I could pick up some fruit besides apples and oranges, and I'd sell an internal organ for a bean burrito."

"Wow. Quite a refined palate you have there. I'm not sure your internal organs would fetch a good price on the open market if all you're eating are bean burritos."

"Oh, I eat other things. Given something other than plastic-wrapped American cheese slices, I can put together a grilled cheese sandwich deserving a Michelin star," she boasted.

"I believe all grilled cheese sandwiches deserve a Michelin star, but you can be snobby if it makes you feel better."

"Some feta, nuts and quinoa would make me feel much better about eating the bagged salads my mom bought me." She took a noisy slurp of the chocolate milkshake she'd ordered, then let her head fall back against the seat. "And I could get some Brussels sprouts to grill."

He shuddered then reached over to swipe an onion ring from the paper bag. "I can't believe you're even thinking about Brussels sprouts while eating these."

"What can I say? I'm multidimensional," she said, gesturing for him to finish the last ring off. "And I can't go on eating potatoes, onions and okra. I'm going to turn into gumbo."

"Well, we can't have that." He crumpled his own wrapper, gathered their trash and reached for the door handle. "I'll go toss this and we'll be on our way. We need to get back. I have work to do."

While Cara shopped, Wyatt called her parents to let them know they were in town longer than expected, but the call went to voicemail. Forty minutes later, they were sailing down Highway 65 hauling a decent sampling from Cara's favorite food groups—cheese, frozen burritos, snack crackers and breakfast pastries.

"Why don't you try calling your parents? Let them know we're heading back," he suggested, nodding to the phone she'd tossed into the console on their way into town.

"Dad said he needed to replace some wire on the western fence," she said as she powered the phone on. "Mom's probably helping him."

Wyatt frowned. "I could have helped him."

Cara glanced over at him, a faintly amused smile tugging at her lips. "You think my mom doesn't know how to stretch fence?"

"I think your mom can do anything," he replied without

missing a beat. "I'm only saying I would have been happy to help."

"And I'm sure they'd appreciate the offer, but they know you're here on other business."

She jolted and they both looked down as the phone in her hand emitted several short bursts of vibration. "Someone was looking for you," he said grimly. "Was it your folks?"

Cara's lips thinned into a tight line. "No."

She snapped the word off so sharply, he checked her again. "Do I need to pull over?"

"It's nothing. More text messages from my biggest fans," she said, her voice tight with bitterness.

He reached over and took the phone from her hand. A quick glance showed a string of text messages from a variety of area codes. A surge of anger pulsed through him. He wanted to pull over to read them, but the stretch of road they were on had little to offer in terms of a shoulder. So he opted for the second-best thing. He pressed and held the power button as he maneuvered a curve one-handed.

"What did they say?" he demanded in a growl.

"I only saw the notification windows, but they looked to be more of the same. I don't deserve my share of LYYF. I should leave the company to the real geniuses. Blah blah blah," she muttered, turning to look out on a broad swatch of pastureland. "I'm so tired of it all," she whispered.

Without thinking, he dropped the phone back into the console and reached across to place a steadying hand on her leg. The moment his palm landed she tensed and he froze for a beat. Then he jerked his arm back, gripping the steering wheel like a fifteen-year-old angling for a learner's permit.

"Sorry," he breathed. "I didn't mean—"

"It's okay," she said, trampling his apology. "And I know. I appreciate you being here. I appreciate everything you're doing, Wyatt." She angled to look directly at him. "I hope you know I do."

"I do."

A horn blared and he glanced up into the rearview mirror. "Holy cow, this guy needs to slow down," he muttered, inching the SUV to the right as a sleek silver sports car swerved into oncoming traffic to pass. "Double yellow, dude," Wyatt complained, gesturing to the markings on the road.

"Missouri plates," Cara observed as the car dropped back into the lane in front of them.

The driver immediately ran up on the bumper of the next car ahead of them. The coupe was so low-slung the driver was barely visible over the headrest. Cara gripped the door handle. Wyatt tightened his hands on the wheel, half-expecting to witness a terrible accident as the erratic driver overtook car after car, heedless of the rules of the road.

"Wanna throw your cop light up onto the roof and go after them like on TV?"

He shot her a wry smile but kept their speed steady as the other car disappeared over a hill. "Sadly, this ride didn't come equipped with a cop light."

"So sad."

Wyatt shook his head in wonder as the line of traffic shaken by the aggressive driving of the speeder settled into a more sedate pace.

They rode in silence for a couple miles. Then turning her attention back to the road, she pointed to a blur of a highway sign. "If you turn off on 14, we can come in the back side. It's hilly and curvy, but it's a pretty drive and we could check to see if Mama and Daddy are in the west pasture on our way to the house."

"Sounds good."

They drove into the small town of St. Joe in tight silence. The *click-click* of the turn signal sounded almost laughably loud to his own ears. Ryan Hastings's warnings about getting too attached to a primary while on protection duty reverberated in his brain. Then again, Ryan knew the dangers firsthand. He'd fallen for Kayla Powers while trying to protect her from a murderer, given up his career with the state police and moved to Bentonville to help her raise the baby she hadn't known was on the way at the time of her late husband's death.

"Cara, I shouldn't have—"

"Please don't, Wyatt," she cut him off, the words quiet but firm. She reached over and placed her hand on his arm. "I don't want things to be awkward between us. I feel… Can't we…?" She stumbled to a stop as he slowed to make the turn onto the narrow secondary road. "I didn't mind. Okay? It's… Wow, things are complicated right now, and I don't—"

"You don't have to say anything more," he interrupted.

"Well, it seems like one of us does," she countered. "Sheesh, I mean…how 'bout them Hogs?"

He laughed, amused by her use of a native's shorthand for, *Let's change the subject, please.*

"How about those Hogs?" He smiled and let off the gas as they wound through a series of curves. "I don't know if they'll make it to a bowl game this year or not."

"You realize I have absolutely no idea how the Razorbacks are doing this year, don't you?"

"I do, but I'm willing to roll with it if you are."

"Okay then. Give me the midseason highlights," she invited. "It is midseason, right? I think I remember football going until Thanksgiving."

"You aren't far off," he said encouragingly. "Okay, here's where we are."

He spent a good fifteen minutes giving her the rundown on how the University of Arkansas football team was performing, who their star players were, and a fairly in-depth analysis on the current coaching staff. For her part, Cara pretended to listen, interjecting the occasional hums and snorts where his commentary warranted response. He was about to launch into his views on the ongoing college athletic conference realignments when she held up a hand.

"Okay, uncle," she cried.

He glanced over and found her smiling at him, her eyes crinkling at the corners. He grinned back at her. "Bet you never pull the old 'How 'bout them Hogs?' on a guy again," he teased.

"Are you kidding me? I've been using that line to distract my father since I was trying to get around his no-dating-before-sixteen rule," she said with a smug smile. "Turn left up here, then we'll take a quick right on the farm road."

He did as instructed. A quarter mile down the dirt road, they came to the section of missing fence Jim had pointed out to him on their tour of the property. The ATV Jim used was parked near the opening. He could see the coils of new wire to be stretched in the bed of the utility vehicle, but Jim and Betsy Beckett were nowhere in sight.

A set of deep ruts was cut into the ground from the edge of the road, the far side of the ditch and through the gap in the fence. Either one of the Becketts had driven the farm truck out to the pasture, or someone had come to call.

Slowing to a stop, he reached for his cell phone, but Cara had beaten him to it.

Her mother answered on the second ring. "Cara, honey, is that you?" Betsy asked, her voice tremulous.

"Mama? Where are you? Where's Daddy?" Cara asked, panic rising in her voice.

"Why, we're up at the house, sweetheart," Betsy cooed, her tone a shade too bright. "Are you almost to Little Rock? You don't want to miss your flight again, sugar. I know you think you have more money than God, but those tickets are expensive," she added with a tittering laugh.

"Mama? What's happening?" Cara demanded.

"Nothin' happening here. Paul Stanton stopped by for a visit. You remember Mr. Stanton? I guess I should say Lieutenant Governor Stanton." Her mother gave a high-pitched giggle and the hairs at Wyatt's nape rippled. "He's so sad he missed seeing you. But listen, I'm bein' rude," she said, her drawl thickening in her rush. "You get on now, and be sure to call us and tell us when you've landed safely. Love you, honey. Your daddy and I love you so very much."

The call ended.

Cara turned to look at him wide-eyed. "She's acting like we're on our way to Little Rock to catch a flight."

He shook his head. "She knows we're not, but whoever is there with her doesn't." He scowled. "Paul Stanton is there? The lieutenant governor?"

She bobbed her head. "Mama went to prom with him back in the day, but Daddy hates the guy. Wyatt, something weird is going on."

"I gathered as much," he said gruffly. "But I have to get you away from here."

"I can't go off and leave them," she argued, shrugging out of her seat belt.

"You can't go in there. Not with whatever is happening," he shot back.

"Those are my parents," she said, agitation pitching her voice high and tight.

"I'm aware, but—"

The next thing he knew, the passenger door was hanging wide open and Cara was leaping across the ditch. He shouted after her, but she didn't look back. He was still fumbling with the clip on his seat belt when he heard the engine on the ATV turn over.

She took off like a shot, careening over the bumpy hill at the edge of the property, headed straight for the house. Cursing under his breath, he lunged across the seat and grappled for the handle on the open door. The moment it was closed, he threw the car into gear and cranked the wheel. The SUV hit the bottom of the ditch so hard his head smacked the roof. He aimed for the opening in the fence, squeezing his eyes shut as he plowed through, a piece of the broken fencing scraping the length of the passenger door.

He couldn't think about damage to the state-owned vehicle now.

He had to catch up with a woman who preached the gospel of staying in the moment, but was proving to be an expert at making a quick getaway.

Chapter Fourteen

Cara spotted the enormous luxury SUV parked in the drive from a quarter mile out. She fixed her sights on it, opening up the throttle and clenching her jaw to keep from clacking her teeth on every rut and ridge hidden beneath browning grass and fallen leaves.

Paul Stanton. Paul Stanton. She'd known the man all her days, but for the life of her, she could not form a picture of him. Brown hair—probably grayish brown now. Brown eyes? Probably. Her overriding recollection of the man was he was bland. Handsome enough in a conventional way.

Neat. For some reason, she recalled shirts pressed to a crisp, khaki pants with knife-edge pleats and loafers polished to a high gloss. In other words, the polar opposite of her ruggedly handsome if not a bit rumpled and work-worn father.

It was no wonder her mother had dumped Mr. Permanent Pressed for her father.

"Gah!" she cried when she hit a bump so hard the rear of the gator skittered to the side. She let off the gas until she regained control, then hit it again the moment she felt all four wheels were under her.

The pearly white SUV parked behind her father's mud-spattered pickup gleamed in the afternoon sunlight. She squinted when the shining chrome trim tossed sunlight back at her. She took pleasure in skidding to a stop right beside the hulking vehicle, sending up a plume of dust and gravel she hoped marred the sparkling paint job.

She killed the engine and leaped from the ATV. She was skirting the back of Paul Stanton's vehicle when she slid to an abrupt stop. Parked beside the massive car was another. This one low-slung and sleek. A matte silver with an all-too-familiar profile. Hurrying to the rear of the sports car, she knew what she would find.

Missouri plates.

The driver who'd been in such a hurry on the highway had been swerving in and out of traffic, endangering the lives of other drivers so he could get here faster.

Here. To her parents' little ranch in the Ozarks. Her safe haven. The place she could hide out without anyone knowing where she was. No one except Paul Stanton.

Cara reached into the back pocket of her jeans for her phone but came up empty.

Cringing, she darted a glance at the field she'd sped across to get to them. She had no doubt Wyatt would be hot on her heels, but he would have to come around via the farm and county roads. She couldn't wait for him. Wouldn't. She was the one who'd brought this madness to her mother and father's doorstep. She would be the one to stop it.

Rolling her shoulders back, she circled the corner of the house and came up the front walk. Only then did she register the steady stream of gruff, rhythmic barks. Roscoe, bless him, was standing at attention, his forehead furrowed with concern and the hair on his back standing on end, barking to be let inside to inspect the newcomers.

Walking softly, Cara crooned the old dog's name as she climbed the shallow steps. She scratched behind his floppy ears, then pressed her forehead to his to calm him. "Who's in there, boy? Bad guys? Guys with bad hair? Why was Mama talking all funny, huh?"

The dog sat at her feet, his hindquarters hitting the deck with a thump.

"Don't worry. I'll get 'em. You stay here and tell Wyatt where we're at, okay?"

Creeping off the porch, she circled around to the kitchen door. Her mother had hung sheets out to dry in the sun. Cara pictured the state-of-the-art washer-dryer set in the laundry room sitting idle while Betsy Beckett's linens snapped in the autumn breeze. She could make out the muffled hum of conversation coming from the kitchen, but was too short to catch a peek through the window over the sink.

As quietly as she could, she took the two steps up the back stoop and pressed the button on the screen-door handle.

The click of the latch opening might as well have been a shotgun blast.

Cara froze, tensing every muscle in her body. She listened intently, but no one inside spoke. She bit the inside of her cheek, figuring she'd give it to the count of five before she proceeded.

She only made it to three.

"Well, hello there, Cara."

She looked up to find Paul Stanton smiling down at her beneficently from the screened back porch. He looked incongruous standing there next to the chest freezer, amid a jumble of discarded boots, rain and cold weather gear and the motley collection of half-dead houseplants her mother refused to give up on entirely.

The man who greeted her lived up to her recollections. His hair was indeed brown, but the close-cropped helmet now sported sleek silvery sidewalls. The buttons on his starched shirt strained across a round drum of a belly. He smiled down at her, but no warmth reached his dark eyes.

"Your mama was under the impression you were headin' down to Little Rock to catch a flight, but my friend couldn't locate any information about a flight booked, so we thought we'd hang around a bit to see if maybe you'd changed your mind. Again." He pressed the flat of his palm to the screen door, and she stumbled back a step as it swung open. "Come on in. We've been waiting for you to get home."

She took two steps back, her sneakered feet crunching the leaves gathered along the side of the porch. "Who's we?"

He flashed a wide politician's smile. "Why don't you come in and we'll all chat a bit. Your mama has poured us all a glass of her delicious sweet tea."

Riled by his ingratiating tone, she stood her ground. "Who? What friend? What are you doing here?"

"We came to talk to you, is all. From what I hear, you can be a very difficult young lady to pin down."

"Cara, honey, you go on," her mother called from inside the house. "I don't want you to miss— Oh!"

The surprise and distress Cara heard in her mother's sharp cry set her in motion. Running up the steps, she brushed past Paul Stanton and his smarmy smile and charged into the kitchen. "Mama!"

Three steps into the room she drew up short. Zarah Parvich was standing in her parents' kitchen, her feet planted wide and her expression disconcertingly businesslike as she pressed the muzzle of a gun to Cara's father's temple. "Hello, Cara. Looks like you missed your flight again," she said without rancor.

Cara raised both hands in a gesture of surrender. "Zarah? Why are you pointing a gun at my father?"

"Hey, now, no one said anything about pointin' guns at people," Paul Stanton said, his forced laugh ringing hollow in the tense room.

The other woman hitched her shoulder in a shrug. "I needed to get your attention."

"Okay. You've got it," Cara said. "Can you lower the gun now?"

She fixated on the semiautomatic pistol in the woman's hand. It was strange to see a gun out in the open after living in Southern California for so long. She wasn't far into her freshman year when she learned to keep her mouth shut about horses, heifers and handguns. Almost everyone she knew was virulently anti-gun. Everyone except Zarah, apparently. Thankfully, the other woman complied.

She choked down the sob of relief squeezing her throat. "You okay, Daddy?"

"I'm fine, sugar," her father responded, his voice even and steady. "Got work to do, though. Not that *he* would know a darn thing about an honest day's labor," he added, jerking his chin in Paul Stanton's direction.

"Hey, now—" Stanton began, grabbing hold of his tooled leather belt and hiking his pants as he stepped forward.

"How dare you, Paul Stanton?" Betsy Beckett said in a low, tremulous voice. "What kind of trouble have you brought into my home?"

"Elizabeth, I swear—" Stanton began, but Cara raised a hand to stop him.

"We can get into the hows and whys later." Turning to Zarah, she scowled at the gun then the sharp-featured young woman who held it. "What do you want?"

"I want what everyone wants," Zarah said as if the answer should have been obvious. "I want what people have been telling you for weeks. I want you out."

"What's it to you?" Cara shot back.

With a huff of impatience, Zarah rolled her eyes. "Oh, I plan to have a vested interest."

Cara looked everywhere but at the back door. The last

thing she wanted to do was tip Zarah off to Wyatt's imminent arrival. She took in the familiar kitchen, the ancient wood napkin holder bracketed by salt and pepper shakers, the iron skillet wiped clean and waiting on the stovetop, the café curtains Grandma June had helped her make for a Mother's Day gift.

The refrigerator's compressor hummed, undercutting the tension in the room. Drawing a steadying breath, Cara forced herself to meet Zarah's gaze. "What interest?"

"She said she's engaged to Tom Wasinski," Paul Stanton chimed in. When her mother shot him a filthy look, the man took an involuntary step back. "I'm sorry, Elizabeth, but Wasinski could be a deep-pockets donor and if I run for Senate, I want him on my side. His company is about to go public."

The Beckett family turned to glare at him as one. If her expression was one-tenth as incredulous as her father's, Paul Stanton had to feel lower than an earthworm.

"I always knew you were about as stiff as a fence post, Stanton, but I never realized you were as dense as one," Jim Beckett grumbled. "Our Cara is an equal partner in their company. Her pockets are every bit as deep as either of those two fellas."

"Now, Jim," Betsy began, long accustomed to stepping between the two men.

"Not for long," Zarah said. She pointed the muzzle of the gun to a plain manila folder on the small dining table. "Cara's about to get out of the business."

Cara wanted to bask in the warmth of her father's pride, but the glint of sunlight off gunmetal made it difficult to enjoy the moment. "You are not engaged to Tom," she said flatly.

"Well, not technically engaged," Zarah conceded. "But once you sign these papers, I'll be able to hook up with him, you know, as an equal, and he won't have to worry about whether he's 'technically' connected to my employment," she said, using a single set of air quotes to dismiss the excuse Tom must have used to rebuff her.

But Cara knew the two weren't and never had been involved. In one of the few confidences they'd shared recently, Tom had confessed he was deeply, but quietly, involved with a woman he'd met on a tech-free weekend yoga retreat he'd attended months ago. One Cara herself had recommended and Zarah had booked. Could it be the mystery woman in Tom's life actually was Zarah? She racked her memory for a name, but couldn't recall him disclosing one.

Cara wondered if she'd missed something big in her old friend's life, or if the young woman she'd trusted with hers was delusional.

"How long have you and Tom been involved?" she asked, her approach cautious.

"We talk all the time." Zarah smiled smugly, pulling her long ponytail over her shoulder with her free hand and stroking it as if she was settling in for some girl talk rather than holding Cara's loved ones at gunpoint. "I know he feels like he can't let things evolve as they stand now, but together, we're going to take LYYF to the next level."

Cara could only hope Zarah had forgotten there was a special agent with the Arkansas State Police staying with them.

"What about Chris?" Cara asked, anxious to keep her engaged.

"Chris won't be a problem. Everyone knows he's going to take the money and run the minute he can cash in." She tipped her chin up. "You and Chris never cared about what it took to keep the company going. Tom is the brains behind it all."

"Tom doesn't create content," Cara pointed out.

Zarah gave an indelicate snort. "Like it's difficult." She rolled her eyes. "I've been helping you churn that stuff out for years. Besides, I'm a better actress. I've booked more roles than you have in half the time in Hollywood."

"I talked to you this morning," Cara said, stalling for time. "How did you get here so fast?"

The younger woman rolled her eyes. "It's not like it was difficult to figure out you were stalling. Plus, TSA's system is ridiculously easy to hack. I've been waiting to see if you boarded a plane going anywhere. When you changed your flight, I booked one to Dallas. When you didn't turn up, I hopped a flight to Springfield, Missouri, and drove down." She pursed her lips. "I guess it's pretty enough with the trees and all, but there's not much around here." She wrinkled her nose in distaste. "And it's so run-down." She glanced over at Paul Stanton. "You might get more people to visit if things didn't look so…poor."

Paul opened his mouth to protest, but Cara spoke first. "So what do you expect to happen here today?"

Without missing a beat, Zarah pointed the gun at Cara's mother's chest. "I expect you to sign over your partnership."

Her father half rose from his chair and Paul Stanton bumbled forward with a hearty "Hey, now—"

Zarah swung the gun from one man to the other and they both subsided, hands raised. Moving closer to the table, Cara placed herself between Zarah and her mother. She was the target here, not her parents. Cara had to make certain Zarah kept her eye on the prize.

"Who am I signing it over to? You?" Cara asked, trying to keep her tone curious rather than accusatory.

"Yes. Sign it over to me, and I will let Tom know we can be together now. Equal partners," Zarah said with a decisive nod. Her pretty face brightened. "I mean, it's not like this is what you wanted to do with your life, right? And if you still want to be involved, maybe we can pay you a salary or something."

Cara glanced down to see her father staring at her intently. He cut his eyes to the window, and it was all she could do to keep from looking over. Wyatt must be out there. *Please let him be out there.* She needed to buy time.

"It was you, wasn't it?" she said softly.

"What was?" Zarah asked, squinting as if confused by the non sequitur.

"All of it. The doxing. The messages. All the...stuff." She closed her eyes, willing herself to hold it together as the pieces fell into place. "You did it."

"Oh, that," Zarah said with a dismissive laugh. She shrugged. "I put some info out there, but the rest... I didn't have to do much."

"Except have me kidnapped," Cara interjected.

"Oh, well, technically, you paid for that yourself. Good thing you never look at your account statements, huh?" She wrinkled her nose. "Anyway, didn't go as expected. He was only supposed to take you somewhere and scare you into signing."

"Now he's dead," Cara said flatly.

"Yeah, well, not my fault. He shouldn't have taken the job if he couldn't handle the pressure." Zarah exhaled in a put-upon whoosh. "I guess I learned a good lesson on outsourcing."

Cara fixated on the gun dangling from Zarah's hand like an afterthought. She didn't look like she had much experience handling firearms. She certainly hadn't been taught how to handle one safely. She was waving what looked like a small nine millimeter around like it was a water pistol. And what if Wyatt came through the door and startled her? She could accidentally shoot any one of them.

Drawing on every acting lesson she'd ever had, Cara forced herself to look into Zarah's eyes with what she hoped were eyes filled with hope and optimism. "You know this was never what I expected to do with my life," she began, faking a quaver into her voice. "I don't know how I got this far off track." She bumped her mother with her hip, signaling the older woman to scoot her chair away. She pointed to the folder on the table. "What is this?"

"It's an agreement to transfer your partnership shares," Zarah said, her customary chipper efficiency slipping back into place. "And you've always been really nice to work with, Cara. I'm not going to leave you high and dry. Once the public offering goes through and prices are up, I'll cover you. In today's cash value, of course," she added.

"Of course," Cara murmured.

Out front, Roscoe gave a woof of greeting and they all turned. Zarah swung the gun around when a floorboard creaked. "Sounds like your hot cop is still hanging around after all," she said, turning back to press the muzzle into the dusty folds of her father's Carhartt jacket. "Tell him to join us," she called out in a louder voice. "But be sure to tell him I'm holding your sweet daddy at gunpoint."

"Wyatt, if that's you, Zarah is here and she has a gun," Cara called out robotically.

"I'm coming in, and I am *not* holding a gun," he announced before stepping into the doorway, his hands raised. To Cara's disappointment, he wasn't lying. There was no sign of a weapon in Special Agent Wyatt Dawson's hand.

"Some cop you got yourself there," Zarah scoffed. "He's got a kind of hot-nerd vibe going on. Too bad he couldn't come in busting down the doors to save you."

Cara raised her eyebrows. "He's a cybercrime guy. I'm not sure kicking in doors is their thing. He tells me they barely leave the office."

She shot Wyatt an apologetic glance and he made a point of scowling at her. But the glint in his eyes was keen and bright. He wasn't insulted, nor did he seem to be worried.

Which made exactly one of them. Had he somehow called for backup? How long would it take someone to get there? Their eyes held for a moment and a veil of calm settled around her shoulders. He wasn't freaking out over a woman who was clearly suffering some sort of break waving a very real gun around like a toy. She wouldn't either.

"So what's the situation?" Wyatt asked, his tone casual, almost disinterested.

"We're talking business," Zarah snapped.

"Talking business with a gun pointed at a person?" Wyatt asked smoothly. "Isn't asking someone to sign legal documents at gunpoint coercion?"

Cara shot him a quelling look. "Don't you worry about it. Wasn't I telling you I was thinking about doing something different with my career? Well, Zarah is here and we're talking about making a deal."

"A deal in which she fronts zero dollars, and you sign everything over?" her father asked with an incredulous laugh.

"I'm going to pay her once the stock offering is complete. Tom and I can combine our shares, pay Cara for her time and efforts to this point and still have controlling interest in the company."

"Sounds like you have it all figured out." Cara nudged her mother with her knee, but Betsy didn't budge. "Mama, you still keep extra pens in your junk drawer?"

When she looked down, her mother was staring at her with naked disbelief. When she spoke, all traces of syrupy sweetness were long gone from Betsy Beckett's voice. "You can't seriously be considering signing those papers."

Cara shifted so Zarah couldn't see the silent stare-down between her and her mother. "Mama, I know what I'm doing." She thought of the old handgun her granddad kept in the kitchen drawer of the old house. Cara knew it made the move to this one along with Grandma June's cast-iron skillet. She'd seen it in the back of the junk drawer. "I know you and Daddy have never approved of what I do. Here's my chance to start over. I can have all my time back to pursue acting…real acting. All I need to do is sign on the dotted line and this will be all over."

"How do we know?" Betsy demanded. "How do we know she won't shoot us all?"

Zarah looked aghast at the suggestion. "You think I like doing this? I hate it. I'm not one of you hillbilly gun nuts," she snarled. "All I want is my share of LYYF and I'll be out of here."

Cara grabbed the folder again and waved it like a flag of surrender. "Fine. You know what? I'm tired of this. I want my life back. My actual life-life. The one I plan on living." She flipped over the folder and dumped the papers out onto the table.

She took the seat across from her father and Zarah and pulled the papers closer. "Mama, please grab me a pen, would you? If I know you, you've got at least six or seven of them you swiped from Buck's stashed in there," she said, naming a local gunsmith's shop.

It was both a request and a prod. The moment she met her mother's fiery gaze she knew the message had been received. With a small nod, Betsy rose and walked stiffly to the drawer on the far side of the stove.

It was time to show her know-it-all assistant from California how hillbillies from run-down little towns in the Ozarks settled their disputes.

She pretended to reread the first page of the documents, her shoulders tensing as she heard her mother rustling through the drawer behind her. "So, how will you work the transfer of funds?" she asked, pitching her voice low so Zarah would be forced to focus on her.

"Crypto?" the other woman replied with a cheeky smile.

Cara snorted. "Nope. Cash."

"I'll wire transfer it to you." Zarah flashed a dimpling smile. "It'll be easy. I already know all your account numbers."

"Yeah, I may need to rework some of those things," Cara murmured, keeping her head down as the rummaging continued behind her. "Mama? You find me a pen?"

"Hold your horses. I'm looking for one that works." To emphasize her point, Betsy tossed a cheap plastic ballpoint to the floor in disgust. "I have got to clean this mess out one day."

"Sounds like you need an assistant, Mrs. Beckett," Zarah chirped.

"Maybe so," her mother murmured. The sifting of clutter finally ceased, and Cara glanced over her shoulder to see her mother reach up and carefully tuck her hair behind her ear, clearing her peripheral vision. "I'm not finding a decent ink pen, but I did find this."

With one fluid move, Betsy Beckett swung around to face the young woman, her father-in-law's old service pistol in her hand and a grim expression hardening her pretty features. "Drop the gun."

Zarah's eyes widened. "No," she snapped, jabbing her gun into Jim Beckett's ribs so hard he let out a soft grunt. "This is my plan. We're going to do things my way," she insisted, her voice climbing with agitation.

"Oh, God," Paul Stanton blurted. Both of his arms raised, he turned toward the front door. Seeing Wyatt in the doorway, he stopped short. "This is too much. It's all too far out of hand."

"You think?" Wyatt asked, unperturbed.

Cara looked up as the lieutenant governor switched directions, then dithered, his arms flailing. "I have to get out of here. I can't be here. I was never here," he babbled.

"Could have sworn I saw you," Wyatt replied, his voice a life preserver of quiet and calm amid the melee.

"I can have your badge," Paul Stanton threatened, spittle flying from his mouth.

"You can try," Wyatt challenged. "But from where I'm standing, it doesn't look good for you, Mr. Stanton."

"You drop your gun," Zarah demanded, stepping back from Cara's father and training her sights on Betsy instead.

You chose incorrectly, Cara thought as her mother released the safety on her weapon.

"You terrorize my daughter, point a gun at my husband and track your muddy shoes on my kitchen floor and you think you get to give the orders here?" Betsy demanded, widening her stance. "I don't think so, honey."

Out of the corner of her eye Cara saw Wyatt lowering his hands. He was cool as a cucumber. It gave her the confidence she needed to end this farce once and for all.

Meeting Zarah's eyes, she spoke slowly and deliberately. "Lower the gun now, or I will never sign this. Mama, you too," she added. "I mean it. Everyone, lower the guns now."

"You mean everyone but me, right?" Wyatt asked, drawing his weapon from its holster at the small of his back as he closed the distance between him and Zarah.

Zarah's head whipped around in surprise, but his aim didn't waver as he took hold of her wrist with his left hand, expertly squeezing at the precise pressure point to make her release her grip. The gun she'd been waving around dropped to the floor as he twisted her arm behind her back.

"Zarah Parvich, you are under arrest. You have the right…"

Cara sat frozen, unable to tear her gaze away from the sight of Wyatt holding both of Zarah's empty hands behind her back.

"Cara, can I ask a favor?" Wyatt asked politely.

"Uh-huh," she said, and nodded.

"I left my coat on the living room floor. I have some zip tie restraints in the inside pocket. Grab a couple for me?"

"Sure," she replied as she rose.

"I'm leaving," Paul Stanton announced.

He took two steps toward the front room and without thinking, Cara snatched Grandma June's skillet from the stovetop and swung. She aimed for his body and not his head, wanting to slow the man, not kill him.

But the lieutenant governor wasn't the least bit grateful for her forethought. Cursing a blue streak, Stanton fell against the fridge, then crumpled to the floor, clutching his right arm.

"Excuse me, Uncle Paul," she said with a sneer as she stepped over his legs. "I think we'd like you to stay a bit longer."

On the opposite side of the room, Jim jumped up from his chair and hurried to embrace his wife. "Girl didn't know who she was messing with," he murmured into her hair.

Her mother gave a watery laugh. "I'm a regular Dirty Harriet," she said, burrowing in.

Cara carried Wyatt's coat back into the kitchen and her mother looked up, shaking her head. "Holy cow, girl, I can't believe you remembered this gun." Betsy wiped her eyes with the heels of her hands. "I doubt it's had a bullet in the chamber in the last twenty years. How did you know it was still there?"

"I saw it the other day when I was looking for a pen," Cara said with a smirk. "You've got everything in the world in there except a working ink pen." Holding Wyatt's jacket by the collar, she turned her attention to him. "What are you carrying in here? It weighs a ton."

"Nothing much. Flashlight, pepper spray, flex cuffs, extra

magazines, a collapsible baton," he said offhandedly. "Standard desk jockey stuff."

She pulled two zip ties from the deep inner pocket and handed one over. Zarah stood, unresisting, her head bowed, her lips clamped shut. Once she was cuffed, Wyatt guided her to a spot on the floor against the wall where she sat silently weeping.

Cara watched as he used the end of the other plastic strap to pick the discarded gun up off the floor. He deposited the weapon on the kitchen table, then looked from Cara to the woman on the tile floor.

"I called for backup from state police and the sheriff's department before I came inside. They should be here shortly. You okay to keep an eye on her while I see to our esteemed lieutenant governor?" he asked.

"I am," Cara responded. And to her surprise, it was true.

Lowering herself to the floor in front of the woman who'd turned her world upside down, she whispered, "Okay. Okay. Easy. Deep breaths, Zarah. Breathe in…"

Chapter Fifteen

Within minutes, her parents' house was a complete circus. Teams from both the state police and the Searcy County Sheriff's Office jostled for jurisdiction, but everyone knew in the end the county would have to give way.

"I knew I should have checked your financials," Wyatt muttered.

"Most people don't hire their own kidnappers," she murmured, her gaze fixed on her former assistant.

"Would have saved a lot of time and grief," he replied.

"Next time," she promised.

They watched as Zarah was properly secured and led to one of the trooper's vehicles for transport to Little Rock. A short distance away, Cara's mother stood behind the EMT checking Paul Stanton's arm to ascertain whether X-rays might be needed, reading her onetime prom date the proverbial riot act. Her father stood off to one side, a faint smile curving his mouth, his admiring gaze locked on his wife.

"She's something," Wyatt said to her father. "Nearly gave me a heart attack when she pulled a gun out of her kitchen drawer."

Jim Beckett looped an arm over Cara's shoulders and tucked her into his embrace.

"My dad didn't like leaving my mother in the house alone

while he was out doing chores, but as he used to say, you can't keep the inside and the outside up at the same time. So, he kept his old service pistol in the kitchen drawer in case trouble came strolling up the road. She must have brought it with her when she moved in with us."

"She did," Cara said quietly. "She told me Granddad would want us to have it to hand."

Without peeling his eyes off the floor show, her father pressed a kiss to the side of her head in a gesture he hadn't made in years, but one she remembered so well it brought a hot rush of tears to Cara's eyes.

"And another thing, Paul Anthony Stanton," her mother said, shaking her finger in the face of the man who held the second-most-powerful office in the state. "The minute they haul you out of here, I'm not only calling your precious mama, but I'm also callin' Delia Raitt. By the time I'm done with you, you won't be able to get elected prom king in prison or dogcatcher anywhere else!"

"I know I should stop her, but it's so darn entertaining," her father murmured to no one in particular. "Better than any show on CineFlix."

"Agent Dawson?" A shorter, powerfully built man with a blankly sober expression stood in the doorway Wyatt had filled mere hours before. "Could we speak to you in private, please?"

Wyatt nodded. "Yes, sir." He glanced first at Cara, then her father. "Y'all okay here?"

"We'll be fine," her father replied, giving her a squeeze as he answered for both of them.

Wyatt hesitated, his gaze lingering on her. Her cheeks heated, but thankfully, her father remained enthralled by the dressing down her mother hadn't quite wrapped up. "I'm good. Go do what you do," she said with a little jerk of her chin.

When he was gone, her father said, "I like him. Decent guy."

"I do too," Cara said quietly.

Satisfied with what he found, the EMT turned to one of the troopers standing nearby. "Doesn't look to be broken, but he should have an X-ray to be sure there's no fracture."

"Too bad," Jim whispered to Cara as the troopers hauled the man up from the chair and out of their house. "Swing for the fences next time, sugar."

She giggled and gave him a playful elbow jab. "Daddy. Behave." She assumed a prim expression. "You know I'm a pacifist."

He pulled back enough to tuck his chin to his chest and glare at her. "What? You only eat fish caught in the Pacific?"

She rolled her eyes and groaned. "Even for a dad joke that was bad."

Betsy Beckett turned to face them, hands planted on her hips. Thankfully, she seemed to have expended her supply of vitriol. "What's so funny, you two?"

"Not Dad's jokes," Cara replied. She slid out from under her father's arm and hugged her mother. "You were fantastic today."

"I guess I learned more than I thought I had, watchin' all those depressing shows your daddy likes."

"I wasn't worried. I know my wife." He leaned in and pressed a smacking kiss to Betsy's lips. "She can take care of herself and everyone else around her." He turned and looked at Cara as he pulled on the heavy work jacket he'd shrugged out of when the first of the patrol cars arrived. "You get it from her, Care Bear. You're like your mama."

A lump the size of a boulder rose in Cara's throat.

"Where do you think you're going?" her mother demanded as he reached for the handle on the back door. "I have a house full of cops and robbers here, and the police are going to want to talk to you some more. If you think you're going to slink off—"

"I'm goin' to see to the feed. I'll be right back," he said, zipping the jacket up to his chin.

He was gone before either of them could say another word. Betsy exhaled an exasperated sigh. "I swear he breaks out in hives if he has to spend more than an hour of daylight indoors."

"Probably," Cara concurred. "Nothing new there." A crime scene team bustled in, and it quickly became clear they were in the way. She caught her mother's tired gaze. "Let's go in the other room?"

"Sounds good," Betsy replied.

But when they slipped into the living room, they found themselves caught in the cross fire between one of the sheriff's men and an officious-looking state trooper. Betsy steered them toward the dining room, but there they found several men and a young woman dressed in dark suits setting up laptops and pulling legal pads from briefcases. Before they could be spotted, Cara took her mother's hand and led her down the hall toward the bedrooms. She could hear the rumble of deep voices coming from the room Wyatt had been using, so they tiptoed down the hall into Cara's room, closing the door silently behind them.

Betsy leaned against the closed door as if bracing against an approaching horde. "Good gracious, there's a lot of people in my house," Betsy said, patting her chest. "I hope they don't look too close at my floors. I haven't swept in days and Roscoe sheds enough for us to build a brand-new dog twice a week."

"Poor Roscoe," Cara said, peeking out her window at the front porch. Close to a dozen patrol cars and SUVs were parked haphazardly in the driveway and on the lawn, and the poor old dog had felt duty bound to greet every one of them. "I hope he's—" She scanned the porch until she spotted a familiar lump parked next to the rail. "Good, he's sleeping." She let the blind fall back into place with a chortle. "Wouldn't want him missing his middle-late-afternoon-pre-supper snooze."

"Supper," her mother groaned, stepping away from the door and dropping heavily onto the side of the single bed Cara had dutifully made before leaving the house.

Dropping down beside her mother, Cara patted her knee. "I think we're going to open the fridge and call whatever falls out supper."

Betsy tipped her head onto Cara's shoulder, and the simple reversal of their usual roles made Cara feel more centered than she had in years.

"Mama?"

"Hmm?"

"I think I am going to sell," Cara said, the words coming out as the thought took hold.

Her mother didn't move a muscle. For a moment, Cara wondered if Betsy had fallen asleep, or simply hadn't heard her, but then she stirred. Sitting up, she took both of Cara's hands in hers and held them tight as she gazed deep into her eyes.

"Don't decide anything now. Whatever you do, you do it in your time and in your way. No matter what anyone says, you created something special. You created it. You are the one who gets to decide what's right for you, and your creation."

"Well, me and Chris and Tom," Cara said with a self-deprecating little laugh.

"No, Cara," her mother said, giving her hands a squeeze. "Only you. Partners can help and support each other, but they can't dictate how we live our lives. You can walk with them, follow your own path or figure out a way to blaze a whole new trail. Make sure, in the end, you choose which it will be." Her mother let go long enough to sweep Cara's hair from her brow. "I imagine it's like a marriage. You have to be your own person, but together. Every day, choosing to be together."

Cara gave a snort of a laugh. "If my business partnership were a marriage, it would be illegal in most states."

Betsy rolled her eyes. "You know what I am saying. I'm only saying not to make any big moves until after this whole stock thingamajig is done. I have no idea if those fellas you're working with were actually involved in all of this mess or not, but I say let the truth come to light. You hang on and get everything you have coming to you, because it's yours and you earned it. After, well, then you can make your choices and your daddy and I will support you. One hundred percent."

Cara flung herself into her mother's arms. "Thank you, Mama."

They rocked as they held one another, Betsy alternately humming and shushing her. Cara was so happy to be assured of her parents' approbation to worry about the mixed messages.

With a snuffle, Cara pulled back a bit. Her gaze landed on the boy-band poster. "Mama, why didn't you ever take that poster down?"

Betsy spared the yellowing print a half glance, then pulled Cara close again. "As long as I kept it up, we'd both know this would always be your room. Whenever you came home, you'd feel…at home."

Cara squeezed her mother tight again and they stayed locked together until someone rapped lightly on the door.

"Who's there?" Cara said, dashing fingertips under her damp eyes.

"It's Wyatt," he replied without attempting to open the door. "Are all three of you hiding in there?"

Cara and Betsy laughed. "Jim has gone out to be with his cows," Betsy called back.

When he still didn't open the door, Cara asked, "You want to hide out in here too?"

The door opened slowly, and Wyatt poked his head in, a sheepish smile crinkling his eyes. "Hey."

"Hi," Cara returned, a single eyebrow raised. "You in or you out?"

His smile dissolved into a wince, and he raised a hand to the back of his neck in a gesture so familiar to her now, it made her chest ache. His gaze dropped to the floor and he shifted his weight from one foot to the other. "Listen, Emma is here with some guys from the FBI and the Department of Justice. It looks like we're talking state and federal charges for, uh, well, both of them and they want to talk to you."

"Okay." Cara rose, smoothing her hands down the front of the jeans she'd been so happy to acquire earlier in this endless day. "Let's do it."

Wyatt took a small step back, then glanced down the hall before turning back to her with an apologetic smile. "Actually, I have to go."

"Go?" she and her mother asked in unison.

Then Cara noticed the packed duffel at his feet. "Oh."

"The guy I was talking to is my section chief, Simon Taylor. He's heading back to Little Rock now and wants me to give him my full report on the way."

"Oh," Cara repeated, the bottom dropping out of her stomach. "Should I...? I'd like to meet him. Thank him."

Wyatt shook his head. "No need. Plus, he's not exactly a people person, you know?" He wrinkled his nose. "Trust me, you aren't missing anything."

The silence stretched several seconds too long. Thankfully, her mother stepped into the breach. "Jim and I can't thank you enough for all you've done," she said as she rose to say her goodbyes. "Let me call him in from the barn—"

"Oh, no. Thank you, ma'am," Wyatt said with a quick, hard shake of his head. "I didn't do much more than try to tug on a few loose threads."

Her mother wrapped an arm around Cara's waist and gave her an encouraging squeeze. "You brought our daughter home safely to us."

Wyatt met Cara's eyes at last, then gave her a lopsided smile. "No. I didn't even do that. Jim was right. Cara took care of herself and everyone else around her. I was nothing more than the guy who got to drive her home."

"Dawson?" a man called from down the hall.

"I have to go." Wyatt raised a hand in farewell. "Take care, okay?" He gave her a winsome smile. "Make sure the guys let you be the one who rings the big bell next week. You deserve it."

He turned away, hoisting his bag onto his shoulder in one fluid move. Cara and her mother followed him down the hall, but stopped short of the living room. Wyatt didn't seem to want to linger. The stern-looking man holding a leather computer bag nodded to her and her mother, then followed his agent—her agent—out the front door.

Cara wanted to call after him, but she couldn't make any sound come out. Besides, what could she say? He was with his boss. She was with her mother. Surely they'd have a chance to catch up later. She sucked in a breath when he stopped to give Roscoe a pat as the other man made a bee-line for a marked state police SUV.

"Ms. Beckett?" the young redhead she'd seen setting up equipment said as she strode toward them, her hand extended. "Special Agent Emma Parker. It's good to meet you in person."

"Oh. Yes. Emma." Cara mustered her best smile, but knew

it probably came across several watts weaker than usual. "Thank you for all you've been doing for the case." She gestured to her mother. "This is my mom, Elizabeth Beckett."

"Betsy," her mother supplied as the two women shook hands.

"If you don't mind, we'd like to ask you a few more questions," Emma said, gesturing to the dining room. "Wyatt said it would be okay for us to set up in your dining room, Mrs. Beckett, but I promise we'll be out of your hair ASAP."

Cara stiffened as a flash of headlights strafed the front of the house. She blinked a couple times, then saw the taillights on the SUV flash bright as the driver tapped the brakes. Her heart lurched. For a second, she thought maybe Wyatt had forgotten something and was coming back. Maybe the thing he'd forgotten was her.

Then she saw the vehicle dip as the driver maneuvered onto the rutted gravel lane and picked up speed.

"You go on with Agent Parker," her mother said in a gentle tone. "Do what you need to do. I'll fix up a mess of sandwiches for whoever wants something." Cara hesitated and her mother leaned in to kiss her cheek. "Go on now. Maybe later I'll tell you about the guy who drove me home from the prom."

Cara took a half step away before her mother's teaser fully registered. "Drove you home from the prom? You said you went to prom with Paul Stanton," she said with a puzzled frown.

"I did," Betsy said, a serene smile curving her lips. "I went with Paul. Danced with him a couple times too, but he was more interested in sneaking drinks with his football buddies." Her smile turned enigmatic as she started toward the kitchen. "Your daddy was the one who drove me home. It's been him ever since."

Epilogue

Cara Beckett strolled through Arrivals at Bill and Hillary Clinton National Airport without a single person recognizing her, and that was exactly the way she liked it. She tossed a glance over her shoulder to be sure her companions were right behind her.

"You're in the fast-paced capital city now. Try to keep up," she called over her shoulder.

"There's seriously only one terminal?" Chris asked, quickening his pace to fall in beside her.

"Yep."

She smiled as they approached the single escalator down to the baggage claim area. Cara paused to allow Chris to go first, waiting for Tom to catch up. With his ever-present computer bag hanging off one shoulder and a small carry-on in the other hand, the man was craning his neck as if the small airport was one of the wonders of the modern world.

"Come on, Captain Moneybags, you can put an offer in on the place another time," she teased.

"It's weird. I guess I've only ever flown into larger airports," he observed, stepping on the escalator behind her.

"When you've flown commercial," she qualified. "We won't count general aviation."

Tom frowned as he pondered her take. "You know, if

you're serious about this, maybe we should look into investing in a company plane after all," he mused.

"Yes!" Chris thrust his fist into the air, garnering the attention of the passengers around them. He didn't shrink from the spotlight. "I've been saying so for years."

"Yeah, well, we haven't been able to actually afford one," Tom shot back.

"And now we can," Chris said, his smile smug.

At the foot of the escalator he hooked a hand through Cara's arm. Tom flanked her left side, and they walked three abreast through the sliding doors into bright autumn sunshine. The late-November breeze swirled around them.

Beside her Chris gave an exaggerated shudder. "I thought it was supposed to be hot in the South?" he complained.

"We're due east of Los Angeles," she reminded him.

"Do I need to call a car?" Tom said, sliding a phone from his pocket.

"No, I have a friend picking us up," she said as she scanned the line of cars depositing and scooping up passengers. She spotted the plain black SUV with the state tags parked in one of the diagonal pull-through spots with a five-minute limit. "There she is."

As they approached, the driver's door opened and Emma Parker stepped out. "You made it," she said, meeting them at the back of the vehicle.

"We made it," Cara called back. "Tom, Chris, this is Special Agent Emma Parker. Be polite. She has a gun."

But it was Emma who was enthralled by the sight of the tech whizzes. "Wow. I'm so thrilled to meet you." She shook each man's hand, then turned to Tom. "I've been hacking multiplayer games since I was eleven. Like you." A pretty peach blush colored her cheeks. "I mean, I know you used to—"

Tom cut her off there. "Don't tell anyone, but sometimes I still do."

"He never had the patience to beat them legitimately," Chris chimed in.

"Me either," Emma said with a grin.

"Some of us actually have skills," Chris said pointedly.

"Okay, okay." Cara waved them both toward the doors. "You can flirt with her while we drive."

Once they were all settled into the vehicle, Emma joined the steady flow of traffic circling the small airport. Cara pointed to the parking deck. "The garage where I got carjacked," she said, using her best impression of a tour guide.

"Not funny," Tom muttered.

"I'm not kidding," she retorted.

"Cara's Trauma Tours," Chris said with a peevish edge. "Not a great selling point for your plan."

Cara turned and found both men scowling at the concrete structure as if it were responsible for the incident. "I don't have to sell you on my plan," she reminded them gently.

"We're still partners," Tom argued.

Smiling, Cara nodded, pleased too with the way they'd reconnected in the two weeks since Zarah Parvich and Paul Stanton were arrested and LYYF had a record-breaking launch on the stock exchange. When Cara told them she was heading back to Arkansas to spend Thanksgiving with her parents, the two men seemed genuinely sad to end the ongoing celebration.

"I can tell you the whole cybercrimes crew is really excited to have you drop by," Emma informed them as they merged onto the highway. She shot Cara a sidelong glance. "Wyatt in particular."

"Well, we appreciate all you did to help Cara," Chris answered. "A quick stopover to thank you in person is the least we could do."

Cara watched the highway signs zip past. This was the same route Gerald Griffin had forced her to take mere weeks before, but looked completely different with her two oldest friends along for the ride. Just a few miles down, Emma signaled her intent to exit. Arkansas State Police Headquarters was located in an old shopping mall on the city's south side.

Within minutes, Emma had wheeled the SUV into a spot designated for official vehicles and killed the engine. "We've got about an hour before I'll need to get you back to check in for your flights out."

"Let's do this then," Chris said, reaching for the door handle and discovering it was useless. He was trapped in the back of the police SUV. "Or not."

"Cop locks," Emma informed them. "Hang on, we'll let you out."

"Yeah. Makes sense," Chris muttered as Emma opened the rear door for him.

Cara smiled at Tom as he stepped out of the vehicle.

"Should I take my bags?" he asked.

Emma wrinkled her nose, then shrugged. "Up to you. This is not a great area, but if they're not safe in this vehicle, they aren't safe in any."

"Good point."

Emma made a point of chirping the locks as they walked away, and they all laughed.

A chuckle tangled in Cara's throat when one of the glass doors leading into headquarters opened and Wyatt Dawson stepped into the sunlight. His hair glinted gold and his shoulders looked broader than ever as he crossed his arms over his chest and waited for them, his lips curved into a smile he was clearly keeping on a tight rein.

Cara hung back, allowing Emma to make the introductions between the men. When Wyatt reached for the door and held it open for them, she hesitated on the sidewalk. Wyatt clocked her position with a glance, then let the door swing shut behind the others.

"Hey," he said, his gaze locked on her.

"Hi," she returned.

Then, unable to hold back a moment longer, Cara flung herself at him. He caught her up easily, strong arms winding tight around her as she buried her face in his neck.

"One minute you were there, and before I could even... you were gone," she mumbled into his skin.

"I wanted to stay. I wanted to stay with you, but I didn't know what you wanted and I couldn't... I love my job, Cara. I didn't know—"

"No. Right, I know," she said, her voice choked.

He held her fast, one hand sliding up her back to hold her to him even tighter. "Breathe," he whispered into her ear.

She gave a soggy chuckle and inhaled deeply. Maybe she got drunk on the scent of his soap, or perhaps he was exuding some kind of pheromone that made rational women lose their minds. She didn't know exactly why she pressed her lips to the exposed skin above his collar, she only knew it was absolutely necessary.

Wyatt froze for a second, and she wondered if she'd gone too far.

Then, the next thing she knew, he gripped the back of her head in his big, warm palm and his mouth was on hers. His lips were warm and firm, the bottom slightly chapped from his habit of gnawing on it, but all in all, the kiss was perfect. Long, lingering and packed with promise.

She pressed her slick lips together when he drew back for air. The last thing she wanted was to do something stupid like apologize. Not when she was not the least bit sorry he'd kissed her.

"I've wanted to kiss you a long time," he confessed, his voice slightly hoarse. "But this probably isn't the best time and place."

"Feels right to me," she said, her voice breathy.

"Complicates things," he said gruffly.

"Not for me," she answered, pulling back to look him in the eye. "This is by far the easiest decision I've made in weeks."

"Is it?"

She nodded. "I'm heading up to my folks for Thanksgiving," she informed him.

To her chagrin, he loosened his hold on her. "Sounds great. I'll be working on shift for the holiday, but probably head down to see my family over the weekend."

"Oh. I see."

She was unable to mask her disappointment, and he was as perceptive as ever. "Why? What's happening?"

"Oh, nothing." Cara flashed a shaky smile, her nerves ratcheting up as they circled one another. Taking a calming breath, she dove in. "I was wondering if you might have some free time this weekend."

His eyebrows rose. "Well, sure. I mean, I didn't have anything set in stone. What did you have in mind?"

"I thought you might like to come with me to check out a piece of property," she suggested, hugging herself as she braced against the stiff wind and possible rejection.

"Property?"

"There's a couple places out near Pinnacle Mountain State Park." His eyes lit with interest when she mentioned the recreational area just north and west of Little Rock. "You know, I was thinking someplace far enough out to have some land to build a studio, but close enough to enjoy the perks of high-speed internet."

"The perks of high-speed internet?" he repeated, his smile stretching wide. "What kind of perks?"

"Oh, you know, cop shows on CineFlix. And maybe, if the connection is as reliable as I think it is, a certain cop might possibly show up at my door to watch cop shows on CineFlix?" she suggested with a hopeful smile.

"I'd love to come look at property with you," he said, looking her square in the eye.

"I'm not going back to California," she told him. "I mean, at least not permanently. I'm sure I'll have to go out there someti—"

He cut her off with another kiss, this one swift and sure.

They jumped apart when someone hit the crash bar on the door with a little extra force. "Hey, Dawson," a gruff voice called out.

Cara laughed, pressing her forehead to Wyatt's shoulder as she tipped her head to the side. Trooper Masterson stood grinning in the open doorway, a small knot of people gathered around Chris and Tom behind him.

"You planning to hold the poor woman hostage or something? I wouldn't try it. I hear she's slippery."

Looping an arm across her shoulders, Wyatt kept her close as he turned toward the door. "Oh, I know. Cara Beckett can take care of herself and everyone else around her," he informed the older man. "Believe me, I plan to stay on her good side."

* * * * *

COLTON'S LAST RESORT

AMBER LEIGH WILLIAMS

To Beardy and the littles,

I've never written a book faster. It's a testament to your love and understanding that I was able to do so during a difficult time. Endless bear hugs and ice cream kisses for all of you!

And to Patricia, Kacy, Kimberly, Charlene, Addison and our editor, Emma Cole.

It has been lovely working with all of you.

Prologue

Allison Brewer didn't belong in a morgue. She was a twenty-five-year-old yoga instructor with zero underlying conditions. She never smoked, rarely drank, and was the picture of health and vitality.

Detective Noah Steele sucked in a breath as the coroner, Rod Steinbeck, pulled back the sheet. How many times had he stood over a body at the Yavapai County Coroner's Office? How many times had he stared unflinchingly at death—at what nature did to humans and what human nature did to others?

She looks like she could still be alive, he thought. No cuts or bruises marred her face. There were no ligature marks. She could have been asleep. She looked perfectly at peace. If Noah squinted, he could fool himself into thinking there was a slight smile at the corners of her mouth. Just as there had been when she'd feigned sleep as a girl.

However, an inescapable blue stain spread across her lips. He could deny it all he wanted, but his sister was gone.

"I'm sorry, Noah," Rod said and lifted the sheet over her face again.

"No." The word wasn't soft or hard, loud or quiet. Noah surprised himself by speaking mildly. As if this were any other body...any other case. His mind was somewhere near the ceiling. His gut turned, and his chest ached. But he let that piece of himself float away, detached. He made himself think like he was trained to think. "What're your impressions?"

"Fulton's already been here. It's his case. And for good reason. You're going to need some time to process—"

"Rod." He sounded cold. He was. He was so bitterly cold. And he didn't know how to live with it. He didn't know how to live in a world without Allison. "Next of kin would be informed of any progress made in the investigation. I'm her next of kin. Inform me."

Rod shuffled his feet. Placing his hands at each corner of the head of the steel table, he studied Allison. "I'm not sure I'm comfortable with this."

"She's dead." Noah made himself say it. He needed to hear it, the finality of it. "If Sedona Police wants me to process that, I need to know how and why."

Rod adjusted his glasses. "Look, maybe you should talk to Fulton."

"She was found at the resort," Noah prompted, undeterred, "where she works."

"Mariposa."

"You were on scene there," Noah surmised. "What time did you arrive?"

Rod gave in. "Nine fifteen."

"Where was she?"

"One of the pool cabanas," the coroner explained.

"Tell me what you saw."

"Come on, Noah…"

"Tell me," Noah said. He knew not to raise his voice. If he were hysterical, it would get back to his CO. He'd be put on leave.

He needed to work through this. If he stopped working, stopped thinking objectively, he would lose his mind.

Rod lifted his hands. "She was found face down, but one of the staff performed CPR, so she was on her back when I arrived. Her shoes were missing."

That could've been something, Noah thought, if Allison hadn't had a habit of going around barefoot where she was comfortable, particularly when entering someone's home.

The temperature had dipped into the thirties the night before. *A little cold for no shoes, even for her*, he considered. "What was she wearing?"

"Sport jacket and leggings," Rod explained. "Underneath, she wore a long-sleeved ballet-like top cropped above the navel with crisscrossed bands underneath. It was a matching set, all green."

"What do you figure for time of death?"

"Right now, I'd say she died somewhere between one and two this morning."

She hadn't gone home to bed, Noah mused. "Any cuts, lacerations? Signs of foul play?"

"Some abrasions on the backs of her legs."

"Show me."

Again, Rod paused before he walked to the bottom of the table. Lifting the drape, he revealed one long, pale leg with toes still painted pink. Noah tried not to see the unearthly blue tone of the skin around the nails. He craned his neck when Rod showed him the marks on her calves.

"She was dragged," Noah said as he realized what had happened. Why did the air feel like ice? The cold filled his lungs. They felt wind-burned, and the pain of it made his hands knot into fists.

"That would be my understanding," Rod agreed. He replaced the sheet gingerly.

"Before or after TOD?" Noah asked.

"After."

Noah's brow furrowed. "She was killed somewhere other

than the cabana and staged there." His voice had gone rough, but he kept going, searching. "Were there any items with her at the scene?"

"Fulton noted there was no purse, wallet or cell phone. She was identified by members of Mariposa's staff."

"Were her lips blue when you got there?"

"Yes." Rod nodded. "Her fingernails and toes were discolored as well."

Noah scraped his knuckles over the thick growth of beard that covered his jawline. "Who found her?"

"From what I understand," Rod said slowly, "it was a staff member. You'll have to get the name of the person from Fulton."

"Who was there when you arrived on scene?" Noah asked curiously.

"There was a small crowd that had been blocked by officers," Rod told him. "Several members of security, one pool maintenance person and all three of the Coltons."

"Coltons." Noah recognized the name, but he let it hang in the air, waiting for Rod to elaborate.

"The siblings," Rod said. "They own and manage Mariposa. Adam, Laura and Joshua, I believe, are their names."

"What was your impression of them?" Noah asked, homing in.

Rod considered. "The younger one, Joshua, was quiet. Laura didn't say much either. She seemed stricken by the whole thing. The oldest one, Adam…"

When Rod paused, Noah narrowed his eyes. "What about him?"

"He did all the talking," Rod said. "He ordered everyone back and let the uniforms, Fulton, crime scene technicians and myself work. There was no attempt to tamper with the scene. Although I did hear him speaking to Fulton as we readied the body for transport."

"What did he say?" Noah asked, feeling like a dog with a bone.

"He wanted Fulton's word that the investigation would remain discreet," Rod said. "They get some high-profile guests at Mariposa. He didn't want their privacy or, I expect, their experience hindered."

The muscles around Noah's mouth tensed. "A member of their staff is found dead, and the Coltons' first thought is how it's going to affect their clientele? Does that seem right to you?"

"I'm not the detective," Steinbeck noted.

No, Noah considered. *I am.* "You'll do a tox screen?"

"It's routine," Rod replied. "As it stands, I don't have a cause of death for you."

"You'll keep me informed?" Noah asked.

"I'll stay in touch."

Noah forced himself to back away from Allison's body. Deep in some unbottled canyon, he felt himself scream.

"Have your parents been notified?"

The question nearly made him flinch. Rod didn't know. No one did. Not really.

It didn't matter, he told himself. He'd loved her, hadn't he? He'd loved her as his own. "She doesn't have parents," he said. "Neither of us do."

"I'm sorry." Rod placed his hand on Noah's shoulder. "I'll take care of her."

"I know." Noah turned for the door.

"Don't get yourself in trouble over this," Rod warned. "Let Fulton handle it. He'll find out what happened to her."

Noah didn't answer. In seconds, he was out of the autopsy room, down the hall, crossing the lobby. Planting both hands on the glass door, he shoved it open.

Cold air hit him in the face and did nothing for the lethal ice now channeling through his blood.

He thought about stopping, doubling over, bracing his hands on his knees.

He could hear her. Still.

Breathe, Noah. Deep breath in. And let it out.

Noah shook his head firmly, blocking out her voice. He thought of what Rod had said—about the scene and his impressions of the people there.

He took out his keys, walking to the unmarked vehicle that was his. Opening the driver's door, he got behind the wheel and cranked the engine. The sun was sinking swiftly toward the red rock mountains in the distance, but he picked up his phone. Using voice commands, he said, "Hey, Google, set a course for Mariposa Resort & Spa."

He studied the GPS route that popped up on-screen before mounting the phone on the dash. Shifting into Reverse, he cupped the back of the passenger headrest. Turning his head over his shoulder, he backed out of the parking space.

To hell with staying out of Fulton's way. Someone was responsible for Allison's death. He would find out who.

And he was going to nail the Coltons' asses to the floor.

Chapter One

Ten Hours Earlier

"Dad wants to meet."

Laura Colton stared at her brother over the rim of her thermos. "You couldn't have let me finish my coffee before dropping that bombshell?"

Her brother Adam raised a brow as he eyed the overlarge bottle. "There are three cups of java in that thing. If that's not enough to prepare you for the day, it's time you rethink some of your life choices."

"I demand coffee before chaos," Laura informed him and took another hit to prove her point. She was no stranger to butting heads with her older brother. They worked closely as owners and managers of Arizona's premier resort and spa.

It was their passion for Mariposa that made them lock horns. The resort wasn't simply the business venture that supported them. Before it was Mariposa, it was the respite their mother had sought when the disappointment of her marriage to Clive Colton had grown to be too much. Laura and her siblings' memories of Annabeth Colton were tied not just to the project she had started shortly after the birth of her third child, Joshua, but the land itself.

The three of them had buried her here at Mariposa after her battle with pancreatic cancer.

Laura loved Mariposa. It was more home than her actual hometown of Los Angeles had ever been. When Adam had asked her and Joshua to join him after he'd taken legal control of the resort at the age of twenty-one, neither of them had hesitated. From there, their management styles had been born out of renovations and the desire to make Mariposa their own.

The Coltons had put the once-small hotel on the map. It had been transformed into a getaway for the rich and famous, with twenty-four acres of spacious grounds northeast of Sedona. It now boasted thirty guest bungalows with stunning views of Red Rock Country, a five-star restaurant named after Annabeth herself, a garden, rock labyrinth, golf course, spa, horse stables and paddocks, and hiking trails.

Laura had learned to work with both of her brothers. They were invested in their shared vision, in this life. She could take their ribbing. Just as she could take the fact that she and Adam were both workaholics whose dedication and zeal left little in the way of private lives.

She drank more coffee and tried not to rue the long chain of failed relationships she'd endured, letting her eyes stray to the view from the conference room windows of L Building.

Shadows were long across the rocky vista with its stunning juxtaposition of blue sky and red geography. From its flat ridge top, Mariposa woke briskly. Staff would be going about preparations for the day. The chef at Annabeth would be arranging its signature champagne breakfast. Below the ridge and the bungalows, the horses would be feeding. The helicopter pilot who transported guests from the airport in Flagstaff would be doing preflight checks.

If she had to scrap her plans to be married with children by her late twenties for this, so be it. *There's plenty of time for all that*, Adam liked to say when anyone commented on his lack of a wife or children.

Plenty of time, she mused. No need to worry about the fact that she was tripping fast toward thirty.

Cautiously, she asked, "What does Clive want?"

Adam chuckled a little as he always did when she called their father by his given name. "He didn't say."

She ran her tongue over her teeth. "Is he bringing Glenna?"

"He didn't mention her," Adam said, referring to their stepmother of four years. Laura imagined it seemed odd to him still, too. Clive's string of mistresses hadn't been a well-kept secret. He'd fathered a fourth child outside of his marriage to Annabeth. Dani had come to live with Adam, Laura and Joshua in Los Angeles for a time. Laura had been only too happy not to be the only girl, and the four of them had been all too aware of Clive's neglect.

Laura had never forgotten that, and she'd never been able to forgive Clive for his carelessness or whims. She knew his affairs had been one reason Annabeth had escaped time after time to Arizona. She'd loved Clive, despite his faults and mishandlings. The heartbreak and embarrassment of knowing he had looked for companionship elsewhere…that he had married her for her money…it had been too much for Annabeth to bear.

No, Laura had never forgiven her father, even if Glenna wasn't like the other women. She was close to Clive's age, for one, and beautiful, like his mistresses. Unlike the others, she was mature and independent. She even owned her own business, and it was a successful one.

It didn't mean Laura's father had turned things around. He'd had little to do with his children's upbringing. Annabeth had raised them practically on her own until the cancer had taken a turn for the worse when Laura was just twelve years old.

"I thought we could arrange Bungalow Twelve for him," Adam continued as he shuffled papers in the file spread on the table in front of him.

Laura pursed her lips. Adam was a businessperson, not a bitter man or a hard one. The snub was subtle. Every bungalow at Mariposa was luxurious, but only bungalows one through ten featured a private outdoor pool and were prioritized for VIP guests. She rubbed her lips together, considering. "You don't think he'll notice?"

Adam picked up a pen and made a mark on the latest budget report he'd likely stayed up late last night reviewing. "Notice what?"

Adam wasn't petty either. Neither was she, Laura told herself as she made a notation in the notes app on her phone. "Bungalow Twelve," she agreed. "When are we expecting him?"

"The day after tomorrow."

"And when is he departing?"

"He didn't say that either."

"He can't just come and go as he pleases," Laura pointed out. "We have guests coming in after him, and the concierge and Housekeeping require notice."

Adam lifted his eyes briefly to hers. Even sitting, he looked lanky despite his broad shoulders. His blue eyes matched hers, and his medium-blond hair was never not short, trim and stylish, even when the rest of the world was waking up. People liked to think he'd been born in a suit, and if she hadn't grown up with him, she'd wonder, too.

"I'm sure you'll let him know when he arrives. Let's move on."

Laura made another notation about her father's visit and

did her best to ignore the unsettled feeling that pricked along her spine.

"The wedding on Valentine's Day weekend," Adam continued. "I'm assuming everything's on schedule?"

"I spoke to the mother of the bride yesterday," she explained. "They've asked for another three bungalows, as the guest list has expanded."

"A little late for that."

"I said we could do it," she admitted, "as long as they agreed to cap the number there."

He let loose a sigh. "I'll have to adjust the price points. How many more plates is that for the reception?"

"Five adults, four children."

He scrawled and started talking numbers.

"We need to talk about this year's anniversary celebration," she interrupted. Mariposa had opened on Valentine's Day almost twenty-two years ago. "Since the wedding is on Valentine's Day, I propose we move the celebration to Wednesday, the eighteenth."

Adam stopped counting to consider. "That works for me."

"We'll have a bandstand, like last year," she said, ticking items off her list. "Live music, hors d'oeuvres, cocktails and fireworks. And you'll make a speech."

He raised his gaze to hers. "Will I?"

"Yes," she said, beaming. "People like to hear you speak."

He waved a hand. "If I must."

"Good man," she praised and put a check mark next to Adam's Speech on her list.

An infinitesimal smile wavered across his lips. "You enjoy painting me into a corner and patting me on the head when I have no choice but to comply."

"I'm sure I don't know what you mean." She tapped the hollow of her collarbone. "Is that the tie I bought you?"

"Yes," he said after a glance at it.

"It looks very nice," she said. "And I was right. It does bring out your eyes."

His smile strengthened. "Clever girl."

The door to the conference room opened. Laura eased back in her chair as Joshua loped in. He smiled distract-edly through dark-tinted shades when he saw the two of them seated on either side of the table. "Greetings, siblings."

"You're late," Adam pointed out.

"Oh, you noticed," Joshua said, unfazed as he pulled out a chair and dropped to it. "How thoughtful of you." He caught Laura's look. "You're not going to tell me off, are you?"

He was so charmingly rumpled, any urge to scold him fell long by the wayside. Joshua was twenty-seven. His dirty-blond hair was perpetually shaggy. When he took off his glasses, his eyes laughed in the same shade as hers and Ad-am's. At six feet, he was trim and muscular. He couldn't claim to eat and sleep work as they did, but he was just as devoted to Mariposa. He was very much at home in his role as the resort's Activities Director.

"No," she replied.

He pecked a kiss on her cheek. "You're my favorite."

"For the moment."

He leaned his chair back and crossed his legs at the an-kles. "What's the latest?"

"Clive is coming," she warned, handing over her thermos easily when he held out his hand for it.

He took a long sip. "And how do we feel about that?" he asked, squinting at Adam across the long, flat plane of the table.

Adam answered without inflection. "Indifferent."

"Oh?" Joshua said with a raised brow. He looked at Laura for confirmation.

Laura cleared her throat. "We're placing him in Bunga-low Twelve."

Joshua laughed shortly before setting the thermos on the table between him and her. "I approve."

"I thought you might," Adam said, again without looking up.

Joshua had been only ten when their mother had died. His memories of Annabeth were the foggiest—most of them mere reflections through a vintage-cast mirror. Though he remembered well how Clive had abandoned them to their grief. As the youngest, he'd needed the most stability and guidance. It was Adam and Laura who had stepped into that role—not their father.

"Glenna won't stand being demoted to anything below the amenities of Bungalow Ten," he warned.

"We don't know she's coming," Laura revealed.

"I'm just saying," Joshua said, holding up his hands.

None of them had gotten to know their stepmother well. But Joshua was right. Glenna may keep her thoughts to herself, and she could be perfectly cordial. But she also had a discerning eye and was accustomed to a certain type of lifestyle. One reason, no doubt, she had been drawn to Clive Colton. As CEO of Colton Textiles, he lived in a Beverly Hills mansion she had already refined to her tastes.

Laura sighed. "I'll deal with that if it comes."

Joshua sketched a lazy salute. "I'll have Knox loan you a helmet."

"I have one," she reminded him. Not that she'd need it. She could handle Clive, and she could certainly handle Glenna. She shook her head. "Are we being unkind?"

Her brothers exchanged a look. "In what way?" Adam asked.

"He hasn't been well," Laura reminded them. "The ministrokes last year and the rumors about sideline business deals going sideways… We could be losing him."

They lapsed into silence. Joshua reached up to scratch

his chin. "Is it not fair to say I feel like I lost him a long time ago?"

She studied him, and she saw the ten-year-old who'd needed a parent. His hand clutched the arm of the swivel chair. She covered it with her own. "It is fair," she assured him.

Adam had shielded his mouth with his writing hand. He dropped it to the table, the ballpoint pen still gripped between his fingers. "Mom left the resort to us in her will not just because she wanted us to have a piece of her and financial security. She left it because she knew the house in Los Angeles wasn't a home. She left us a place we could belong to. Dad never provided that for her or us. She made sure after she was gone we wouldn't need to rely on him, because she knew all he would ever do was disappoint us. Like he disappointed her."

"She left us fifty percent of the shares in Colton Textiles, too," Joshua added. "If it'd been him...if he had gone first... would he have done the same?"

Laura shook her head. "I don't know." But she did, she realized. She knew all too well.

Adam dropped the pen. He folded his hands on the table-top. "If we have an opening, we can slot him into one of the VIP bungalows. Would that ease your conscience?"

Laura considered. She opened her mouth to answer.

A knock on the door interrupted.

"Come in," Adam called.

The panel pulled away from the jamb. Laura felt the tension in the room drain instantaneously as Tallulah Deschine peered into the room. The fifty-year-old Navajo woman was head of housekeeping at Mariposa. She'd been with the Coltons since the renovation. In the last decade, she'd become more of a mother to them than a member of staff, and she was one of the few workers at the resort who, like

Adam, Laura and Joshua, lived in her own house on property. "I'm sorry to intrude."

Joshua sat up straighter. "No need to apologize, Tallulah. Come sit by me." He pushed out the chair next to his.

Worry lines marred her brow. "There's a situation. Down at the pool."

"What kind of situation?" Adam asked, his smile falling away in a fast frown.

Tallulah's attention seized on Laura. She opened her mouth, then closed it.

Laura saw her chin wobble. Quickly, she pushed her chair back. "What is it, Tallulah?" she asked softly, crossing to the door. She heard Adam and Joshua get up and follow suit. "What's happened?"

Tallulah's eyes flooded with tears. She spoke in a choked voice. "The maid, Bella… She noticed one cabana was never straightened after hours last night. When she went inside to do just that, she found someone there."

Adam touched her shoulder when she faltered again. "Someone who? What were they doing there?"

"Oh, Adam." Tallulah shook her head, trying to gather herself. "Bella thought she'd fallen asleep there, so she tried waking her up. She couldn't. There's something *really* wrong…"

"Who is she?" Laura asked. There was a hard fist in her stomach. It grew tighter and tighter, apprehension knotting there. "Tallulah, who did Bella find in the cabana?"

"It's Allison," Tallulah revealed. "The yoga instructor. Knox knows CPR. He's trying to bring her around—"

"Did you call 9-1-1?" Adam asked, his phone already in hand.

"Alexis made the call."

"EMTs should only be ten minutes out," he assured her.

Joshua pushed through the door. "If she's not breathing, that's not enough time."

Laura tailed him. He'd already broken into a run. She didn't catch up with him until they came to the end of the hall.

If Allison wasn't asleep in the cabana...if she wasn't breathing... What did that mean?

Laura hastened her steps and nearly ran into Alexis Reed, the concierge, and Erica Pike, Adam's executive assistant, in the lobby.

"What's going on?" Alexis asked urgently. "Is Allison okay?"

"I don't know," Laura said. Joshua didn't stop. He hit the glass doors. They swung open. She followed him out into the mountain air. Her heart was in her throat as they raced to the pool area.

The drapes on the farthest cabana were still closed. The pool maintenance person, Manuel, stood outside with his hat in his hands. Their head of security, Roland, stepped out, expression drawn.

"How is she?" Joshua asked. "Did Knox bring her around?"

Roland shook his head.

Laura fumbled for speech. "What?"

Joshua swept the curtain aside.

Laura moved to follow him, but Manuel brought her up short. "I don't think you should go in there, Ms. Colton."

She shook her head. "Why? What's wrong with her?"

Roland took a breath. "I don't know how to say this, but I don't think she'll be coming back around."

Laura couldn't wrap her head around the words. She slipped past Manuel and Roland, ducking through the parting of the drapes. Her footsteps faltered when she saw Joshua and Knox Burnett, the horseback adventure guide, leaning over the still, white face of the woman lying supine on the outdoor rug. Neither of them moved. "Why did you stop?" she asked Knox. "Why aren't you helping her?"

"Laura…" Joshua mumbled. "You need to go."

She crouched next to him. Her hand lifted to her mouth when she saw the tint of Allison's lips.

Knox's face was bowed in an uncharacteristic frown.

Even as she denied what she was seeing, she looked at him. "Why did you stop?" she asked again.

He was panting, his long hair mussed. His face inordinately pale, he said, "She's cold. So cold. I couldn't get a pulse. She never had a pulse…"

Laura looked down at Allison's face. Her dark eyes stared, unseeing. "Oh, God," she said with a shaky exhalation.

Joshua's fingers closed over hers. He spoke in a whisper, as if afraid Allison would hear. "She's gone."

Chapter Two

Laura frowned at the water glass on the table in front of her. She wished for her thermos. Hell, she wished this interview could take place at L Bar. The bartender, Valerie, knew Laura's drink of choice.

Allison, she thought. *Oh, God. Allison...*

Detective Mark Fulton of the Sedona Police Department sat across the table. He hadn't allowed either of her brothers to join her. They had each been questioned separately, as had Bella, Knox, Tallulah, Manuel and Roland.

"I understand you were the one who initially hired the deceased," Fulton commented.

She studied the small corona on top of his shiny, hairless head, a reflection from the wide chandelier above them. Forcing herself to look away, she traced the pattern of his tie with her gaze—circles overlapping circles in various shades of blue, each edged with a thin gold iris. "Allison," she said. She swallowed. She hadn't let herself cry.

Not yet. She'd been surrounded by people—her brothers, the staff, the guests—since the discovery of Allison's body.

Her voice split as if the strain of not crying had injured her vocal cords.

"Sorry?" Fulton said, looking up from his notepad distractedly.

"Her name is Allison," she told him. He needed to stop calling her *the deceased*. It sounded discordant, inhumane.

"Of course," he allowed. He spared her a brief smile. "You hired Allison. Ms. Brewer. Is that correct?"

"I did," Laura answered. "Two years ago last September."

"And when did you see her last?" he asked.

Laura thought about it. "Yesterday. She teaches... I mean, she taught a yoga course in the meditation garden at the rock labyrinth at sunset. I saw her coming back from that around dusk. It was between six and six thirty. I was on my way to check on our chef at Annabeth. He had to have stitches the day before. He cut himself during the lunch rush. I wanted to make sure he was okay to work through dinner. I saw Allison walking from the meditation garden toward C Building, which is where the staff locker rooms, break rooms and café are located. It's also where they park their cars when they arrive for work in the morning."

"Did you speak to her?"

"I did," Laura said with a nod.

"How would you describe her demeanor?"

Laura frowned. "I'm not sure what you mean."

"Did she strike you as happy, tired, angry, upset...?"

It took a moment for Laura to settle on the right description. "She was upbeat. Allison was always upbeat. Even when she was fatigued, which I imagine she was after a full day of classes. She does guided meditation for guests and for anyone on staff who wants to join after hours. One reason I was so excited about hiring her was because she had wonderful ideas for improving the wellness of not just Mariposa's guests but the resort as a whole. She wanted fellow members of staff to have the opportunity to rest and recharge."

"That was generous of her."

Laura nodded. "Allison was always generous with her time and attention. Everyone liked her."

"What did you speak to her about when you saw her yesterday evening?"

She narrowed her eyes, trying to recall the exact words of the conversation. "She wanted to grab dinner and was looking forward to a few moments to herself in the break room before the guided meditation with the staff. Sometimes, she liked to join the stargazing excursion after dinner. She was excited about seeing last night's meteor shower before she went home to Sedona. She had a house there."

"Would you mind telling me what she was wearing at the time?" Fulton asked.

Laura fumbled. She thought again of Allison lying between Knox and Joshua. Her blue-tinged lips. Her blank stare.

Something wormed its way up Laura's throat. The taste of acid filled her mouth. She had to force herself to swallow it back down. "Workout clothes. The same ones we… we found her in this morning."

"Was she wearing shoes last night?"

She narrowed her eyes at him. "That's an odd question, Detective. Do you mind me asking how that's relevant?"

"I'm just trying to get a full picture of the deceased… I mean, Allison…in the hours leading up to her death."

He said it gently. Even so, *her death* sounded so final. Laura reached up for her temples, feeling off balance. "Ah… I believe so. Yes. She wore flexible, lightweight footwear between classes. For the classes themselves, she preferred to go barefoot." Laura remembered the tiny lotus tattoo on Allison's ankle. Her eyes stung. "Do you mind me asking, Detective, if you have any idea *how* she died? It just seems strange for someone so young to just…"

Fulton nodded away the rest. "That's why I'm trying to

go through all the details. It will help me understand what happened to her."

"Did she have a heart attack?" Laura asked. Even that seemed nonsensical. Allison was so healthy. She was vegan, preferring to bring her own meals instead of having them prepared by others. "It could have been a stroke, I suppose. Or an aneurysm?"

"Again, Ms. Colton," Fulton said in as kind a voice as he could muster. "I assure you. I will do everything I can to figure out what happened to your employee."

Employee? Allison was her friend. Laura opened her mouth to correct him, but she faltered.

"Was there anyone on staff who Allison didn't get along with?" Fulton asked.

"No. As I said, everyone liked Allison."

"What about guests? Have there been any disgruntled students from her yoga or meditation classes?"

"No," she said, finding the idea ridiculous. "None."

"In two years, she never had a dissatisfied student?"

"Not one," Laura said. She would have known. Allison would have told her.

"Did she have a personal relationship with any of the guests?"

"What do you mean by that?" Laura asked.

"Was she closer to any particular guest?" he elaborated. "Beyond the classes. Maybe one she got to know during the stargazing excursions."

Laura frowned. "Allison would never overstep. She knew where to draw the line. She was the perfect mix of friendliness and professionalism, and she never would have thought of mixing business with pleasure, if that's what you're implying."

"You're sure of this?"

She met his level stare. "Yes."

He made several notes before he asked, "Do you know anything about her personal life? Was she involved with anyone on staff?"

"No, Detective. Relationships among staff members aren't encouraged."

"No one on staff seemed especially interested in Ms. Brewer?"

"I don't think so," Laura said. "There was a flirtation with our adventure guide, Knox Burnett. But Knox flirts with everyone."

"What about outside the resort? What was her personal life like in Sedona?"

"She was in a relationship when she first came to the resort," Laura remembered suddenly. "But it ended a few months after she started."

"Did she seem upset?"

"She enjoyed being single again. Prioritizing herself was important. She enjoyed living alone." She came to attention as something occurred to her. "Oh my God! Have you told her family? She didn't talk about her parents, but there was a brother she was close to. She talked about him regularly. Does he know? Should we have contacted him already? I'm sure she put him down as her emergency contact."

Fulton held up a hand. "We have contacted her next of kin. You don't need to worry about that."

"Still, I'd like to extend the condolences of the family and staff," Laura explained. "There must be something we can do."

"I'd be happy to get you in touch, if you like."

"I would," she said. "Very much."

"I'll have that information sent to you as soon as possible," he stated. "One more question, and I'll let you get back to your day. Can you tell me about your whereabouts between one and two o'clock this morning?"

She felt heavy in her chair, as if gravity were exerting more force than necessary. "Is that when Allison died?"

"Yes, ma'am."

"Why do you need to know my whereabouts?"

"It's simply a matter of routine."

"I was in bed," Laura explained. She'd gone to bed early, her large tabby cat at her side.

"Can anyone corroborate that?"

"No." Was her word not enough? "I took off my smart-watch to charge it. I'm sure there's a time stamp, probably around 11:00 p.m. My alarm goes off at 5:30 a.m."

"Your brother informed me there are no security cameras on the property."

"No. The privacy of our guests is very important at Mariposa."

"He said that, too. I just hope it doesn't make matters more complicated for you."

"Why would it?" she asked.

He closed his notepad and pushed his chair back from the table. "I think that's all I have for now. Thank you for sitting down with me. If I have any more questions, I'll let you know."

If he had any more questions for her? She was the one with all the remaining questions, and none of them had been answered. She sat frozen as he rounded the table. Before he could reach for the door, she snapped to attention, standing suddenly. "Detective?"

He stopped. "Ma'am?"

"You will keep my brothers and me informed of any developments?" she requested. "We all cared about Allison a great deal."

"I will," he agreed. "Have a good day."

She waited until he was out the door before she sank to the seat. Her legs weren't steady enough to stand on.

She should've asked why Allison's lips had been blue. Would Fulton know how long she had been in the cabana?

Had she suffered? Was she scared? How long had she been alone and frightened?

How could this happen? What was she going to do now? How was she supposed to go about their day as if nothing had happened?

Laura's posture caved. She rarely let it, but she folded under the weight of shock and pressed her fingers to her closed eyes.

She hadn't lost anyone close to her since her mother's passing and hadn't forgotten how it felt—the staggering weight of bereavement. It was impossible to forget. But she hadn't expected... She hadn't been prepared to feel it all again.

The shock was wearing away fast. Once it was gone, the grief would sink in. And it wouldn't give way to anything else. She pressed her hand to her mouth, choking it back.

She was afraid of it. Grief. How it gripped and rent. As a child, it had come for her on wraith wings, real but transparent. She hadn't been able to see it, but it had held her. It had hurt her. And it had transformed her into something she hadn't recognized.

Panic beat those wings against her chest now. Her pulse rushed in her ears. She tried to breathe, tried to think through it, but it didn't allow her to.

It was already taking hold.

She'd seen it coming before. Her mother had warned her there wasn't much time. She had told all her children what to expect at the end of her cancer battle. She had prepared them and armed them for the hard days to come.

This wasn't the same. And yet it was.

She thought of her brothers waiting outside the door. Coming to her feet, she walked the length of the conference room. She paced until the panic subsided—until her breathing returned to normal and her heart no longer raced.

Adam might be the oldest, but her brothers had looked to her in the past. For strength. For stability. When their mother died, she had stepped into Annabeth's power—to carry them, to ground them and to keep them together.

They were grown now, but they would look to her, still. They would need her to handle this…and they would need to lean on her. And so would the staff.

She dried her eyes, fixed her makeup and made herself down the entire glass of water in front of her.

A knock clattered against the door. She checked her reflection in the window before she said, "Yes?"

Alexis stepped in. "Hey. How are you holding up?"

Laura made herself meet her friend's gaze. "I'm fine."

Alexis raised a brow. "You want me to pretend that's true?"

"I'm going to need you to," Laura requested.

Alexis nodded. "Okay." She, Allison and Laura had gotten to know each other well. Besides Tallulah and Laura's brothers, redheaded, smiling Allison and dark, no-nonsense Alexis were the members of staff Laura felt closest to. In some ways, they had been her saving grace over the last few years. There were things she couldn't discuss with Adam and Joshua. Just her girls. The three of them had made Taco Tuesdays at Sedona's Tipsy Tacos a weekly escape from the pressures of the hospitality business. Laura lived and worked at the resort. Alexis and Allison had taught her that getting away, even for a few hours, could be crucial for her well-being.

"How about you?" Laura asked. "How are you handling this?"

Alexis's hazel eyes raced across the length of the table, as if searching for the answer there. "I think I'm still processing."

"It's a lot."

"Yeah, and it doesn't make sense, Laura."

"No," Laura agreed.

Alexis glanced over her shoulder before closing the door at her back. She leaned against it. "That detective. Did he say whether she was attacked in any way?"

Laura had to stop and take another steadying breath. "You think someone hurt her?"

"She can't have just died."

Fulton's final battery of questions came back to Laura. She shivered and rubbed her hands over her upper arms. "But who would do such a thing? Who would want to hurt her?"

Alexis's brow furrowed. "I don't know. But it won't take long for the police to find out exactly what killed her. And I have a feeling they're not done questioning everyone."

Laura thought of that, the implications… "Murder doesn't happen at Mariposa. It never has."

"Maybe not," Alexis said, subsiding. "Look, if you need to go home, Erica and I can cover for you."

"No," Laura said quickly. "You're working through this. Adam and Josh are working through this. I'm going to do the same. We have to get through the day."

"Knox is shaken up pretty badly," Alexis told her. "He should go home."

Laura nodded. "Right. I'll handle that." It would give her

something to do, someone to take care of for the time being. "I'll check back in with you in a little while."

Sadness leaked across Alexis's features. "Oh, Laura," she said as she grabbed her into a hug.

"I know." Laura fought the knot climbing back into her throat. "What are we going to do without her?"

Chapter Three

Laura knew her presence at Annabeth that evening was re-assuring to people. She just wished she was able to reassure herself as she made a point of going from table to table.

For years, she'd watched her mother do this. The real Annabeth had exuded just the right mix of politeness, gratitude and grace to put even the most harried guest at ease. Laura tried to emulate that. She channeled her mother's energy and hoped people bought the illusion.

Under the surface, her duck feet churned. She prayed the diners missed the sweat she felt beading on her hairline and the devastation she knew lurked behind her eyes. Joshua was doing the same at L Bar while Adam did his best to bolster the staff.

Allison's death had hit the heart of the resort.

Laura hadn't found a chance to pull Adam or Joshua aside to ask if Fulton had presented the same questions to them or how they had handled them. Alexis's warning came back to her as she noticed the table with a Reserved card standing empty near the window. The police weren't done asking questions if foul play was involved.

Lifting a hand, Laura flagged the nearest server, a young woman named Catrina. "Isn't this Mr. Knight's table?"

"The actor?" Catrina nodded. "Yes. He normally comes in around six."

Laura checked her watch. "He's running behind. Have someone place a call to his bungalow, please, and see if he'd still like to dine here tonight. If he's decided against it, there are people waiting who can be seated here."

"Yes, Ms. Colton," Catrina said before hurrying off.

"Laura."

She turned to find Erica Pike. The executive assistant stood eye to eye with Laura at five-nine, and her long brown hair was pulled up in a loose bun. Glancing at the table, she asked, "Is everything okay?"

"I was just wondering why CJ Knight hasn't shown up for his six o'clock table," Laura said.

"Oh." Erica's spine seemed to stiffen. "He checked out."

"Checked out?" Laura repeated. "When?"

"Early this morning," Erica explained. "I thought you knew."

"No," Laura said. "A lot's happened."

Erica nodded, her green eyes rimmed with shadows. "I know. Poor Allison."

Laura tried to think about the situation at hand. "Mr. Knight had spoken to me about extending his stay in Bungalow One for a week or more. Why the change of heart?"

"He didn't say," Erica replied. "Roland asked me to find you. The detective from the Sedona Police Department is back."

"So soon?" Laura said and missed a breath.

"A security person from the gate escorted him to C Building," Erica told her. "He's waiting in the break room."

The police were back with more questions, just as Alexis had predicted. Laura offered a soothing smile to a passing patron before striding toward the exit, doing her best not to rush.

C Building was built in the same style as L Building and the bungalows, but the interior was spartan. Music piped softly from speakers. A fountain in the center of the atrium burbled and splashed pleasantly. Both had been Allison's ideas. Extending the same sense of calm ambience to the employees' building that guests enjoyed everywhere else had brought the Mariposa environment full circle.

Tears stung Laura's eyes again. Allison had left a large footprint on Mariposa. She'd made it better for everyone.

Laura faced the closed doors of the break room. Halting, she took a minute to breathe and get her emotions under control. She couldn't seem to still the little duck feet paddling under the surface. To make up for it, she encased ice around her exterior. Donning her professional mask felt as natural, as fluid, as freshening up her lipstick.

She pushed the doors open and stepped in. "Detective Fulton…"

The man who stood from a chair at one of the small bistro-style tables was not Detective Fulton.

She blinked in surprise. He was younger, taller, more muscular. His build distinguished him. He carried himself more like a brawler than a police officer. He had brown hair that grew thick on top and short on the sides, a full beard and mustache. A bomber jacket lay across the table. His black button-down shirt was tucked into buff-colored cargo pants, his belt drawn beneath a trim stomach with a bronze buckle. The pants looked almost military. So did his scuffed boots. He'd rolled his sleeves up his forearms while he'd waited, revealing a bounty of tattoos.

No, she decided. This definitely didn't look like a detective. While his attire might have been military-inspired, he didn't carry himself like a military man. More like a boxer. Shoulders square. Hands balled, ready to strike. His hair and ink made him look like a rock star.

He wasn't restful on his feet. He shifted from one to the other, twitchy. His direct stare delivered a pang to her gut, a quick one-two. It was dangerous. Deadly.

Not a rock star, she discerned. A criminal.

She took a step back. "Who are you?" she demanded. The building was empty. The bulk of the staff was in the meeting with Adam at L Building. There was a phone on the desk in the atrium. She placed one hand on the parting of the doors. Should she make a run for it?

That direct stare remained in place. It felt like an eternity before one hand unclenched and sank into a pocket. A badge flashed when he pulled it out. "Detective Noah Steele. Sedona PD."

She wanted to examine the badge. It looked authentic from a distance, but she hadn't studied Fulton's all too closely when he'd arrived this morning. She wished she could go back and implant the image on her mind so that she at least had something to compare to.

"What do you want?" she asked, forgetting her professional demeanor. Her feet itched to run.

His expression didn't change. Neither did it lose its edge. "Are you Laura Colton?"

"There was another man here earlier," she told him. "Another detective. Mark Fulton. He said he was the lead on the case."

His gaze narrowed. She swore she'd seen a rattlesnake do that once on the hiking trails. Part of her tensed, waiting for the buzzing sound of the rattle.

"So, what are you doing here?" she challenged. "Are you really even a cop?"

"Lady, you'd do well not to insult me at the moment."

She dropped back on one heel and crossed her arms. *Lady?* "Should I call Security and have your identity certified by them?"

"It was Security who dumped me here, away from everybody else," he retorted. "Take it up with the meatball at the gate if you don't like it."

Erica did say that security personnel had escorted the detective to C Building. She frowned, opening her mouth to apologize.

He cut in, "You didn't answer my question. Are you Laura Colton?"

"I am," she said and watched, perplexed, as his eyes darkened and his fists clenched again. "It's been a long day... Detective. I'm sorry for the misunderstanding."

"A long day," he repeated, low in his throat. He let out a whistling breath. Was that his excuse for a laugh? Mirth didn't strike his expression. If anything, it tensed. "*You've* had a long day?"

"Yes," she said. She had the distinct impression that he was mocking her—that he disdained her. The level of malice coming off him was insupportable. She'd just met him. What could he possibly have against her? "I'm sure you're aware one of Mariposa's employees was found this morning...dead." She swallowed because her voice broke on that unbelievable word. "Isn't that why you're here?"

He came forward, stepping quickly between the tables. "You're damn right that's why I'm here."

She dismissed the inclination to put her back up against the door. There was a gun in a holster on his hip, she noticed. Her pulse picked up pace. He had no reason to hurt her. None whatsoever. And yet he looked capable of murder. "*Why* are you so angry?" she demanded.

"Why is your family so determined to keep Allison Brewer's death quiet?" he challenged.

She searched his eyes. They were green. Not leafy green, or algae, or even peridot. They were electrodes. Vibrant, steely, stubborn. She saw downed power lines, snapped electrical cables, writhing and sparking—about to blow her world off the grid.

She had to focus on the music, flutes and pipes, something merry and soothing Allison would have loved, to maintain a sense of calm. "What are you talking about?" she asked.

"Your brother Adam told officers at the scene this morning that Allison's death should be kept quiet," he seethed. "You'll tell me why. Why do you and your brothers want this buried? What happened to her?"

"You're acting like there's some sort of cover-up."

"Is there?"

She would have laughed if he were someone...*anyone* else. "No. This is a resort. People come here for privacy. To get away from the world."

"So close."

"What?"

"Close the resort," he said. "Let the police come in and investigate properly."

"There are over eighty people booked at Mariposa through this week alone," she explained.

"If you really care about Allison—"

She stepped to him, fears squashed as her ire rose. "Allison Brewer was my friend. She was one of my closest friends. And I will *not* be accused of covering up her death. Who are you to march in here and accuse me of that?"

If she'd expected him to cower, she was sorely disappointed. He closed the marked bit of space between them, lifting his chin. "If you're so close to her, why has she never mentioned you before?"

He spoke in present tense, just as she had even after witnessing the coroner carrying Allison's body away under a sheet. His fury...his near lack of control. It was cover for something else.

Adam had done this, she realized. After their mother's

death. He'd been angry, precarious, until he'd learned to put a lid on it. Until he'd developed control and that laser focus that was so vital to him. "You knew her," she realized. "You knew Allison."

He blinked, and the tungsten cooled. Going back on his heels, he moved away.

She watched him rove the space between tables and chairs, his head low.

Allison hadn't had a type, Laura recalled. But Laura couldn't see her with someone this high-strung. Someone this lethal. She had, however, spoken of her brother often— her foster brother. *As thick as thieves*, Allison had said regarding the two of them.

Laura's brow puckered. "Your last name is Steele."

He turned his head to her, scowling. "So?"

"You don't share a last name," Laura pointed out.

He cursed under his breath. Was he mad that she'd made him so quickly?

"Are you really a detective?" she asked, bewildered.

"Of course I'm a detective," he snapped, pacing again from one end of the room to the other. "Why else would I be here?"

"Other than to accost me and my family?" she ventured. "You act like we're culpable."

"Everybody's culpable," he muttered.

Her eyes rounded. "So…there *was* foul play involved in whatever happened last night?"

He stopped roving. His palm scraped across his jaw, the Roman numerals etched across his knuckles flashing. "Nothing else makes sense."

"Murder at Mariposa doesn't make sense," she said. "The people here aren't prone to violence."

He dropped his hand in shock. "You actually believe that?"

She didn't answer. His mockery locked her jaw.

"Here's a news flash," he said. "Most people are inherently violent."

"If you actually believe that," she countered, "then I'd say you have a very narrow view of humanity. And so would Allison."

He flinched. "Someone at your resort killed my sister, Ms. Colton," he said. "I'd advise you to watch your back, because I won't rest until I have proof."

The quiet warning coursed through her. She sensed, if this man had his way, Mariposa would be reduced to rubble before he was done.

Chapter Four

Goddamn it. She had to be beautiful.

Inside C Building, Noah watched Laura Colton and her brothers through the glass doors of the atrium. Legs spread, arms crossed, he listened to harp strings and water cascading cheerfully from the fountain to his left, trying to read the exchange. Trying to discern what was on her face.

He didn't have to. He recognized it, and it drove a knife through him. She was grieving. The tension around the frown lines of her mouth were indicators, just like her heartbreakingly blue eyes drawn down at the corners. She eyed him, too, through the glass doors as Adam and Joshua Colton stood on either side of her, debating what to do about the situation.

Although he gathered sadness and confusion from her face, she didn't waver. She was a winking star at the edge of the galaxy—remote, out of reach and somehow constant.

His shoulders itched. He didn't roll them, but the urge bothered him. It raised the hair on the backs of his arms and neck. The supernatural sense strengthened as she continued to stare.

He could be constant, too—like a roadblock. An obstacle. He would stop traffic. He would dent fenders. He would do anything to find out what had happened here.

It didn't matter if it made waves for these people. Nothing mattered except Allison.

He hadn't been there. The hopeless thought burned on the edge of his conscience. It burned and smoked, and he hated himself.

He hadn't been there for Allison. Not in the last few months. Not like he should have been. He'd been distracted by work, his closure rate at the SPD and the rise in homicides around the area.

And now Allison was dead. If it wasn't someone else's fault, it was his.

He was responsible…until he found who was to blame.

He couldn't live with her death on his conscience. That sweet little girl. She'd had no one, and he'd promised her. He'd *sworn* he would be there for her—until the last breath.

That last breath was supposed to be his, not hers. It wasn't supposed to be her. It should be another person lying under a sheet at the coroner's office.

He'd known she was too soft for this world—too pure. Too good. And, like a son of a bitch, he'd neglected her.

Her voice came to him. *I'm an adult. Noah, you don't have to chase my monsters out of the closet anymore.*

Are you sure about that? he'd challenged.

She had laughed, dropping her head back and belting. Allison never did things halfway, especially when they brought her joy. She'd taken his hand as she'd said, *There are no more monsters. We're free of them now.*

He was the monster, he realized. He was a monster who'd abandoned her to the real world, and she was dead because of it.

As if she could read his thoughts, Laura Colton shivered. She broke the staring contest by turning to gaze at her younger brother, folding her arms around herself.

She was cold, he mulled. Of course she was cold. She was

standing outside with the barest of snow flurries falling at a slant from the north. Her white dress was long-sleeved, with a leather belt cinched at the waist and a rustic blue handkerchief tied elaborately at her throat in a Western knot. The handkerchief wasn't meant to keep out the cold. It was silk, for Christ's sake. The dress may have been long, but there was a slit on one side.

As she shifted, he saw a flash of creamy skin. Her boots, the same blue as the handkerchief, with custom floral tooling, rose to just below the knee. Her shoulder-length blond hair swung as the wind flurried and spiraled. She shivered again, visibly.

Noah clenched his jaw. *Morons*, he thought of her brothers. Couldn't they see she was cold? Couldn't *one* of them loan her a jacket?

Adam caught on first. He swung his jacket off in a quick motion and draped it across the line of her shoulders.

Not enough, Noah chided even as Laura acknowledged the gesture by touching Adam's arm just above the elbow. Joshua braced his arm across her shoulders and huddled her against his side. He rubbed a hand up and down her arm for friction.

Good, Noah thought. Maybe he could stop feeling sorry for her long enough to separate the woman from the adversary.

She was beautiful. So what? He'd seen icebergs. He'd seen one calve and flip over, churning the sea like a bubbling witch's cauldron, exposing its breathtaking glass underbelly. Unspoiled, untouched. Secret and forbidden.

Laura Colton was that kind of beautiful. And damned if it was going to distract him.

Icebergs were roadblocks, too. Sure, they contained multitudes, and they were frigging fascinating to boot. But they could be upset. They melted. They flipped. And when they flipped, their spires crumbled.

I won't let you get in my way, he determined as her heartbreaker eyes seized hold of him again. Frost wove delicate swaths around the edges of the door pane, framing her.

Friend? Allison had never mentioned her. He was sure of it. If he wasn't sure, it was because he had forgotten.

He couldn't bear to think that he'd forgotten.

You forgot the last lunch, a voice in his head taunted.

He and Allison normally met for lunch on the first Friday of every month. Tipsy Tacos, the little cantina close to her place that served vegan options alongside the ones with meat he preferred, was her favorite restaurant.

It's perfect, isn't it? she'd practically had to yell over the mariachi music, her dark eyes laughing.

Noah dug his phone out of his pocket. He unlocked the screen, then scrolled through his texts. Her messages popped up on-screen.

There was one from a week ago.

Allison: TGIF! Music fest this weekend?

Noah: TGIF. Gotta work overtime. Don't go home with a stranger. Call me if you need a ride.

Allison: Will do!

Then a week before that…

Allison: Did you read the meditation book I gave you?

Noah: Covered up in work. I'll get to it.

Allison: Promise?

Noah: Promise.

Emojis had followed. Then the exchange before that dated two weeks past.

Allison: Thinking of you.

Noah: Thinking of you, too. You ok?

Allison: Worried about you. Let me book you a massage. You need you time.

Noah: I'm fine. Don't go out with that guy again. He's bad news.

Allison: LOL. He said the same about you.

Noah: Never trust a guy in an El Camino.

Allison: I miss you!

Noah: Miss you, too. Sorry about lunch.

Allison: It's NBD. I know work's crazy. Hugs!

Noah: Hugs to you.

Noah winced as he scrolled through the next exchange.

Allison: I'm at the cantina.

Noah: Damn. I'm across town. Had to make an arrest. I'm sorry, Al.

Allison: It's ok.

Noah: I'll pick you up.

Allison: It's nice out. I can walk.

Noah: Let me know if you change your mind.

Allison: Will do.

A smiley face capped the message.

He looked for subtext. He searched for anger on her part. Blame. Disappointment. Anything to beat himself up with. As ever, he found nothing. Just happy, look-on-the-bright-side Allison.

The only other person who'd loved him like this...who'd worried about him like this and looked out for him...was his mother. Before she was killed and he had gotten dumped into the system.

He'd let her down. Even if Allison didn't know it, he'd let her down.

He had to live with that. He had to live with the fact that there would be no more text messages at 10:00 p.m. telling him to *relax...unwind...life's short...live well...*

Forcing himself to swallow, he took stock of his emotions. He felt raw, unspooled. He'd gone at Laura Colton too hard. If she really was Allison's friend, did she have a litany of cheerful, forgotten text messages that broke her heart in hindsight, too?

There was movement, he noticed. He stuffed the phone back in his pocket as a security guard moved into the Coltons' circle. He placed a hand on Joshua's shoulder. They all turned to listen. Joshua nodded and walked away.

Laura and Adam spoke quietly, nodding back and forth before moving toward the door.

Maybe he should apologize to her, Noah thought. He could have waited to question the Coltons, done some digging into them and Mariposa first... But he hadn't been thinking with his head when he'd left Allison at the coroner's office.

He'd done this before with his mother. There had been grief, and he'd been alone then, too. Nobody had cared about him, much less commiserated with him. He didn't know how to expose the hurt and had no idea how to talk about it. The shock of Allison's death had put his fists up and his head down like a brawler.

He'd swung at Laura Colton, Noah reflected as Adam escorted her into C Building to face off with him again. Noah did his best to relax his stance. *Breathe*, Allison said in his ear as Laura's gaze climbed back to his.

"It was a mistake," he said without taking a beat to think about the wording. He backtracked. "Yelling at you in the break room. It shouldn't have happened. I apologize."

Her hands balled together over the parting of Adam's jacket. After a moment, she nodded shortly. "I accept your apology."

"That doesn't resolve everything that happened here this evening," Adam said evenly. "I intend to call the Sedona Police Department for some clarity on the situation. They wouldn't let you lead this investigation if Allison was a relation of yours, which is why Fulton was the detective on scene this morning. Not you. Does your commanding officer know you're here now?"

Noah studied Laura and her cold, white-knuckled hands. Then he asked the man, "If it was your sister, what would you do? Would you sit around, bury your head in the sand, hoping somebody else figures out what happened to her? Or would you use every skill, every resource at your disposal, to make sure what happened to her is brought to light?"

Adam tilted his head. "I understand why you're here, Detective. As a brother, I sympathize, and I'm deeply sorry for your loss. If I didn't have Laura..." His shoulders lifted, then settled as he deflated. "I wouldn't be standing here."

"Adam." Laura spoke her brother's name in a whisper. She raised her hand to his arm as she had outside. This time, she held it.

"But the fact remains that we don't know what happened to Allison, precisely," Adam went on. "We don't know that anyone at Mariposa is responsible or if she died of natural causes. That's for the coroner to decide, yes?"

Noah jerked his chin. "Yes."

"So you'll agree that your demand we close the resort is premature at this point?" Adam ventured.

"What happens when the coroner's word comes down?" Noah asked. "What happens when we're certain it was homicide? What then?"

"If that's the case," Adam said carefully, "we'll reevaluate. But I see no reason to close Mariposa."

"You're worried about your bottom line," Noah growled.

"No, Detective," Adam said coolly. "I'm worried about the same thing Allison was, too, every day. The privacy and comfort of our guests."

"You sure it's not the Colton reputation?" Noah countered.

Laura unfolded her hands. "It's late, and the snow's coming in. I'm sure you'd like to get home, Detective Steele, in case the roads become impassable. Why don't we all reconvene after the coroner decides on the manner of Allison's passing, then proceed from there?"

She said it in such a way, Noah felt every argument die.

He didn't want to go home. At home, it would be quiet.

He'd have nothing to distract him from the voices inside his head that said Allison's death was on his hands. "Fine."

She offered something of a smile. It wasn't the real thing. Her eyes weren't involved in it. "I'll walk you to L Building."

"That's unnecessary," Adam cut in. "I'll walk the detective back to his vehicle. You go home, Laura. It's cold."

"I'll be fine," she assured him. "I'd like a moment with Detective Steele." When Adam only frowned at her, she added, "Alone."

Adam exchanged a look with Noah, one that warned he'd better tread carefully.

Laura started to remove his jacket. Adam stopped her quickly. "Keep it. And promise to go home as soon as you see him out. You need to get off your feet."

"I will," she vowed.

"A promise is a promise, LouBear," he reminded her. He dropped a kiss to her brow.

The sentiment rang through Noah's head. *A promise is a promise.* He hated himself all the more. Before she could open the door, he reached for the handle.

"Thank you," she said before ducking back out into the cold.

"We'll see each other again, Detective Steele," Adam said in closing.

"You can count on it." Noah left the statement hanging in the air like an anvil. He zipped his jacket as he and Laura followed the well-manicured path back to L Building.

She walked in long strides. "Normally, I love the snow. Tonight, it just makes me sad."

"Allison loved snow." He closed his mouth quickly. He hadn't meant to say it.

"She did," Laura said. "I remember the first winter she worked for us. There was so much that year, she had to move classes inside. She liked watching the snowfall from the windows at Annabeth. She said it was like being trapped in a snow globe."

That sounded like Allison. The black hole in Noah's chest opened further. He felt gravity reeling him in toward it. He hoped it would wait until he was alone to absorb him.

"I need to apologize, too," she revealed.

"For?" he asked.

"I misjudged you," she explained. The cold stained her cheeks. "Back in the break room. I didn't think you were with the police."

"What did you think I was?"

"A criminal." She winced. "I don't like labeling people. But I labeled you right off the bat. And I'm sorry for it."

He didn't know what to feel, exactly. He glanced down at his hands where Roman numerals riddled his knuckles and a spider crawled up the back of one hand. The etchings on the other made it look like a skeleton hand with exposed joints and bones that went all the way up his fingers. On some level, he could understand. He'd spent a fair amount of time undercover because he was good at inserting himself into a certain crowd.

He remembered how in the break room she'd all but backed herself up to the exit door when he'd approached her. Had she thought he was going to hurt her…take her jewelry…worse? A growl fought its way up his throat. He choked it back, along with everything else, and punched his hands into the pockets of his jacket. "I don't expect you to lose sleep over it, Ms. Colton."

"It's Laura," she said as they came to the doors to L Building. She turned to him, the golden light over their heads crowning her. "We're probably going to be seeing a lot of each other. And we both knew Allison. So Laura will suffice." She stuck out a hand for him to shake.

He stared at it. Then her. There were snowflakes in her

hair. If someone gave her a scepter and horse-drawn sleigh, she would be a glorified ice princess.

Unwilling to let her shiver a moment longer, he closed his hand around hers. It felt like ice, and it was as smooth as the surface of a mink's coat. He took his away quickly, unwilling to watch his tattoos and calluses mingle with her fancy digits. He pulled the door open for her.

She cleared her throat. "I'm going to miss her, too."

Whatever he could have said was trapped beneath his tongue.

Her lashes lowered, touching her cheeks, before she lifted them again. "As soon as you make the arrangements, I'd like to know. I'd like to say goodbye."

Arrangements. The portents of that barreled down on him. He was Allison's next of kin, her only relative. It was up to him to plan her funeral.

He couldn't bury her. He couldn't even contemplate it. She didn't belong in the ground any more than she belonged in a morgue.

An unsteady breath washed out of him.

Her hand came to rest over his. "I can help you. I've helped plan a funeral in the past. I was young, but I think my brothers and I managed to pull it off well enough. If you need help—"

"It's fine." He barked it, desperate to be away from her so he could unleash the panic and anguish building up inside him. He held the door open wider. "Good night, Ms. Colton."

Her lips firmed. She strode inside. He watched her long after the door closed. He watched through the glass until she disappeared down the hall, the tail of her white skirt the last thing to disappear. The lights went off seconds later and he was left staring at his own reflection.

A funeral.

Another breath wavered out, vaporizing in front of him.

He pinched the bridge of his nose, hard. That black hole had him by the balls.

He'd go home, he decided. And when he got there, he'd drink himself into a stupor.

Chapter Five

Laura opened the door to her bungalow the next morning to find Joshua on her front stoop. His messy hair hid underneath a burnt-umber ski cap with Mariposa's pale yellow butterfly logo. Ice crunched under his boots as he moved his toes rapidly to keep them warm. "I brought pastries," he announced.

She eyed the long white box in his hands. "You mean you brought the bakery?"

"Had it delivered," he boasted. He handed her a large cup. "With coffee."

The way to a man's heart might be through his stomach, but Laura was convinced the way to a woman's was by crossing cell membranes with caffeine. She wrapped her hands around the to-go cup, absorbing the heat through the gloves she'd donned. "It's no wonder every man I meet is a disappointment." Tipping the cup to him in a toast, she added, "You are the standard."

He offered his arm. "Watch your step. It's slippery."

She trod carefully until they reached the golf cart he'd parked in front of her house. "Have you spoken to Knox?"

Joshua got behind the wheel. He waited until she was seated, tucking her long skirt around her legs before he released the brake and shot off. "I checked on him last night. He's okay. Still shaken up. Hell, I am, too."

"Did you tell him he doesn't have to come in today? Carter's already agreed to cover for him. The horseback excursions will be canceled because of ice and snowmelt."

Joshua nodded. "He agreed to take the morning off, but he wants to come in after lunchtime. He said working with the horses will help him through things."

Laura could understand that. As the golf cart careened around the corner, she stopped the doughnut box from slipping across the seat. She opened it, then indulged, choosing a chocolate éclair. Nibbling, she balanced the pastry in one hand and her cup in the other. "I don't know if I should tell you this."

"Well, now you've got to." He nudged his elbow into her ribs playfully. "Spill it, ace."

She watched the gardens whoosh by. White coated everything. Mariposa looked enchanting under a crystal frost.

Underneath, was some part of it—or someone inside of it—deadly?

She shuddered, blamed the cold, then polished off the éclair. "She had a crush on you."

"Who?" When he glanced over, she canted her head tellingly. He gawped. "Allison?"

Laura sighed. "She wasn't the type to hold back. But she worked with you. She valued her job. So she sat with her feelings." Reaching over, she cupped his chin in her hand, helping him to close his mouth. "I promised her I wouldn't tell. But I think you two could have made each other happy, at least for a time, and… I don't know. All this reminds me not to waste time if you know what's right for you."

Joshua looked shocked, bereft and everything in between.

He jerked the wheel onto the scenic path, along the wall that fell away from the ridge where Mariposa dwelled. She looked out over the countryside. Snow, red rocks and the Sonoran Desert clashed to make the view that much more spectacular. "We're going to be okay. Right?"

"We've done this before."

She nodded. The three of them had weathered quite a few storms together. "Should I have kept my promise? Should I not have told you?"

He shook his head. "I liked Allison. I liked her a lot. But I have rules, same as she did."

Joshua liked to have fun, but he didn't date anyone in-house. Mariposa was as sacred to him as it was to Laura and Adam, and that included every single person under its umbrella. "I didn't mean to make this harder for you. I just didn't get much sleep last night, wondering whether you two missed out on something special. She was special, Josh."

"I know." His Adam's apple bobbed. He reached for her hand and clutched it. "It's going to be okay."

She had told him that after their mother's death, every night he'd cried himself to sleep. Eyes welling, she turned them away, feeling his fingers squeeze hers. "It's coming up on that time of year."

He kept driving, pushing the golf cart as fast as it would go. If Adam saw him driving like this on the guest pathways, he would chastise him for it. Laura said nothing, however. When Joshua didn't reply, she added, "The anniversary."

"I know."

Every year on the anniversary of Annabeth's death, the three of them took the day off. They'd disappear for a day, first bringing mariposas to her grave, then embarking on a hike. The date coincided with the bridge between winter and spring. Snow gathered in places along the trail. Snowmelt tumbled down passes, rushing for valleys. And early spring growth punched through the bedrock, clawing for purchase like hope incarnate.

They never spoke much on the hike. They never took photos to capture the day. And while Joshua was a more proficient hiker than both Laura and Adam, he never left them behind. They didn't turn back for the resort until they reached the high point—Wrigley's Rough, a jagged fall of rocks with a view of the architectural site of the ancient ruins of the Sinagua people. From the top, they could see every piece of land Annabeth had left them.

Laura couldn't help but think that this year, the anniversary would be especially hard to navigate.

They pulled up to L Building. "Adam doesn't like when you park here," she reminded him.

"It's freezing," Joshua said, engaging the brake. "I'm not making you walk from C Building. Hey," he said before she could step out of the vehicle. "We really are going to be okay."

She adored him for saying it. "When I figure out when the service will be, would you like to go with me?"

"Of course," he agreed. "Are you ready for what comes next?"

"What comes next?" she asked curiously.

"Drink," he advised as they walked to the door that led to their offices at the back of the building. "I got you the big gulp for the meeting with Dad."

She raised her face to the clouds. "Oh," she said.

"You forgot."

"I forgot," she admitted. Pressing her hand to her brow, she shook her head. "It completely slipped my mind."

"That wasn't something else keeping you awake?"

"I didn't think about it at all." She groaned. "Oh, Josh. He's going to waltz in, being all Clive, and I've had no sleep, no prep..."

He nudged the coffee toward her mouth. "Drink, ace."

"Right," she said, tipping the to-go cup up for a steaming swig. She quickly covered her mouth with her hand. "Lava."

Erica waited for them near the closed door of Adam's office. "Good morning," she greeted them. "Your father's flight gets in soon. The helicopter will pick him up around eight thirty. He asked for a meeting in the conference room at ten."

"How does Adam feel about him running the schedule?" Joshua asked.

Erica arched a brow in answer.

"Oh, boy," Joshua muttered. He offered the box of doughnuts to Erica. "Lady's choice."

Erica eyed the contents when he opened it. "I want the one with the sprinkles."

"Excellent," he said, using a parchment square to pinch the corner of the pastry and hand it to her.

"Thank you," she said, cradling it.

"Did you get in touch with CJ Knight's people?" Laura asked. She didn't miss the way Erica tensed, just as she had the night before.

She shook her head, lowering the doughnut. "No. Do you still want me to reach out?"

"Yes," Laura said. "I'd like to know why he vacated Bungalow One so suddenly. He's a valued guest. If his departure had anything to do with the resort, we could offer incentives to bring him back. I have his manager's number. His name's Doug, I think."

"Doug DeGraw," Erica confirmed. "He rarely leaves CJ's side."

Laura frowned at Erica over the lid of her to-go cup.

"What is it?" Erica asked, alarmed.

"Nothing," Laura said. "That'll be all. Thank you, Erica." As Erica moved down the hall, Laura grabbed Joshua by the collar and pulled him into her office.

"Hey, what—"

She shut the door, closing them in. "She called him CJ."

"So?"

She frowned. "Josh, when was the last time you called a guest by his or her first name?"

He thought about it. "Over the summer, maybe. There was that competitive rock climber. The blonde one with the killer— Oh!" He took a step back, holding up a hand. "Wait a minute. You think Erica and CJ Knight…"

"I don't know," Laura replied. "But Erica is a professional. And calling one of our VIPs by his first name was a sight less than professional. You should look into this."

"Me?" he asked, aghast. "Why me?"

"Because the majority of people, including Erica, don't just respect you. They love you. You also have a tendency to meddle in other people's affairs," she stated.

"I do not."

She placed her finger over his mouth to quiet him. "Please. For me."

He frowned, then tugged off his hat and ran a rough hand through his hair. "Fine," he said reluctantly. "But I'm not comfortable with this. What are we going to do if something did happen between Erica and Knight?"

"I don't know," she said. "She's the best executive assistant we could ask for. And I doubt CJ Knight left because of Erica, even if they crossed the line. They could just be friends. If she is close to him, she may have more insight into why he left or if he plans to return. Adam's worried about any hint of wrongdoing coming off Allison's death. Celebrity guests get nervous when bad press starts to circulate. And if word leaks to the media that someone like CJ Knight left Mariposa—"

Joshua nodded off the rest. "I get it. Damage control. I'll talk to Erica."

"I appreciate it," she told him. "Truly."

"I've always got your back, ace," he murmured. "You know that. And, for the record, I didn't sleep last night either. If you toss and turn again tonight, call me. If we're going to be awake, we might as well talk each other through it. Or drink about it."

She raised her hand to his lapel, flipping it the right way out. Smoothing it, she offered him a small smile. "I like that idea."

Someone knocked on the door. Before she could answer, Adam stepped in. "You heard?"

"About our ten o'clock?" Laura asked. "Erica told us."

Joshua lifted the pastry box. "Doughnut?"

Adam frowned over it. "Jelly-filled?"

"Lemon or raspberry?"

"Lemon," Adam said and took the parchment around the doughnut when Joshua offered it to him. "Thanks. By the way, I called Greg. He'll be sitting in on the meeting."

Joshua gave a little chuckle.

"I missed the joke," Adam said critically.

"You're the one who wants our attorney to sit in on a family meeting," Joshua pointed out.

"Why is that?" Laura asked.

Adam shifted his jaw. "I have a feeling Greg should be a part of this."

Laura trusted Adam's instincts. Still, there was another matter. "Clive won't like it. It'll put his back up."

"So will the fact that you still call him Clive," he noted.

"Have you heard anything about Allison's case?" Joshua asked.

"No," Adam said. "I couldn't sleep last night, however—"

"Disturbed, party of three," Joshua inserted.

"—and I had a thought," Adam continued, ignoring him.

"I'd like to set up a fund for her family to help cover funeral costs."

"Adam," Laura breathed. "That's a wonderful idea."

"I second that," Joshua said. "And she should have a plaque to go in the meditation garden. It was her idea, her design. It should be in her name."

"Just like the restaurant is in Mom's," she mused. "Of course."

Joshua's phone beeped. "That's Carter. I offered to help him with the morning work down at the stable. I'll be back for the meeting."

"Preferably on time," Adam called after him.

Joshua tossed a wave over his shoulder and shut the door behind him. Adam looked at her. "Since Detective Steele is the only relative so far who's contacted us, do you think we should send the offer through him, or would you be more comfortable speaking with her parents directly?"

"He's her foster brother," she explained. "I don't think her parents are in the picture. She never spoke of them. Only him. And, you should know, last night, I got the sense Detective Steele was overwhelmed by the idea of planning a funeral for her. I offered to help. He refused. Judging by his behavior, I'm not sure he'd be willing to take on financial help."

"Was he a jerk to you, Lou?"

"Hey," she said with amusement, measuring the width of his straight-backed shoulders. He was wearing his best suit today and his muscles were knotted, ready, beneath it. "Easy there, knuckles."

"He threatened you in the break room," Adam reminded her.

"He threatened all of us," she amended. "And underneath…" She sighed, remembering. "My God, Adam. He looked broken."

"I don't envy him," Adam muttered.

"I'll speak to him about the fund," she said.

"Are you sure?" he asked. "Erica can see to it."

"I know she can," Laura said. "But this is personal."

Adam conceded. "Are you ready for Clive?"

Laura eyed the to-go cup she'd set on her desk. "Ask me again after coffee."

AT SIXTY-ONE, CLIVE COLTON looked shrunken. He still had his spine. Admitting weakness was distasteful to him. But now he cut a less imposing figure, more compact and slightly stooped compared to his once-distinctive six-foot frame. More salt than pepper tinted his hair. His suit was conservative, tasteful and impeccably bespoke.

He hugged her upon entering the conference room, just as he embraced Adam and Joshua. The latter pulled away after a brief clutch. The hug wasn't about warmth or familiarity. It was for form's sake, something Joshua didn't give a fig about.

Greg Sumpter, the siblings' private attorney, shook hands with Clive. "It's been a long time, Clive."

"Sure," Clive said, his smile falling away. "How are you, Sumpter?"

"Oh, just fine, thank you," Greg replied jovially. Tall, fit, Greg was dressed casually. No suit or tie for him. He wore his collar open. His relaxed demeanor, paired with his legal savvy, had appealed to Adam, Laura and Joshua right away. He visited the resort often, not just for business, but to check in personally with the three of them and to see Tallulah. He was forty-eight and unmarried, and Laura knew he had a one-sided love for their head of housekeeping.

"I didn't expect to find you here," Clive told him.

Adam spoke up from the head of the table, where he stood behind his usual chair. "I asked Greg to join us."

"Why is that?" Clive asked.

Greg answered quickly. "He thought you and I could play a round of golf later. It snowed last night, but it should melt off quickly. Do you still get out on the course?"

Clive lifted a shoulder. "Now and then. Can't swing it like I used to."

Joshua groaned.

"We'll tee off this afternoon," Greg said. "How's that sound?"

"Fine," Clive said, pulling out a chair for himself.

Greg sent Adam a wink before taking a seat. Laura folded into a chair between her brothers, smoothing her skirt over her legs. "What do we owe the pleasure of a visit?" she asked Clive directly. "You didn't bring Glenna with you?"

"Not this time," he said, running a hand down his tie.

"And your health?" Adam mentioned. "How are you feeling?"

"Spry enough," Clive said, cracking a smile. That smile had caught the imagination of his wife and mistress and the other women he'd taken a shine to through the years. "Thanks for asking."

"Would you like coffee?" Laura offered. "Tea?"

"Mylanta?" Joshua muttered, earning a nudge from Laura.

Clive didn't seem to hear him. "No. Thank you, though, Precious." His grin broadened. "Anybody tell you lately you look just like your mother?"

"No," she answered.

"Pretty as a picture," he said proudly. "Just like Annabeth. She was stunning. Before the cancer did its bit—"

"What did you call this meeting for?" Adam interrupted as Laura tensed and Joshua muttered under his breath.

"Are you in a hurry, son?" Clive asked.

"We've got meetings scheduled for the conference room at eleven thirty and after lunch," Adam told him. "Spring means nuptials, and Mariposa has become the place for destination weddings."

"Congratulations," Clive said. His eyes were drawn to the view from the windows. "You've built something impressive here. You were so young when you took it on. I didn't think you'd last long in Arizona. Now you've got something to be admired."

"Yes," Adam replied.

Laura's tension refused to drain. Adam had been right to invite Greg. There was something Clive wasn't saying.

They waited him out. He swiveled back to the table. "I've come to ask for your help."

"Our help?" Joshua asked.

Adam rolled over his brother's incredulity. "Are you in trouble?"

"No, no," Clive said, waving a dismissive hand. "Nothing that drastic. The company's just seen better days, is all."

"What could we do?" Laura asked.

"I understand the resort's made some significant gains," Clive said. "I also understand that you've got plenty of capital at your disposal."

"How do you know that?" Joshua asked.

Clive chuckled. "If there's one thing I understand, son, it's business."

"A business you stole from Mom's inheritance?" Joshua parried.

Clive stared at him. "Colton Textiles is in my name, son. Not your mother's. And I'm not sure I care for your tone."

"This is me playing nice," Joshua informed him. "And you may come from money, but you never made your own. You play with everybody else's. You married Mom for hers. If not for her, you wouldn't have a leg to stand on."

"Josh," Adam cautioned. "Maybe you should take a walk."

Joshua looked at his brother. "I have a right to be here, and somebody has to speak for her."

A headache was brewing behind Laura's left temple. She wished for coffee. "It's okay," she said to Adam. "Let him speak for her."

Adam relaxed gradually. He addressed Clive again. "What did you have in mind?"

"A loan," Clive revealed.

"How much?"

"Two fifty to start."

Joshua scoffed. "Two hundred and fifty thousand?"

"If that doesn't get the company back on its feet, then another," Clive added. "This is your inheritance, too, don't forget. My legacy to the three of you. You each have a stake in Colton Textiles. Adam, you especially."

Laura thought about it. Colton Textiles was a fine-fabrics importer. When Annabeth had died, she had left shares to each of her children. Adam had eighteen, and Laura and Joshua each had sixteen. Clive had wound up with the lion's share.

"Don't do this, Adam," Joshua implored. His eyes burned.

Adam considered. "That's a lot of money."

"You'll make it up in no time," Clive said smoothly. "And it's a loan. You'll have a return on your investment in due time. With interest."

Laura shook her head. "You can't expect us to decide on the spot. We'll need to discuss it and come to an agreement. Together."

"The three of you?" Clive questioned.

"That's how things are done around here," Adam informed him.

Clive eased back in his chair. "Good for you, kids. Good for you."

Did Laura imagine his condescension, or was it real? Her father wasn't just the face of Colton Textiles. He was a chameleon who could easily mask his true feeling and intentions when it suited him.

When there was something he needed to hide.

Adam rose and the rest of them followed suit, Clive coming to his feet at last. "We should have a decision for you soon."

"Tomorrow," Clive requested as they hovered around the door. "By the end of business hours. If I'm to make gains, too, I'll need that money as soon as possible."

Adam gave a nod. "Fine."

"How 'bout you and Laura join me for lunch?" Clive asked, putting his hand on Adam's shoulder. "Just the three of us. I hear your restaurant's five stars. What's it called again?"

"Annabeth," Joshua retorted.

Clive smiled, nonplussed. "Of course it is."

"I'm due in Flagstaff at lunchtime," Adam explained.

"Laura?" Clive looked to her, expectant.

No plans came to her mind. "All right."

"Splendid," he replied. Reaching out, he gave her chin a light pinch. "Are you still seeing Quentin Randolph?"

The name struck her off guard. "No. How…how did you know about Quentin?"

"I knew him before you did," he said. "I told him about Mariposa. And about you."

She stared, unable to believe a connection between her father and the man who had grossly betrayed her was possible. "He never mentioned you."

"A shame it didn't work out," he said. "You were quite the power couple. What happened this time?"

He'd turned out to be just like Clive—a chameleon. She ignored the question and moved to the door to open it.

Joshua beat her to it. "I need some air," he muttered to her.

"Same," she whispered.

"THERE'S SOMETHING SKETCHY going on," Joshua said. He pointed to Laura. "You know it. And I know it."

Adam crossed his arms. "Why do you think I had Greg sit in on the meeting? I knew there was something off when Dad called initially."

Next to him, Greg planted a hand against the wall in a relaxed stance. "I can look into him. See what's really going on with Colton Textiles."

"If he needs that kind of money, it's bleeding," Joshua said. "It's bleeding badly. And if he needed money, why didn't he go to Glenna? She's got plenty. Why did he come all this way?"

Laura chewed over it. "He was right about one thing. We all have a stake in Colton Textiles. It was Mom's company, too. It's as much a part of her legacy as Mariposa. If it is bleeding, could we really just watch it die?" Wouldn't that be like watching a part of Annabeth die all over again?

Adam turned to Greg. "Can you look into it by tomorrow afternoon?"

"I'll make the necessary calls," Greg said. He pulled a face. "I may miss my tee time with the man of the hour…"

Joshua cracked a smile for the first time since Clive's arrival. "Aw, shucks."

"Let us know what you find out," Laura said. She hugged him. "And thanks for sitting in. If you don't go soon, you'll miss lunch with Tallulah."

Greg grinned. "You know me too well."

"She's taking her lunches with the kitchen staff now," Joshua pointed out, "since her nephew, Mato, got hired on as sous-chef."

"Thanks for the tip." Greg gave the men a salute before strolling off.

Joshua waited until he was out of earshot. "He's loved Tallulah as long as we've known either of them."

"Yes," Laura said with a soft smile.

"I don't know if I could wait that long," Joshua confessed, "for someone to decide whether she wanted me."

"Yeah, you're much more of the now-or-never type," Adam drawled. "Or now *and* never. Never being next week when you decide you've had enough."

Joshua pursed his lips. "Is that any worse than the kind of man who's married to his desk?"

"Enough," Laura said. "Both of you."

"What was all that business about Quentin Randolph?" Joshua asked. "Clive was the one who set you two up?"

"No," she said automatically. She didn't want it to be true. The idea made her feel ill.

Adam's phone rang. He took it from his pocket. "I have to leave for Flagstaff shortly." He glanced up at Laura. "You can cancel lunch. Dad can dine alone."

"I'm not afraid of him," she claimed.

"I never said you were, Lou," he told her.

"You don't owe him anything," Joshua chimed in.

"I'll be fine," she explained. "Maybe I can get some more information about Colton Textiles out of him."

Joshua sighed. He patted her on the back. "Good luck with that, ace."

Chapter Six

The following afternoon, Noah flashed his badge at the man in the Mariposa security booth. The uniformed guard waved him in. He steered his car into the same lot he'd parked in two nights prior. Then he followed the path to L Building and ventured into the open-air lobby.

The clerk at the front desk's name tag read Sasha. She smiled, waving him forward. "How can I help you?"

"Laura Colton." Noah didn't know why her name was the first thing out of his mouth, but there it was.

Sasha picked up the phone on the desk. "Do you have an appointment?"

"She's expecting me," he said, sidestepping the real question.

"Name?"

"Steele."

"Just a moment."

After placing a call, she revealed, "Ms. Colton is at L Bar. Go through the doors here and take a left."

Moving briskly, Noah heeded her instructions. He found himself inside an impressive room. On one side, liquor-stocked shelves sprawled from floor to ceiling. The bartender moved tirelessly from one patron to the next. Music played at just the right volume, not too soft, not too loud. Here, the atmosphere felt easy, not stodgy, like he'd expected.

He saw her at the same time she saw him. Laura's dress flowed around her, long and red with turquoise necklaces stacked above the V-necked bodice. Her boots were black leather to match her wide belt. Large earrings dangled from her ears. She'd swept the strands of hair that framed her face back in a subtle half-do.

She looked perfect. Noah felt his joints lock up in response.

What was it about this woman?

She walked to him slowly, offering a nod to a patron who acknowledged her in passing. "Detective Steele," she greeted him. "Back so soon?"

He could see the apprehension lurking behind her icy blues. "Is there a place we can talk?"

"Detective Fulton didn't mention an update in the case," she said. "Is that why you're here?"

The envelope from Steinbeck weighed heavily in Noah's pocket. "Is there somewhere we can talk?" he asked again.

She looked around and seemed to decide that the bar was not the place to have this conversation. "Follow me."

She led him to a back hallway with windows where paintings would have been in any other setting. The Coltons' resort decor leaned heavily on their natural surroundings.

She swept keys out of the small jeweled bag she carried and unlocked one of the closed doors. "Have a seat," she said as she pushed the door open and switched on the light.

Her office, he decided. With its buttery-leather ergonomic desk chair and the wide crystal vase overflowing with fresh desert blooms, how could it be anything but?

"Coffee?" she asked as she rounded the desk.

"No." He didn't sit, although the plush chair looked inviting. Was that a real cowhide or just for show?

She remained standing, too. "Well?"

He pulled the envelope from his pocket and handed it across the desk. "Coroner's report."

She held it for a moment, then turned it over. The flap wasn't sealed. She pulled it back, then pried the report from its pocket. Unfolding it, she gathered a steadying breath in through the nose.

He watched her eyes dart across the page, reading Steinbeck's findings, and knew the exact moment she learned the truth. She raised her eyes to his in a flash of disbelief before staring at the paper again. "She died of an overdose?"

"Of fentanyl," he said grimly.

She shook her head. "That can't be right. That would mean…"

"Somebody drugged her," he finished, advancing another step toward the desk. "The coroner showed me the entry site. The needle went in above her left hip."

The page and envelope fluttered to the surface of her desk. Her hands lowered, limp, to her sides. "You were right," she breathed. "How is that possible?"

"She was killed," he reiterated. "At your resort. And you're going to let me find who did it. That was the deal."

Fumbling for the arm of her chair, she sank into it.

He gripped the edge of the desk, fighting impatience. Fighting the inclination to circle the thing and put his hands on her. Whether it would be to help her snap out of it or just to see if she would let him, he didn't know. "Look, my CO doesn't want me on this. He asked me to back off. Stay home. Wait for Fulton to tie up the case."

"Something tells me you're not going to do that," she said wearily.

"If I had your cooperation," he replied, very close to begging, "if I had your permission, I could dig through back channels. I could find what's under the surface. The underbelly."

Her throat moved in a swallow. "This morning, I would've argued that Mariposa doesn't have an underbelly. But this..." She touched the edge of the autopsy report. "Who could have done this? Who here could be capable...?"

He went around the desk. Instead of touching her, he gripped the arms of the chair. He pushed himself into her space and watched her eyes go as round as pieces of eight. "I'll help you. I won't rest until the person responsible is behind bars. But you have to help me."

She bit her bottom lip carefully. It disappeared inside her mouth as she searched his eyes. Her guarded expression closed him off and he was certain the answer would be no.

Her lip rounded again, pink. Perfect, like the rest of her. She canted her head to the side. "You need a reason for being here," she said. "In case Fulton or your CO catches you on-site."

She was...saying yes? He missed a breath. "If I could pass under the radar...if everyone could see me as something other than a cop...a guest, maybe, or a new member of staff, they could be inclined to talk. That would make my job easier."

"Not staff," she said contemplatively. "That wouldn't be right."

He frowned at the tattoos on his hands. They were right there for her to see. "What, you don't hire criminals?"

"That's not what I meant," she said defensively.

"Then what did you mean?"

"A guest, maybe," she decided. "That would get you in the restaurant, the bar, the spa, the golf course and stables... everywhere but C Building." Her eyes cleared. "Oh."

"What?" he asked, feeling his stomach muscles tighten as he watched her pupils dilate.

Her gaze trickled down his throat, over his shoulders and down his chest. "It's that simple...and that complicated."

"Throw me a bone here, Colton."

"You need to immerse yourself among staff and guests. You need a cover. Being my boyfriend would guarantee access to pretty much anything."

"Your boyfriend." He heard his tone flatline. It was the worst idea he'd ever heard.

And it was the best idea he'd ever heard.

She was right. Being Laura Colton's paramour wouldn't just open doors. It would make people openly curious about him. Those people would lower their guard enough…maybe be clumsy or trusting enough to let something slip. To let him in.

The possibilities came tumbling down as reality set in again.

Who the hell was going to believe that she would date *him*? She ruled this high-class joint. She was Mariposa's princess. He lived on a city salary, drove a decade-old city-issue sedan that ran rough in the winter, and he had no family left to speak of.

Who would buy that Laura Colton would choose to slum it with Noah Steele?

He backed off. "Yeah, that's not gonna work."

"Why not?" she asked his retreating back. She gained her feet again. "If someone here killed Allison, they have to be found. They have to be brought to justice. What if they strike again? What if someone else is killed? I have to protect the rest of the staff, the guests, my family… You're the man to help me do that. Not Detective Fulton."

Fulton had cop written all over him while Noah…didn't. "I don't exactly fit into the woodwork around here either. I'm not the country-club type."

"I told you I don't like labels, and we get many people here of different backgrounds, Detective."

"I bet I don't know a single person who could afford a night in one of your bungalows. What's the going rate these days?"

"For a night?"

"Yes."

She paused. "Five thousand."

A strangled laugh hit his throat. "Holy sh—"

"That includes food and all resort amenities except alcohol, spa packages and special excursions," she explained. "Our guests are happy to pay the price because they know it means we take care of their privacy and security while they're here. They can immerse themselves in the resort and landscape."

"And there are no cameras anywhere," he recalled.

"No."

He cursed. "That's going to make my job difficult."

"All staff members also sign nondisclosure documents when they join the Mariposa team," she warned.

"Then you're wrong," he said, crossing his arms. He eased back against the wall, tipping his head against the plaster. "It's the perfect place for a murder. And I bet Allison's killer knew it."

"That doesn't make me feel any better."

"I'm not here to make you feel better," he reminded her. "I'm here to catch a killer."

She drifted into thoughtful silence. Finally, she came around the desk. "What if you weren't Noah Steele from Sedona? What if you were Noah Steele, the politician's son?"

"Do I look like a politician's son to you?"

"You could be the son of a shipping magnate. Or you could be an entrepreneur."

"I knew I should've packed my sweater-vest."

Defeated, she sat on the corner of her desk. "You're not making this easy."

He swallowed the inclination to apologize to her. Again.

Her chin snapped up. Her stare roamed his boots, his hair. As she perused him, it made him come to attention. "What're you doing?" he asked, bracing himself for whatever thought bubble she'd conjured.

Prospects flashed across her face. They practically glittered. "When I first saw you, I thought you could be a rock star."

"I can't carry a tune."

"You don't have to," she said. She crossed to him. "You're not here to entertain. You're here to get away from shows. Touring. The loud party atmosphere. You're here to disconnect. Recharge. It's a commonality many of our guests share, so you'd have a good jumping-off point for conversation."

She was close enough he could see the beauty mark she'd tried to hide under her concealer. It lived, camouflaged, near the corner of her mouth. "And what band am I supposed to be from?"

"I don't know. You could be a cover band, a good one that tours nationally. And you don't have to be the front man. You could be a bass player. A drummer."

"Maybe I just got out of rehab," he muttered, his voice imbued with sarcasm.

"The people who know me will never buy that I'm dating an addict."

"Speaking of people who know you," he said, "Adam knows who I am. He won't buy any of this."

"Adam will have to know," she agreed. "Josh saw you through a window two nights ago. If he remembers you, we'll let him in on the scheme. If not, then I'll tell him. I prefer not to."

"Why?"

"Because he can be terrible at keeping secrets," she admitted. "I love him, but he wears his heart on his sleeve. When would you like to start?"

They were really doing this—this fake dating thing? He took a long breath. "As soon as possible if I'm going to make headway."

"Tomorrow morning, then. Be here at nine. We'll have a champagne breakfast at Annabeth. That way, I can start introducing you as—"

"The boyfriend." He shook his head. "If I saw you and me together, I wouldn't buy it."

"Not everyone's a detective," she said. "Most people take what they see at face value. They don't analyze. If we play it off right…if we're convincing…then you have free rein over Mariposa for the foreseeable future."

"You'll need to tell big brother," he warned. "Tonight. He'll need to play along, too. I have a feeling he won't approve."

"Let me worry about Adam." She hesitated. "You should come earlier than nine. Can you be at my place at eight? To be convincing as a couple, we'll need to establish history. Basic facts like where we met, how long we've been dating and so on."

"Why not now?" he asked. Last time they'd been together like this, one-on-one, he'd been desperate to get away from her. Now the space between them was no longer a minefield of fresh-turned grief. It felt…warm and, yes, precarious. But he wasn't alone. Here, with her, he wasn't a victim to his thoughts and the self-blame that had plagued him since finding out Allison was gone.

Laura drooped like a flower without water. "I have a meeting tonight. It's a family matter. My…father's in town."

Why did she pause before the word *father*? He still knew very little about the Coltons and Mariposa. He could use the time tonight to research. "Eight o'clock."

"I'll tell Roland you're coming. You won't have trouble getting in." An indentation appeared between her brows.

"What?" he asked.

"I'm sorry," she said, shaking her head. "I didn't know how to say goodbye for a second."

Amused, he wondered what path her thoughts had gone down. "No one's looking. I think a handshake will do, Ms. Colton."

"Of course." She offered her hand. "And no need to call me Ms. Colton anymore, remember?"

He gripped her hand softly. Cradled it. What else did someone do with a hand like hers? "Laura," he said, hearing how it left him like a prayer.

The other night, he'd dropped her hand like a hot potato. Now he made himself hold it. He made himself picture it—her and him. Together. If he was going to convince anyone else they were an item, he had to convince himself first. For one dangerous moment, he let himself imagine pulling her closer. He imagined holding her, the smell of her hair, pressing his lips to the curve between her neck and shoulder, running his hands up the length of her spine...

He imagined the shape of her under his hands, how a woman like her would respond to his touch...

"Noah," she replied.

Heat assaulted him. Before he could hit the safe button, a vortex of flame swept him up. It refused to spit him back out.

Noah took a step back. The doorknob bit into his hip.

Shaking her hand had been too much? What was he going to do tomorrow when they had to convince Laura's family, friends, employees and guests that they were a couple? Flame-retardant gear wouldn't keep him safe from this inferno.

Allison's death had ripped his defenses wide, exposing him.

He couldn't let Laura Colton take advantage of the fact.

"Good night," he said shortly.

"Good night," she returned, and the slight smile on her face stayed with him long after he left.

"HAVE YOU LOST your mind?"

Laura stood her ground. "It's a good plan, Adam."

"He's the wrong cop," Adam reminded her. "He's emotional. According to his commanding officer, he's not even supposed to be anywhere near this."

The guy in her office hadn't seemed emotional. Determined? Yes. Standoffish? Absolutely. Underneath, Laura was certain Detective Steele—*Noah*—had to be hurting. But his clear-cut focus had struck her, inciting her own.

Someone had drugged her friend, cut her life short... She couldn't walk away from that. "I'm doing this," she told Adam. "We're doing this—him and me—whether you think it's advisable."

"Laura—"

"This happened on our watch," she said, and the horror of that made her stomach lurch. "Someone killed her here. This is our home, Adam."

Adam planted a hand on her shoulder. "You are not responsible for Allison's death."

"Then help me catch who is," she insisted. "Don't get in the way. Please."

The last word splintered. He closed his eyes in reaction.

Voices down the hall echoed toward them. Adam's hand lifted from her shoulder. "We'll finish this discussion later," he concluded.

She raised her chin in response. Recognizing the voices as those of Joshua, Greg and Clive, she braced herself for what was to come. The family attorney stood as a buffer between father and son as he escorted them down the hall to the conference room. His Hawaiian-print shirt seemed loud and cheery, his smile in contrast with Joshua's scowl and Clive's expressionless face.

The only nondescript thing about Greg was the beige folder he was holding. He raised his free hand to wave at Adam and Laura. "We're not behind schedule, are we?" he asked them.

"We arrived early," Adam replied. He stepped aside, motioning for Clive to go ahead into the conference room. As his father moved beyond him and Laura, they both raised questioning looks at Greg.

He offered them a slight nod.

Laura's lips parted. She glanced between her brothers, noting Joshua's grim intent. She watched Adam button his suit jacket, the galvanized rods of his business mien snapping into place. He let Greg follow Clive into the room first. "Shall we?" he asked the others.

Laura wished she knew what was in that folder. As she and Joshua entered the conference room, she leaned over and whispered, "Did Greg tell you what he found?"

"Nothing," Joshua answered.

She took her seat. They would each have a vote, she knew. It was how they handled anything that involved their mother's estate, resort capital or unnecessary risk. She folded her hands on the table, watching Clive settle in. He seemed relaxed. Expectant.

His statement about Quentin Randolph from yesterday came back. Had her own father sent a wolf to her door? She could hardly stand to look at him with that knowledge. Throughout lunch the day before, she'd wanted to ask if it was true. Had he known who Quentin was?

Would it influence her vote if she knew he had? She prided herself on separating business Laura from personal Laura. That was part of her success, just as it was Adam's.

That task was hard enough knowing how Clive had

treated her mother through the years, and how he had neglected Adam, Joshua, her and their half sister, Dani. Adding the implications surrounding Quentin's place in her life would make being objective that much harder.

Clive adjusted his cuff links. He grinned. "Who calls the meeting to order?"

"It's nothing so formal as that," Adam informed him. "Though this time, I will ask Greg to start."

Greg took a pair of reading glasses from the neckline of his shirt. He put them on and opened the folder. "After yesterday's meeting, I placed a couple of calls to colleagues with a vested interest in Colton Textiles."

"Why?" Clive drawled. "This is a simple family matter. Nothing worth meddling in."

"I asked Greg to look into it," Adam told him.

Clive's serene smile dimmed on his eldest. "You don't trust me?"

Laura spoke up. "If we agree to your terms, we could risk as much as half a million dollars."

"Risk." Clive batted the word away. "Come now, Precious. I said it was a loan, and that I'd pay you back with interest."

"You wanted us going into this blind," Joshua surmised. "Look around you. We built this place because we were smart. You still think we're children you can easily bait and switch, don't you?"

"I'll ask you again to modulate your tone when you speak to me," Clive told him.

"Greg," Adam prompted again, "tell us what you found. Once the cards are on the table, the three of us will put it to a vote, yes or no, and that majority decision will be the one we go forward with."

Greg cleared his throat. "Right. The reality is that Colton Textiles is going under."

Palpable silence cast the room in a long shadow.

"I knew it," Joshua said under his breath.

Laura stared at her father in disbelief. "Going under? How?"

Adam frowned. "How long has it been in the red?"

"Two years," Greg revealed. "There are other investors, none of whom have seen a return on their investment."

"How could you let it get this far?" Laura asked. "If you were going to come to us, you should've done it from the moment there was trouble."

"Well, I'm here now," Clive said, dignified. He spread his hands. "You must want to save your birthright."

"If you cared about our birthright, you would have told us the truth," Joshua retorted.

"You owe me this."

Laura froze, feeling her brothers do the same. "What did you say?"

"You owe me," Clive stated again. "I paid for it all, didn't I? The house in LA. The private schools you attended."

"Let me stop you right there," Adam said. His hands slid onto the table, palms down. He leaned forward. "Because I sense this discussion going sideways. Our mother may have died when we were young, and you weren't exactly there to take her place. But I'm fairly confident when I say a proper parent doesn't talk like that."

"Now wait just a second—"

"No." Adam's voice invited zero rebuttal. "She paid for the house in LA. And she paid every dime of our tuition. And before you claim you put me, Laura or Josh through college, we paid our way through the trusts she left in each of our names, the remains of which we pooled to make Mariposa what it is. You have no fingerprint here. If you're going to come running to us to save the family company, I suggest you avoid leading with lies and grandiosity. That may have worked with your investors, but we know you. We know the real you."

"What good's a vote when you're all prejudiced against me?" Clive demanded.

"In this room, we're not your sons or your daughter," Adam pointed out. "In this room, we're owners and directors of Mariposa Resort & Spa, and we'll vote accordingly. All in favor of loaning Clive Colton half a million dollars to save Colton Textiles, say 'aye.'"

Neither Laura nor Joshua spoke up.

Adam raised a brow. "The nays have it."

Clive leaned back. In a jerky motion, he pulled down the front of his vest. "Very well." Climbing to his feet, he took turns frowning at each of them. "I should have expected as much. You chose your side years ago."

"Right around the time you made it clear you wanted nothing to do with us," Joshua returned. "How does that feel, by the way?"

Laura crossed to her father, keeping her voice low. "If you had come to us as soon as the trouble started, we would have helped you. We could have saved the company together."

"You can't dress betrayal up with excuses, Laura," Clive said. "Didn't your mother teach you that?"

She felt the breath go out of her. "No. But she did teach us common decency."

"Then why not throw the company a lifeline?"

Joshua stepped up behind Laura, supportive. "You can't save a man from drowning when history tells you he won't hesitate to hold you under water to save himself."

"Or bring down the entire ship," Adam chimed in as he stacked papers on his end of the table.

"*And* he insults your mother," Joshua added. He made a face. "I mean, come on. That's just wrong."

Laura couldn't look away from Clive's angry face. "I've

been trying to forgive you for over a decade. She taught us to forgive. She forgave you—more times than any other woman would have had the grace to do so. And it didn't stop you. Still, I thought I could—one day—offer my forgiveness. And maybe I will. But not today."

"You know what I learned from your mother?" he asked. "Beauty can be all ice. She must've taught you that, too. Cold suits you."

Heat flooded her face. She felt it in the tips of her ears. "Please, leave."

Clive held her gaze for several seconds before his eyes cut over her shoulder and locked on Joshua. He glanced to the head of the table at Adam. Without saying another word, Clive stepped toward the door.

Laura didn't breathe easily again until he was gone.

Joshua echoed her thoughts. "He'll be back."

"Maybe," Adam granted. "He's wrong, Laura. You're not cold, any more than Mom was."

"Of course not," Greg chimed in.

But the cold had seeped into every part of her, and she couldn't think how to comfort herself with Clive's accusations loud in her ears.

Chapter Seven

Laura woke the next day with her father's words still echoing. Would they bother her so much if they didn't correlate with Quentin Randolph's remarks when she had broken off their engagement a year ago?

She switched on the kitchen light and went straight to the coffeepot to wake it up, too. She left it running before bending down to scoop up the mass at her feet. Her long-haired tabby, Sebastian, cried out as she dropped kisses to the back of his head. She cradled him against her. His purring reverberated into her chest, easing the dregs of another terrible night of sleep.

She closed her eyes for a moment, pressing her cheek to his soft fur. "Good morning, handsome," she whispered.

Feeling generous, Sebastian let her cuddle him, only growing restless when the coffee maker hissed as it percolated. When he wiggled, she set him on his feet and followed him to his food bowl. "Breakfast," she agreed and set about preparing his morning noms.

Her mother had adored big hairballs like Sebastian. When it had come time to leave the house in LA, her brothers had agreed that Laura should take the cats. She had cared for her mother's felines for the rest of their natural lives.

Sebastian was the first cat she'd brought home after burying the last of her mother's. While shopping in Sedona one afternoon on her own, she'd stopped at the animal shelter. It hadn't been the plan, but two hours later, she'd returned home with Sebastian in her arms.

After the relationship with Quentin had blown up in her face, her failures regarding marriage and starting her own family had trapped themselves in an echo chamber in her mind. The humiliation of learning Quentin's true intentions had almost been too much. If not for Sebastian, work and her brothers...she'd still be living in that echo chamber.

Allison and Alexis, too, had helped. Their girls' nights had increased in frequency. As Laura slid aside the long glass door leading onto her patio, she thought of all the evenings she and the girls had spent talking, laughing and commiserating.

She closed the door so Sebastian would stay in. Unknotting her robe, she slid it off. The pool beyond the deck chairs and firepit was heated. She cast off a shiver at the cool kiss of winter's chill, setting the robe on the back of a chair. When she'd moved from her suite at L Building, she'd asked the bungalow's designer to include a starting block next to the pool. She stepped onto the platform and hooked her toes over the edge. Folding, she gripped the edge of the block with her fingers. She counted off, imagined the starting bell and sprang forward, streamlined from fingers to toes.

No sooner had she hit the water than she started swimming. She flutter kicked, rotating to one side as her arm swept over her head, digging into the water, before she repeated the motions on the other side. The freestyle strokes took her to the end of the pool and back before she flipped over and started backstroking. She did a lap down and back this way before she flipped again and crossed the pool by butterflying. Finally, she finished with the breaststroke.

She'd done the relay so many times, she knew how many

repetitions of each stroke it took to get from one end of the pool to the other. She knew, down to the inch, how much space she needed between herself and the wall to flip and change direction. When she finished, she gripped the edge of the pool, catching her breath.

Her time was slower today. Hooking her arms over the lip, she tilted her head to one side to let the water drip from her ear. Maybe it was the sleepless nights. Maybe her thoughts were weighing her down. She wanted nothing more than to cast them off. She no longer wanted to dwell on her father or Quentin Randolph.

Boosting herself over the edge, she sat with her feet dangling in the water, letting the cold prickle across the wet skin around her one-piece bathing suit. She watched her legs circle under the surface and contemplated another relay to drown the voices in her head.

She heard Sebastian scratching at the glass door. Her coffee would be done, and she would need to eat, shower and complete her hair and makeup routine before her morning meeting.

She toweled off, then draped the robe over her shoulders as she went inside. The house felt warm. She sat before the glass door with Sebastian at her side, watching the colors of breaking day stain the sky over silhouettes of peaks, enjoying the ritual of her first cup of coffee.

As she washed and dried her mug, she heard the knock at her front door. She set it on the drying rack and sidestepped Sebastian so she wouldn't tread on his tail and upset him.

Joshua normally didn't show up for another hour. She snatched open the door regardless.

Dressed in a leather jacket and blue jeans that looked like a flawless fit, Noah Steele brooded behind a pair of dark sunglasses.

He stared at the parting of her robe and the black bathing suit with cutouts above each hip. His frown deepened. "You always answer the door like this?"

She drew the robe around her, belting it tight. "You're early."

"Yeah, well," he rumbled, removing the sunglasses. "I figured the sooner you and I figure out how to do...whatever the hell it is we're doing...the better."

"Come in," she said, stepping back to admit him. As he moved inside her bungalow, she dragged a hand through her wet hair. "I'm sorry I'm not dressed. If you give me a moment, I can—"

"No need for formality," he said. He stared at her in the low morning light from the windows. "Seeing the princess of Mariposa at the start of the day without makeup or any of the polish..." His mouth shifted into a side-cocked half smile. "It's a trip."

She looked away quickly. "There's coffee, if you'd like some."

Sebastian jumped onto the counter, eyeing the newcomer. Noah eyed him in return. "Who's this?"

"This is Sebastian," she said, dragging her fingers through the fur over his spine.

"You're a cat person."

"Yes," she said. "What about you?"

"I don't have pets."

"Oh," she said. She tried to contemplate coming home after a long day with no creature there to greet her.

He looked around, cataloging her everyday surroundings. "It's too neat."

She glanced around at her living space. There wasn't much out of place other than the throw blanket she had used the night before on the couch and the hardback she had left face down on the coffee table. "I have someone who cleans for me once a week."

"Must be nice."

She fought the inclination to sigh over his presumptive tone. "If you don't want coffee, we should get started."

"It's why I'm here."

She sat on the sofa. Because her legs were bare and the robe reached midthigh, she twitched the throw blanket into place over them as he sat on the other end. She curled her legs up on the sofa beside her to disguise the move. "I thought about it a lot last night. I think, if people ask, we should put our relationship at six months."

"Why six?" he asked.

Sebastian hopped up between them. When he sought the space next to her, she waited until he folded into a rest position to pet him. "Because that's enough time for us to get to know each other. Since we decided you're a musician and I'm here at Mariposa, we've been courting mostly over a long distance. Calls, texts, the occasional rendezvous."

"'Rendezvous,'" he repeated. "So the relationship's sexual."

She found she could blush. And he hadn't even smiled at the suggestion. "Do you know many rock stars who abstain from sex?"

"I don't know one rock star, period," he replied.

She eyed the leather jacket. It was soft from wear, scarred in places and sheepskin-lined. He hadn't bought it just for the cover story. And he wore it all too well. "Have you considered which place in the band you would like to be?" she asked, changing the subject. "Bass? Keyboards? Drums?"

"Rhythm guitar," he responded readily.

"Can you play the guitar?" she asked, curious.

"No," he admitted. "But, as you say, I'm not here to entertain. I'm here for a little R and R. And to see my girl."

She tried to ignore the sudden rush of feeling…the wave of sheer heat at hearing him refer to her as his girl. Tamping down on it, she turned her attention to Sebastian's belly when he rolled to expose it. "Six months will have given us plenty of time to grow loved up enough. There will be hand-holding involved. Hugging. Maybe kissing, to seal the illusion. Are you okay with that?"

"Are you?" he challenged.

"Yes." She hoped.

"I've done undercover work," he revealed. "It's all part of the act."

She opened her mouth to ask if he'd ever pretended to date another woman for the sake of work. The question washed away quickly. That wasn't what she needed to know about him. "How old are you?"

"Twenty-nine."

"So am I," she said, offering a stilted smile. "My birthday's May sixth. When's yours?"

"November seventeenth."

She nodded, filing the information away in case she needed it. "My middle name is Elizabeth."

"Why do I need to know that?"

"It's the sort of thing lovers would know about each other after a time," she commented.

He looked away. "My full name's Noah Nathaniel Steele. Nathaniel for my dad."

She felt a smile warm her lips. Nathaniel seemed awfully formal. Like a nice tie he kept tucked away in a drawer because he'd decided it didn't suit him. "Your real dad?"

"For this," he said carefully, "maybe I shouldn't be Noah Steele, former foster kid. Maybe the rhythm guitarist, Noah Steele, comes from a traditional home. A normal one. It's less complicated."

"Great artists rarely come from normal homes. But that's your decision. Where do you want the new Noah Steele to come from—California?"

"Washington," he decided. "I spent some time there with my mom before…"

As he trailed off, she willed him to say more. Was he speaking of his biological mother or his foster mom, the one he'd shared with Allison?

"Before…?"

He shook his head. "It doesn't matter. I'm from Washington State."

"I'm originally from LA," she pointed out. "Just for the record."

"I know."

She blinked. "Oh. You looked into me."

"Part of the job," he excused. "You want me to apologize?"

"No," she blurted. "There's nothing available that most people don't know. And it's good you know. For the sake of what we're doing."

"In that case," he said, "why don't you tell me what happened with Quentin Randolph a year ago? Why did you break off your Page Six engagement?"

She should have seen the question coming. It hit her like a wall. "He wasn't who I thought he was."

He lifted both brows when she said nothing more. "That's it?"

She felt her shoulders cave a bit. "Quentin loved the idea of my wealth more than he loved the idea of me. He wanted the connections that come with the Colton name more than he wanted me. And he fooled me into thinking otherwise for a little over a year before my brothers caught on to his schemes." She paused in the telling, then asked, "Is that enough or do you need more?"

Noah's tungsten eyes flickered. "Did you love the guy?"

"Would you agree to marry someone you weren't in love with?" At his marked silence, she rethought her answer. "I loved the version of Quentin he built for me—the one that turned out to be false. So, in a way, I suppose I didn't. Not really. And that makes it easier...until the humiliation sets in."

"He's a moron."

She blinked. "I beg your pardon?"

He spoke clearly, drawing each word out. "The guy's a stage-five moron. If someone like that had come sniffing around Allison, I would've taken care of him."

He would have, she realized. A shiver went through her. She blamed it on her wet hair and bathing suit, gathering the lapels of her bathrobe together. "When was your last long-term relationship?"

Rebuke painted his hard features.

She stopped his protest before it began. "These are things couples know about each other."

A disgruntled, growly noise lifted from his throat. "Six... seven years ago?"

"And how long did it last?"

"Five months."

"That's long-term?" she asked.

"I don't know." He cast off the admission. "What's your idea of a long-term relationship?"

"A year," she stated. "Or more."

"Women tend not to stick around that long," he revealed.

"Maybe you're dating the wrong type," she advised.

"What type should I be fishing for?" he demanded. "You know any trust-fund beauties who wouldn't mind slumming it with an Arizona cop?"

Laura chose not to answer.

"Before Randolph, did you date anybody else?" he asked.

"Yes," she said. She didn't want to talk about the other men. But she had probed him about the women in his life. It was only fair.

"Who?"

"Dominic Sinclaire."

"The diamond guy?"

"Why do you sound so derisive?" she asked.

"I don't know. Who ended things there?"

"I did," she said without thinking.

He narrowed his eyes. "I'm sensing a pattern."

"Should I have stayed with someone with a wandering eye?" she asked.

"The son of a bitch cheated?" he said, voice going low.

"Yes."

"He cheated. On Laura Colton."

Exasperated, she repeated, "Yes."

"What an ass."

"Charming," she commented.

"Sounds like he was charmless."

"Dominic has a great deal of charm," she explained. "The problem came when he employed it elsewhere. We're off topic." She tried to think of another question for him. The ink peeking out from underneath the collar of the jacket drew her gaze. "How many tattoos do you have?"

"I stopped counting." When her eyes widened, he asked, "Is that too many for you?"

"No," she said. She'd never known someone with too many tattoos to count. "Which one is your favorite?"

"I don't have a favorite," he claimed.

"I don't believe that for a second," she told him. "Even Francis Bacon had a favorite painting."

"Who?"

She redirected the conversation again. "It's your turn to ask a question."

"Okay," he said. "Morning or night?"

She frowned. "Really? You think that's relevant?"

"It would be," he weighed, "if we were really into each other."

"Ask something else," she demanded.

"Fine," he consented. "What's your drink of choice? No, let me guess. White wine spritzer."

"Martini," she corrected. "Dry. Yours?"

"A boilermaker."

"That's not a real thing," she assumed.

"Yes, it is. It's a glass of beer with a shot of whiskey."

"You can't have one, then the other?"

"I like to multitask."

Trying to plumb the depths of this man was more difficult than she had imagined. Noah didn't have quills. He had a hide like a crocodile.

Wanting to dig deeper, she asked, "What do you do for exercise?"

One corner of his mouth tipped into a grim smile. "I'm a morning guy."

She fought the urge to strangle him with her terry-cloth belt. "You wanted to do this, too. If you won't make something of an effort, what's the point of being here with me?"

The smirk fell away. A breath left him in a tumultuous wash. Shifting on the sofa, he leaned over, planting his elbows on his knees.

"I'm sorry," he said after a while. "I'm not used to this."

"Answering personal questions?" she asked. "That makes sense. You're the investigator. You ask the questions. Don't you?"

"No. I mean I don't really get close…to people," he told her.

"Weren't you close to Allison?" she asked.

"We met when we were kids," he muttered. "She was my sister in all but blood. That may not make sense to you—"

"It does," she explained. "I have a half sister. Dani. She lives in London. We don't see each other much anymore. But it doesn't change the fact that she's my sister."

"Your father had an affair."

So he'd found that corner of the family history. She tried

not to bristle. "He had many affairs. He paid off his main mistress. As a result, she gave up custody of Dani. She was mourning the loss of her mother as Adam, Josh and I were, too. The four of us... We were a mess." The house in LA had felt like a cavern of lost hopes. They had been four sad children, desperate for someone who wasn't there.

"I'll try harder," he said. "For Allison."

"Me, too," she promised. She nearly reached for his hand, then stopped, uncertain.

No, if they were going to do this, one of them had to break the intimacy barrier. Her heart flipped as she eyed the denim covering his thigh. She touched it in a gesture of support.

When his eyes swung to hers in surprise, she felt her face warm. A chain wrapped around her navel flashed to life, glowing orange, as if it had been living in hot coals.

He didn't move, didn't look away. His tungsten eyes brought to mind electrical storms. The severe line of his mouth didn't ease as his gaze swept over her. She saw it land on her mouth.

She wasn't just playing with fire. This was a California brush fire with the wind at its back. Out of control. Destructive.

It would devastate her if she let it.

Her hand shied from his thigh. She gripped the edge of the cushion, wishing she knew what to say next. Wishing she knew what she was doing.

Would helping Allison's brother burn her to the ground?

He was still watching her. She felt his stare drilling into her profile. His voice was rough when he spoke again. "Do you want to keep going?"

Could she? Closing her eyes, she gathered herself, wishing the flush in her torso would cool. The robe felt stifling suddenly. She flicked the blanket off her legs, planting her feet on the cool tiles of the floor. "Where do you live?" she asked quietly.

"Sedona. I have a house there. And I row."

"What?"

"It's how I stay in shape," he revealed. "Rowing. There's a park near my house with a small lake. During the winter, I use a rowing machine at home."

Rowing. It made sense, she thought, judging by the muscles packed underneath his jacket. She tried not to think about muscles bunching along his back and stomach as he worked the oars. The flame inside her kicked up regardless. "Do you like to dine out or in?"

"Eating out is expensive."

"So you drink your boilermakers at home," she discerned.

"I'm more of a social drinker, I guess."

"You don't really strike me as a social guy," she admitted.

He made a satisfactory noise. "We *are* getting to know each other better," he murmured.

The rumble of his voice was appealing. She shrugged to release the knots of attraction digging in everywhere. "Is there anything else about you I should know?"

He was quiet for a moment. Then he said, "I was in the navy."

Her eyes went to his boots. They were the same ones he'd worn the first night. She'd thought some part of him was military—or militant. "For how long?"

"I enlisted out of high school. I left when I was twenty-three."

"That's when you became a cop," she realized.

"A rhythm guitarist for an Eagles cover band," he corrected.

She nodded swiftly. "Right." *Stick to the story, Laura.* She checked her smartwatch and stood up. "I really must get ready. Please, have a cup of coffee while you wait."

"So we're still on for breakfast?" he asked, getting to his feet, too.

"Of course." A romantic champagne breakfast for two at Annabeth with the entire resort watching. Nerves flared to life. "Give me forty-five minutes to make myself presentable," she insisted. "Then you can get started on your investigation."

"What should I call you?" he asked suddenly.

"I told you last night. Laura will be fine."

"Yeah, but don't most couples have sentimental names for each other?"

Distracted, she replied, "I believe I can trust you to come up with something."

"Are you sure about that?"

"Yes," she decided. Then she paused. Couldn't she?

"ARE YOU READY?"

Noah cataloged the faces milling beyond the open restaurant doors. Turning to Laura, he thought again of the way his tongue had practically lolled out of his mouth when she had emerged from her bedroom back at her bungalow perfectly coiffed and dressed to the nines in a black maxidress. This one had a transparent lace collar and sleeves, with a line of ruffles below her clavicle. The skirt was a mix of ruffles and lace. A buff-colored belt tied it together with a hat in the same color. The keyhole in the back of the dress had made his palms itch as much as the cutouts in her bathing suit.

He'd wanted to say something then.

You look stunning.

You're too fine for the likes of me.

Instead, he'd just stood there with his mouth hanging open like an idiot.

He took a steadying breath. "Let's get this over with."

"Take my hand."

Cursing inwardly, he snatched her fingers up in his and hoped to God his palms weren't sweaty.

"There's Tallulah," she murmured. "She's our head of housekeeping and has been with the resort as long as my family has. She lives on property like Adam, Josh and me, and she knows everything there is to know about her staff and the guests."

"Good to know," he said, sizing up the woman of average height and weight. When she saw Laura, her face lit up. "Last name?"

"Deschine. And she's not a mark," Laura warned under her breath. His steps had picked up pace and she hurried to catch up. "Everyone adores her. *I* adore her."

"Everyone's a mark," he informed her.

"Tallulah," Laura greeted her, going straight into the woman's arms.

Noah relinquished her hand as she hugged Tallulah. The woman placed both hands on Laura's shoulders and searched her face, speaking quietly. "How are you doing—with everything?"

Laura's smile dimmed slightly. "I'm okay. Are you?"

"I'm still in shock, I think," Tallulah murmured. "Poor Bella. She remains out."

Laura nodded. "Knox has taken some time off, too, but he's returning full-time today. We need him, but I hope it's not too soon."

Tallulah eyed Noah. "Who is this?"

Laura pivoted to him. She took his hand again, fixing that poised grin into place. "Tallulah, this is Noah. My boyfriend."

"Boyfriend?" Tallulah's focus flitted over the tattoos on his neck and hands, the leather jacket and rustic boots. She shook her head. "You didn't tell me you were seeing anyone."

"I've been keeping it quiet," Laura explained. She placed her hand low on Noah's back. "*We've* been keeping it quiet."

"We haven't had enough time together over the last few months," Noah said. "Have we, Pearl?"

Laura's gaze snapped to his. After a beat, she remembered herself. "No. But once Noah heard everything that's happened, he flew in to be with me."

"That's nice," Tallulah said, a smile warming her mouth. "She needs someone. It's good to meet you, Noah."

"It's nice to meet you, too, ma'am," he returned.

When Tallulah swept away, Laura took a moment to gawk at him.

"What?" he asked. "Have I done something wrong already?"

"No," she said with a slight shake of her head. "You called her 'ma'am.'"

"Shouldn't I have?" he asked.

"You absolutely should," she agreed. "It was just odd hearing something that polite come out of your mouth."

He rolled his eyes. "Right. Because I'm uncivilized."

She sighed at him. "Never mind."

As they ventured into the restaurant, heads swiveled in their direction. He tried not to squirm under the attention. Up front, he'd known that being Laura Colton's boyfriend would make people openly curious.

He had been right. The maître d' took his coat. Noah had put more thought into his appearance, for once. The black T-shirt with the Metallica logo exposed the web of tattoos down both arms. He placed his hand on Laura's waist as they were led to their table and could practically hear the buzz of speculation surrounding them.

"Thank you," she murmured when he pulled out her chair, aiming a high-wattage smile over her shoulder.

There was a flirtatious note in those baby blues. When

they heated like that, they no longer reminded him of ice floes. They made him think of hot springs, and his body tightened. His hands hardened on the back of the chair. Leaning over her shoulder as she lowered to the seat, he whispered, "Don't lay it on too thick, Colton. Neanderthal like me might get the wrong idea."

He saw the tension weave through her posture again. She said nothing as he moved to the chair facing her and dropped to it. Without opening the menu, she told the server, "Billy, may we have the champagne breakfast?"

Billy looked back and forth between them, owl-eyed. "Just for the two of you?"

Laura smiled Noah's way. "Just us two."

Noah shook out his napkin. Billy skipped off to the kitchen, no doubt to spread the gossip. "We're an organized spectacle."

"You wanted in," she said, not losing the smile. "Too late to turn back now."

"You could make a scene," he pointed out. "Scream at me. Throw something at me. Demand that I sleep with the horses tonight and be on my way in the morning."

She shook her head. "I don't believe in making a scene."

He shot off a half laugh. "You enter a room and it's a scene, regardless of what you say."

She propped her chin on her hands. "I believe you're trying to give me a compliment."

"I'm telling you the truth, Pearl."

Her nose wrinkled. And even that looked pretty on her. "'Pearl'?"

"You said I could call you whatever I want."

"It makes me sound like a member of *Golden Girls*," she complained.

"What's wrong with *Golden Girls*?" he countered.

"Nothing," she said. "But I am still three months shy of thirty."

A woman passed their table. She did a double take and skidded to a halt. "Laura?"

Laura beamed. "Alexis! Noah, this is our amazing concierge, Alexis Reed."

He dipped his head to her. "Nice to meet you, Ms. Reed."

"And who're you?" she asked, skimming her gaze over his torso.

"This is Noah Steele," Laura said. "He's my…boyfriend."

Alexis slowly turned her stare on Laura, her shock plain. "Girl, you've been holding out on me."

"Noah's in a band called Fast Lane," Laura said. "We've been keeping things quiet because he's been touring."

Brows arched high, Alexis turned her stare back to Noah. She offered him her hand. "Is this your first time at Mariposa?"

"It is," he granted, taking her hand in his. He squeezed it lightly.

"How long are you staying for?"

"As long as it takes to make sure Laura's okay. The last week has been tough on her."

"I'll say it has," Alexis seconded. "Well, I'll let you two get back to it." She sent Laura a meaningful look. "You owe me a long talk over white wine."

"I do," Laura agreed. "Are there any problems I need to see to this morning?"

"Nothing I can't handle," Alexis answered smoothly. "Enjoy your champagne. I'll check in later."

Noah waited until Alexis walked away before speaking. "Fast Lane?"

"It's an actual band," she said. "If I'd given her a fake name, nothing would pop up if she googled it."

"Let's hope she doesn't google Fast Lane and Noah Steele together," he said. "That may blow my cover."

Laura shook her head. "I hate lying to the people I care about. This is going to be harder than I thought."

"Relax," Noah advised. "Once I find out who's responsible for Allison's overdose, you can tell everyone the truth."

Laura didn't appear to be consoled. Billy came back, setting a bottle of champagne and glasses on the table. He popped the cork, let the champagne breathe as he set a plate before each of them with a fruit medley and a croissant that smelled incredible. Then he poured the champagne into a pair of crystal flutes. "Can I get you anything else?" he asked.

"This is perfect," she complimented him. "Thank you, Billy."

As he walked away, Laura sipped her champagne. She lowered the flute, tapping her finger to the side. "I like your arms," she noted.

He glanced down at his forearms. The spider went up one wrist. Webbing chased it up his forearm. The primary feathers of the falcon on his upper arm peered out from underneath his sleeve. On the other arm, more bones. "Sure you do."

"I mean it," she said. "You're practically a work of art."

"Well, that was the idea," he drawled.

"You have to get better at this."

"At what?" he asked. Eating the croissant with his hands didn't seem right. Not with a grand piano snoozing nearby and crystal dripping from the ceiling. He picked up his knife and fork and sawed off a corner.

"Letting me be nice to you," she added.

"Hmm." The croissant practically melted on his tongue.

Carefully, Laura set the champagne flute down. "We've got Adam incoming."

Noah set his fork down. He lifted the napkin from his lap and wiped his mouth. "How did he take the news?"

"Not well," she warned. "Please, be good."

"Really? 'Be good'?"

She gave him a squelching look before greeting her brother. "Adam. Will you be joining Noah and me for breakfast?"

When Adam only turned a discerning eye on Noah, Noah lifted his hand. "Howdy."

Adam didn't respond. Noah noticed that both his hands were balled at his sides. Amused, he asked Laura, "Is he going to call a duel or what?"

She frowned at him. "Noah."

"Will he accept pistols, or should I borrow someone's small sword?" Noah continued, undeterred.

"You're both being stupid. And everyone's watching."

Adam glanced around at the interested parties. His fists relaxed. But the sternness refused to leave his face. "Do you know what you're doing?"

"Of course we do," she said.

"I'm not asking you," Adam said.

Laura looked at Noah, pleading.

He stood up from the table and stepped into the aisle to face Adam squarely. "I'm here to see that Laura's okay," he told Adam, planting a hand on the man's shoulder. He had the satisfaction of seeing a nerve in Adam's temple vibrate. "She's lost a good friend, and she needs someone to lean on."

"And you're that person?" Adam asked skeptically.

"You're damn right I'm that person," Noah snapped. "The real question is whether her big brother is going to stand in the way of that."

Adam looked as if he'd rather swallow a handful of broken glass than allow Laura to continue this charade. He measured the hand on his shoulder with its skeletal ink. "All right," he said, his hard jaw thrown into sharp relief when the words came out through clenched teeth.

Laura stood, too. "I think Noah should stay in a bungalow."

Adam's eyes shuttered. "I think that's asking a bit much."

"There are a couple of empty ones," she stated. When he remained unmoved, she tilted her head. "I'll pay for it, if you're worried about that."

"Don't be ridiculous, Lou. This has nothing to do with money."

"Then say yes," she insisted. "The sooner Noah finds the perpetrator, the sooner everything can go back to normal."

Adam groaned. "He can stay in Bungalow Fifteen. It's better than him bunking with you at your place, which is where you'd put him if I refused."

"Thank you," Laura said. "You won't regret this."

Adam waited until she settled back at the table before turning fully to Noah. He leaned in, lowering his voice to a fine edge. "My sister just vouched for you. Don't let her down."

"And let you run me through with your princely sword?" Noah ventured. He shook his head. "I don't think so."

Adam shrugged his hand from his shoulder before he walked away.

Amused, Noah sat again. "I think he's starting to like me."

Laura gave him a discreet roll of her eyes, reaching for her champagne again. He didn't miss the way her lips moved around a whispered prayer before she tipped it back.

Chapter Eight

"You're dating again?"

Laura didn't think she could take another brother's dis-approval. She swallowed, watching Joshua's expression as he took in the news.

"Why didn't you tell me?" he asked.

"I was being cautious," Laura tried to tell him. "Can you blame me?"

Joshua squinted off in Noah's direction. The pair had come to the stable so she could familiarize Noah with the grounds and introduce him to other members of staff. She hadn't expected Joshua to be there at this hour. His shock was palpable.

"Laura." Joshua's face broke out in a grin. "This is great!"

She blinked. "It is?"

"Of course it is," he said. "I didn't think after the Quentin situation you'd put yourself out there again. But look at you."

A relieved laugh tumbled out of her as Joshua gathered her in for a hug. "You're not upset?"

"Why would I be upset?"

"After everything with Quentin... You were so angry."

"He hurt you," Joshua told her. "He broke trust with all of us. Tell me you trust this guy, and I'm here for you."

"I do trust him," she breathed.

"That's fantastic," he said, pulling away. "Do I know him from somewhere? He looks familiar."

"You must've seen his band," she blurted. "Fast Lane."

"Maybe."

Before he could think more of it, she asked, "Did you speak with Erica?"

His smile tapered off. "Yeah, I did. She said nothing to make me think her and CJ Knight are more than they should be. Apparently, his manager—that Doug guy—isn't answering her calls."

Laura thought about that. "That's not good."

"Is there anything we can do about it?" Joshua asked. "What we should be worried about is Dad causing trouble for us."

"You think he will?" she asked.

Joshua nodded. "He's going to get that money somehow. And we know he plays dirty when he has to. Roland's been informed not to let him on the property without notifying one of us first."

"That's good, I suppose," Laura conceded. She watched Noah pet one filly who had come to the corral fence. The horse nickered as she nudged her muzzle against his chest. Noah's hands roamed into her mane before teasing her forelock and stroking her ears.

"Does he make you happy, ace?" Joshua asked.

Laura watched Noah and the horse, and something somewhere softened. It was difficult to associate the gentle horseman with the bullheaded one she knew. "Yes."

"Then I don't care who he is," Joshua explained. "I don't care where he comes from or what he does for a living. You deserve to be happy."

She looked back at her brother. "Thank you."

She would have hugged him again, but Knox hailed him. Joshua tossed her a wink and roamed back into the stable.

Laura crossed to the fence where Noah stood. "Penny has a taste for rebels."

"She's got spunk," he said, patting the horse's flank when she sidestepped for him to do so. "I like that in a filly."

She tried not to watch his hands. She couldn't miss how Penny nodded her head, as if agreeing with his every touch. "Do you ride?"

"I used to take Allison horseback riding on her birthday," he said.

"That's sweet," she said, trying to align him with Allison's indulgent brother. The pieces wouldn't have fit together so well if he wasn't giving Penny everything she wanted, including a treat he'd nabbed from the feed room.

Noah's head turned her way. "Do you ride?"

"I did," she replied. "My horse, Bingley, died last fall. I bought him when I moved to Arizona. He colicked overnight and…that was it."

"And you haven't ridden since?"

She shrugged. "I haven't had the heart to."

"You know what they say," he suggested.

"What?" she asked when he left the words hanging.

"To get back on the horse."

Her lips parted in surprise. "Allison said the same thing."

He stilled. "Did she?"

"Yes."

He looked away quickly. "If I'm going to stay on-site, I need to go back to my place to pack some clothes. I also need to go by Allison's."

"Why?"

"To look for anything that may point to her killer," he said. "She might have written something down. She could have received a note or a gift from someone. Since I don't have CCTV footage to fall back on, I thought that would be the best place to start."

"Let me come with you," she blurted.

He lifted his shoulders. "What good would that do?"

"Her killer is linked to the resort, and apart from my brothers, no one knows the resort like I do," she explained. "You could miss something I won't."

He shook his head. "I don't know…"

"I won't get in your way," she pledged. "If you need to take a minute when we get there, I can walk outside." She wrapped her hand around the spider etched on his forearm. "Please, Noah. This is something I need to do as much as you do."

He rocked back on his heels, pulling a breath in through his teeth. "You talked Adam into letting me stay and investigate," he said. "I owe you one."

"Is that a yes?"

"It is," he admitted.

"We can take my car."

"At what time does it turn into a pumpkin?"

"Ha." She gave his shoulder a light pinch. There was no give in the tight-roped muscle underneath his sleeve. He didn't even flinch.

Rowing, she thought in wonder. Turning away from him and Penny, she looked across the corral. "Oh," she said as Knox and Joshua looked away quickly. She dropped her voice. "Maybe you should kiss me."

"Now?"

"We have an audience," she whispered.

He stopped himself from looking around. Just barely, she sensed, as the muscles of his throat and jaw jumped warily. Somewhere far away, she thought she heard her heart pounding. Or was that his? She didn't see his chest rise. Was he even breathing?

The chain around her navel heated again. She still held

his arm. Of its own accord, her thumb stroked the spider's spinnerets, soothing the cords of sinew underneath.

He took a half step closer.

Her pulse skittered. Every inch of her was aware of him, tuned to him.

He seemed to hesitate, uncertain. Then his head lowered, angled slowly.

He dropped a kiss onto the corner of her mouth. His hand skimmed the outside of her lace sleeve, and he lingered, head low over hers.

She wished he'd take off his sunglasses. Would the storms reach for her as they had on the sofa this morning? Would his eyes be tender? Were they capable of that?

She wondered what that would look like.

"We should go," he said.

The words skimmed across her cheek. Then he moved away, and she drew in a stuttering breath.

"THIS ISN'T A CAR."

Laura kept her eyes on the road and her hands at ten and two. "What are you talking about? Of course it's a car. It's got an engine and tires—"

Noah held up a hand to stop her. "This is a Mercedes G63 AMG. Calling this bad boy a car is like calling Cinderella's glass slipper a flip-flop."

Her lips curved. "You should see how she handles off-roading."

"You off-road?" When she lifted a coy shoulder, he tipped his head back to the headrest. "Don't take this the wrong way, Colton. But that is *sexy*."

"I've opened her up a couple of times on the interstate." She bit her bottom lip. "She goes really, really fast."

Reaching up, he gripped the distress bar. He shifted in his seat. Was she *trying* to turn him on? "You're killing me."

She snuck a glance at him over the lowered, fur-trimmed hood of her puffer jacket, her smile climbing. She wore large sunglasses that hid her eyes, but the smile may have been the first full, genuine one he'd seen from her. "Maybe we should take this time to keep getting to know each other."

"We're only a few minutes from my condo," he claimed. Their morning session of Twenty Questions had nearly been his undoing. It had exposed more than he'd intended.

His walls were already down, he reminded himself. He may not have completely come to terms with Allison's death. But he was an open wound, one Laura's questions had gone poking at without mercy.

"One quick question, then."

He tried not to squirm. "Fine. One question." Damn it, he could handle *one question*.

She took a minute to consider. Then she asked, "Tell me a secret."

"A secret?"

"Something about you no one else knows," she added.

He shook his head. "I don't have any."

"None?"

"No," he said.

She looked pointedly at his tattoos. "Do you really expect me to believe that?"

"Sure." He glanced at her. "How about you? What're your secrets?"

"I'll tell you mine if you tell me yours," she offered.

"This match is a draw," he concluded. He pointed to the end of the street. "Turn left there. My condo's on the right."

She made the turn, then swung into the inclined drive. She leaned over the wheel to get a look at the white two-story. "This is you?"

He popped the handle and pushed the passenger door

open. Dropping to the ground, he dug his keys from his pocket. "You don't have to come in."

Laura was already out of the vehicle. She walked around the hood, zipping the silver puffer to ward off the dropping temperature. "You don't want me to come in?"

He'd been in her place, he thought. What did it matter if she saw the inside of his? "It won't take but a moment."

"I think I can handle that," she said, on his heels as he followed the path to the front door. He'd dumped rocks into the garden beds so that only the heartiest of desert plants jutted up through them.

There were two dead bolts on the door. He unlocked them both and the knob before pushing it open. After scooping up the mail on the welcome mat, he tossed the keys on the entry table. "Make yourself comfortable," he said, eyeing the return addresses. He set aside the bills for later and tossed the junk mail into the kitchen trash on the way to the bedroom.

He took down his old duffel from the top of the closet. Then he opened and closed the dresser drawers, selecting what he would need for a few days at the resort. He tossed his toothbrush, toothpaste, shampoo and beard trimmer into a toiletry bag. It fit inside the duffel.

On his bedside table, he exchanged his everyday watch for his good one, flipping his wrist to fasten it. In a small ceramic dish, he saw the leather bracelet Allison had given him when he'd left for the navy to match her own.

The evil eye in the center of the braided cord stared at him, wide-eyed. It was blue—like Laura's eyes.

He frowned as he scooped it up. Shoving it in his pocket, he knelt on the floor and opened the door on the front of the nightstand. His gun safe was built in. He spun the lock once to the left, then the right, left again. It released and he turned the handle to open the lead-lined door.

Inside, he palmed his off-duty pistol. It was smaller than

his service weapon. Since his work at Mariposa was off the books, he couldn't carry his city-issue.

He tucked the pistol in its holster before strapping it in place underneath his leather jacket. He picked the duffel up by the handle. Through the open closet door, he could see the black bag that held his suit.

Steinbeck hadn't released Allison's body. But that time would come. There would be a funeral.

Noah had to bury her. He drew his shoulders up tight, already hating the moment he would have to unzip that bag, don the godforsaken suit she'd helped him pick out for a fellow cop's funeral years ago and stand over her coffin.

He pushed his fist against the closet door, closing it with a hard rap. Then he switched off the overhead light and walked out of the bedroom.

Laura stood in the center of the living room.

He followed her gaze to the large painting above the couch. Looking back at her, he raised his brow. "You look like you've seen a ghost."

She lifted her hand to the painting. "It's Georgia O'Keeffe."

"Is it?"

She squinted at him. "You didn't know?"

"Allison bought it shortly after I moved in," he said. "She said it was a replica. But she thought it'd look good in the space. She teased me for never putting anything on the walls. I waited a long time to own a home, and I didn't want to put holes in the plaster. I put the damn thing up to make her happy." And it had, he thought, remembering how she'd beamed and clapped her hands when she'd seen it on the wall for the first time. His chest ached at the memory. "What about it?" he asked, wanting to be away from it. There was nothing of his sister here. And yet there was too much.

"The painting's called *Mariposa Lilies and Indian Paint-brush, 1941*," Laura stated. "It…was a favorite of my mother's."

Noah made himself study the painting again. This time he shifted so they stood shoulder to shoulder. "Yeah?"

"Mariposas were her favorite flower," Laura breathed.

"Hence the name of the resort," he guessed.

She nodded silently. Abruptly, she turned away from him. "I need some air."

He veered around her quickly. If she cried…here, of all places…he didn't know how he'd handle that. Opening the door to the back patio, he held it wide.

She didn't thank him. Head low, she stalked out on long legs.

He gritted his teeth, wondering whether to follow or hang back. Watching, he tried to gauge how unsteady her emotions were.

She crossed the terra-cotta tiles to the railing. Clutching it with both hands, she viewed the sheer drop to the crevasse below. In the distance, the sun slanted low over white-tipped mountains. The clouds feathered overhead, wild with color. Her shoulders didn't slope. Her posture didn't cave. She stood tall, another exquisite fixture on the canvas he saw outside his back door.

After a while, she said in a voice that wasn't at all brittle, "I can see why you picked the place."

Noah tried to choose a point on the horizon just as fascinating as she was. His attention veered back to her, magnetized. "It was this," he admitted. "And the quiet. It's far enough outside the city, I don't hear the traffic."

She folded her arms on the railing and didn't speak. It was as if she was measuring the quiet. Absorbing it.

Quiet strength, he thought. It came off her in waves. He opened himself to it, wishing he could make room in his grief for it. How had she learned to do that—move past it? Or was he supposed to move *through* it?

Was that why he felt like he was losing this race? He had to stop trying to go *over* the grief and go through it?

Somehow, that seemed harder.

He jangled the keys he'd picked up from the counter. "We should get to Allison's."

She waited a beat. Then she turned and crossed the tiles to him, placing one boot in front of the other. She gathered her jacket close around her, her breath clouding the air.

As she breezed past, her scent overcame him. He felt his eyes close. Even as he wondered what he was doing, he caught it, pulled it in deep and held it.

It was a classy fragrance, something no doubt with a designer price tag.

He swore it was made to chase his demons.

That was his secret. And he'd take it to his grave.

He shut the door and locked it, promising himself he'd come back to the view when Laura no longer needed him. When she was gone. When he'd found Allison's killer, put him or her in a cell...if he didn't kill the person first.

He'd come back here and learn, somehow, to wade through the fallout.

ALLISON'S ONE-STORY HOUSE was a little Spanish-style residence across town. Noah had a key to the door on the same ring as his. Silently, he worked it into the lock before pushing the door open.

The lights were out. He switched them on as the door squeaked, echoing across hard floors.

It was the opposite of his place, Laura observed. It smelled faintly of incense. The walls were bright yellow and cluttered with artwork. There were little eight-by-ten paintings, woven dream catchers, and a whole quilt draped on the wall of the dining room. The plush rugs sank under Laura's boots. As Noah flipped on more lights, Laura caught herself clasping her elbows. There was a hammock hanging in the dining room where a table should have been.

A pair of UGGs sat by the back door.

Noah bent over a table where books were stacked. He went through them one by one.

She circled the space once before she saw the little notebook on the edge of the bar. She opened it and was confronted with Allison's pretty, sprawling handwriting. "I might have something," she whispered.

Noah looked up. He saw the notebook splayed across her palms and rose.

As he crossed to her, she turned so he could see what Allison had written. "It's not really a journal. It's mostly Zen proverbs." She flipped a few pages and shook her head fondly. "She dotted her *i*'s with hearts."

He said nothing as he pried the notebook gently from her hands. Lowering to a stool at the bar, he journeyed through the pages, one after the other.

She turned away. His expression might be inscrutable, but she could feel the sadness coming off him.

The photo on the fridge caught her attention. It was a stunning snapshot of Allison in dancer's pose on top of Merry Go Round Rock. Underneath, a flyer was pinned with Allison's yoga class and guided meditation schedule for the New Year. She'd made small notes next to each time to help keep track of repeat students with their initials and Vinyāsa sequences.

Laura took down the flyer and folded it in two, wondering if Noah would find something useful on it.

The photograph behind it slipped to the floor. Laura crouched to pick it up and was shocked to recognize a young Allison next to a fresh-faced Noah.

In the photograph, Noah was clean-shaven. The wide,

uninhibited smile underneath squinty green eyes and the brim of a navy dress-blue cap struck Laura dumb. His smile made him ridiculously handsome, not altogether innocent, but happy.

She stood to pin the photo back to the fridge with a Buddha magnet. A glass of water had been left on the counter. There was an empty breakfast bowl in the sink, unwashed. Alstroemerias in a vase next to the sink drooped.

She couldn't stand to think of them being left to die. Laura picked the vase up by the base and lowered it to the bottom of the sink. She turned on the tap and filled it halfway.

Noah stood. He tucked the notebook into the back of his jeans under his jacket before wandering toward what could only be Allison's bedroom.

Laura didn't want to follow. But she couldn't imagine him facing everything in there, in his sister's most private space, on his own. She tailed him.

The bed was half-made. Dirty clothes were still in the hamper. Noah had switched on the bedside lamp and was dragging the tip of a pen through the little ring bowl on her dresser. He opened a drawer, then another.

"What are you looking for?" she asked.

"Bracelet," he said, riffling through a jewelry box.

"I can help," she told him. "What does it look like?"

He shut the box, then thrust his hand deep into his pocket. He opened his fist to reveal an evil-eye pendant on braided leather strings.

"That's Allison's," she realized.

"This one's mine," he argued. "I picked it up at the condo just now. She wore hers, always."

Laura frowned. She couldn't remember Allison without the bracelet either. "Wasn't it on her when she…?"

He shook his head. "I viewed the personal items found on her person. The bracelet wasn't among them."

Laura looked around. "If it's not here..."

"Then it's lost," Noah finished, "or her killer has it."

"I'll look over here," she said, pointing to the bathroom.

They searched for another twenty minutes, combing each drawer, cabinet and closet space. The bracelet was nowhere to be found. Laura gathered the scarf she'd bought Allison for Christmas. She'd seen the warm, cozy wrap with its bright rainbow pattern and fun fringe at a local arts and crafts festival and had instantly thought of her friend.

She ran her hands over it and felt tears burn behind her eyes.

"Did you find it?" Noah asked from the door.

She lifted her gaze to his.

He froze, wary, and turned his stare elsewhere. "You need to come out of there."

Relinquishing the scarf, she stepped to the door. He let her pass under his arm before he closed it. Once more, she hadn't let tears fall, but she rubbed her hands over her cheeks anyway, to be sure. "I didn't find the bracelet," she told him. "I take it you didn't either."

"No dice," he replied.

There was violence in him, she saw in his taut jaw, his electrode eyes. He barely had it restrained. She saw him as she had the first night. Only this time, the readiness and anger weren't gunning for her.

She wasn't sure why she did it or what compelled her. She simply thought of the way he'd kissed her at the paddock. Just that brush of his mouth at the corner of hers and the softening she felt inside herself...

Fitting her hand to the bulge of his shoulder under the jacket, she held him.

His brows came together. "What are you doing, Colton?" he asked, hoarse.

She didn't answer. She didn't have to lift herself all the way to her tiptoes to stand chin to chin with him.

Just enough, she thought, touching the hard line of his jaw. She brushed her thumb over the center of his chin. The hair there was thick and soft. Up close, he didn't smell nearly as dangerous as he looked. He smelled like worn leather and clean sweat.

She leaned in. Even as he tensed, she closed her eyes and touched her mouth to the corner of his.

She felt his hands gather in the material of her jacket over her ribs, but he didn't wrest her away. Nor did his body soften, even as she pulled away, lowering to her heels.

His eyes searched hers, scrambling from one to the other and back in escalating questions. "What was that for?" he asked.

She considered what was inside her—what he was fighting. "You're not alone."

His brows bunched closer. The skin between them wrinkled in confusion.

She licked her lips, tasting him there. "I have something to tell you."

"What?" he asked, the line of his mouth forbidding.

"Adam's setting up a fund in Allison's name," she informed him. "It's to help pay for funeral costs."

He shook his head automatically. "I don't need your money."

"Noah, please. We just want to help. Let us. You must be overwhelmed by all this—"

"I'm fine." He moved away.

"She told me once that for the longest time you were the only person she had in this life," she blurted. "It's the same for you, isn't it? She was the only person you had. And now she's gone and a big part of you is lost. Even if you don't want anyone to see it."

"I think we're done here," he said.

She rolled her eyes heavenward. She might as well bang her head against the wall.

In the living room, he'd switched off all the lights. As he went to the front door to leave, she caught sight of the alstroemerias. The petals were so delicate, she could see the light from the window through them.

She'd take them home. She'd care for them, as Allison would have. Then she'd return the pretty crystal vase to Noah when they wilted.

As he locked up, she cradled the vase against her chest and frowned at the stiff line of his back. "What was Allison's favorite flower?"

"How should I know?" he grumbled, checking the handle to make sure it was locked. Shoving his keys in his pocket, he stalked back to her Mercedes.

"You can't expect me to believe that you never bought your sister flowers," she retorted.

It wasn't until she'd fit the base of the vase in the cup holder between the driver and passenger seats that he spoke again.

"Orchids."

She fastened her seat belt and paused, then started the car. "What?"

"Allison liked orchids," he said again, his expression flat as he stared out the windshield. "Not that I know why. They're fussy. She was the opposite of fussy. I got her these blue and purple ones once. She cried when she had to throw them out."

Laura was happy she'd taken the flowers from Allison's. She couldn't think about them falling to the countertop one petal at a time. Methodically, she shifted the Mercedes into Reverse. "Let me know when you decide the funeral should be."

"Why?" he asked.

She set her jaw, watching the backup camera and turning the wheel as the Mercedes reversed onto the street. She could be stubborn, too. "If you won't accept my family's help with the service, you can expect several dozen orchids to grace the proceedings."

Noah thought about it. Then he bit off a laugh. "Before this is all over," he contemplated as she pointed the vehicle toward Mariposa, "you're going to drive me crazy."

She mashed the accelerator to the floor and watched the needle on the speedometer climb. "The feeling's mutual."

Chapter Nine

Bungalow Fifteen had every amenity Noah didn't need. The decor was tasteful and minimal. He could have eaten off the bamboo floors. Fresh flowers populated surfaces and there were no paintings here either. Just lots and lots of windows framing more showstopping views of Arizona. The bathroom off the bedroom had given him a moment of pause with its plush, all-white linens, marble tub and glass walk-in shower. On the back deck, there was a hot tub.

What Bungalow Fifteen lacked was a murder board.

So the coffee table in the living room had become Noah's work area. There, he'd arranged maps of the resort, lists of names, including staff and guests from the time of Allison's murder, pictures of the discovery scene at the pool cabana, Allison's notebook, and the schedule Laura had pulled from her fridge.

On the couch, folders were open to the Coltons' history. The section on the patriarch, Clive Colton, was doubly thick.

One manila folder lay closed. Inside lurked pictures of Allison's body at the pool cabana and others from the morgue, close-ups of the entry wound from a needle and abrasion marks on the backs of her legs.

She hadn't died in the pool cabana. The killer had drugged

her at an unknown location and then transported her to a public place that would appear less incriminating.

Was Allison aware when the needle had gone in? Was she afraid? Or had she simply floated away like the dandelion tufts she often picked from the cracks in the sidewalk and blew into the wind?

Noah locked down that train of thought as the ache inside him let out a train-whistle scream. He avoided looking at the photos unless absolutely necessary.

He picked up the list of names, culling members of staff, crossing off those he'd been able to pin down alibis for with a few well-placed phone calls. Most people had been at home in Sedona. The exceptions were, of course, those who lived on property—Tallulah Deschine and the Coltons.

The tip of Noah's pen hovered over Laura's name. He wanted to strike her from the list of possibles. He knew on a primal level she had been precisely where she had told Fulton she was during the interview process—alone at home in bed.

But the cop in him wouldn't allow it. Not because he doubted her innocence. Because striking anyone from a list of suspects was impossible without corroboration. The only witness to Laura's activities during the time frame of Allison's murder was the tabby cat, Sebastian.

Noah would have sat the feline down and questioned him if he could have.

Tallulah, Adam and Joshua were still on the list, too. All claimed to have been in bed, sleeping, according to Fulton's notes. Knox Burnett, the horseback adventure guide who had tried to revive Allison the morning her body was discovered in the pool cabana, hadn't been able to confirm his whereabouts in the wee hours of the morning. He had also taken several days off from his work at Mariposa, claiming emotional distress.

Noah had cleared the concierge, Alexis Reed, whose

neighbors had seen her arrive home around dinnertime that evening and whose car hadn't left her driveway until sunrise. But he hadn't crossed off Erica Pike, the executive assistant whose whereabouts hadn't been as easy to establish.

Between security, housekeeping, maintenance, transportation, the spa, gym, restaurant, bar, stable and front desk, there were one hundred staff members at Mariposa. There could also be one hundred guests if the bungalows were booked solid.

They hadn't been, he noted, the day the murder took place. February was supposedly the calm before the storm of the long hospitality season that stretched from March to October. Still, the chill and intermittent snow flurries hadn't deterred everyone. Seventy-two guests had been booked at Mariposa for the week the crime had taken place. With some legwork, Noah had obtained some alibis there as well.

This left less than two dozen possibles on his short list.

Noah rubbed his chin, reading the four names he had circled. There were more questions around these names than others—like actor CJ Knight. Knight had checked out ahead of schedule the morning Allison was discovered in the pool cabana. Noah's calls to his manager, Doug DeGraw, had been pointedly ignored.

He eyed his notes where he'd cross-checked possible suspects with those who had attended Allison's meditation or yoga classes. There were fewer names on the list he'd cross-referenced with the late-night stargazing excursions she had tagged along on.

The bracelet she had given him lay among the maps, photos and notes. The evil eye stared at him baldly. He'd searched the pool cabana. It had been swept already by crime scene technicians, and the police tape had come down, clearing it for use. Noah had found nothing in or around the area they had missed.

He lamented the absence of security cameras. The pool area was along a major thoroughfare. CCTV could have easily picked something up if the Coltons weren't so concerned with the discretion of their overclassed clientele.

A knock made him drop the sheet of paper in his hand. He felt the weight of his off-duty gun on his belt. Rising, he grabbed the leather jacket from the back of a chair and swung it on as he approached the door.

Peering through the peephole, he scanned the two people on his doormat. His teeth gritted. Trying to relax his shoulders, he did his best to cast off the pall of tension that shadowed him everywhere. He snatched open the door and fixed what he hoped was a devil-may-care grin on his face—something befitting a rock-and-roll guitarist.

Adam and Joshua Colton may have shared similar heights, builds and coloring. But they couldn't be more different. Adam stood as high and straight as a redwood. No trace of a smile touched his mouth.

On the flip side, Joshua grinned widely, a sly twist teasing one corner of his mouth higher than the other. His hair was longer than his brother's and carelessly wind-tossed. While Adam's eyes injured, Joshua's practically twinkled. "Hey, Fender Bender!" he greeted Noah, earning a groan from Lurch at his side.

Whether it was because Joshua's enthusiasm reminded him of Allison's or because his ready familiarity with Noah made Adam uncomfortable, Noah felt a strong chord of amusement. "Fender Bender?"

Joshua lifted a shoulder. "Adam told me not to lead with 'Motherplucker.'"

A choked laugh hit Noah's throat. He covered it with a cough as Adam cast a disparaging look over at his brother. The elder Colton shifted his weight and attempted to start over. "We're going for a morning run."

"Okay," Noah said uncertainly.

"You should come with us," Joshua suggested.

"Or not," Adam dropped in. "I'm sure you're booked."

Joshua nodding knowingly. "With Laura."

Adam shifted gears fast. "You're coming with us, Steele. No ifs, ands or buts about it."

"Pretty please," Joshua added, posthaste.

Noah lifted a brow. He glanced at his jeans. "You know, I'm not really dressed for—"

"We'll wait," Adam inserted.

When Joshua moved forward, Noah stiffened. He wouldn't have time to hide the mess on the coffee table. "Ah... It won't take long for me to get changed."

Joshua's smile turned stilted. "What're you hiding in there, Keith Richards?" He craned his neck to get a look. "Burned spoons? Coke? Heroin? Women?"

On the last word, the younger Colton's voice dropped to a dangerous bass. Noah would've been offended if he wasn't so impressed by the hard gleam in his eyes. He tried to laugh it off. "None of the above," he said. "I just don't want it to get back to Laura that I'm a slob."

Joshua lifted his chin slightly. "Sure. We'll wait."

"Just a minute." He shut the door and shrugged off the jacket, cursing viciously. Throwing it over the back of the chair, he then unlaced his boots. In the bedroom, he removed the gun holster and tucked it safely under the mattress.

Quickly, he exchanged the jeans he wore for an old pair of sweatpants. He left on the 1969 Johnny Cash San Quentin State Prison T-shirt and grabbed the sneakers he'd stuffed in his duffel as an afterthought. Happy for the foresight, he scrubbed the back of his hand over his bearded jaw, left his jacket on the chair and opened the door to find the Coltons waiting with varied levels of patience.

Stuffing his bungalow key card into the pocket of his

sweats, he injected a hint of nerves into his voice as he asked, "You two are going to go easy on me, right? Being on the road doesn't leave a lot of time for exercise."

Joshua and Adam traded a glance as they led the way up the path. "Sure thing," Joshua replied before he broke into a jog, getting a head start.

Noah caught up with Adam and muttered, "Thanks for your help back there."

"You want Josh's trust," Adam retorted, "earn it yourself."

Adam pulled ahead, trailing behind his brother. Noah was forced to kick it into gear. A cloud of warm air plumed from his mouth as the cold slapped his face.

He kept up with them just fine, even as the path turned rough around the edges and the bungalows fell behind. They passed signs for a trailhead. The path declined, forked, inclined, forked, declined and inclined again. Caution signs zipped past, as well as guardrails looking out over long drops.

They reached a high point and Adam and Joshua let up finally. Adam doubled over, holding his hamstring while Joshua paced, panting.

Noah tried not to grope for the trunk of a nearby shrub tree. He liked to think he was in good shape, but he sipped air that felt thin. They'd pushed him, either to test his mettle or as some kind of Colton initiation rite.

They would need to work harder to throw him off the scent, he thought with a lick of triumph as he caught Adam's wince. "Is this the halfway point?" he called out.

Joshua spared him a look over his shoulder. "This is as far as we go, Steele."

No more "Fender Bender." Not even a "motherplucker." Noah circled, swept up in the panorama. "Hell," he whispered, impressed. He could understand why people paid thousands of dollars to stay at Mariposa. The state parks were littered with people. To find a solitary hike these days, a person had to wander off the map.

Here, there didn't seem to be anyone around for miles. The quiet struck him. He raised his face to the sun. No wonder Allison had been in love with this place.

I get it now, he told that part of his mind that still felt connected to her somehow.

Another thought struck him. He'd been lured away from other guests with only Laura's brothers for company. He eyed the long tumble of rocks down to the bottom of the hill. "Is this where you kill me?"

A laugh left Adam. It sounded grim. "I wish."

At least big brother's honest, Noah mused.

Joshua turned on him, hands pressed into his hips. "What do you want with Laura?"

The question shouldn't have caught him off guard. He'd have done this, too, had Allison brought a man around to meet him. He searched his mind.

And found that some part of him could answer the question. Something inside his chest that had cracked like an oyster.

What did he want with Laura?

Everything.

No, he schooled himself. That wasn't the right answer. That couldn't be the answer at all. He didn't want anything from Laura.

Except her mouth. Her smile—the real one he found so elusive. Laughter he'd never heard. Her banter. Hell, even her rebuttals.

He wanted her hands, he thought, unbidden. Soft, clean, manicured fingers tangled up in his, spreading through his hair…

He shifted when that image alone turned him on. Shifting away from the Colton men, he put some distance between them and him. He didn't think they would be amused if they saw what the simple thought of their sister did to him.

Joshua didn't let up. "Answer the question."

Noah thought about it, vying for an appropriate response that would appease them both. What came out was "I want her to know she's safe."

"Of course she's safe," Adam snapped at his back. "Mariposa's safer than anywhere else."

Noah whirled on him. "Is that right?"

The light of challenge died in Adam's eyes.

"Would I be here if she felt safe?" Noah pressed.

Joshua shook his head. "I'm not sure how you could make her feel any safer than Adam and I can."

"Someone was murdered under your noses," Noah pointed out. "Someone she cared about."

"She blames herself," Adam mumbled.

"Allison's death had nothing to do with Laura," Joshua said.

"How do you know?" Noah asked. "How do you know she's not the next target?"

Both men froze. Noah struggled against the need to press further, to question them more about Allison. But Laura had warned him not to give himself away to Joshua if he could help it.

If Joshua did have loose lips, then Noah's cover would be blown before he could avenge Allison. "She needs me," he said and wondered if it was true, because he knew all too well that the next part was. "I can't let her do this alone."

Adam and Joshua remained studiously silent. After a few minutes, Joshua stretched for the return run.

It wasn't until Joshua had started back for the trailhead that Adam spoke up again. "Allison gave private lessons to some guests."

Noah nearly skidded on a patch of ice. "Why didn't you mention it before?"

Adam chose not to answer that. Instead he told him, "She'd go to them."

"Their bungalows," Noah muttered.

"Yes," Adam replied. "When she came to me with the idea, I advised against it. Our goal is to keep the staff presence to an absolute minimum, in and around the bungalows. Maintenance crews and Housekeeping don't go there unless a guest has a spa treatment or excursion scheduled. All requests are seen to personally by the concierge."

"You asked her not to do it?"

"Allison has a way of talking you into things." Adam grimaced. "Sorry—she *had* a way. I told her she could start taking on a handful of private lessons at a time, as a trial run. If everything went well, she could take on more in the spring."

"Do you know which guests signed up?" Noah asked. "Do you know which ones had private lessons scheduled during the week she was murdered?"

"I don't know their names," Adam explained. "I just know she had three signed up during that time, two she taught that same day. She was excited. She enjoyed helping people, whether it was in a group setting or one-to-one." Adam cursed under his breath. "Did she die because I gave in—because I let her go into people's bungalows against my better judgment?"

If the private lessons had led to Allison's undoing, what were the three names on her exclusive list?

Chapter Ten

Laura hurried toward the front desk. A raised voice had brought the lobby to a standstill and one of the front desk clerks seemed to shrink before a painfully thin platinum blonde whose designer handbag swung in a threatening motion. "I don't want Bungalow Eighteen! My husband and I always stay in Bungalow Three! My last name is Colton, too, you know!"

At Laura's side, Roland spoke briskly. "I'm sorry, Ms. Colton. The guard at the gate didn't realize who she was until she was past the checkpoint."

"It's all right, Roland," Laura assured him. Someone needed to rescue poor Clarissa from her stepmother's rant. She picked up the pace to intercept.

"I can escort her out."

"No, that will just make things worse." Laura had never known her stepmother to visit without Clive or to make a scene. But she knew the indicators of escalation. She could feel the open curiosity and horror from people gathered around. "I can handle this."

Alexis breezed in, planting herself behind the desk in front of Clarissa. "Ms. Colton," she greeted Glenna smoothly. "How very nice to see you again."

"Don't patronize me," Glenna snapped. "I've been on a plane for two hours. I want my bungalow!"

"Clarissa has informed you that Bungalow Three is currently occupied," Alexis informed her. "If you had called ahead, we could have told you it wasn't available."

"I don't care that it's not available—"

"Ms. Colton, reservations are required for Mariposa's bungalows," Alexis went on. "We need at least six weeks to see to personal requests. This is a five-star resort. Not a fly-by-night motel. Because you showed up without prior notice, you will enjoy all the amenities Mariposa offers with a complimentary spa package from the comfort of Bungalow Eighteen or I can call Sedona's Hampton Inn. I'm sure they'll be happy to give you their best room."

Glenna bristled. She hissed. But Laura saw the handbag droop as her arm dropped. "I see I've been painted into a corner."

"No, ma'am," Alexis said, her incisive gaze not leaving Glenna as Clarissa handed her the welcome package, complete with key card and spa vouchers. "Our policy is bungalow by reservation only. Anyone who behaves as you have is normally showed the door. And yet *you* are getting a key card and a free massage from Arizona's very best masseur." She thrust the envelope at Glenna. "We hope you enjoy your stay at Mariposa, Ms. Colton. If you need anything further, my name is Alexis Reed. I'll be your concierge. My number's in the packet. Please, *do* call me."

Glenna took the envelope slowly, as if afraid the thing contained anthrax. She tossed her hair over her shoulder and strutted out the entry doors, no doubt to hail one of the golf cart operators to take her to her assigned bungalow.

People roamed the lobby freely again, and Laura approached the front desk. She caught Alexis's eye and mouthed, *You are my hero.*

Alexis lifted both hands in a prayer pose and tipped her chin down.

"Drinks on me at L Bar tonight," Laura told her.

Prayer pose turned into a discreet fist pump. Alexis stopped when the next check-in appointment came forward. Brushing Clarissa out of the way, she said, "Take five. I'll handle this."

"Thank you," Clarissa breathed and practically fled. She looked at Laura. "I'm sorry, Ms. Colton. She just started yelling. I didn't know what to do."

"It's all right," Laura assured her. "Go to the break room. Brew a cup of tea. I believe Tallulah left a dish of brownies for everyone there. Come back in half an hour. I'll help Alexis and Sasha cover the front desk."

Clarissa lit up. "Thank you so much! I was doing the meditation classes with Allison. Since something happened to her, I've been out of sorts…"

"I know exactly what you mean," Laura said. "This has been a difficult time for everyone."

"People keep asking for yoga classes. I just keep handing them spa vouchers."

"That's the best we can do for now," Laura reminded her.

"Any idea when a new yoga teacher is coming?"

Distress trickled down Laura's spine. She hadn't given a thought to hiring anyone else. It would be her responsibility to do so. "Not at this time."

Clarissa nodded solemnly. "I'll be back in thirty minutes, on the dot."

As Clarissa speed-walked out of L Building, Laura pressed her hand to her stomach. The idea of putting out the call for a new yoga instructor, conducting interviews and placing genuine effort into finding a replacement for Allison made her feel sick.

Roland took her elbow. "Are you all right, Ms. Colton?"

She gave him a tight nod. "Sure. Please let me know if Glenna makes any more waves."

"Will do," he agreed. "I'm going into a briefing with Adam. Should I tell him she's arrived?"

"Yes," she said. "The snow's melted off, so Josh is directing Jeep tours. He'll be off property for the better part of the day. I'll text him and warn him before he returns."

Roland walked toward the offices but snapped his fingers and backtracked. "I've got something for you."

"Oh?" Intrigued, she watched him dig a folded piece of paper out of his pocket. "What's this?"

"I ran into your friend Mr. Steele out by the stable earlier," he revealed. "He said he was looking for you."

Laura thought quickly, her fingers tightening reflexively around the note. "I did tell him to meet me there. I suppose I forgot."

"I wouldn't worry about it," Roland returned consolingly. "He was friendly enough."

Laura tried not to laugh at Noah being referred to as "friendly."

"He gave you this?"

"Yeah. He said he knows how busy you are. He knew I'd be seeing you, so he wanted me to pass along a message."

"Thank you, Roland," Laura said. When he nodded and walked away, Laura unfolded the small slip of paper and stared at the tidy, slightly slanted handwriting.

Pearl,
I missed you. There's a new gelding here you need to check out. He's calm and sweet, like you. His name's Hero if you're still interested in getting back on the horse. If you're not busy later, meet me at L Bar at six. I'll have a martini waiting.
Yours,
Noah

Laura lingered on the closing. *Yours.* She felt herself soften again.

The note hadn't been sealed, which meant Roland could have easily read it. Noah would have guessed that. That was why he'd used the nickname he'd picked for her. Was that why he had invited her to drinks this evening? Or why he'd said such sweet things about the new gelding's nature and her own?

She folded the note again, trying to shove the questions into a drawer. What she couldn't ignore was how the written words had made the waves of sickness she'd felt moments before ease.

She made a mental note to drop by both Glenna's bungalow for a chat and L Bar for a date.

L BAR HUMMED with activity. Still, the atmosphere felt comfortably intimate. Patrons hovered around high-topped tables or the long bar where the personable bartender, Valerie, built drafts and mixed cocktails.

"You're Laura Colton's man," she guessed when he introduced himself.

"I am," he said.

"How'd you manage that?"

He chuckled because she meant it more as a ribbing than an insult. And she had a point. "Beats the hell out of me."

"Is she joining you tonight?" Valerie asked.

"I hope so," he said, looking at the doors—as if he couldn't wait for Laura's arrival.

Who was he kidding? He'd glanced toward the doors half a dozen times already. "She'll have a martini, dry. I'll have a Corona and lime."

"Coming right up," she said as she built his beer. "You arrived just in time, if you ask me. The boss doesn't burn the candle at both ends. She's too smart for that. But word is, she's broken up about what happened."

"You're right." He tried to think how to broach the subject without drawing eavesdroppers into the conversation. "You never forget the shock when something happens like that. I lost a friend of mine a few years back. It's tough."

Valerie passed the beer to him. She grabbed a cocktail shaker for Laura's martini. "I don't think anyone who knew Allison will get over it."

Noah folded his arms on the bar. He allowed his shoulders to droop over them. "I don't think anyone ever really gets over it. I'll never forget what I was doing when I heard the news about my buddy."

"I won't forget either," Valerie replied. "I closed the bar that night same as always. It was close to the weekend, so it was open later than it is on weekdays. My roommate woke me up the next morning with a phone call from Laura. That's who hired me and everybody else. If there's a staff bulletin, she makes sure everyone knows about it. Even those of us who aren't scheduled to come in until later. That must've made things harder for her—having to call around and deliver the news to all the staff."

Noah nodded. He made a mental note to track down Valerie's roommate and confirm that she had been home around the time of Allison's death.

"I'm glad she has someone," Valerie mentioned as she poured the cocktail into a martini glass. She topped it with an olive. "You're a real sweetheart for being there for her."

He flashed a smile. "Wouldn't have it any other way."

"Is your band coming to Arizona soon?" Valerie asked. "I'd like to check it out."

"I'll have to check our schedule," he said. "We're taking a break right now. We've been touring for a while."

"Enjoy it while you can," she advised. "Nobody knows more about burning the candle at both ends like a genuine rock-and-roll superstar."

"I'm no superstar," he said.

Valerie leaned toward him over the bar, lowering her voice. "Her stepmother showed up this afternoon."

He searched his memory files for a name. "Glenna?"

"That's the one. Made quite a scene at the front desk. I hear there's trouble with her father, too. She and her brothers turned down his request for a loan. Now he may be out for blood."

Lifting the beer to his mouth, he made a noncommittal sound.

"That's how the old man operates, from what I understand," Valerie said, easing back with a shrug. "He never gave a hoot for his kids. But when the chips are down…"

"How else do you expect an eel to operate?" Noah groaned.

Valerie laughed. "Hey, it was nice to meet you."

He dipped his head. "Nice to meet you, too." Backing away with the drinks, he let her move on to the next customer. He saw the empty table in the back corner and made a beeline for it.

Laura arrived moments later in another fur-trimmed jacket—this one camel-colored. It looked as soft as he knew her skin to be. The hem floated around her knees. She stopped to speak to Valerie for a moment, then let a guest snag her attention. She passed around smiles and assurances in a manner any PR representative would have admired.

The smile didn't dim when she found him lurking at the back table. "I'm behind schedule," she said when she reached him. "I apologize."

"No need," he said, standing to take her coat as she slipped it from her shoulders.

Her bare shoulders. *Christ*, he thought, seeing the delicate ledge of her clavicle on display above the off-the-shoulder blouse. Every lover-like thing he could have said seemed too real. Too sincere.

You're a knockout...

I am the envy of every man in this room...

What the hell are you doing with me, Pearl?

He held out her chair for her. When she settled, smoothing the pleat of the sunshine-yellow linen slacks she wore, he draped her jacket on the chair behind her. And, because this was L Bar—because he could feel every Tom, Dick, Harry and Valerie watching—he took her shoulders.

She turned her head slightly, and he felt her spine straighten.

He told himself it was all for show as he dropped his mouth to her ear. "I'd've waited," he murmured for her. "I'd've waited all goddamn night for you, Colton." Even as he chastised himself for being a moonstruck moron, he closed his lips over the perfumed place beneath her lobe.

She tilted her head. Not to shy away. He knew it when she released an infinitesimal sigh, when her pulse fluttered against the brush of his mouth as he lingered, sipping her skin like a hummingbird. He cupped the other side of her face as she presented him with the regal column of her throat.

Her shiver pulled him back. It roped him to the present, to what was real and what wasn't. He wrenched himself away, watching his hands slide from her skin. "You're better at this game than I am," he muttered before slinking off to his chair where he belonged.

She watched him as he set the martini in front of her and tipped the beer up. It took her several minutes to taste her drink, sipping in a ladylike fashion that drove him to distraction.

"What kept you?" he wondered aloud.

She set the glass down without a sound. "My stepmother

arrived unexpectedly this afternoon and was disgruntled when she didn't receive the VIP treatment she thought she deserved."

"It fell to you to unruffle her feathers?" he asked. "Don't you have enough to handle?"

"Glenna's family," she said cautiously. "At first, I thought their marriage was more business than anything. Her and Clive's courtship happened swiftly. Before we knew it, they were married. But I know Glenna takes care of him. He's getting older. When they married, I won't lie and say I wasn't relieved."

"Because that meant he was no longer your responsibility."

She winced. "Does that make me callous?"

"Not if the rumors about Clive Colton are true," he said. "Not if he only comes to you and your brothers for money."

Her gaze riveted to his. "How do you know about that?"

"I've spoken to over half your staff over the last few days," he reminded her. "While they respect you, Adam and Joshua, they talk."

She looked away, noting those at the surrounding tables. In a self-conscious move, she ran her fingers through her straight-line bob.

He wanted to tell her how surprised he'd been by the loyalty of her employees—how the ones who knew about Clive's recent visit to Mariposa had sided with the siblings, bar none. Not one disparaging word had been spoken about Adam, Laura or Joshua. Noah knew that had nothing to do with the nondisclosure documents everyone had signed and everything to do with how Mariposa was run, how staff were treated, and how devoted the Coltons were to the resort and the people who worked for them.

She wasn't the princess of Mariposa; she was the queen, and her subjects loved her dearly.

She sighed. "I just want to know why she showed up without warning. Why she came alone. Her behavior is outside the realm of anything I've seen."

"Breaks in patterns of behavior are tells," he advised. "Dig deeper and you'll find a motive."

"Have you made any headway in the investigation?"

"I have a short list of people with no alibis."

"Who?"

He tried dousing the question with a warning look.

She braced one elbow on the table's edge, rested her chin on her hand and leaned in. From the outside, it looked intimate. Especially when her eyes roved the seam of his mouth. "Are we still in this together, Noah?" she murmured.

He, too, leaned in, setting both arms on the table. He hunched his shoulders toward the point of hers. Wanting to rattle her chain as much as she was rattling him tonight, he dipped his gaze first over her smooth throat. Then lower to the straight line of her bodice. For a split second, he wondered what was keeping it in place. The curves of her breasts were visible, and she wore no necklaces to detract from the display. The effect made him lightheaded, slightly giddy. Did L Bar have an antigravity switch?

His gaze roamed back to hers and latched on. He was half-wild with need. The effort to steer his mind back to the investigation and Allison felt arduous.

Frustration flooded him, anger nipping at its heels. *Damn it.* It shouldn't be this easy to make him forget why he was there. "Why didn't you tell me Allison was giving private lessons to guests in their bungalows?"

Her eyes widened. "She…what?"

"I thought you were her friend," he hissed. "You say you knew her. How could you not have known what she was doing?"

Laura's lips parted. "She didn't tell me."

"I'm supposed to believe that?"

Her eyes heated. "Do you really think so little of me?"

"Adam knew."

She gripped the stem of the martini glass. "Why did neither of them think to involve me?"

"You'll have to take that up with your brother. He said she had three clients the week of her death, two the day she died. I need to know who they were."

"I don't have that information," she said coolly, pulling away from him. "You didn't answer my question."

She'd asked about his list of suspects. "You won't like it."

"It's a little late to spare my feelings," she informed him.

Remorse chased off his anger. He fell prey to so many mixed emotions around her, and it floored him. He'd never known anyone who could make him *feel* like this.

"Tallulah," he said.

She laughed shortly, without humor. "If she's at the top of your list, you're reaching."

"Erica Pike," he continued. "Knox Burnett. Adam. Joshua. You."

Laura stiffened. "Me?"

"You don't have an alibi for the time in question," he said. "Not one anyone can corroborate. I can't cross you or the others off my list until you give me one."

"I'm a suspect." On the outside, she was all ice. "This may be the worst date I've ever had."

"It's not personal, Laura."

"No," she agreed. "You've made that very clear. Haven't you? And it's surprising."

"What is?"

"That a guy like you can be so by the book."

He felt a muscle in his jaw flex. "A guy like me?" he repeated.

"You don't really think I hurt her," she said.

"No, I don't thi—" Fumbling, he course-corrected quickly. "That's not the—"

"You don't really think my brothers killed Allison either," she surmised.

He caught his teeth gnashing together and stopped them before he ground his molars down to the roots. "It doesn't matter what I think. I go where the facts are."

"Speculation figures into detective work," she said. "I've read enough true crime to know that. What would be Adam or Josh's reason for drugging our yoga instructor? For that matter, why would Tallulah or Erica do such a thing?"

"I don't have motive," he said. "Just a list of people who claim to be sleeping at the time of her death."

"You've ruled guests out?"

"No," he said. He tossed a look toward a man in an open-collared shirt who was lifting a glass of whiskey in a toast to Valerie. "Roger Ferraday doesn't seem to know where he was or what he was doing during the night in question. As it sits, he's Fulton's chief suspect."

"Ferraday," Laura said numbly. "He's staying here with his teenage son, Dayton."

"Who has a list of hushed-up misdemeanors back home in Hartford," Noah revealed, tipping his beer to his mouth to drain the glass.

"He's fifteen," she said.

"Doesn't make him or Daddy innocent," Noah told her. "I'm also taking a look at CJ Knight."

Her gaze pinged to his, alarmed.

He narrowed his eyes. "Does that name ring a bell?"

"Yes," she said. "He left the morning Allison's body was discovered. We haven't been able to reach his manager to find out why."

"DeGraw won't return my calls either."

"CJ Knight was one of Allison's repeat students," she

whispered. "And I understand he has Bungalow One booked again after Valentine's Day."

"Think he'll show up?"

"I can't say at this point."

"If he keeps his booking, I want to know the second he checks in."

She rubbed her hand over her arm, discomfited. "I don't know how you do this—look at everyone…every person without an alibi and peel back the layers to see which one of them has murder written on their heart."

"With some people, it doesn't leave a mark," he said. "For some people, killing is in their nature."

"God," she said with a shiver.

"There are those, too, who don't seek to harm others," he said. "They start small and escalate. Or they claim it was an accident. Throw in the occasional plea of insanity."

"It must do something to you," she said, "to do this every day. To look at the dead."

"You get used to it."

"Do you ever have trouble sleeping?"

All the time, he thought. He didn't grimace, but it was a near thing. "Somebody's got to speak for them. The victims. Somebody's got to fight for them."

Her expression softened at long last. "My brothers took you running this morning."

He rolled his eyes. "If that's how they treat all your suitors, I'm starting to understand how so many dickheads slipped through the cracks."

"Meaning?"

"Meaning if they wanted to warn someone off, they wouldn't do it at first light. They'd do it at night. They'd rustle them out of bed, blindfold them and drop them off in the middle of the desert. See if they can make it back on their own before daybreak."

"Why does it sound like you've done this before?"

"I plead the Fifth."

"Is this why none of Allison's boyfriends ever lasted all that long?" she asked.

Before he could answer, he spotted Alexis cutting through the crowd. "I think your friend's looking for you."

Laura turned and waved. "I wasn't sure if you'd join us," she said. "I'll fetch a glass of white for you."

"Not just yet," Alexis said. She placed her hand on Laura's. "We have a situation."

Laura's smile dropped like a stone. "What kind of situation?"

"There's been a leak," Alexis answered. "There's a van from the local news station at the gate and the front desk is getting calls. It's about Allison."

Laura rose quickly. "Does Adam know?"

"Yes," Alexis said. "He's waiting in his office."

"Tell Roland to delay the news crew at the gate as long as possible while Adam and I reassess," she said. "We'll need at least ten minutes to shift into damage-control mode."

"I'm on it," Alexis assured her. "Who could have done this? Who would have talked to the press?"

Laura shifted her eyes to Noah.

He understood the question she was asking. "Leave it with me."

She nodded shortly. "I have to go."

"Go," he urged. When she leaned in, he did the unthinkable. She'd meant her pursed lips to skim his bearded cheek. He turned his head automatically and caught the kiss on the mouth.

Her hand gripped his arm. Her fingers dug through his sleeve.

Again, he didn't think. If he had, he wouldn't have opened

his mouth. Her eyes watched his. He didn't close his either as he grazed his teeth lightly over her round bottom lip.

A noise escaped her. He pulled back. The heat refused to bank. His heart racked his ribs.

She stared at him, as shocked as he was.

Did she feel the heat, too?

Alexis said her name. Laura blinked. She backed away from him, turned, and followed Alexis to the doors and out.

He caught the curious looks he'd earned from those around him. Turning away, he saw the jacket Laura had left on the back of her chair.

Noah dug the cash out of his pocket, dropped it on the table, gathered the coat and left to fade into the night.

Chapter Eleven

"Why are you here?"

Noah ignored Fulton as he escorted his guest into the station. She'd fought the cuffs like a wet cat. As she bristled against his lead, he warned, "People get tossed into lockup for fighting custody, sweetheart. I'd calm down if I were you."

Glenna Colton twitched in indignation. "You're hurting me!"

"I'm not," he said firmly, guiding her toward the back of the Sedona station, where the interrogation rooms were located.

"I want my lawyer!"

"You're entitled to a representative during questioning," he acknowledged. "You'll need one when this is all over."

"I still don't understand what I'm being charged with," she said.

"Assaulting a police officer, for one," Noah said, knocking on the door of Interview Room 1. When no one answered, he opened it and poked his head in. The room was clear. He maneuvered her inside. "Sit down, be a good girl, and we'll see about getting the cuffs off."

She sneered at him. "I get a phone call. I *want* my phone call."

"In a minute, Veruca," he said.

No sooner had he shut the door behind him than he heard, "Steele!"

Noah stopped, gritted his teeth, then turned to face his superior office. "Sir."

Captain Jim Crabtree, a weathered barrel of a man with twenty-plus years on the force, bore down on him. "Aren't you supposed to be on personal leave?" he asked. "Who is this woman?"

Fulton peered through the blinds of the interview room and cursed a stream. "That's Glenna Bennett Colton. Wife to Clive Colton. His children own Mariposa Resort & Spa."

Crabtree spoke in a steely, quiet manner that wasn't any less threatening than the sound of his yelling. "We went over this. You asked if you could approach Mariposa. You asked me for my permission to investigate your sister's death and I told you it's against departmental procedure."

"Yes, sir," Noah said.

"You are *not* about to tell me you picked this woman up on the streets of Sedona," Crabtree warned.

"No, sir."

A knowing gleam entered Crabtree's dark eyes. "How long have you been poking around the resort?"

Noah pressed his lips together. He respected the hell out of Crabtree and couldn't lie. "Several days."

Fulton let out a disgruntled noise. It was cut off by Crabtree. "You went against orders. That makes you eligible for administrative leave. I could send you before the review board."

Hell. He couldn't lose his badge. Not with Allison's killer on the loose.

Not when being a homicide detective was the only job that had ever made sense to him. It was the only box he'd ever fit in. "Respectfully, sir, I'm asking you not to do that."

"Give me one reason I shouldn't."

Noah caught Fulton's fulminating stare and wasn't cowed in the least. "I've been operating at Mariposa on and off for the last week without the primary investigator any the wiser."

"Jesus, Steele," Fulton tossed out. "You're a son of a bitch. You know that?"

"Also," Noah said, moving on, "with the help and permission of the Colton family, I've been operating undercover. People don't see a cop walking around. They see the man staying in Bungalow Fifteen. Laura Colton's boyfriend."

"How the hell did he pull that off?" another detective, Ratliff, muttered behind him. General assent went up through the ranks of watching cops.

"I have a short list of suspects and inside access to guest quarters and staff buildings," Noah continued. "I've built a rapport with regulars and employees alike, and I'm looking at a handful of people who were close to Allison while Fulton fights for crumbs from the table. If you pull me out now, we lose our best chance of tying up this case."

"You expect me to believe you can think clearly—objectively—when your sister's the victim?" Crabtree challenged.

"I know how to do my job," Noah said. "I've got the best closure rate in my division."

"Yes," Crabtree granted. "But she was your family."

"I'm going to close this case," Noah informed him, "just as I've closed dozens of cases before hers."

"I don't need a loose cannon on my hands," Crabtree warned. "If you find her killer, how do I know you won't take matters into your own hands?"

It was a fair question, one Noah had asked himself a dozen times. When he found the man or woman who'd killed Allison…when he looked them in the eye at last…would he be able to follow procedure? Was his belief in due process strong enough when confronted with the person who'd squashed what was most precious to him?

Noah took a breath. "I won't let you down, Captain."

Crabtree stared him down. "When you're ready to make an arrest, bring Fulton in and let him handle it. Do not approach the suspect. If you so much as touch them, Steele—"

A muscle in Noah's jaw twitched in protest, but he made himself answer. "Yes, sir."

"Now explain to me why the Coltons' stepmother is in interrogation," Crabtree demanded.

"I believe she's responsible for the news leak at Mariposa," Noah said. "When I approached her with evidence, she swung at me. I cuffed her and brought her in for booking."

"Did anyone see you do this?"

"No. My cover's still in place."

Crabtree nodded in Fulton's direction. "Fulton will take care of it. Either go home and clear your head or go back to Mariposa and find me an actual suspect."

"Yes, sir." Noah subsided and let Fulton pass into Interview Room 1 to finish his job.

"IT WAS GLENNA?" Laura asked. "She leaked Allison's homicide?"

Noah nodded. "The timing was right. From there, it was just a matter of pressing the right buttons. Once cornered, she didn't hold back."

"She always seemed so even-tempered," Laura said, struggling to understand. "Why would she do this?"

"You can't think of any reason?" Adam asked from behind his desk. "We had Security watching the gates for Clive."

Her lips parted in surprise. "So he snuck Glenna in here under our noses to cause trouble on his behalf?"

"She said something as I was hauling her in," Noah added. "She said her husband would get what he wants, and Mariposa only exists because he allows it to."

"That's inaccurate," Adam said mildly.

Laura's brow furrowed. "Roland asked me if he should escort her out when she made a scene in the lobby. I should've let him. Valentine's Day is this weekend. I should've thought about the wedding party coming in. Once the families hear about the murder…"

"They signed a contract," Adam assured her. "If they cancel, they'll pay the cancellation fee."

"If that wedding falls through, then who's saying the next one won't?"

"How long will Glenna be detained at the SPD?" Adam asked Noah.

"She wasn't just booked on assaulting an officer," Noah said. "You and Fulton had an understanding that the investigation would be kept quiet to aid in the search for the killer. By leaking it to the press, Glenna interfered in a police investigation. Her lawyer's there now, doing his song and dance. She'll likely be released on bail tomorrow morning. But she won't get away scot-free. She's facing charges."

"And she's going to be angry," Laura pointed out.

Adam rolled his pen between his fingers. "We might as well have poked a beehive."

Laura felt tired just thinking about it. "You have to finish this," she told Noah. "You have to find who did this and get them away from the resort."

"I will."

For once, he didn't argue. The little ship in a bottle she carried inside her anchored up to his strength. It was a port in this storm. "We're running out of time."

"So am I," he said. "My CO found out what I'm doing. He's not wild about it."

"You're not leaving."

His eyes didn't stray from her. "I'm not going anywhere."

The assertion made her feel lighter, if only for a moment.

She thought things over, picking through the cluttered mess in her mind. She sought something…anything they'd overlooked. "The schedule from Allison's fridge. Do you still have it?"

"It's at my bungalow. Why?"

She faced Adam. "You said Allison had taken on three people for private lessons?"

"As a test run," he said, "yes."

Laura remembered the letters on the piece of paper. "There were three sets of initials written on the schedule. I thought they were repeat students. But what if they're the names of the guests who requested private lessons?"

Noah's eyes cleared. "*CJK*. Those initials were on there."

"CJ Knight," she clarified. "Is that enough evidence to issue a warrant for him?"

Noah shook his head. "I need him to come back to Mariposa. I need him to keep his reservation."

Laura thought about it. Then, injecting as much promise into her voice as he had at L Bar, she said, "Leave it with me."

Chapter Twelve

Laura couldn't cast off the tension. Since she'd learned Noah had taken Glenna into custody, she felt as if she was waiting for the other shoe to drop.

Sebastian was in no mood for a cuddle. Alexis had gone home for the night, so an impromptu girls' night was out of the question. She couldn't call Joshua to confide in him because she was still lying to him about Noah's part in all this.

She winced at that, hating that she and Noah continued to keep him in the dark. What would he think when he discovered her subterfuge?

Laura told herself not to think about that now. She told herself not to think about anything, but her mind was so full, she couldn't relax.

A hard rap on the front door of her bungalow made her jerk. Sebastian hissed. She dropped the book she had been trying to read to the coffee table and rose from the sofa. Tiptoeing to the door, she peered out through the peephole.

At the sight of Noah, she felt a stir. Snatching open the door, she asked, "What are you doing here so late?"

He held up Allison's schedule. "I thought we'd go over this."

"Oh," she said and stepped aside. "Come in." Before Sebastian could dart out between her legs, she scooped him up. "Naughty," she muttered and waited until Noah shut the door before setting him down again.

"If he wants to be an escape artist," Noah stated, "he should lay off the Fancy Feast."

"He's not fat," Laura said. "He's fluffy."

Noah smiled the knowing, self-satisfied smile that never failed to get her dander up. "Whatever you say, mommy dearest."

"That's my coat," she said, pointing to the camel-colored jacket draped across his arm.

"You left it," he explained, handing it over, "at L Bar the other night."

"You didn't have to bring it to me."

"If you don't leave your things around for others to steal, I wouldn't have to."

Laura tucked her tongue into her cheek. As she led him into the kitchen and den, she indulged herself by asking, "Did my stepmother really hit you today?"

"She grazed one off me," he replied. "What about it?"

"At the moment, I'm having trouble blaming her. You have a very slappable face."

He threw his head back and laughed. A full-bodied laugh, straight from the gut.

It went straight to hers. She sucked in a breath as the corners of his eyes crinkled and his teeth gleamed. For a split second, she saw the man as he had been in the navy uniform in the photograph at Allison's, and her heart stuttered.

He caught her staring at him, aghast, and the laughter melted in a flash. "What? Why are you looking at me like that?"

It took her a moment to speak. "I didn't think you knew how to smile—really smile…much less laugh."

His frown returned, all too at home among his set features. "You sound like Allison. 'You don't smile enough, relax enough. You don't put yourself first enough.'"

The words echoed in her head. Allison had said something similar to her. She shook off the odd feeling it gave her. "What about the piece of paper?"

Paper crinkled as he straightened out the creases and handed it to her. "*CJK* is obviously CJ Knight. But what about these initials? *DG*."

She studied them. "You couldn't find someone on your short list to match them?"

"No," he admitted. "Is it possible you missed someone when you gave me the names of staff and guests?"

She shook her head. "No. There's another set of initials. *KB*."

"That's Kim Blankenship, your guest in Bungalow Seven," he proposed, "or your horseback adventure guide."

"Kim Blankenship is in her late sixties. She's here with her husband, Granger. She built a cream cosmetics empire and is here taking a well-deserved break. And Knox?" Laura instantly rejected that idea. "The private lessons were for guests."

"Maybe Allison made an exception," Noah pressed. "Didn't you say he was flirtatious with her?"

"Yes," Laura granted. "But Knox is flirtatious with every woman. Even me."

"Don't like that," he muttered.

"Why not?" she challenged. "It's not like you and I are really…"

As she trailed off, his gaze became snared on her. "Really what? Kissing? We've done that. Touching? We've checked that box. The only thing you and I aren't doing right now, Pearl, is sleeping together."

Her mouth went dry. She forced herself to swallow. "It's not real."

His eyes tracked to her mouth before bouncing back to hers. Her body reacted vividly. Her heart rammed into her throat.

She wanted his mouth on hers. She wanted to know what it would be like, she realized, for Noah to kiss her and mean it. Not for show—for himself and her.

She demurred. They wouldn't be able to uncross that bridge. Once they went to the other side, she wasn't sure she could swim back to safety. She feared what she would find with him. Fire and brimstone, perhaps? Too much, too hard, too fast?

It sounded wonderful. She reached for it even as she turned away. "Knox Burnett didn't kill Allison," she said clearly, walking into the kitchen.

Noah's voice dripped with sarcasm. "The queen of Mariposa has spoken."

She reached for a wineglass. "Quentin called me 'queen.' Or 'queenie.' Sometimes, he just called me Q. Except when he left. Then he just called me a cold hard bitch who would get what was coming to her." She pulled the cork out of the bottle next to the coffeepot and poured a liberal dose. "Dominic thought I was cold, too—in bed and out of it. Do you want some?"

He didn't spare the wine a glance. "You never should've given those assholes the time of day."

"But I did," she said, raising the wine to her lips. She tasted, let it sit on her tongue, then swallowed, swirling the liquid in the glass. "Which makes me either stupid or desperate."

"It's simple," he stated. "Stop dating pretty playboys."

"Who should I date instead?" She gestured with her wine. "You?"

He cracked a smile that wasn't at all friendly. "You'd run screaming in a week."

She lowered her brow. "Why is that, exactly? Do you have pentagrams drawn anywhere on your person?"

"No."

"Are you mangled?"

"No."

"Do you keep tarantulas or dance with cobras?"

The lines in his brow steepled and she sensed he was trying not to give in to amusement. "I told you. I don't have pets."

"Do you have some sort of fetish most women find offensive?"

"No."

She shrugged. "Then why would I run from you, exactly?"

"I'm not Prince Charming."

She clicked her tongue. "I've looked for Prince Charming. No luck there."

"Doesn't mean you and me are meant to be," he asserted.

Some part of her wanted to challenge that. Even the part of her that knew better wanted to know what it would be like…the hot mess they would be together. When heat fired in her again, she drowned the images with more wine.

"And, for the record," he said, "you're not hard or cold. You're calm and together, and you have a strong sense of what's right for you and what isn't. You know how to take out the trash. That's why the playboys have come and gone. And so has your father."

She looked away. "My father has nothing to do with this."

"Your daddy's got everything to do with it," he said. "It was him who taught you what toxic people look like."

She thought it over. "If I'm together or strong, I learned it from my mother. She kept my brothers and me together through the upheaval. Even when she was sick, she had spine. She was incredible. I can't fathom why she never kicked my father to the curb. They lived separate lives by the time she bought this place, but she never divorced him."

"Maybe he made it impossible for her to do so," he intoned.

She felt the color drain from her face. "You're having a glass," she decided, handpicking another piece of stemware. She poured him one and passed it to him over the countertop. "I don't believe in drinking alone."

He lifted the drink, tipped it to her in a silent toast, before testing it.

She watched his throat move around a swallow. Her own tightened. She was growing tired of the tug-of-war between her better judgment and the side of her that wanted to dance in the flames. She was having difficulty quantifying both. "What was your mother like?"

His glass touched down on the counter with a decisive *clink*. "I don't talk about my mother."

She culled a knowing noise from the back of her throat. "That's what's wrong with you."

A laugh shot out of him, unbidden.

Another one, she thought, satisfied.

He shook his head. "God, you're a pest."

Even as he smiled, she recognized the pain webbing underneath the surface. "She died, didn't she?" she asked quietly.

The smile vanished. He masked the hurt skillfully with his hard brand of intensity. "So what if she did?"

She took a moment to consider. "That would mean we have something in common."

He stared at her...through her.

There was a lost boy in there somewhere. The foster kid who'd been dumped into the system while he was still coming to terms with losing the woman who'd raised him. She ached for that child, just as she ached for that part of her that had listened to Joshua cry himself to sleep every night and had been helpless against the tide of grief.

The line of his shoulders eased. He lifted the glass and downed half the wine in one swift gulp. Frowning at the rest, he cursed. "She'd just kicked my stepdad to the curb. He was a user with a tendency for violence. We moved around some to throw him off the scent. I didn't mind. Stability's fine and all, but I had her, and she had me, and that was... everything."

He chewed over the rest for a time before he spoke again. "There was this STEM camp I wanted to go to. I didn't think I'd get to go. It cost money, and she was working two jobs to keep the building's super off our backs. She put me in the car one afternoon, said we were going out for groceries. She drove out of town and pulled up in front of the camp cabins. She'd packed me enough clothes for a week. I was so happy. I don't remember hugging her goodbye. I just remember running off to join roll call."

She waited for him to go on. When he didn't, she asked, "Is that the last time you saw her?"

"Alive?" He jerked a nod. "The son of a bitch found her. Bashed her skull in with a hammer. Next time I saw her, she was lying in a casket."

"I'm sorry." She breathed the words. "I'm so sorry, Noah."

"He got off," he added grimly. "Broke down on the stand and got sent to a psych ward instead of doing his time up-state."

The wine on her tongue lost its taste. She winced as she swallowed. "No closure for you, then."

"Hell, no. All things considered, it's better than what Allison went through before she got shuffled into foster care."

"What happened?"

"The truth's too ugly to speak here," he grumbled.

"Where else could you speak it?" she asked.

Turning up the glass, he swooped down the rest of the

wine and reached across the counter to place it in her deep-basined sink. He gripped the edge of the counter, bracing his feet apart. "Her mother was killed, too. Her father did it, right in front of her, before he shot himself."

"Oh," Laura uttered. She closed her eyes. "She never... She never told me."

"And you'd never know." He gave a shake of his head. "Even as a kid, she was all sunshine and rainbows. She had this raggedy stuffed bunny she carried around by the ear. There was nothing anyone could say to convince her it wasn't alive or that it should be washed or thrown away. She called it Mr. Binky."

Laura found she could smile after all. "You wound up in the same home she did."

"I'm not sure what would have happened to her if I hadn't."

"Why?"

He hesitated again. "She didn't have anyone else."

"Your foster parents—"

"—didn't give a damn. I was fourteen when I went out and got my first job. I had to. Otherwise, Allison and I wouldn't have eaten. I had to teach myself to cook. There's nothing more motivating than that pit in your stomach—that one that's been there for days because someone drank away the grocery budget for the week. I was scared the reason Allison's cheekbones stood out was because she'd gotten used to that feeling. She was so used to it, it wasn't remarkable to her anymore. She'd just come to accept it. So I worked, and I cooked so she'd never have to know what hunger was again."

"I had no idea it was like that for her," Laura said.

"In that home, nobody hit us," he explained. "Nobody snuck into our rooms at night. Nobody screamed at us. But there's a different kind of abuse and that's straight-up neglect."

Laura had felt neglected, too, but not like that. It wasn't the same. Her father's indifference didn't compare to being left to starve or fend for herself.

She had starved, she realized. For his approval. For affection. After her mother died, she'd had to learn to stop. Men had disappointed her, even those before Quentin and Dominic—because she'd half expected their approval and affection to die off, too. She'd taken the safe route out every time.

"Allison told me the same thing she used to tell you," Laura mused. "That I don't live enough. Smile enough. Put myself first enough." Suddenly, what she'd told Joshua the day after Allison's body was found rushed back to her...

I think you two could have made each other happy, at least for a time, and... I don't know. All this reminds me not to waste time if you know what's right for you...

Behind him, she saw the blue glow of the pool through the glass door to the patio. Air filled her lungs, inflating her with possibilities. She set aside her glass and rounded the counter. "Let's go for a swim."

"What?"

"Let's swim, Noah," she said, grabbing his hand. She tugged him toward the door. "Just you, me and the moon."

"Wait a second," he said, trying to put on the brakes. "I didn't exactly bring a bathing suit."

Be brave for once, Laura, she thought desperately. Buoyed by wine and a spirit she'd ignored too long, she told him, "Then I won't wear one either."

Noah's eyes lost their edge. His resistance slipped and he turned quiet.

She slid the door open and stepped out into the cold. "Don't worry," she said when he hissed. "The water's heated."

He stared at the steam coming off the surface, then at her as she took off her socks and untied the drawstring of her loungewear pants. "So we're doing this," he said.

She frowned at his jacket and boots. "Are we?"

When she shimmied out of her pants, his brows shot

straight up. He shrugged off the jacket one shoulder at a time. "I can't let you swim alone."

"And you say you're not a hero," she said, pulling her shirt up by the hem so that she was standing in the cold in her gray sports bra and matching panties. She shivered, dropped the shirt and crossed her arms over her chest. "Hurry up, Steele, before I lose my nerve."

The jacket hit the ground. He grabbed his T-shirt by the back collar and pried it loose.

Muscle and sinew rippled and bunched under a tapestry of black-and-white pictures. The wings she'd gleaned under the sleeve of his shirt took the shape of a large falcon. It spread across his upper arm and shoulder, finishing with another wing that reached as far as his left pectoral. The designs boasted more bones mixed with clockwork, as if he had tried to convince the world that he was half human, half machine. They were vivid and detailed. Although some lines and shapes had faded more to blue than black with time, none of them bled into others.

The effect was…breathtaking, she found. She was stunned by her own reaction.

Laura tried not to stare at him—at all he was—as he unzipped his fly and pushed the denim down. He fought with his boots before discarding them and the jeans completely, leaving him standing in his boxer briefs.

She reached for him, happy when he let her lace her fingers through his. Drawing him up to the top of the starting block, she grinned. "On three."

"One," he began.

"Two…"

"Three," he said and pushed her.

She flailed for a second before breaking the surface. She opened her mouth to shout at him but shrieked when he cannonballed in after her. The residual splash was impressive.

She swept the water from her eyes as he surfaced, grinning. "Prick!" she shouted, tossing water in his face.

"You look good wet, Colton."

She felt more than stirrings of heat. The tendrils of steam off the water's surface could've been from her. Unsure what to do with herself, she floated on her back. The moon was directly overhead. She drifted for a moment, watching it and the stars before flipping onto her stomach for a lazy freestyle lap.

She'd drowned parts of herself in this pool. The pool hadn't been installed for fun or leisure. She'd needed it to stay fit and sane. Water purified. It cleansed. It took away her doubts and reinforced what she needed.

Usually. Still unsure of herself, she did another lap.

"Hey, Flipper," he tossed out when she came up for air.

She swept the water from her face. "What?"

He nodded toward the starting block. "Want to race?"

She laughed at the idea. "Sure. But, fair warning—I won the California state championship two years in a row."

"Do you still have the trophies?"

"Maybe."

"Of course you do," he said knowingly. He gripped the edge of the pool and pulled himself out.

She tried not to groan. He wasn't just ripped and inked. He was wet, his boxer briefs clinging. Peeling her eyes away from him, she climbed the ladder to join him. She slicked her hair back from her face. "Ready to lose?"

He didn't answer. Glancing over, she caught the wicked gleam in his eye as he gave her a thorough once-over. She felt her nipples draw up tight under her sports bra. "Would you like to frisk me, Detective?"

His gaze pinged back to hers. He blinked. His mouth fumbled.

Without warning, she threw her weight into him so that he tumbled into the pool.

Before he could come up for air, she executed a dive. Without looking back, she pumped her arms and legs into motion.

She felt the water churning to her right. As she raised her arm in a freestyle stroke and tilted her face out of the water, she saw him gaining, cutting through the water like a porpoise. She quickened her strokes.

They were coming up to the wall. She reached out blindly, groping for it.

Fingers circled her ankle, bringing her up short. She spluttered, arms flailing, as he held on.

Then she heard laughter—deep, uninhibited. She stopped fighting. As he drew her back against his chest, she abandoned the competition for lightheartedness. Delighted, she dropped her head back to his shoulder and belted a laugh to the sky.

His arms had hers pinned, and he tightened them. She could feel the reverberations of joy from his chest along her back and listened to the colonnades of his laughter. She closed her eyes, absorbing them.

The laughter wound down slowly and his body stilled, an inch at a time. He said nothing, holding her as steam curled around their joined forms.

She felt his breath on her ear. Then the bite of his teeth on the lobe, light and quick. "Laura?"

She shuddered at the sound of her name. "Yes?"

"In our game of Twenty Questions, I never asked you the most important one."

She tilted her cheek against his as he drew her closer still, his lips grazing her jaw. "What's that?"

"How do you like to be touched?"

The breath left her. It bolted. She felt the flush sink into her cheeks. It sank lower, deeper. And it turned darker, more shocking and satisfying.

Take what you want, Laura, she told herself.

She touched the back of his hand. Raising it to her breast, she brought it up to the ache, snug beneath the heavy curve. Spreading her fingers over his so that he mirrored the motion, she let her fingertips dig into his knuckles and encouraged him to grasp, take.

He obeyed. Her mouth opened on a silent cry as he molded her, kneading her through her sports bra.

"Don't be a lady," he told her. "Don't be quiet."

She swallowed, the sounds clawing up her throat. "You... you want to know my secret?"

"All of them," he said, brushing his thumb over the unmistakable outline of her nipple. "I want to know every last one of your secrets, Pearl."

A bowstring drew taut between her legs. Urgency quivered there. "I hate when you call me that," she said. "And I think about you even when I shouldn't."

"When?"

He is so good at this, she thought, arching back as the kneading quickened. "All the time."

"When?" he said again, the note dropping into his chest as his hold tightened.

"I think about you when I work," she rattled off. "I think about you when I'm with others, when I'm alone. In bed. In the shower."

He groaned. Turning, face-to-face, she saw the answering heat and need behind it. "I think about you kissing me... touching me..."

"Is that what you want?" He was close, but he pulled her closer, so his mouth brushed her own. "You want my hands on you? My mouth?"

She heard herself beg, "Please."

His eyes closed but not before she saw his relief. "As you wish," he whispered before taking her mouth in a decisive kiss.

He didn't kiss softly. He took, and she clung. She wrapped her arms around his neck and held on for dear life.

His hands spanned her waist. They cruised, flattening against her ribs, as he licked the seam of her lips, encouraging. She parted for him. One hand rose to the back of her head as he plumbed, touching his tongue to hers.

Her body bowed against his. Every inch of him was hard and fine. She spanned her fingers through the short hair at the nape of his neck, looking for purchase.

There was none. With him, there was nothing but that slippery slope of want and need, and she was going under.

She felt the pool tiles on the wall at her back. Pinned, she felt her excitement focus, sharpen. It arrowed toward her center.

With a harsh noise that sounded almost angry, he snatched his mouth from hers. He cursed, placing his hands safely on either side of her head.

She sucked her lower lip into her mouth. It stung. The tip of her tongue tingled.

His jaw muscle flexed. It was rigid. His eyes were alive, knife-edged, electrifyingly tungsten. The hands planted against the wall clenched in on themselves. She felt him go back on his heels and grabbed him by the arms. "Where do you think you're going?" she demanded.

He shook his head. "I'm no good for you."

"I don't care," she blurted. When he opened his mouth to protest, she reached up to cover it. "You're not Prince Charming? Fine. But I want this, and you want this." She replaced her hand with her mouth, skimming softly in a gliding tease.

His hands dropped to her shoulders and latched as she lingered. He drew a quick breath in through the nose.

She broke away and saw the ardor on his face. "I won't

run from you tomorrow or the next day. I'm here." She kissed him again, deeper. "Take what you want," she invited.

He winced. "There's nothing you could ask me that I wouldn't give. That scares the hell out of me. I don't care what those other fools told you. You're not ice. You're a four-alarm fire. And I'm burning, damn it. I can't afford this. I can't afford you or what you do to me."

"I'm not going to run," she whispered. She thought of Allison, his mother... "I won't be gone tomorrow."

His hands still clutched her shoulders, firm, but they were no longer keeping her at arm's length. They pulled her into his circle of danger and heat. His muscles were still rigid, his grimace unbroken. But she felt him give... With her hands sliding from his waist to the backs of his hips, she angled her mouth to accept his.

It wasn't an onslaught this time. His tongue flicked across hers and he nibbled her lip, but the clash took on a different hue. She ached with it, the ball of need inside her roughening. It grew diamond bright.

"Tell me again," he instructed. "Tell me what you want me to do to you."

Fitting her palms to the backs of his, she used them to sweep her body from throat to thighs. She slowed the motion down as they followed up the seam of her legs where her thighs came together, up her belly, over her breasts, cheeks, hair...

He raked his fingers through the damp strands, then did it all again on his own. His hands slid firmly down her torso, teased her inner thighs before putting on the brakes, slowing the motions, skimming the folds of her sex so that her hips circled and she sought. She clamped her hand over the back of his, encouraging.

He didn't whisper so much as breathe the words again. "Show me. Show me exactly how to make you come alive."

Her touch worked urgently against his, demonstrating.

He caught on. "Like this?"

She nodded, then stopped when he increased the rhythm. She gulped air.

His hand slipped beneath her underwear. She moaned and churned.

This would break her, she decided. That was his endgame. He wanted to watch her come apart one molecule at a time. The flames inside her raced and leaped as she climbed the ladder fast.

She came, biting the inside of her lip.

"Let it go, Pearl," he bade. "For Christ's sake."

She couldn't leash it. A cry wrenched from her, unpolished and visceral. Everything he made her feel.

"Yes," he encouraged, his mouth on her throat.

She shuddered as she came down off the high, messy and resplendent. Something bubbled up her throat. It crested, escaped. A sob, she heard, distressed. "Oh, God," she uttered. She felt rearranged and so sparkly and sated, she thought she could taste stars.

"Hold on," he said, tossing one of her loose arms around his neck, then the other. Grabbing her around the waist, he hoisted her out of the water.

She fumbled over the ledge of the pool, coming to rest on her hands and knees. Every limb felt like a noodle. "Oh, sweet Lord," she said, then snorted a laugh. Quickly, she covered her mouth, wondering where it had come from. When he didn't follow, she asked, "Coming?"

He swiped his face from brow to chin, gave a half laugh and glanced down at his waist.

Understanding gleaned. He may have slaked her need,

but not his own. Looking toward the wicker cabinet where she kept towels and a robe, she dragged herself to her feet.

She retrieved two towels, the long ones that wrapped around her twice. She folded herself into one, knotting it beneath her collarbone.

Behind her, she heard a splash and turned to see him emerging from the water. He passed a hand over his head as he turned from her, slicking the hair back away from his face.

She went to him. "Here."

"Thanks," he said and reached for the towel.

She pulled it away, trying to compress the sly impulse to smile.

He saw it form on her lips anyway. "You think this is funny?" he asked.

"I do," she admitted, holding the towel high.

He cursed and rearranged his feet so that he was facing her.

She saw what he'd been trying to hide from her. His erection was at full mast, the soaked boxer briefs straining to contain it. "I think it wants you to let it out."

"You're right." He snatched the towel.

She watched him scrub the terry cloth roughly over his face and hair. He toweled off his chest and arms before wrapping the towel around his waist. "What's stopping you?"

"What if you don't like what happens when I do? What then?"

She considered him. "What wouldn't I like?" When he didn't answer, she gripped the towel on either side of his waist and yanked him toward her. She stole a kiss while she had him on the back foot, hardening her mouth over his to prove a point.

He hummed in unconscious agreement.

She pushed him away abruptly and watched him fumble for a second in protest. "You want to know another secret?" she asked when he opened his eyes.

"I told you," he said after a moment. "I want all your secrets."

"There's nothing I don't like about you, Noah Steele," she revealed.

His chest lifted in a rushing breath.

"Why not show me the rest?" she suggested.

"You don't do this," he ventured. "You don't just take a man to bed. Not without flowers, dinner. Hell, candles. Silk sheets. Some ridiculous dress meant to tie your man's tongue in a knot."

"Maybe."

"We didn't have dinner," he noted. "I didn't bring you flowers."

"No," she admitted.

"I don't see any candles."

The candles were all inside her, she thought desperately. They stood tall under columns of flame. The wax melted away and puddled, refusing to cool. She wanted his hands all over her again, and it was driving her wild.

She wouldn't beg this time. She wanted him to beg.

She would make him.

"I'm not wearing a dress," she pointed out.

"You're not wearing much of anything and damned if that helps."

She smiled. "But I do have a bed with silk sheets."

"And you want me to mess them up?"

"Don't you get it?" she challenged. "You can shred my sheets, for all I care."

A slow grin worked its way across the forbidding line of his mouth. "You are, far and away, the most bewitching woman I know."

She closed her hands over the knot of her towel, untying it. Letting it fall to her feet, she grabbed him by the hand. "You know what's better than flowers?"

"What?"

"That."

Chapter Thirteen

The room was dark. The sheets were blue. Their skin was damp and bare. She clung to him. Afraid she'd see all the dark and treacherous ridges of his desire, he touched her gently, feathering his hands in and out of her curves.

She rained kisses over him as she braced her hands on either side of him. "It's your turn to tell me."

"What?" Indulgent, he blindly traced the raised surface of a mole on her navel.

"How you like to be touched."

He chuckled, then stopped swiftly when she closed her mouth over his nipple. It tautened and grew pebbly. The skin at the small of his back drew up tight and goose bumps took over. She would drive him over the edge.

He rolled over her, pinning her to the sheet. Taking her hand, he moved it between them.

Her gaze didn't stray from his in the dark as he showed her how to stroke him. How to drive him over the edge—a firm-handed hold, a deep-seated stroke, slow to start, then quickening.

She kissed him as he let her take control, curling his hand into the sheet. He breathed hot against her mouth.

"More," she told him.

Something like a growl leaped from his throat as he took

her wrist. Taking her hand away, he turned it up against the pillow over her head. "Not yet." He thought about his wallet on the pool deck. Out in the cold. "Damn it."

She pointed to the nightstand. "Top drawer."

Turning her loose for a second, he pulled out the drawer. Relief whistled out of him. "Were you a Boy Scout, Pearl? Because you prepare like one." He tore the corner off the wrapper with his teeth.

She snatched it from him, then shoved his hands away when he tried to fight her for it. "Lay still, hard-ass," she said none-too-gently.

Not only did he obey. He laughed deeply and fully. Then choked when she took her time rolling the condom into place, drawing out his needs. Her eyes glowed at him in the dark, watchful.

"I'm not sorry you're not a hero," she told him. "Or a prince."

"That's good," he said helplessly. He tugged her back to him when she was done. Then he flipped their positions, so she was beneath him. He turned her knee outward with his. "Because I'd hate to disappoint you, like all those other bastards."

He slid home. Her nails dug into the bed of his shoulder blades. They scraped as he took her through the first glide.

It wasn't soft. When she bit her lip, he wondered if he should be.

She has silk sheets, you meatball, he thought. *Of course she wants it soft.*

She sighed, tracing the line of his vertebrae with her fingertips. "Then don't stop."

He lost himself and didn't look back.

She was perfect. The way she held on. The way she met him stroke for stroke. The way she pressed her heels to the bed and said his name. He forgot why they shouldn't be together as she pulsed around him and her fingers found his, clinging.

Raising them above both their heads, he wove them together like a basket. He took her mouth as he tripped toward the edge and flung himself over like a man on fire.

He fell hard, tumbled end over end and face-planted.

Had that coming, he thought. The landing wasn't any softer or safer than their lovemaking. He lay panting, wreathed in sweat, tuning in slowly to the brush of her fingers through his hair.

"Noah?" she said, muted.

"Hmm?" he managed.

"Are you all right?"

He opened his eyes, saw the afterglow shining off her so brightly it made his eyes water.

She was so beautiful it made his eyes hurt.

He swallowed, still unable to catch his breath. "Why wouldn't I be?"

"You're shaking a little."

He took stock and felt the fine tremors in his joints. "I'll be all right. Just give me…"

He trailed off because she was caressing his face in soft, loving strokes that made him still.

Her eyes were all too blue in the dark.

His heart stuttered, banged, fired and drummed. And it hit him.

He'd never loved a woman. Naturally, it took him a minute.

It hit him like a Sherman tank going max speed, artillery firing.

He released her hands, sliding his away. Careful not to hurt her, he pulled out of the nest of her thighs before rolling to his back beside her.

She turned onto her side, skimming a kiss across the ridge of his shoulder. Laying her hand on his chest, she placed her head on the pillow and closed her eyes. "Stay."

It wasn't a question. Still, the answer was there before he could make himself think. "Yeah," he said.

"Your heart's still racing. Are you sure you're all right?"

He gathered her hand from its warm spot on his chest and pulled it away, up to his mouth. He kissed her knuckles to distract the both of them from what was happening inside him. "Pearl?"

"Yes?"

"Go to sleep."

She gave a little sigh. Her fingers played lightly through his beard until she dozed off and he lay awake—wide the hell awake—trying to fathom how far and fast he'd fallen.

LAURA BOLTED UPRIGHT in bed, alarmed at the sight of sunlight peeping at her from between the curtains and the sound of knocking from far away. "Oh, no," she said to Sebastian, who peered sleepily at her over his mustache of orange fur.

She slid out of bed, groping for the robe over the back of the purple wingback chair in the corner. She fumbled it on, tied the belt, then combed her fingers through her hair.

Scenting coffee like a bloodhound, she spotted the mug, still steaming, on the nightstand next to the framed portrait of her mother. There was a small scrap of paper next to it with Noah's handwriting.

L.,
Fulton called. I have to run. We'll talk later.
    Made you something. It's in the oven.
N.

The knock clattered again, louder this time, followed by Joshua's voice. Laura stuffed her feet into her slippers and padded quickly from the bedroom to the entry corridor.

When she snatched open the door, Joshua looked immensely relieved. "Ah, jeez, Laura. You had me worried."

"I'm fine," she blurted. "Sorry. I slept through my alarm."

Joshua gave her a puzzled once-over. "You never sleep in."

"I know," she said, frazzled. "I was up late and must have crashed hard."

"Noah spent the night here."

She shook her head automatically. "I don't know what—"

"Come on, ace." Joshua rolled his eyes. "I saw him head out just a few minutes ago."

"Oh." She cleared her throat and reached for it awkwardly. "It's not what it looks like."

His brows came together. "Why not? Haven't you two been together for six months?"

"I…" She caught back up and nodded, clutching the lapels of her robe together over her collarbone. "Yes. Yes, we have."

He lifted his hands. "Hey, I'm not judging. You say he makes you happy. I believe you."

"You took him running," she recalled.

Caught, he lifted both shoulders in a sheepish shrug. "Adam's idea."

"Oh, give me a break, Josh," she snapped. "I heard you were the pace car. I also heard you took him up the advanced hiking trail. Even Adam thought his legs were going to fall off."

Joshua pursed his lips. "It's not my fault I'm in better shape than everybody else."

She gave a half laugh. "If you'd believed me when I told you he makes me happy, would you have put Noah through his paces?"

"He kept up just fine."

He didn't sound pleased about the fact. "You like him."

"Maybe," Joshua said. "And he said something that scared the hell out of me."

"What?" she asked.

Joshua took a breath, rolled his shoulders back as if trying to dislodge tension and said, "He said he was here to keep you safe. He said you could be the next target of whoever killed Allison."

She shook her head. "Nothing's going to happen to me."

"That's what she thought, too," Joshua said. "I may be your brother, but I like that he's staying the night with you. I like that you have someone watching over you when Adam and I can't. Until the police find out who killed Allison, I'm willing to look the other way when Noah's around. Bonus points that he looks like he could scare off a grizzly."

She smiled. It wobbled around the edges. "You don't have to worry about me so much."

"That's the thing," he drawled. "As long as Steele's around, I worry less. Where'd he go, anyway?"

"Sedona," she said. "He had something to do there."

Joshua lifted his chin. "Right. Valentine's Day's tomorrow."

"Valentine's…" She shrieked and ran back into the house, leaving the door open for him. In the bedroom, she dressed quickly, did her hair and applied makeup faster than she ever had before.

How could she sleep in the day before the wedding?

She snatched the coffee off the nightstand and downed half of it as she eyed the cat still curled up at the foot of the bed. Normally, Sebastian woke her if she even thought about sleeping past her alarm. He required a prompt meal at the break of every day.

As she ventured into the kitchen, where she found Joshua pouring coffee from the pot into a mug of his own, she peered into the cat food bowl. The remnants of a feast were scattered across the bottom of the porcelain dish.

Noah had fed her cat? Stunned, she took the bowl to the sink to rinse it. Then she remembered the note. Turning to the oven, she pulled open the door.

One of her china plates sat in the center of the upper rack. She pulled it out and found a still-warm western omelet.

Joshua peered over her shoulder as she set it on the range. "That looks incredible."

"It smells incredible," she said in wonder.

Joshua was quiet for a moment. "You used to make us breakfast—Adam and me. After Mom died."

"Yes." She remembered.

Regret tinged his voice. "Nobody's ever made breakfast for you in return, have they?"

She didn't reply. The note had said Noah had had to run. But he'd made her coffee, fed Sebastian and thrown together a whole omelet?

The walls of her heart gave a mighty shake.

A fork clattered onto the range next to the plate. She turned to see Joshua grin. "Eat your heart out, ace."

THE MORNING MEETING wasn't quick, but it was concise. Laura let Adam lead, still reeling from her naughty night with Noah.

Alexis lingered after Adam called the meeting to an end and the other members of staff bustled out to prepare for the next day's event. "I did what you asked," she told Laura. "I called the number you tracked down. It was CJ Knight's cell phone."

"Did he answer?" Laura asked hopefully.

"I left a message." She took her phone from the pocket of her blazer. "He texted me a reply."

Laura tilted her head to read the phone's display.

Ms. Reed, I apologize for leaving Mariposa on short notice. Yes, I will keep my reservation for 2/16.

"He's coming," Laura said to Adam.

"That's good," he said with a nod. "Thank you, Alexis."

"Yes," Laura chimed in. And because she was so sick of withholding information from Alexis, Laura added, "Mr. Knight may have information."

"What kind of information?" Alexis asked, narrowing her eyes.

Adam cleared his throat, warning Laura to tread lightly.

"About Allison," Laura answered.

Alexis assessed them both. "You think he had something to do with what happened to her?"

"No," Laura said quickly. "But he departed Mariposa the next day. Police couldn't question him. It's possible he saw something or heard something that could lead police to the person responsible."

"That makes sense," Alexis allowed after a moment's contemplation.

"If you could avoid mentioning this to him when he arrives, that would be great," Adam added. "We need to let the police handle their investigation."

"Right," Alexis said.

Laura walked with her to the door of the conference room. "You'll see that the other concierges have their assignments as the wedding party filters in today?"

"I will," Alexis replied.

"I appreciate it," Laura told her.

"That was clever of you," Adam noted after Alexis had departed. "You didn't lead her to believe the police are considering Knight as a suspect."

"I want this to be over," she blurted. "I hate hiding things from the people I care about. Alexis. Josh. Tallulah."

"This was your idea, Lou."

"I know," she said with a wince. "I didn't think it through."

"You were thinking about Allison," he discerned.

She nodded, silently knitting her arms over her stomach. It twisted with guilt.

Adam changed the subject quickly. "I just got a call from a friend of mine, Max Powell."

"Yes," she said, remembering. "The celebrity chef. You went to college together."

"Your attention to detail is one of your many strengths," he said fondly. "Max is taking a break from his TV show's filming schedule and wants to spend a few weeks at Mariposa."

"Let me know the date of his arrival," she replied. "I'll make sure he receives the best treatment."

"Thank you." A smile climbed over the planes of his face. It was a relief for her to see it and the light in his eyes. "The bride and groom check in at eleven?"

"Yes," she said. "Alexis and I will escort them to their bungalows. From there, she'll take them to their first spa treatment, and I'll check in with the parents and wedding party at Annabeth. They're surprising the happy couple with a prewedding margarita lunch. I've enlisted Valerie and her bar staff to help the kitchen staff with the drink rotation. I expect the celebration will go on for some time. I also expect every member of the wedding party to be tipsy when the minister arrives for the rehearsal on the golf course at five."

Adam thought about it. "Talk to the transportation staff. See if they can't have shuttles ready to drive them there. We don't want tequila behind the wheel of the golf carts."

"Good idea," she said.

"How's it going with Steele?"

Her smile froze. Joshua knew Noah had spent the night

with her. How long would it take for Adam to find out?
"It's going."

"When's he coming back from Sedona?"

"I'm unsure," she realized. "He didn't say, exactly."

"He may be keeping his distance."

"Why?"

He paused, planting his hand on the jamb. "Valentine's
Day comes with certain expectations."

She lowered her chin. "Are you speaking from experience?"

He evaded the question. "Let me know of any problems
between arrival and luncheon. I'm crunching numbers again
with the father of the bride."

"Have fun with that," she muttered.

SHE FELT LIKE she was walking on eggshells for the rest of
the day. Weddings and talk of murder mixed like oil and
water. She felt she and Alexis handled the wedding party's
questions about the investigation well, though.

Laura spotted Fulton lurking around the bungalows before
the intendeds' surprise luncheon. His badge and gun were
in full view. She wrung her hands and wondered what he
was up to and if Noah had returned to Mariposa with him.

Thinking about Noah was doing her no favors. Vivid,
distracting memories of the night before followed her everywhere. The things he had done to her…the things she
had done to him… The heat in her cheeks refused to leave.

Her body carried its own memories, its own markers. She
couldn't cross her legs without the tender ache of coupling
causing her nerve endings to remember. She'd worn a high-
necked blouse to ensure that the marks from Noah's beard
on her neck and chest were tucked away from prying eyes.

Wishing he were feeling the aches as he went about his
day, she hoped it was distracting him from his work as much

as it was distracting her, if not more. And she wondered if she'd left any guilty marks on him to remind him of their exploits.

By the luncheon, her thoughts turned to speculation. Had he really had to return to Sedona—or was he just avoiding her? She had no missed calls from him, no texts. Just the note he'd left with Sebastian and the empty omelet plate at home.

Was Adam right? Was Noah steering clear of Mariposa because he was allergic to Valentine's Day? Would she even see him tomorrow? She'd thought about calling him again to tell him what she'd learned about CJ Knight. To ask if he knew what Fulton was up to, but her doubts had given her other ideas.

"You look ready to tear the heads off those shrimp."

Laura glanced up from where she'd been hovering next to the buffet. Alexis had finished her to-do list in time to witness the end of the luncheon. Laura stepped away from the shrimp bowl. "Sorry."

"Don't apologize," Alexis said, turning to angle herself toward the festivities. "I just thought you'd like to know your face says, 'Approach me and die.'"

Laura smiled a bit. "I'm in a weird headspace today," she admitted.

"Want to talk about it?" Alexis asked.

Did she ever. She wished she could confide everything to Alexis—the whole confusing fake relationship that didn't feel fake but might still be. She felt terrible for making her friend believe that she and Noah were actually... Wait, but weren't they? What did last night mean? Would Allison approve? Or would she hate what Laura was doing with the brother she'd adored?

Laura tried to think about what to say exactly. Something—anything—to make sense of her actions and his. "Noah spent the night last night."

Alexis arched a brow. "Did he?"

"Mmm."

She frowned. "Haven't you two done that before?"

Laura wanted to curse. "Yes." Fighting for an explanation, she continued. "But last night... Last night was..."

"Oh," Alexis said significantly. "What you're trying to say is last night, you and Noah had *the* night."

"Precisely," Laura replied.

"All right." Alexis grinned. "Now that you mention it, I do detect a strong afterglow."

"I'm...*glowing*?"

"Like a menorah."

Laura snorted a laugh and covered her mouth as Alexis folded her lips around a muted chuckle. It took them both a moment to contain themselves.

Laura sighed. "Allison lived for conversations like this."

"She did," Alexis said reminiscently. "She'd say these are the talks that keep us young."

Laura sobered. "Taco Tuesdays won't be the same."

"No," Alexis granted. "She would want us to keep doing it, though."

"Then we will," Laura determined. "After the memorial."

"When is the memorial? Have you spoken with her family?"

"A little." Every time she'd brought it up with Noah, he'd shut her out. She wasn't looking forward to having the same conversation again. "The coroner's office hasn't released her, so I don't think they've put burial plans into motion yet."

"Adam's coming," Alexis said swiftly. "And...good Lord. What is it with you Coltons and your collective wrath today?"

Laura glanced up and found Adam pushing toward her on fast-moving legs. His face wasn't friendly. Her stomach knotted.

"May we speak in private?" he asked.

"Of course," Laura said. She nodded to Alexis, who moved off to give them a moment to themselves.

Adam's eyelid twitched. "Josh tells me Steele was at your place this morning."

"He was," Laura replied.

"Alone. With you."

"Yes, Adam," she said, feeling weary.

"What are you doing?" he demanded.

"It wasn't supposed to happen like this," she began.

"Jesus, Laura." He pressed his fingers into his eyes before remembering himself. He glanced around and lowered his voice. "Are you buying into your own cover story? Is this all some fantasy you had to indulge?"

"No," she said, offended. "Of course not."

"He's not a rock star," he told her. "He's a cop."

"I know that!"

"And he's not actually in love with you!"

Ouch, she thought. Shaking off the strange pulse of hurt, she straightened her posture. "I know."

"Every bit of this with him is pretend," he went on, undeterred. "And you're setting yourself up to get hurt all over again."

"Stop it, Adam."

"I'm not going to let you get hurt again!"

"Please," she begged, eyes brimming with a sudden wave of hot tears. "I said stop."

He saw the tears and his expression darkened. "I'm not a violent man, Laura. You know this. But if he's making you do this, I swear—"

"It was me," she said. "I was the one who told him to stay. He didn't make me do anything. I wanted him."

His jaw loosened.

She shook her head. "Don't act so shocked. I'm a grown

woman. I choose who I go to bed with, just like Josh. I'm responsible for my own actions, just like you. If I get hurt, then that's my problem. Not yours."

"I have to watch," he said from the pit of his stomach. "I have to watch you pick up the pieces and move on. And it guts me every time."

She touched his arm. "It's going to be okay. I... I know what I'm doing."

"Are you sure about that?" he asked.

She wasn't, but she nodded. "I do."

He shook his head in disagreement. "You're always so careful. You're not considering the consequences from every angle."

"Maybe not." She could grant him that. "But ask me if I have any regrets."

"I think it's a little early for that," he considered.

"Do not talk to Noah about this," she said, knowing him. "I don't need you chasing him off like a coyote before—"

"Before what?" he challenged. "Before he shows you what kind of man he really is?"

"Don't pretend to know who he really is," she advised.

"Fine," he returned. "Then you shouldn't either." He turned and left her with the shrimp.

She looked around the tables, making sure no one had caught wind of the argument. She caught Alexis's sympathetic gaze from across the room and tried to erect a reassuring smile.

It slipped as she glanced toward the exit and saw Noah standing just outside the doors of the restaurant.

Chapter Fourteen

"Your stepmother made bail."

Laura nodded slowly. "We knew she would."

"You should prepare for whatever else she's planning," Noah cautioned. "I know her type. She's a schemer—a wrench in the system. She'll make trouble for Mariposa and your family again. I guarantee it."

Laura's brow furrowed. "I think you might be right."

"Fulton believes he has enough to close Allison's case by the end of the week."

Laura frowned. "How can he? There's not enough evidence to convict anyone. Is there?"

"No," he said.

"Then why the urgency?" she asked.

Noah shifted uncomfortably as the laughter from the open doors of Annabeth spilled out into the afternoon air. "I told you he was looking hard at Roger Ferraday. While I was at the station, I looked closer at his background and his son's." He showed her the folder in his hand. "Roger Ferraday has one DWI on his record. There were others that've been expunged because he's got money and power and he's got a high-priced lawyer who plays racquetball with judges and prosecutors alike." He opened the folder and angled it toward her. "This is his son's rap sheet."

Her hand touched her mouth as she read the felonies and misdemeanors. "How is he free to come and go as he pleases with a record like this?"

"Papa Ferraday flew his bouncing baby boy to Arizona on their private jet because whispers of date rape and drug abuse are getting the attention of people who don't care who he or his lawyer are," Noah revealed. "There's talk of locking Dayton Ferraday up for good."

"How does this tie back to Allison?" she asked.

Noah didn't want to spell it out for her. "Dayton has used fentanyl at least once in a case of date rape. The victim was a minor and charges were dropped, thanks to Roger's influence. But the connection's there."

She stared at him, distress painting her. "You think Allison's death had something to do with...rape?"

"Fentanyl is a date rape drug," he confirmed. "Come on, Laura. Think. For what other reason would her killer inject her?"

This time, both hands rose to cover her face. She stood still for a moment. Then her shoulders shuddered.

Noah wanted to take it all away. The likeliest truth was too ugly for him to process. He didn't want her to have to do so as well. "Hey," he said, sliding his palm over her shoulder. When she didn't raise her head, he rubbed circles over her back. "Hey, it's okay."

He didn't know why he said it. Nothing about this was okay. But he needed her to be. If she broke down, he didn't know what he would do. The confluence of rage and violence he felt for whoever had hurt his sister didn't mix well with a lack of self-control.

Laura had to know, he reminded himself. If there was a rapist at Mariposa, no one was safe. Not the maids. Not the concierges, front desk clerks, masseuses... Most especially not its queen bee, who drew playboys like flies and slept alone a heartbeat away from where Allison was killed.

The need to protect her whistled in his ears. He wanted to get her out of there, away from the resort. The danger was too close to her.

Sweeping the soft strands of her hair aside, he lowered his lips to the nape of her neck. His anger and torment over Allison lived shoulder to shoulder with his panic over what he felt for Laura, his need for her. He felt too small to contain everything inside him. Something was going to have to give soon or he would explode.

"I can't believe..." She took several shallow breaths, trying to get the words out. "...someone would do that to her... take advantage of her like that... Did he mean to kill her or did he just...want to have his way with her?"

"Either way, the son of a bitch is going to spend a long time behind bars. Unless Fulton rushes it, screws it up, and the guy gets off on a technicality. I have to make this right."

Even as her eyes flashed with tears, her voice was firm. "We both do."

He'd denied it for the better part of the day. He'd held himself back from the truth of what he felt. But he felt himself fumbling over that blind, terrifying cliff again. He felt himself go over the edge. Fear chased him, but he couldn't not see her. He couldn't stop feeling what he felt. In what he hoped was a perfunctory motion, he lifted his hand to her face to wipe the tears with his thumb.

Her eyes went soft, and he knew he'd failed. "Thank you for the coffee and omelet this morning."

"It was nothing," he lied.

"You fed my cat."

He had. "I didn't want him to wake you."

"You were trying to sneak out?"

"I told you. I got called into the station."

"Adam knows about us. About last night."

"You told him?" he asked incredulously.

"Josh did. He saw you leaving my bungalow this morning."

He rocked back on his heels. "I'm surprised I made it through the gate."

"Do you still want to talk to CJ Knight?"

He nodded. "Someone needs to."

"He's returning to Mariposa on the sixteenth," she told him. "Looks like you're going to get your shot."

"What's he booked for—spa, golf, excursions?"

"I'll have to check with the front desk," she replied.

"Find me an in," he told her, "and I'll find out if he's Allison's killer."

"I will," she promised. She looked across the grounds, past the pool to the tumble of rocks on the far horizon. The sun was low. It fanned across her lashes, and he saw they were still wet. Something inside him constricted. "Do you want me to keep Bungalow Fifteen available for you?" she asked.

She could smell the distance he was trying to erect between them. "Yes," he said, hating that he was too spineless to spend the night in her bed…too terror-struck to put himself at her mercy again.

He'd be a fool to let her play with his heart again.

"Very well," she said stiffly.

Before she could veer back through the doors to the restaurant, he took her by the elbow. Without thinking, he pulled her in.

As always, he went a step further. He kissed her. Her arms linked underneath his. They fanned across his back, and she made a noise that flipped his restraint like a wrestler's hold.

He opened his mouth to hers, recapturing the heat from last night. He let it coil around him. It was as if he'd never left.

He tipped his head up and away from hers. Her nails scraped across his scalp, making his mind go dangerously blank.

"Last night, you left a path of little reminders across my skin," she told him. "I've spent the whole day hating you for it."

Last night, she'd drawn little maps across his soul in carbon black. He'd spent the better part of the day trying to come up with enough elbow grease to erase them. He'd failed miserably.

"Hate me, Laura," he invited. "It's better for both of us." He touched her shoulders and held her away from him. "I'll see you."

Her expression folded, but her eyes glinted with promise. "Yes, you will."

BETWEEN THE WEDDING and resort operations, Laura stayed busy. Too busy to think about the man in Bungalow Fifteen or the path between his bungalow and hers that, as promised, remained scant on foot traffic over the next few days. No one questioned why they didn't spend Valentine's Day together. The wedding was an all-day spectacle that had her limping back to her house well after hours on Saturday. She found Sebastian waiting for her there alone, demanding Fancy Feast and cuddles on his terms. *Just like a man*, she thought as she juggled a martini and Sebastian's large, round form in her favorite corner on the couch.

She ran into Roger Ferraday a handful of times on Sunday and struggled to maintain her demeanor. She skirted Adam, his warnings and assumptions.

Most of which she had to admit were true. She had gotten carried away by the illusion of her and Noah. But not rock star Noah. The real Noah—the one she'd thought she knew. And maybe she *was* setting herself up to get hurt.

Maybe she was her mother's daughter. Maybe she sought the one person she knew would never let her stand beside him without pretense.

When Tallulah tapped on the open door of Laura's office in L Building on Monday morning, Laura couldn't have been more relieved to see her. She closed the proposal Adam had prepared for her about a new line of more efficient bulk washing machines he wanted to splurge on for housekeeping. "Right on time, as always," she greeted her.

Tallulah stepped into the office and closed the door. "Were you expecting me?"

"No," Laura said, propping her chin on her hands as she watched Tallulah settle into one of the faux cowhide chairs across the desk. "But your visits are always welcome."

"You look tired, Laura," Tallulah murmured, studying her.

"Things have been busy," Laura said by way of excuse.

"Yes, they have," Tallulah agreed.

"Do you want to have coffee with me?" Laura asked, already reaching for the Keurig she'd tucked lovingly into the corner with mugs with the Mariposa logo.

"I would," Tallulah admitted, "but I have something I need to speak with you about."

"I'm all ears," Laura said, easing back into her chair.

Tallulah folded her hands carefully in her lap. "It's about Bella."

"The maid?"

"Yes," Tallulah said. "She came to me this morning in tears and handed in her resignation."

Laura blinked in surprise. "I'm sorry to hear that."

"So was I," Tallulah stated. "She's wonderful at her job, and she's a good girl."

"Did she give you a reason for leaving?" Laura asked.

"Not at first," Tallulah said. Her dark eyes flickered. "But when pressed, the story came out."

"'Story'?" That didn't sound good.

"She says she was assaulted," Tallulah said quickly, as if in a hurry to get the words out. "By a guest."

Laura stiffened. "Assaulted?"

"Yes," Tallulah replied. "It happened Friday, and she didn't tell anyone. She didn't tell me."

Laura wrapped her hand over the edge of the desk. "Tallulah, what kind of assault was it? Did she say?"

Tallulah's eyes grew wide. "Oh, Laura. She said she was manhandled, sexually. She was cleaning Bungalow Three because she thought the guests there were out for the day and she was attacked."

"Bungalow Three." Laura bit down on the urge to scream. "That's where—"

"The Ferradays," Tallulah confirmed with a nod.

"Which one?" Laura asked and heard her voice drop low where anger coiled.

"The younger," Tallulah answered. "And after what she told me, I'm in a mind to march down there and pour boiling water over his head."

Laura pushed back from the desk. She stood. "We need to report this."

"She doesn't want to involve police," Tallulah said. "I could hardly get her to talk to me."

"You don't understand," Laura said as she picked up her phone and dialed Noah's number. "This has happened before."

"With the maids?" Tallulah asked, shocked.

"No," Laura said. "Back in Connecticut, where the Ferradays live when they're not here."

"You knew this?" Tallulah stared at her, aghast.

Laura hated herself for it. "He's already under investigation. That's why his father brought him here. Probably in hopes that things would quiet in his absence." She swallowed hard. "Tallulah. I didn't think he'd do something like this. I'm so sorry."

Tallulah nodded in a vague, distracted motion.

Laura wrestled with her guilt. The call went to voicemail and she redialed. "Come on, Noah. Pick up."

"Why are you calling him?" Tallulah queried.

Laura knew she couldn't explain. She waited through a second procession of rings, then all but growled when it went to voicemail. "Noah. It's Laura. I need you to call me back as soon as you get this. It's urgent." She dropped the phone back to the cradle. "Where is Bella now?"

"I had Mato drive her home," Tallulah admitted. "She was too upset to drive herself."

"We'll need her to make a statement," Laura said. "She's already told her story to you. Do you think she'll do so again if you're there with her?"

"Maybe," Tallulah offered after a moment's thought. "But she was adamant, Laura. No police."

"She may not have a choice." Laura headed toward the door. "Can you call Roland and have him meet me at Bungalow Three? I'm going to have a word with Roger Ferraday."

"Ms. Colton." Roger Ferraday grinned winningly when he found Laura on his doorstep. "This is a surprise."

"Mr. Ferraday," she greeted him. Roland hadn't arrived yet, but she'd knocked on the door of Bungalow Three regardless. "Is your son here?"

"Dayton?" Roger gave her a puzzled look. "Why?"

"There's been a security breach. We're just checking to make sure all guests are present and accounted for."

"Security breach?" Roger's smile tapered. "Should I be concerned?"

"We don't believe so," she blurted. "If you could assure me your son is in residence, please…"

"He is," Roger assured her. "I think he's still in bed."

"When was the last time you saw him?" Laura asked.

"You're scaring me, Ms. Colton," Roger said, visibly paling.

"Have you checked on him this morning?" she asked. "Are you sure he's in his bedroom?"

"I'll go check," Roger said, and he left the door open as he fumbled away. He called his son's name, rushing.

Laura took the open door as an invitation and stepped inside the bungalow. She smelled men's cologne and take-out. The table was crowded with to-go containers, and she spied a pile of wet towels through the door to the pool deck. Housekeeping hadn't come through yet.

Thank goodness, she thought.

"Here he is," Roger announced with obvious relief as he returned to the living area with his son. "He was sleeping in, just as I told you."

Laura eyed the slouch-framed boy with a messy lid of black curls. He peered at her, unhappy to have been roused from sleep.

"What's the big deal?" he asked in a baritone. He was of medium height, skinny, but she saw deceptive strength in the long arms that hung from the sleeves of his oversized Ed Hardy T-shirt.

If she searched his room, would she find fentanyl?

Had he killed Allison?

She unscrewed her jaw so that she could speak. Fury tried to bite down on the words. "I'm going to have to ask you to stay here."

"Me? What did I do?"

She glared at him. "You know exactly what you did."

His eyes narrowed, and he took a step forward. "Are you accusing me of something?"

Betrayal and disbelief worked across Roger's features. "You...tricked me?"

"Our security team will be here any moment," she stated. "They'll take your son into their custody and await police."

"Dayton didn't do anything," Roger said with an expansive gesture. "Listen, Ms. Colton. I'm sure there's something I can do, some arrangement we can come to—"

"I'm afraid not, Mr. Ferraday," she said with a shake of her head. Where was Roland?

"In that case, I'd like to speak with your brother," Roger requested. She could see sweat forming on his upper lip. She noted how he'd planted himself between her and Dayton. "Adam, isn't it?"

"You're lucky I'm the one handling this matter," she informed him. "Neither of my brothers would wait for Security to haul your son out."

"You know." Dayton spoke up, inspecting Laura. His pupils were as black as water beetle wings. "You're a smart-mouthed bitch."

"Shut up, Dayton!" Roger snapped. "I'm handling this!"

"No," Laura said, staring back at Dayton. "Go ahead."

"Okay," Dayton said, and his shoulders squared. "You're a big, loud, smart-mouthed bitch and you're going to eat your words. Just like the rest of them."

She took a step forward, drawing herself up to her full height. "You're right about one thing, Dayton. I'm a really big, really loud, really smart bitch. And I'm going to make sure you never hurt another woman again."

Roger held his hands up. "Ms. Colton, please. I'm sure we can solve this unfortunate matter together. There's no need to involve Security or the police. Dayton and I will leave your resort quietly. Just name your price."

"Bribery won't work here," she told him.

He had the nerve to smile. "Only because I haven't named the right price."

"Maybe I haven't made myself clear," Laura said, raising her voice. "Your son is a rapist and, possibly, a murderer, and he's leaving Mariposa in handcuffs."

"A murderer?" Roger repeated, smile fleeing. His face reddened, and he advanced on her. "That's a lie!"

"Yeah," Dayton spit. "What the hell?"

"Get out!" Roger shouted at her.

She heard the knock on the door. "Ms. Colton?" Roland called as he stepped into the open entryway. "Are you all right?"

Roger Ferraday's arm snaked out, hooking her around the throat. The other pinned her arms to her sides.

"What are you doing?" she cried out.

"Back off!" Roger warned Roland. "Back the hell off or I'll hurt her!"

Roland's Taser was already in hand. He didn't back away. "Mr. Ferraday," he said, focused on the face next to Laura's. "You're making a big mistake here. The police are right behind me. If they see you've taken Ms. Colton hostage, you'll be charged with holding her against her will. And the accommodations at the state penitentiary lack the luxury you're accustomed to."

Laura could smell the fear and sweat pouring off Roger. It dampened his shirt and hers as he pressed his front to her back. It slicked across her ear as his cheek buffered against it. Holding herself still, she kept calm, knowing her fright might encourage him to carry this through.

The tension shattered when the glass sliding door exploded. Glass rained, skidding across the floor, and a dark figure darted through the opening, gun between his hands. "Hands in the air!" he yelled.

Laura barely had time to register the lethal focus on

Noah's face before Roger shoved her aside. Her boot heel slid across a loose piece of glass, and she went flying. She reached out to grab the table's edge, but she was going too fast. Her head arced down to meet it and she was helpless to stop her momentum.

Little white lights broke across her vision. Then the world came rushing back to her as she met the floor, little glass shards poking through her blouse. She reached for her head as pain split her temples.

When she pulled her hand away, blood smeared her fingers.

Chapter Fifteen

It was well after dark when Noah returned to Mariposa. He wasn't able to go back to Bungalow Fifteen. Not after going several rounds with Roger and Dayton Ferraday at the police station.

He hadn't accepted Captain Crabtree's orders that Fulton be the one to question them. He'd gone about the task himself with grim determination.

Roger Ferraday would do time. The Coltons' lawyer, Greg Sumpter, had shown up with Adam on Laura's behalf to demand that he be brought up on assault charges while Joshua had escorted Laura to the hospital to get checked out.

The younger Ferraday wouldn't get away from rape accusations this time. Bella, the maid, had changed her mind about not testifying after Adam and Tallulah had spoken to her personally. She was traumatized and scared but had seemed determined to put Dayton away once she found out about the other girls he had assaulted in Connecticut.

Fulton, certain Dayton was Allison's killer, had Bungalow Three searched, confident fentanyl would be recovered from the scene.

Instead, small quantities of Ecstasy were found in Dayton's mattress.

When Noah had leaned harder on Roger, the man cracked

under the pressure and admitted the reason he had no alibi for the night of Allison's homicide was he had found the bulk of his son's drug stash and the two of them had snuck out under the cover of night to dump it on the hiking trails.

By the end of the interview, Noah had wanted to lock Roger up on more than assault. He'd expressed no regret about holding Laura against her will or harming her, and he'd blamed Bella and the other girls for his son's criminal behavior.

Noah had thought of little more than punching the bastard in the face. But he'd known Crabtree was watching through the two-way glass, anticipating the moment Noah lost his cool.

He'd kept it—but only just.

Now he trudged up the walk to Laura's place. The door opened before he could get to it and Joshua, Adam, Tallulah and Alexis stepped out together. They stopped talking collectively when they spotted him.

Tallulah reached for his hand. "Laura's okay. It's good you're here. She doesn't need to be alone tonight."

The feeling of her hand in his felt foreign, but it was pleasantly warm. "You had dinner with her?"

"You weren't exactly here to keep her company," Joshua said in accusation.

Adam surprised Noah when he argued, "Go easy on the man, Josh. I'm sure he has his reasons."

When the four of them looked at him expectantly, Noah said, "I had to go up to Flagstaff. I got delayed there and didn't get Laura's message until she'd left the hospital."

"That was hours ago," Joshua pointed out. "Flagstaff's half an hour away."

Noah swallowed. "I'm sorry."

Alexis eyed the bag in his hand. "Do you come bearing gifts?"

He thought of what was in the bag. A blip of panic made him itch for something more—a better offering. "Yes."

"Good," Alexis noted. "There's no concussion, but doctors advised her not to imbibe for the next twenty-four hours."

"Noted," he said.

"Good night to you, Noah," Tallulah murmured before walking away. Alexis followed her. Joshua said nothing as he moved off.

That left Adam. "Anything you have to say to my sister can wait until the morning."

Noah searched for the right words. "I'd like to see her."

Adam studied him. "You were good with Bella. You made giving her statement easier."

"So did you," Noah said, "and Tallulah."

"Roland told me what happened at Bungalow Three," Adam explained. "He told me how Roger had her in a choke hold and how you apprehended him."

"She got hurt," Noah noted dully. The scene was on a loop in his mind. Ferraday shoving Laura away to save his own ass, her skidding into the table, knocking her head against it and falling to the floor, bleeding.

"I've asked Roland not to reveal your real identity," Adam pointed out. "Not until your investigation comes to a close."

"Thank you," Noah said.

"Laura says Dayton Ferraday may have killed Allison."

Noah shook his head. "He and his father confirmed each other's real alibis for the night in question."

"So you're back to square one?"

"Not if you tell me CJ Knight checked in this morning," Noah told him.

"He did," Adam confirmed.

Noah breathed a small sigh of relief. "That's something."

Adam gave him a tight nod. He started to go, then stopped. "Go easy on Laura. She puts up a good front for all of us, but she's raw tonight."

"I will." He waited until Adam had gone before knocking. He lingered for two minutes. When she didn't answer, he tried the door and muttered something foul when he found she hadn't locked it behind the others.

"Laura?" he called through the house as he stepped inside.

The door closed behind him. Everything was quiet, eerily so.

"Laura!" he shouted.

He checked the bedroom. Her sheets hadn't been turned down. The door to the connected bathroom was open, and the light was off. He moved to the kitchen. Five plates and cups were stacked in the dish drain next to the sink. The couch in the living room was empty except for the unimpressed tabby who flicked his bushy tail at him. "Where is she?" he asked.

Sebastian lifted a paw and started to clean it.

"You're no help," Noah groaned. Then a movement on the other side of the glass caught his eye. He peered out. The steam of the heated pool rose to meet the cool night. In the blue glow of the pool lights, he could see arms cutting across the water like sharks.

He slid open the door, similar to the one he'd thrown a brick through earlier. Walking out on the patio, he watched her lap the pool four times without stopping, hardly coming up for air in between.

She cycled through freestyle, then backstroke, butterfly, then breaststroke. By the time she stopped, finally, he was ready to go in after her.

She gripped the edge of the pool, gasping. He saw the shaking in her limbs.

"Are you trying to hurt yourself?" he asked.

She jerked in surprise. "What are you doing here?"

He stared at the goose egg on her forehead. She'd taken off the bandage. There were no stitches, but bruises webbed across her brow.

As he surveyed the damage to her face, the fury came sweeping back in stark detail, and it crushed him.

She looked away. Using her arms, she pulled herself from the water.

He gripped her underneath the shoulder, helping her to her feet.

"I've got it," she said, taking a step back.

He dropped his arm. "Sure you do."

She reached for the towel she'd set on the nearby lounge chair. She patted her hair dry, then her face, hissing when she pressed the towel to the bump on her head.

He reached for her even as she turned away to dry her arms and legs. Then she wrapped the towel around her middle and knotted it as he'd seen her do before. Finished, she bypassed him for the door.

He tailed her, feeling foolhardy. "I should've punched him," he grumbled.

"That would have been counterproductive," she muttered. "Isn't your CO scrutinizing you?"

"Why did you go into that bungalow?" he asked. He'd needed to ask from the moment he'd found out she'd gone. "You thought Dayton Ferraday killed Allison, and you went to confront him and his father? Why?"

"It's my fault," she said. "He could only assault Bella because I didn't warn Housekeeping or others that he was a predator. I should've told them to steer clear of Bungalow Three. I went because I wanted to be the one to tell Dayton Ferraday that he will spend the rest of his life paying for what he's done."

"Ferraday didn't kill Allison," Noah told her.

She stopped. "What?"

"Father and son gave their real alibis," Noah explained weightily. "They check out."

"But the date rape…the fentanyl…his attack on Bella… It all fits."

"Small traces of Ecstasy were recovered from Bungalow Three," Noah went on. "There's no sign of fentanyl."

"What does that mean?"

"It means CJ Knight is now the chief suspect in this investigation. But that's for me to worry about. You can't do this to me again. You can't go charging into a suspect's bungalow and try to take matters into your own hands. Whoever killed Allison will most likely kill you."

"I am not Allison!" she said, raising her voice.

"The man had you in a choke hold."

"I was doing my job."

"So was my sister," he reminded her. Unable to stop himself, he reached out to feather his touch across the first stain of bruising. "It's starting to hurt. Isn't it? And he scared you. That's the reason you were doing laps out there. Because you were alone long enough to feel the fear again." He pressed his cheek to hers, felt the shaking in her limbs and pulled her close, not caring that she was wet and he wasn't.

When he lifted her into his arms, she protested. He quieted her by touching his mouth to the rim of her jaw. "It's a soak in the tub for you. Then bed."

"You sound like Tallulah."

"Do you listen to her?"

"Sometimes." She pillowed her head on his shoulder, giving in as he sidestepped through the door to the bedroom so she wouldn't catch her toes on the jamb. There, he set her on the wingback chair.

"Take off your suit."

"Do you want me to dance for you when I'm done?" she drawled.

He ignored that and went into the bathroom to draw her a bath, throwing in some Epsom salts. When he came back for her, she was naked and shivering still. He bundled her up again, took her into the bathroom and lowered her into the water.

She let out a sharp breath as she sank in.

"Too hot?" he asked.

"No." She tipped her head back against the lip. "No. It's perfect." She flicked a glance at him when he lingered. "I'm not going to drown."

Reaching into his back pocket, he took out the little bag he'd brought to her door. "I bought this while I was in town."

She eyed the box he held with mixed levels of curiosity. "For me?"

When she didn't reach out, he opened it himself. "I found it while I was in Sedona." On a small cushion, a delicate strand of gold held a single pearl teardrop.

Her eyes rushed up to meet his. "You bought this—for me?"

He bit his tongue, trying to come up with the right thing to say. "It's not flowers."

"No," she said.

"Or dinner. But it looked…right."

She only stared.

He groaned at her reticence. "If you don't want it, I can take it back. I've got the receipt right here—"

"Shut up," she said without heat. "Just…shut up and put it on me."

She straightened, her shoulders rising above the water. Lifting her hair, she turned.

He took the necklace out of the box, unclasped it and lowered it over her head. Securing it at the base of her neck, he eased back as she turned to him again. The pearl rested just above her sternum in the dip between her breasts. She touched it. "How does it look?" she asked.

He shook his head. "It looks like I brought feldspar to an empress."

She leaned over the tub wall, meeting his mouth with her own, silencing him and his doubts.

He brought his hand up to her face. *Easy*, he told himself, feeling the quaking in his bones again. Not fury this time. The fear was there and the need, too. Always.

She pulled away. Her eyes flashed blue. "Stay with me?"

It was impossible to argue. "That's a hard yes."

Her smile was a tender curve meant for him alone as she reclined again against the tub wall and gripped his fingers on the ledge.

He watched over her until the water cooled. Then he helped her dry and dress for bed.

Back in her sheets, he held her until he felt her soften into repose. It took a long time to follow, but when he did, he had his nose buried in her hair and his arm tight around her middle, unwilling to let her go in the silent, anonymous hours between night and day.

Chapter Sixteen

Noah was relieved when Laura took Tuesday off after waking with a fierce headache. It took everything he had not to stay and take care of her. He made her coffee and breakfast and fed Sebastian again. As he ate over her sink so he wouldn't get crumbs on her spotless countertops, the cat bumped his cheek against Noah's ankle, then, purring, started weaving figure eights around his boots.

Noah watched, puzzled. When his plate was clean, he scooped the feline up in one hand. "It's your turn to watch her," he informed him as he carried the tabby back to the bedroom where Laura dozed. "Don't screw it up."

His phone rang. Sebastian twisted, unhappy as Noah juggled him to dig the device out of his pocket. Setting Sebastian down, he swiped at the long strands of cat hair clinging to the front of his shirt before answering.

"Steele," Adam greeted him.

"Colton," Noah replied just as flatly.

"I have a proposition."

Noah braced himself. "I'm listening."

"I don't expect Laura to come to work today."

"Damn right," Noah said.

"I'll be stepping in for her," Adam told him, "to help with the investigation."

"Thanks," Noah mused, "but I'm good."

"Meet me near the paddock in an hour," Adam said, ignoring Noah's refusal. "Dress for a riding excursion."

The line clicked. Noah looked at his phone and saw that Adam had ended the call. "Sure, cupcake," he muttered, sliding the phone back into his pocket.

An hour later, Noah said, "You know, I don't think me and you kissing is going to have the same effect on people as Laura and I do."

"Just once," Adam said mildly, "I'd like to see you go an entire day without vexing me."

"Not likely," Noah responded. He adjusted the Stetson he wore low over his brow as they walked to the paddock together. "You're sure Knight signed on for this thing today?"

"Yes." The corner of Adam's mouth curled. "But if he backs out at the last minute, I won't lose sleep knowing you're Josh's problem. Not mine."

"You realize I know how the internet works, right?" Noah said. "If baby brother abandons me like a lost calf on the trail, I'm dropping a one-star review for Mariposa on Tripadvisor."

Adam's smile morphed. "You wouldn't."

"How do you figure?"

"Because what you've done for your sister these last few weeks tells me you're a man of honor," Adam admitted. "If you have as much regard for Laura as she has for you, you'll leave Mariposa alone when this is all over."

Noah scowled, eating up the ground with long strides. He could smell the horses, the saddle leather… He could hear the chink of cinches and stirrups and the nickers and snorts of the animals as the guides and riders readied them for the long drive ahead.

All he'd wanted to do over the last few weeks was find Allison's killer. He hadn't considered what would come after. Once the perpetrator was caught and Noah's actual reasons for being at the resort were revealed, would he be welcome there?

He couldn't think about Laura and what he wanted with her when this was all over. He couldn't think about losing her. Leaving her.

"I know you spent the night with her again last night," Adam revealed.

Noah felt a muscle in his jaw tic. "She was in pain."

"So you didn't sleep with her?"

He chose his next words carefully. "I slept next to her." At the sight of Adam's grimace, Noah nearly gave in to his own frustration. "I know the hospital said she didn't have a concussion. I wanted to make sure." He'd *needed* to make sure. "She didn't need to be left on her own. Ferraday didn't just hurt her. He scared her." And for that, Noah wanted to drive back to Sedona and toss the man across his holding cell.

"She shouldn't have been there to begin with."

Finally, something the two of them could agree on. Noah saw the knot of people in the horse paddock and scanned for his mark. "Where is he?"

"There," Adam said with a jerk of his chin to the left.

Noah had memorized the file on CJ Knight. He knew the man was twenty-seven, approximately five-eleven, one hundred and eighty pounds, with brown hair and blue eyes. Noah also knew he was unmarried and that he resided primarily in Los Angeles as an up-and-coming film actor.

CJ removed his cowboy hat, so the wind tousled his wavy locks. Under his plaid button-down shirt and jeans, he had the trim body of a gym rat.

Like a true actor, he'd dressed the part for the day's trail-riding adventure, led by Knox and Joshua. Noah's goal was to ride next to CJ and get to know him and hope Joshua didn't have other ideas—throwing Noah into a gorge, for example.

Among the others assembled, Noah recognized Kim Blankenship and her husband, Granger. He remembered the initials on Allison's refrigerator schedule: *CJK*, *DG* and *KB*.

Maybe today Noah could knock out two birds with one stone. Was Kim Blankenship *KB* or did Noah need to look harder at Mariposa's cowboy, Knox Burnett?

He needed to find the identity, too, of the mysterious *DG*.

Joshua spotted Noah and Adam on the approach and he nodded in their direction. "The gang's all here. Where's your riding gear, Adam?"

"I'm not staying," Adam stated. Everyone fell quiet as he brought his hands together. "I'd just like everyone to know that Joshua and Knox are the two best guides in Red Rock Country. You're in expert hands today." He patted Noah on the shoulder, either in assurance or warning. "Come on. I'll introduce you."

Noah walked with him to CJ Knight and the mare that had been chosen for him from the stable. "It's good to have you back, Mr. Knight," Adam said.

CJ shook Adam's offered hand. "It's good to be back. I'm sorry I left with so little notice before. I got called back to LA without warning."

"Is everything all right there?"

"It was a callback on an audition," CJ said. "And it wound up getting canceled, anyway. I wish I'd never left."

"Let us know if we can do anything to make your stay with us better this time," Adam replied. He turned to Noah. "I don't believe you've met Noah Steele. His band Fast Lane's making a splash. He'll be riding out today, too."

"Nice to meet you," CJ said, reaching out to grip Noah's extended hand.

Noah pasted on a smile. "Likewise. Have you done this before?"

"A few times," CJ said. "I love Red Rock Country. Are you new to trail riding?"

"It's been a long time," Noah admitted. "I hope I can keep up."

"Knox normally rides behind with the stragglers," CJ informed him. "Josh keeps pace, but most of the time it's leisurely, so we can enjoy the view."

A man flanked CJ. He had light hair and dark eyes and an unrelaxed posture that looked almost unnaturally upright. "Doug DeGraw," he introduced, shaking Noah's hand. "I'm CJ's manager."

"Noah Steele," Noah returned. He glanced down at the man's feet. "I believe you're wearing the wrong shoes for this."

CJ chuckled as Doug looked down at the business-like brogues he had donned. He patted Doug on the back. "Doug's not used to riding." He lowered his voice and said to his manager, "I told you I'd loan you a pair of boots. And you didn't have to come. You hate horses."

"I'll be fine," Doug said with a slight wince, looking around at the bay he had been assigned. "I'm told fresh country air does the body good."

"I can vouch for that," Adam agreed. "I'd better be getting back to L Building. Enjoy yourselves." He exchanged a significant look with Noah before departing.

Knox brought around a familiar horse that had been saddled. "Mr. Steele. You remember Penny?"

Noah couldn't help but smile as he raised his hand to the filly's mouth for a nuzzle. "I do. Is she mine for the day?"

"She is," Knox said. "She's new to the trails, but she's done well in practice. Want to give her a shot?"

"Absolutely," Noah said as Penny blew her whiskered breath across his palm. He took the reins. "Thanks. Hey, by any chance, do you know when a new yoga instructor will be hired? I've got this pain between my shoulders blades, and I really need a stretch."

Sadness lay heavy on Knox's face. "I don't, no. I'm not sure management's even thought about it. You could ask Laura."

"I will," Noah returned. "Sorry I brought it up."

"It's okay," Knox replied. "Allison hasn't even been buried yet. It's hard thinking about a replacement for her."

"It's a shame she died," CJ added. "I liked Allison. I'd just started private lessons with her."

"Oh?" Noah said, feigning surprise. "I didn't know she offered that sort of thing."

"We got one session in before I had to leave," CJ explained. "I didn't hear of her passing until it hit the news. She was so full of life. I don't understand how anyone could hurt her."

"Are you talking about the yoga instructor?" a voice said from the right. Noah looked over and saw that they'd drawn Kim Blankenship into the conversation. "Allison?"

"Yeah," Knox said, his voice lost in his throat somewhere.

"I knew her!" Kim said with wide gray eyes in a heavily made-up face. Under her hat, her bottle-blond hair was perfectly curled. She mixed a down-home, don't-mess-with-Texas attitude with vintage movie star glamour. "She came to my bungalow the morning before she was killed and led me through a personalized yoga routine. I'd overdone myself hiking a few days before, and she knew exactly what to do to help me work out the kinks. She was so sweet and personable." Kim planted a gloved hand on her hip. "Why, if I knew who did such a thing to her, I'd tie them behind my horse and drag 'em across the desert."

"I'm with you, sweetheart," her husband, Granger, agreed.

This struck up talk among most other members of the excursion. Noah watched CJ nod and concur as others voiced their opinions about Allison and the person who had brought her life to an untimely end. Noah wondered how good an actor the guy really was.

"You ride well, Steele."

Noah looked around as Joshua pulled his big, spirited stallion, Maverick, alongside Penny. "I detect disappointment."

Joshua laughed. "Did Adam tell you I'd leave you for the coyotes?"

"Something like that," Noah drawled.

"You can stop looking over your shoulder, Fender Bender. Accidents on the trail are bad for business."

"That's reassuring," Noah grumbled.

"You've been talking to CJ Knight."

"And you've been keeping tabs on me," Noah acknowledged.

"Part of my job," Joshua explained. "Did he mention Erica Pike?"

"Your brother's secretary?"

"Executive assistant."

"He didn't. Why?"

"No reason," Joshua said quickly.

"Why?" Noah pressed.

Joshua nickered to the stallion when the animal bobbed his head impatiently. "Laura thinks something may have happened between her and Knight. I asked Erica. She said it didn't."

"You don't think she's being truthful?" Noah asked.

Joshua shrugged, obviously uncomfortable with the subject. "It's no good—relationships between staff and guests. Or management and staff, for that matter."

"No wonder you think so little of Laura and me," Noah noted.

"That's another matter," Joshua told him. "You met her before you came here. And you're hiding something." He spotted Noah's look of surprise and snorted. "I'm the second son of Clive Colton. I know when a man isn't being truthful. I don't expect you to tell me what you're lying about, but I will ask you not to lie to Laura. Come clean with her or coyotes will be the least of your worries."

Noah knew what it was to be a brother. It was a shame Joshua would never know that he and Noah had something so crucial in common. "Laura knows who I am."

"I hope so," Joshua said sincerely.

Noah glanced back at CJ Knight. He was lifting his canteen to his mouth and taking a long drink. His manager, Doug DeGraw, unsettled on his mount, struggled to keep up. "That guy's a nuisance."

"Who?" Joshua turned in the saddle. "CJ's manager? We rarely get inexperienced riders on challenging drives like this one. But he insisted."

"Doesn't look like he's having much fun," Noah said.

"The man's sweating bullets," Joshua observed.

"I'm surprised he hasn't turned back."

"Knox offered to take him. He seems determined to stay by Knight's side."

Noah frowned. "Seems more like a nanny than a manager."

"I'm surprised you and Knight are getting on so swimmingly."

"Why's that?"

"Unlike you," Joshua said, "he's a Boy Scout."

"You think so?"

"Yeah. Like any celebrity, he values his privacy. But he's personable with other guests and staff. He's uncomplaining. He tips well and not because it's expected of him—because he's grateful."

"You like him," Noah stated.

"I do," Joshua said.

This coming from the guy who claimed he could spot a liar at fifty paces. If Joshua had guessed that Noah wasn't being entirely truthful, wouldn't he have been able to do the same with Knight if he was the killer?

Joshua tapped Maverick with his heels and rode ahead. He turned the horse to face the riders. "Congratulations! You've all reached the south point. We'll rest our mounts for a while before the return journey. Dismount. There's a creek down at the bottom of the hill where you can lead your horse to water."

A resounding thump brought Noah's head around.

Doug DeGraw sprawled beneath his horse.

CJ shook his head as his boots hit the ground. Gathering Doug's horse's reins, CJ extended a hand to him. "Something tells me you're going to need a masseuse."

"Forget that," Doug said, brushing himself off. He struggled to his feet with CJ's help. "Get me a stiff drink and an hour with a nimble woman."

Kim Blankenship rolled her eyes. "That one's a winner," she muttered as she led her horse down the hill past Noah and Joshua.

Noah took Penny to the creek. "Good girl," he said as she bent her head to the water that burbled busily over its smooth rock bed. He took a moment to admire where they were. There was no fence to mark the boundary of Mariposa, just an old petrified tree trunk with a butterfly carved into its flank. He could see familiar formations from the state park in the distance.

He'd always been drawn to that perfect marriage between the cornflower blue sky and the red-stained mountains, buttes and cliffs that jutted toward it. The wind teased his hair as he took off his hat and opened his canteen for a long drink.

Someone stumbled over the rocks, making Penny sidestep. Noah patted her on the neck until she settled. Then he watched Doug pry off one dirt-smudged brogue. "I told you those were the wrong shoes."

Doug groaned as he rubbed the bottom of his socked foot. "I miss LA. I can't understand why CJ keeps getting drawn back to this place."

Noah lifted his eyes to the panorama. "Can't you?"

"No." Doug stilled as a woman from their party brought her horse to drink. He lifted his chin to her in greeting. "Ariana, right?"

"Yes," she said. "And you're Doug, CJ's guy."

"Just Doug," he said. "You're the host of that new game show—*Sing It or Lose It.*"

"I am," she said, beaming. She was young, a redhead with large green eyes and long legs encased in jodhpurs. "Well, I don't exactly host. I'm the DJ."

"You should host," Doug asserted. He slid a long look over her form. "The network would draw far more viewers if they made you more visible."

She favored Allison. The resemblance jolted Noah, and he fought a sudden overwhelming urge to put himself between her and Doug.

Ariana stepped back a little, as if she didn't care for the way Doug was coming on to her either. Politely, she fixed a smile into place. "Thanks."

Noah cleared his throat, doing his best to draw Doug's attention away from her. "Your shoe's making a break for it."

"Huh?" Doug did a double take when Noah pointed out the brogue racing across the surface of the creek. He swore viciously and ran after it while Ariana giggled.

With Doug out of earshot, Noah moved toward her. "Here," he said, taking her horse's bridle. "They're building a fire. You go get warm. I'll make sure your horse is taken care of."

"Oh, thank you," she said, surprised. "Her name's Autumn. She's a sweetie. But I will join the others. That guy's vibes are way off."

"I'm starting to get that," Noah said.

"Hey." She touched his wrist. "That's an evil eye."

He looked down at the bracelet peeking out from under the cuff of his shirt. "Yeah. My, uh…" Licking his lips, he absorbed the pang above his sternum. "My sister gave it to me," he finished quietly.

"Did you know the evil eye dates back to 5000 BC?" she asked. "It's also used in symbolism across various cultures—Hindi, Christian, Jewish, Buddhist, Muslim…not to mention Indigenous, pagan and folk societies."

"I didn't know that," he said truthfully.

She rolled her eyes at herself. "I sound like a geek. But I love that sort of thing. You've got a light blue eye. It's supposed to encourage you to open your eyes to self-acceptance and the world around you."

"Interesting," he said.

"Is it?" Doug snarled as he returned with one dripping shoe.

Ariana stiffened. "I'll go get a seat by the fire."

"Sure," Noah said. He blinked when she was gone. For a moment, it had felt like he was talking to his sister again.

"Look at that ass work."

Noah sent Doug a long scowl. "A little young for someone like you, wouldn't you say?"

"I like them young," Doug said as he worked his foot into his shoe. "Things tend to be more high and tight, if you know what I'm saying." He chuckled nastily, cheered by his own imagery.

If the man didn't shut up, Noah was going to shove both brogues down his throat.

Doug stood finally and grabbed the reins of his mare

roughly. She rebuked him with a jerk of her head. "I knew someone with one of those."

On the verge of telling him to can it, Noah looked warily to where Doug pointed.

To Noah's wrist. He was pointing at Noah's wrist and the evil-eye bracelet.

Noah felt his jaw clamp and his stomach tighten. "Yeah?" he managed to drawl.

"Yeah." Doug lifted a brow. "That one... Ah, man. She was a real peach."

Was?

Under the watchful gaze of a high-noon sun, Doug led his mount up the hill, limping a little as he went.

"Son of a bitch," Noah muttered, clutching Penny's reins. He fit his hat to his head and led her and Autumn to the cluster of riders, wishing hard for his badge.

"YOU'RE SUPPOSED TO be resting."

Laura looked up from her desk and spied the dusty man framed in the open door to her office. She noted the Stetson and the wide silver buckle on his belt. Noah looked dirty and dangerous, and her heart caterwauled as he propped the heel of his hand on the jamb above him.

The man was the human equivalent of devil's food cake.

Setting the papers in her hands flat against the desktop, she studied his comfortable scowl and smiled broadly despite the ache in her head that had persisted throughout the day. "You're probably going to take what I say and run with it, but...you look good enough to eat, cowboy."

The scowl wobbled, and warmth chased the moody slant of his eyes. Pushing off the jamb, he closed the door.

As he came around the desk, she turned the swivel chair to face him. Angling her chin up, she tilted her head. "I'm happy to see Josh didn't bring you back to me in splints."

Noah leaned over, pressing his hands to the arms of her chair, caging her in. He scanned the mark on her brow and its ring of dark bruises. Then he searched each of her eyes in a way that made her lose her breath. By the time his gaze touched her mouth, she was shivery with anticipation. She clutched the collar of his shirt to pull him down to meet her.

His arms locked, resisting, when he found the gold chain around her neck. Gingerly, he slid his first finger between it and the skin at the high curve of her breast and lifted it, so the pearl drop rose from the V-cut neckline of her plum-satin blouse.

His eyes crawled back to hers.

"I've been thinking about you," she whispered.

He made a low noise.

Her chest rose and fell swiftly. She wished she could catch her breath. He made it difficult. "And I've missed you," she admitted.

He tensed. Then he lowered to his knees. His arms spanned her waist, and he tugged her to the edge of her chair.

When he buried his face in her throat and pressed his front to hers in a seamless embrace, she melted. Spreading her fingers through his hair, she latched on.

She couldn't handle him like this—urgent, tender, sweet. It disarmed her.

She swallowed. "Did something happen?"

His lips pursed against her skin. His breath across the damp circle left by his mouth made her skin hum all over. "I have to go back to Sedona."

"Why?" she asked, pulling back far enough to scan his face.

He stiffened. "I think I know who killed Allison."

"CJ Knight?" she asked.

"He was taking private lessons. I confirmed that. But I think I've been looking in the wrong place."

"Talk it through with me," she invited.

He eased back some, his hands lowering to her outer thighs. "*KB* is Kim Blankenship. Allison went to her bungalow for a lesson the day she died. But I don't think it's her either."

"Then who?" Laura asked.

His eyes hardened. *"DG."*

"You know who that is?"

"I think it stands for Doug DeGraw."

She squinted past the thumping behind her temples. "Isn't that CJ Knight's manager?"

"Yes."

"What makes you think he's guilty?"

"Other than that he's a complete and utter douchebag?" Noah drawled.

She sighed, nodded. "Yes."

"He was trying to flex on one woman. Ariana."

"Fitzgibbons," she said, plucking the name out of her memory files. "She's a new television personality. Beautiful, smiley, bubbly—"

"Like my sister."

She stopped. "They look similar," she granted.

Noah swore. "She's a dead ringer for Allison. And she knows things about spiritualism and symbolism. I felt like I wasn't just looking at Allison. I felt like I was talking to her, too."

"Noah," she whispered. "I can understand how that must have felt. I know how it would have affected me. But is the fact that Doug DeGraw was hitting on Ariana Fitzgibbons the only reason you believe he killed Allison?"

"No," he said vehemently. "He saw the bracelet. He recognized it."

When he lifted his arm, she saw the evil-eye pendant

around his wrist. "How do you know he recognized it? Did he say something?"

"Yeah." Noah's jaw locked from the strain. His hands gripped the arms of the chair again. His knuckles whitened. "He said he knew a woman who wore one. He said she was a real peach. I could've killed him on the spot."

"Okay," she said soothingly, laying her hands across his shoulders. "Let's just take a minute." For all his wrath, she could feel the grief emanating off him and she wanted to hold him until those waves came to shore. "I don't think you're in any condition to drive back to Sedona tonight." When he started to refuse, she spoke over him. "There's rain coming in. The roads will be wet, possibly icy. And it's after six—too late for you to make any headway."

"I need to nail this guy," he told her. "I need to look into his history, his record, his behavior—"

"Come home with me." She touched his face. "We'll soak in the pool, order dinner, then turn in before nine. That way, you can be up and out the door first thing in the morning. And you'll have the whole day to do whatever it is you need to do."

His frantic gaze raced over her. "It's him, Laura. He's the one who took Allison's life. He must've lured her to his bungalow, drugged her, then…"

A sob wavered out of her. She shook her head quickly. "Stop. Please, stop."

He released a long, ragged breath, dropping his head. "I still want to kill him. Crabtree was right. If I find something on DeGraw, I'll need to hand the arrest over to Fulton. If it's me… I don't know if I have what it takes not to put a bullet in him."

Her hands gentled on his face. She kissed the broad plane of his cheek. Then the space between his eyes before placing both palms around the back of his head and drawing him against her once more. "It's okay," she said, blinking back tears. "It's going to be okay."

He didn't pull away. They remained that way, still in the upheaval, for a while.

"Noah?" she whispered.

"Hmm?"

"Will you?" she asked. "Come home with me?"

He shoveled out a breath. Then he nodded, reluctantly.

When he stood, he extended a hand. She took it and let him pull her to her feet. Switching off the lamp on her desk, she grabbed her purse. On their way out, she stopped to lock the door.

"You lock your office but not your front door," he grumbled.

She stuffed the keys in her purse and reached for the handle of the glass door that led out of L Building. He beat her to it, shouldering it open and propping it until she'd passed through. He took her hand. "Wait."

She stopped moving. At the sight of his frown returning, she gave in. "I'll start locking my front door if it bothers you that much."

"Yes," he said with a nod. "But there's something else."

She was stunned when he gathered both her hands in his. As his thumbs stroked her knuckles in fast repetitions, she tried to read him. "What is it?"

"Promise me, Pearl," he murmured. "Promise me you won't approach DeGraw while I'm off property. I can't leave you here if I think you'll put yourself in harm's way for even a second."

She nodded. "All right."

"You promise?" he pressed.

"I promise." Unable to watch the conflict clash on the inside of him, she raised her lips to his.

As he inclined his head toward hers and his hand cupped

the back of her head, he let it be soft—let himself be, drawing out her sigh with a head-to-toe shudder.

He took her home, where they soaked in the pool. He remained close to her as she reclined on the steps. It was easy with him, she thought, not to cut through the water but to rest and let the moment stretch.

She offered to order in, but he found pesto, grape tomatoes, green beans, tortellini and chicken in her fridge. As she sat with her wine and watched him throw it all together in a pan over the stove, she saw someone channeling his demons. Filling another glass, she took it to him. He stopped long enough to clink it to hers, holding her gaze as he took the first sip. She did the same, then rubbed the bones that had been etched on the left side of his spine, leaving the right side blank.

She half expected to feel the inscribed tears in the flesh that separated the unmarked side of his back from the tattoos as she ran her fingers across his vertebrae. Warm, smooth skin greeted them instead, and she marveled again over the level of artistry he'd placed upon his body.

Noah mixed and flipped the contents of the pan so that the pesto coated everything.

He'd stirred, mixed and flipped her, Laura mused. He'd come at her like a demolition expert, knocking down walls, making a mess, hauling complete sections of those walls out.

He'd rearranged things.

Allison had called Laura a "classic Taurus," no more open to change than she was to heartbreak. *It's why you won't play with risk*, she'd told her.

Laura had shrugged that off. *Risk is overrated.*

Maybe, Allison had replied. Her wise eyes had flickered knowingly. *I'm just afraid that when you find someone who's right for you—really right for you—you'll shy away from the risk and lose the chance to get everything you've ever wanted.*

The sentiment had made Laura reevaluate everything. What if she'd already done that? What if she'd missed her shot because the risk scared her?

She and Noah were so different. Night and day, as a matter of fact. But as she watched the hair on the back of his head fan through her fingertips, as the tense line of his body eased and he lifted his face to the ceiling briefly to dig into her touch, she caught her lower lip between her teeth.

Could they be this different and this right for each other all at once? All the candles he lit inside her just by being whispered *yes*.

"You keep this up and I'm going to burn the first dinner I prep for you," he noted.

The first? Her heart leaped. She swallowed all the deeper questions and asked, "What's your sign?"

"What sign?"

"Your astrological sign," she clarified. When he gave her a long sideways look, she let a slow grin play across her mouth. "Come on. With a sister like Allison, how could you not know?"

"Please tell me you don't put as much stock in that as she did," he groaned.

"Not really," she said. "But it's a fun question. And I'm curious. You were born in November."

"You remember that?"

"Of course I do," she murmured.

He lifted the wineglass, taking a break to study her.

She smiled. "November either makes you a Scorpio or a Sagittarius. Which is it?"

Ever the man of mystery, he chose not to answer and took a long sip instead. Then he picked up the spatula and continued to stir. "I'm not a wine drinker. But this one's fine."

"It is," she agreed. "It's a rare vintage. One I've been saving."

He raised a brow. "For me?"

Why did he think he was worthy of so little? "Yes," she said, moving closer. "And after we eat, I'm going to find out how it tastes on your tongue."

The spatula clattered to a halt and his eyes fired. The tension hardened his features, but it had nothing to do with anger this time and everything to do with what they had made the last time their bodies had come together in a fit of urgency. He remembered that clash, she saw, and its sensational conclusion every bit as much as she did.

"Is that right?" he ventured.

She saw the smile turn up the corners of his eyes even as his mouth remained in a firm, forbidding line. "How much longer?" she asked.

"Not long," he guessed. He cursed. "Too long."

She wondered if his body had responded as eagerly as hers was. Crossing one foot over the other, she tried to tamp down on it. By pressing her thighs together, she only fanned the flame. She ran her hand over the small of his back, just above the line of the towel he'd wrapped around his hips, and made herself step away. "I'm going to change."

She made it to the corner before he spoke up again. "Scorpio."

She glanced back in surprise. His head was low, intent on the work of his hands. And she grinned because she saw the pop of color in the flesh leading from his collarbone to his ear.

His body *had* responded, and she could think of nothing more than unknotting his towel and letting dinner burn.

Taking a steadying breath, she said, "Of course you are."

In her bedroom, she opened the top drawer and pulled out the black nightie she'd bought online on impulse a few nights before. Lifting it by the straps, she considered. She hadn't thought she'd have the nerve to wear it for him. She'd thrown out all her nighties after the fiasco with Quentin, deciding she wouldn't need sexy finery again.

Carrying the gown into the bathroom, she closed the door after letting Sebastian follow her inside. She discarded her towel and the wet bathing suit underneath and hopped into the shower.

When she came back out, tying the belt of a black silk robe that had lived at the back of her closet for some time, the smell of pesto hit her. She followed the seductive aroma to the dining room table, where he had already plated dinner for them.

She stared at the candle he'd found on her side table in the center of the dining set. "My goodness," she said, at a loss for anything else.

He topped off her wine. "From the moment we met, I knew you were the candlelit-dinner type."

He pulled out a chair for her. Inwardly, she sighed. The hard man in the towel, quietly and devastatingly courteous, had no idea how irresistible he was. "Thank you," she said, turning her mouth up to his for a breathy kiss.

His eyes remained closed when she pulled back. His head followed hers as she lowered her heels to the floor. "You smell good. You always smell good." When his eyes opened, they were unfocused. "I could eat you alive."

"Tortellini first," she insisted.

He dropped his gaze to the silk covering her. "Are you wearing anything under that?"

Later, she cautioned herself when, again, adrenaline and desire surged. "All good things," she whispered before she lowered to the seat, tucking the robe around her legs when it parted over her thighs.

He pulled out the chair next to hers. Lifting her glass, she drank before lowering it back to the table and picking up her knife and fork. "This looks excellent."

"It'll get you by."

"Mmm," she said after the first bite. The different flavors gelled. Together, they were perfectly delectable. "Noah. This is fantastic."

"I just threw things together in the pan."

She jabbed her fork in his direction. "Modesty doesn't suit you. I watched you make this. You'll take credit for it."

"Or?" he asked and popped a long green bean into his mouth, chewing.

She reached for the bottle of wine. "I could pour this fine vintage over your head."

"You'll taste it on the rest of me, then," he said darkly. Wonderfully.

Images hit her brain, inciting more answers from her body.

"What's it going to be, Colton?" he asked, amused, when she didn't let go of the bottle. The delicious light of challenge smoldered behind his eyes.

Jesus. Did he play with fire often? Because he was good at it. She placed the bottle back on the table. "Fortify yourself," she told him, nodding at his plate. "You're going to need it."

Shaking his head, he muttered, "A little over an hour ago, I didn't think there was anything that could make me forget what's going to happen tomorrow. But you could make me forget the world if you put your mind to it."

That had been her goal. Hadn't it? Now she could only think about wanting him in her bed again. He'd been there since that first night they'd made love. He'd slept beside her. But this time, she wanted more. To make him forget, yes. But also because...

Because she *needed* him. "Eat," she said. It was the only safe word she knew.

They cleaned their plates, and he cleared them. She polished off her wine. Before he could think about washing dishes, she took his hand. "Follow me?" she asked, grabbing the soft faux fur blanket draped over the back of the couch.

As she led him to the back door, he said, "Anywhere," before sliding the glass panel open for both of them.

She held that inside her, letting it feed her, as she led him around the chairs and pool to the path that tumbled down one flagstone at a time to the base of the natural hill her bungalow dominated.

The sound of trickling water led her. Little lights on either side of the path would be turned off soon in adherence to Dark Sky Community guidelines. The stargazing party would leave soon in the Jeeps provided by the resort, with the blankets and hot cocoa offered during cooler nights. The chill in the air was sharp.

"Is there a stream here?" he asked as the tumble of water grew louder.

"When I was a kid, it was a river," she told him. "This is all that's left." A small swath of moonlight shimmied over stones as water hurried across them. "My mother would walk here every morning. Sometimes she would bring me and the boys. But mostly this was her spot."

"Is that why you built your place at the top of the hill?"

"Yes," she said. "It was my way of feeling close to her."

His hand didn't leave hers as they stood listening to the water babble. "Do you find that fades…more and more as the years go on?" he asked quietly.

Her eyes sought his silhouette. As they adjusted to the dark, she carved him out of the night. Hooded brow, firm jaw, solid as the mountains that held the sky. "Yes," she admitted.

He nodded slightly. "So do I."

She tightened her hold on him, bringing his attention to

her. As his feet shuffled to face her, she let go to reach for the belt of the robe.

He stopped her. "You'll freeze."

"It's why I brought the blanket," she said. "Will you hold it?"

He took the furry coverlet. Anticipation high, she untied the knot.

She wished she could see him better, but the moon was behind him. Knowing it bathed her, she parted the silk and let it slip from her shoulders.

She heard his breath tear out of him. Trailing her fingers over the low-cut neckline and transparent lace, she followed the cascade of silk to her navel. "What do you think?"

"I knew you'd drive me wild."

Intrigued, she planted the heel of her hand against the granite slab of his chest. "You feel okay to me."

"Laura, I—"

She bit her lip when he stopped. "Yes?" she breathed, wanting to hear exactly what he'd censored himself from saying. She waited long enough that she shivered.

"You are cold," he confirmed. He swung the blanket around her shoulders. "Let's go back to the house."

"No." With her hand still on his chest, she backed him up to the large chaise underneath a collapsed red umbrella.

He went down hard, grunting. She knelt on the thick cushion. It was cold, too.

They'd warm it, she knew.

She felt his hands close around the blanket on her shoulders. Using it, he brought her against the heat of his chest and rolled her beneath him.

She did taste the wine on his tongue. She tasted herself there, too, as she lay beneath him, shivering not from the cold anymore but the storm of worshipping open-mouthed kisses. They started somewhere around her instep and spread to the back of her knee, up the inside of her thigh, between them where he lingered, using lips, tongue and beard to push her over the edge. Then his kisses continued over her hips, navel, breasts, to the bridge of her collarbone where he found the pearl. He sipped the delicate ridge of her jaw, and at last took her mouth.

She'd brought him here to seduce him. The thick fur blanket lay heavy over their tangled forms as he joined with her. Long, deep strokes built fresh waves of sensation. The cold didn't penetrate the lovely languid haze of his loving, and she knew she was the one who had been completely, utterly seduced.

"Look at me."

Her eyes had rolled back into her head. She made her lashes lift.

His face was half shadow, half light. His hips rocked against hers in an unbroken rhythm and she found she had swallowed the fire. It burned so good, she wanted to bathe in it.

His mouth parted hers. His eyes remained fixed. "Again," he breathed into her.

She shook her head slightly even as the next climax gathered steam. His hand was between them, coaxing her at the point where their bodies met. She was trembling all over, a string about to break even as his touch made her pliant and soft for him.

His chin bobbed in a listless nod. "Do it," he bade, need bearing the words through his teeth.

She didn't have it in her to shy away. And she realized she'd thrown caution with him to the wind days ago. She burned, feeling like a phoenix as she let the firestorm take her. All of her.

He groaned, long, low, satisfied. "That's right," he whispered and added, "Stay with me," when she pooled beneath him. "Stay with me," he said again, quickening.

The base of his erection pitched against the bed of nerves at her center, and she dropped the crown of her head back, gasping at the assault of unending pleasure. He had to stop. She was going to catch fire.

No one… No one had ever brought her this close to blind rapture. No one had made her bare her soul like this before.

"Noah."

His response hummed across her lips as his brows came together.

Ardor painted his face, and she moaned. "I'm yours."

He swore. The word blew through the night as he buried himself to the hilt. His body locked, arcing like a current, and he slammed his eyes closed, suspended in the rush.

When his muscles released, he made a noise like a man drowning. She raised her hands to him, stroking as his lungs whistled through several respirations and his heart knocked like a ram against hers. Lifting her legs, she crossed her ankles at the small of his back and dragged his mouth back to hers, not ready to give up the link.

"I'm crushing you," he said when he caught his breath at last.

"No."

"Laura, baby. I'm heavy."

Baby. Her smile was as soft as the blanket. "You're perfect, Noah Steele."

He stilled in her embrace. It even seemed like he stopped breathing.

"A little while," she sighed soothingly, running her nails lightly over his upper arms. "Let's stay just like this a little while longer."

He made another noise, this one of assent.

Eventually…eventually, she agreed they had to get out

of the cold. And when he wrapped her in the blanket and carried her back up the flagstone steps to her house, she was speechless.

Chapter Seventeen

Mariposa's anniversary always felt bittersweet. Twenty-two years ago, Annabeth Colton had escaped Los Angeles for Red Rock Country, where she'd purchased the hotel.

Today was cause for both celebration and reflection. As Laura went about her duties, she couldn't help but wonder whether Mariposa reflected her mother's vision two decades prior. For Annabeth, it had been both home and a place of hope and renewal.

Laura tried to focus on that and not everything she had learned from Noah the night before.

When CJ Knight and Doug DeGraw crossed her path, however, she thought even Noah would agree the mission verged on impossible.

"Ms. Colton," the actor called out, forcing her to stop on the path to S Building. "I hear there's going to be a show tonight."

"Yes," she replied. "We'll have music and canapés in the rock labyrinth from six to seven this evening, with fireworks to follow. Will you be joining us?"

"Wouldn't miss it," CJ asserted.

Laura looked at Doug. "And you, Mr. DeGraw?"

"If it's better than the excursion yesterday and today's massage." Doug rolled both shoulders back in a discomfited manner. "I wonder why Mariposa is the go-to destination for the rich and famous. I can't find much to recommend it."

As Laura's face fell, CJ cleared his throat. "Come on, Doug. You don't mean that." To Laura, he offered an apologetic smile. "I enjoyed the horseback excursion, and my massage was more than satisfactory. We're booked for lunch at Annabeth. I've told Doug your chef never disappoints."

She returned the smile. "I'm glad you think so." Uncomfortable, she looked at Doug again. "Is there anything I can do to make your stay more enjoyable, Mr. DeGraw?"

He raised a discerning brow. "You wouldn't know what bungalow Ariana Fitzgibbons is staying in, would you?"

"I'm afraid I can't divulge that information," she told him when she regained her voice. "It's against our policy to invade the privacy of our guests."

"Pity," Doug drawled. His mouth turned down at the corners, dissatisfied. "I guess I'll have to find out myself."

"I'd advise you not to do so," she cautioned.

Doug gave a small laugh. "Can't anyone around here take a joke?"

As he walked away, limping slightly on his right leg, CJ's smile deteriorated. He lowered his voice. "I'm sorry. He isn't normally like this. I've noticed he's been out of sorts lately. He practically begged me not to come back here."

She tried to appear as unaffected as possible. "Red Rock Country doesn't agree with everyone."

"I'm not sure how," CJ noted. "I get that Doug's a city guy. He's LA to the bone. But there's nothing I don't love about this part of the country."

"I'm happy to hear it," she said truthfully. "If there's anything you or your manager can think of to make your stay better, please let me know. I'll see to it."

"I appreciate it, Ms. Colton," he returned before hurrying to catch up with Doug.

Laura rubbed her hands across the surface of her arms. The chill had gone deep into her bones despite the desert sun doing its best to ward off the nip of late winter. Thunder rolled in the distance. She looked out across the ridge.

Steel wool storm clouds converged in the east, washing away everything except the foreboding that had been with her since Noah had kissed her goodbye in the wee hours of the morning. He had thought she was still asleep as he'd bent over her still form and skimmed his lips across the point of her bare shoulder before brushing the hair from her neck to repeat the motion there.

She'd wanted to turn onto her back then, ring her arms around him and roll him into the sheets with her. But she'd kept her eyes closed as he'd kissed her cheek and lingered there, his hand moving down her spine to rest warmly in the curve of her hip.

He spooked so easily when he was like that—tender and unguarded. She'd continued to feign sleep, absorbing the sweetness and tranquility.

It wasn't a simple thing, giving her heart to a man who could so easily break it. And yet, in that moment, she'd had no choice. She'd given it as she never had before. Freely.

Laura stared those storm clouds down, daring them to intrude on tonight's festivities. She wanted to follow Doug, track his movements, make sure he stayed far away from Ariana Fitzgibbons and every other woman at Mariposa.

"Come on, Noah," she whispered desperately before continuing to S Building.

THE STORM SPLIT and spread its quilting across the sky. Sunset burned ombré shades across, so the clouds glowed terracotta and apricot one moment, then orange and mauve the next. At last, the day died in a somber cast of mulberry, inspiring a round of applause from the multitude of guests who gathered at the rock labyrinth over steak and blue cheese bruschetta bites and spicy blue crab tapas.

"And that wasn't even the part we planned," Joshua said, amused, as he passed Laura a tall glass of champagne.

"No," she said. She sipped. "You cleaned up well."

"Thank you," he replied, running a hand down the front of his blue button-down. He'd popped the first few buttons on the collar, but the shirt was pressed, and he'd combed his hair back from his face, leaving his striking features to be admired by all and sundry. He glanced over at her. "Let's not pretend I'm the one turning heads tonight."

She peered down the front of the glittering, long-sleeved cocktail dress she'd donned. Its color brought to mind champagne bubbles, and its open back from the waist up made her aware of the swift decline in temperature. "A girl needs to shine now and then," she mused.

Joshua's lips curled knowingly as his champagne hovered inches from them. "If Steele were here, he'd swallow his tongue."

The thought brought out a full-fledged grin. "Perhaps that was the idea. It might've worked if he'd made it on time."

Joshua raised his wrist to peek at his watch. "He could still make it."

"I've learned not to hold my breath."

Joshua sipped, swallowed and looked at her contemplatively.

She narrowed her eyes. "What is it, Josh?"

"Is there something you want to tell me?" he asked. "About you and Fender Bender?"

"What makes you think there is?" she asked, tensing.

Joshua lowered the glass. "Because I looked him up. Noah Steele has never played for Fast Lane."

Her smile fled swiftly.

"How could he when he's been working for the Sedona police for seven years?"

Oh, no. "Josh," she began.

He stopped her with "Is he really even your boyfriend?"

She couldn't miss the light of hurt beyond the forced jocularity on his face. "No. Yes." Closing her eyes quickly, she shook her head. "I don't know. I—"

"How could you not know?" he asked, bewildered.

"I don't know how to explain," she tried to tell him, but he was on a roll.

"Is this about Allison?" he asked. "Is that why he's here? Did he manipulate you into being part of his cover?"

"He didn't *make* me do anything," she argued. "It was my idea."

"So he's not the reason you've been lying to me all this time?" he asked. "You decided that on your own?"

"I'm sorry." She grabbed his arm before he could walk away. "I couldn't tell you. He needed intimate knowledge of Mariposa's staff and guests. He needed to know the resort from the ground up, every operation, inside and outside."

"I knew he was hiding something," Joshua muttered. "I just didn't think you were in on it. We've always told each other *everything*, Laura."

"I know," she said, forcing herself to look him in the eye, however much the accusation in his wounded. "I'm so sorry."

"What's going on?" Adam asked.

Joshua pointed. "Our sister's been keeping things from us."

"About?" Adam prompted.

"Steele," Joshua said. "He's a cop."

"I know."

Joshua stared, aghast. "You know?"

"Yes," Adam said.

"So you've both been keeping things from me."

"Mariposa had to continue as usual," Adam stated, not missing a beat, "with no one the wiser except Laura and myself."

"Why not me?" Joshua asked. "You didn't think you could trust me?"

"Of course we trust you," Laura told him.

"But you have a tendency to wear your heart on your sleeve," Adam informed him. "You also party and socialize more extensively than the two of us. I'm sure you would have had every intention of keeping Steele's actual reasons for being here to yourself. But it would have been all too easy to let something slip."

Joshua's jaw worked as he digested the information. His accusing gaze sought Laura again. "He spent the night with you."

Adam shifted uncomfortably beside her. Awkwardness pressed against her. It clung like shrink-wrap. "He did," she said.

"You don't think that's taking your role a little too seriously?" Joshua questioned.

She swallowed when the taste of anger coated her mouth. "I'm not going to take that—from you or anyone else. I don't have to explain what Noah and I have to either of you."

"I'm not asking," Adam pointed out.

"Not now," she granted. "But you have questioned it."

"Because I thought you would get hurt."

"I'm in love with him," she blurted. "If we're being honest, I might as well throw it out there. I've fallen in love with him and we're all going to have to come to terms with that."

Neither of her brothers seemed to know what to say anymore. Laura was relieved by the reprieve, though she sensed this wasn't over. They would need to discuss this more at another time and place. She and Adam would need to address Joshua's hurt. He would need to know the full details of Noah's investigation. There was no going back, no hiding anything from him anymore.

"He's making an arrest soon," she told them both.

"When?" Joshua asked. "Tonight?"

"I don't know precisely," she said. "I haven't heard from him since this morning. But he's gathering evidence to secure a warrant. Soon, he'll go, and this will all be over." There was relief and dread in the finality of that. With luck, Allison's killer would be locked away for good.

But Noah would be leaving Mariposa.

"Who?" Adam asked quietly.

She searched the crowd for the person she couldn't deny she had been keeping tabs on since the party began. She located him over at the buffet table, not far from CJ. "I'm afraid I can't say. Not without Noah's authorization."

Joshua wasn't heartened by the news. "Fantastic. I can't believe I actually liked the guy. I can't believe I trusted him with you."

Laura glanced around quickly to make sure no one would overhear. Then she hissed, "Allison was his sister!"

"What?" Joshua exclaimed.

"She was his sister," she repeated. "He needed help. I gave it—for her."

Joshua stepped back. He pinched the skin at the bridge of his nose, closing his eyes. "This is a lot to process."

"Then take a beat," Adam advised. "We'll speak about this, however much you need to. But come back when you're ready to do so civilly."

Joshua dropped his hand. He glanced in Laura's direction but didn't quite meet her eye. "I've said some things tonight I'm going to regret later."

"Adam's right," Laura said. She tried swallowing the guilt and hurt. Together, they formed a knot that was anything but small. "We'll talk more when you're ready."

He lifted his empty glass. "I need another."

As he moved off, Laura dropped her face into her hand. "Oh, God, Adam. He's so angry at me."

"He's angry at us."

"I made you keep this from him," she reminded him. "You didn't have to take any of the blame."

"I may not understand all the reasons you did this," Adam explained. "But I will never not stand beside you. I thought you knew that."

His ferocity was something to behold. She wanted to tell him she loved him—that she was sorry that he had to weather Joshua's resentment and accusations, too.

Before she could put any of that into words, Erica said, "Excuse me?" In a black cocktail dress and heels, she looked elegant, but her beauty was subdued by the frown playing at her mouth.

"Yes, Erica?" Adam asked kindly.

"They're ready for your speech," she said, gesturing to the stage.

"Right." Adam downed the last of his champagne. He took the note cards Erica had at the ready, then straightened his collar and tie. "Wish me luck?"

"You always bring down the house," Laura murmured. "But good luck."

He gave her a single nod before taking the steps to the bandstand two at a time.

"I was wondering if I could speak to you," Erica said to Laura. Embarrassment and hesitancy battled for purchase on her face.

"Certainly," Laura told her, trying to inject some measure of cheer into her voice. It didn't work as well as she'd hoped.

"I heard a rumor," Erica said. "About the investigation."

"What kind of rumor?" Laura asked.

Erica coaxed the words out, paling as she did so. "They say that CJ Knight is a suspect."

Laura pressed her lips together, wondering what exactly to say. "He may be," she said, hesitant.

Erica shook her head. "That isn't right. I mean, you see, I…" Releasing a breath, she lifted a trembling hand to her head. "He has an alibi."

"He does?" Laura asked, surprised.

"Yes," she decided. "I lied to you and to Joshua. I'm not entirely sure what came over me that night. The night Allison was killed."

"You were with him," Laura intoned.

"I was with him," Erica agreed with a nod. "CJ and I… were intimate. It happened in his bungalow. So he couldn't have done it. He couldn't have killed Allison. And he wouldn't have. He may be the one-night-stand kind of guy. But he's not the type of man who would murder someone."

Laura set her champagne aside. She placed her hand considerately on Erica's arm. "You need to tell the police. You'll have to in order to clear Mr. Knight of all suspicion."

Erica absorbed this news. Her eyes widened, but she nodded slightly. "Of course."

Laura squeezed her arm gently. "It's a good thing you're doing, Erica."

"Do you think Adam will fire me?" she whispered faintly.

"It hasn't interfered with your ability to do your job," Laura noted. "I think we can all vouch for that. I'll speak with Adam, and we'll see about moving forward from this once the investigation's over."

Erica nodded. "Thank you, Laura—for being so understanding."

Laura simply nodded. As Erica slipped away, Laura looked around. She found Joshua near the bar, talking to Valerie. Adam was at center stage, cuing the band for his speech. Alexis and Tallulah stood shoulder to shoulder as they chatted with Greg and Tallulah's nephew, Mato, who held a tray of canapés on an upraised palm.

She spied CJ Knight at last as he spoke with Knox and Kim Blankenship.

If CJ had been occupied with Erica at the time of Allison's death, Noah was right. Guilt now lay squarely at the feet of...

"Ms. Colton."

The chill started at the base of her neck. It trickled down her spine as she pivoted on her heels to confront Doug De-Graw. He wore a suit in charcoal gray with a black shirt underneath. He'd gone without a tie, and the shirt was buttoned to his throat. His Adam's apple jutted over its neat collar and his cool smile turned her blood to ice.

"Mr. DeGraw," she greeted him. "I see you decided to join us. How was your lunch at Annabeth?"

"Superb."

She forced a smile. "Mr. Knight is correct. Our chef rarely disappoints."

"The food was all right," he said with a wave of his hand. "It was the company that was divine."

Her brows came together. "The company?"

"I slipped the maître d' a fifty. He seated CJ and me next to Ms. Fitzgibbons's table."

The smugness of his grin...the light that entered his eyes... They made Laura take a steadying breath. "Is that so?"

"Yes." He took a step toward her while Adam spoke into the mic on stage and those around them quieted. "You needn't worry. Ariana knows she will benefit from the attention of a man like me. And she's more than willing to take it."

Her lips numbed, and she realized she was pressing them hard together. "What did you do to her?"

"Do?" He chuckled. "Nothing she didn't ask for. In her

own way." With a wink, he slithered off to stand with CJ and the others.

Laura's heart drummed. She barely resisted the urge to place her hand over her mouth as she searched the crowd desperately for the red hair of Ariana Fitzgibbons.

When she couldn't find her, she walked briskly to Roland. When he leaned down to hear what she wanted to say, she kept her voice low. "Doug DeGraw. Do you know who he is?"

"CJ Knight's manager," he said.

She nodded. "Can you keep an eye on him for me?"

"Yes."

"If you see him leave the party, I'm going to need you to call me on my cell phone," she explained. "Immediately. Can you do that?"

"Of course I can." His wide forehead creased. "Should I be concerned about anyone's safety?"

"Not at this time," she said, again looking around, wishing Ariana's face would pop out of the crowd. "The moment DeGraw exits the rock labyrinth…"

"I'll place the call," he finished. "You have my word."

"Thank you," she murmured, then walked away as Adam's speech wrapped to the roused clatter of applause.

"Ms. Fitzgibbons?" Laura called. She knocked again on the door of Ariana's bungalow, louder this time. "Ms. Fitzgibbons!"

No answer came. The windows remained dark. Laura cupped her hands around her face to peer through the nearest one.

A shaft of moonlight revealed an empty couch and table.

If Ariana had returned to the bungalow before sunset, she would have left a light burning before she'd departed again.

Trying not to panic, Laura sprinted along the path to the VIP bungalows.

When she reached Bungalow Two, where she knew Doug was staying on CJ's dime, she slowed.

Noah had made her promise not to approach a suspect. That promise made her hesitate on the doorstep.

She wasn't approaching a suspect, she reasoned. Doug was back at the rock labyrinth, where she knew Roland would watch him.

Raising her fist, she knocked on the door. When she heard nothing inside, she pressed her ear to the door, willing her pulse to stop knocking so that she may better hear a call for help.

When none came, she peered through the window. The blackout curtains had been drawn.

Frustrated, she tore open her beaded handbag and extracted her master key. If Ariana was in there and she wasn't answering, Laura could only assume she had been drugged, like Allison. That maybe she, too, had been given too much and was…

She swiped the master key. The lock chirped and a green light blinked. Laura pushed the door open and stepped inside.

She switched on the light beside the door.

There was no sign of a struggle. As she shut the door behind her, she peered at the couch. The cushions weren't mussed. A pair of men's shoes sat tidily near the door to the patio. There was a glass of wine, unfinished, on the kitchen counter.

Laura stared at the last sips of dark red wine. She saw the faint impression of lips on the rim. No lipstick.

Through the glass door, the pool sat undisturbed. Folded towels lay in the corner on a raised surface, compliments of Housekeeping. Laura counted one, two, three. None of them had been used.

She twitched the curtain back in place. There was no sign of a woman here. No sign that anything nefarious had taken place.

She eyed the short passage to the bedroom and clutched her handbag tighter.

If she could find proof…if she could help Noah nail Doug DeGraw…this would all be over. Allison's killer would be caught.

Laura stepped toward the bedroom door. It was open. She turned on the overhead light, illuminating the white linens on the bed.

She scanned the space, wondering where to start. Doug's toiletry bag lay on the dresser. His suitcase was open on the rack near the bathroom.

She searched all the outside pockets first, then lay a hand flat between folded shirts. After running her hand around the inside rim to no avail, she checked the toiletry bag. Careful not to disorganize the high-end men's products she found inside, she shifted them one by one. Nothing hid underneath them except a sample sleeve of under-eye cream.

She stepped back, making sure everything looked exactly as it had before she'd begun her search. Frowning, she turned a slow circle.

Where else would a guilty man hide evidence of wrongdoing?

She opened the drawer on the nightstand. Nothing there— not a single dust mote.

The corner of the sheet stuck out kitty-corner underneath the coverlet. It had slipped from its holding under the mattress.

…under the mattress…

Hadn't Fulton found Dayton Ferraday's drug stash under the mattress or inside it?

She went down on her knees. Like she had with the shirts, she reached underneath the mattress and felt around.

Her hand met something cold. It rolled, then tinkled against something else. She grabbed the thin item and pulled it out into the light.

The vial was translucent, but she could see the liquid within. On the side, there was a label.

Fentanyl.

Holding her breath, she reached underneath the mattress and found the other vial and a ten-milliliter syringe, empty and capped. It looked like the kind used for insulin.

She placed them on top of the bed and dug into her bag. Remembering to breathe, she pulled out her cell phone and stood. When she unlocked the screen to place the call to Noah, she paused.

She'd missed a call—from Roland.

She checked the time stamp. He'd tried calling ten minutes ago.

It hasn't rung, she thought.

She checked her notification settings and her heart dropped.

After exiting the party, she'd forgotten to take her phone off Silent.

Don't panic, she coached herself. She'd simply take a picture of the evidence, then replace it and slip safely out of Doug's bungalow.

Quickly, she framed the vials and syringe in her camera view. She tapped the screen when it tried focusing on the fibers of the comforter underneath and ignored the sound of her heartbeat in her ears.

She snapped a couple of pictures, then stuffed her phone back in her bag. Replacing the vials, she left the covers on the bed as they should be. Then she stood and took two steps to the door before an item on the floor made her stop.

It lay innocently enough underneath the hook where Doug had hung his overcoat. A leather string with an evil-eye pendant.

Laura bent down to retrieve it. She raised it to get a better look and her lips trembled.

It must've fallen from the pocket of his coat without his knowing.

A sob rose as she studied the evil eye. Unlike the one she had given Noah, Allison's was light green. She'd once told Laura it granted her success in dreams, good health and contentment.

Laura felt a whisper of air across the bare skin of her back and the hairs on her arms and neck stood on end.

Before she could turn, he took her down at the waist.

She met the wall with a clatter, knocking the lamp over on the bedside table. The impact knocked the wind out of her.

Fingers raked through her hair and drove her face into the wall.

A dull gray film slanted across her vision. Her ears rang. She blinked, trying to bring everything back into focus as he spun her roughly around.

It took several seconds for Doug's face to solidify in front of her.

"Ms. Colton," he said with a sneer.

She saw his fist raised to strike. Before he could swing, she took up the fallen lamp on the bedside table. The lampshade fell. She arced the neck of the lamp toward his face and threw her weight into it.

It hit him. The bulb shattered and he toppled sideways on a shout.

She made a break for it, fumbling for the door.

She slipped in the hall. Her heel came off. She left it, scrambling to her feet as his footsteps chased her.

She ran out of Bungalow Two, screaming.

Chapter Eighteen

Fireworks crackled and thundered. Their lights sparkled across the path to L Building, illuminating her escape route in intermittent bursts.

She melded into the manicured hedges and cacti that lined the path, willing the rocks under her feet not to give her away. She'd lost her other heel. The sharp edges of stones bit into the undersides of her feet. She didn't slow. With her knowledge of Mariposa, she could locate help before he found her.

There was blood in her mouth. She'd bitten her tongue when he'd mashed her face into the wall. She swallowed it and kept going. Something dripped across her lips. She licked them and tasted blood there, too. Reaching up, she swiped the space above them. It came away wet and warm.

Her nose was bleeding. The pulse of pain around the bridge alerted her to the damage there.

Her fist was still knotted around Allison's bracelet. She hadn't lost it in the altercation.

She wouldn't lose it, she determined as she pushed on. The roof of L Building was visible through the foliage. She could see the lights of the pool. Her heart lifted. She was almost there. Someone would be there. Someone had to be.

First, she had to cross the open pathway. She glanced around. Hearing no footsteps, she made a break for it.

A cut on the bottom of her foot slowed her, but she half sprinted for the shape of the first pool cabana—the one where they'd found Allison.

Before she could reach it, fingers dug into her arm. She fought them, reaching for escape.

Doug shoved her off the path into the rocks on the other side. Her hands and knees scraped across them.

He covered her mouth before she could scream. "You couldn't leave it alone, could you? Couldn't live and let live?"

His hand covered her nose. She fought for air, her nails digging into his hand. Desperate, she threw her head back into his face.

He grunted. His hold loosened.

She turned over, scrambling away from him. Her back met the long stalk of a cactus plant. Its fine needles dug into the exposed skin of her back.

Doug was on her in a flash. She did scream now—before he could silence her.

He struck her across the face. The shock of the blow silenced her, as did the fingers he wrapped around her throat. The pressure he exerted made little rockets of flame blossom before her eyes. Her ankles kicked against the rocks. The stones scattered, preventing her from gaining purchase. Again, she clawed at his hand. The bracelet dropped.

He glanced down at it, then back up at her. "I don't like killing," he groaned as he watched her struggle. He shook his head to emphasize the point. "I never meant to kill anyone. If she'd been willing...if she'd just spread her legs for me... I wouldn't have had to subdue her. I wouldn't have given her too much."

Her lungs burned. Her eyes went blind.

"It was such a waste," he muttered. "Wasn't it? I hate

thinking about it. Just as I'm going to hate thinking about you, Ms. Colton. Such a beautiful waste."

She fought to stay conscious. She fought to see something other than the whiteout she found when her eyes rolled back. Still, her kicking slowed and she hooked her hands over his arm because they'd fallen away from his fingers. The ocean roared in her ears. It was so loud, it drowned his words.

His grip fumbled away from her. His weight lifted. She gasped, choked, wheezed and coughed. As she fell sideways across the rocks, she reached for her neck, where the phantom hold of Doug's fingers stayed even as she took a breath that raked across her airways.

In the light from the path and the stunning bright lights screaming into the sky—the fireworks' grand finale—she saw two figures, one on top of the other, struggling on the ground.

Her hearing sharpened with the whistle and boom of rockets overhead and shouting. The haze around her vision broke and she realized what she was seeing.

Noah, his face a mask of fury, arced his fist down to meet Doug's face again and again.

Someone else—Detective Fulton—raced forward to pull Noah off. Noah fought him. Fulton didn't let go.

Doug stayed on the ground, curling in on himself. His face was a mess of blood. He didn't get up.

Noah shrugged Fulton off him. Rocks slid underneath his feet as he scrambled over them. He crouched, his hand going to the back of her head. "Laura."

She was afraid to speak. Her throat felt bruised. Sucking air in and out in careful repetitions, she watched his features sharpen.

There was fury there. But more, there was desperate fear. "Hey," he said. "Can you hear me?"

She gave a faint nod.

He blew out a breath, then cradled her to him. She closed her eyes because the cold had gone deep into her bones. She didn't know if it was the temperature or nearly being choked to death, but she lay still, absorbing the heat of him as he held her.

He pulled away. His gaze seized on her throat. "I need to get you to the hospital," he said gruffly.

She opened her mouth, but the words got trapped behind the pain. Looking around over the rocks, she fumbled a hand over them, searching.

She found the little braided cord and lifted it.

When she offered it, he took it from her and raised it to the light. At the sight of the evil eye, he stilled. "Where did you find this?" he asked.

Afraid, she locked her lips together.

He searched her face. Then he shook his head. "You didn't."

She lifted her chin in a half nod. A tear slipped past her guard. She wished she could look away. Then she wouldn't have to watch his disbelief meld into disappointment.

"Laura," he said. "You promised. You *promised* me."

His voice broke and her stomach twisted. *I had to*, she wanted to tell him.

His grimace was complete. It went through her. As he looked away, closing his hand around the evil eye, she felt it as keenly as a knife.

NOAH SPENT AN hour at the police station, watching Doug DeGraw be questioned, booked and processed. Even if he couldn't be the one leading him through it, he needed to watch, just as he needed to hear the bars roll into place as the man who admitted to killing Allison was locked in a cell.

An accident, he'd claimed. Allison had shown up at his bungalow after dark for his private yoga lesson. When she didn't respond to his attempts at seduction, he dosed her with fentanyl and waited for the drug to take effect before having his way with her.

"After, she didn't come around like the others do," Doug had claimed. "She just lay there. She didn't breathe. I checked and realized her pulse wasn't right. It was too slow. I tried to make her come around. She just lay there. Lay there and died."

"You handled yourself well," Captain Crabtree told Noah after they both watched Doug sign a confession.

"He's beat to hell," Noah pointed out, surveying the damage he'd done to Doug's face.

"You saved Laura Colton's life."

And nearly killed the man who'd almost taken it. If not for Fulton, Noah knew he would have done worse. Each of the knuckles of his right hand ached like a sore tooth from the impact with Doug's nose, jaw and cheekbone. "I've still got a job on Monday?"

"You closed the case," Crabtree noted.

Noah had spent the entire day on the phone, tracking victims in the wind. He'd finally found one—a twenty-three-year-old colleague of Doug's who had quit her job a year ago and moved to Tallahassee to live with her folks. She'd been reluctant to talk, and Noah had thought he would have to fly to Florida to speak with her face-to-face. But then she'd broken, and the story had come out. Doug had drugged and raped her, too, similarly.

There were others, Noah knew. A half-dozen women Doug had sedated and terrorized. Noah would find them all. He would bury the man for hurting them, for killing Allison and for nearly killing Laura.

"He tried to frame CJ Knight," Noah said. "He assumed calling him away from Mariposa soon after Allison's death would throw suspicion on him. It might have worked, too, had Erica Pike not come forward."

"Knight was here while you were in interrogation. He confirmed he was with Ms. Pike during the time in question, but not much more."

"What did he have to say about his manager being the killer?" Noah asked.

"He was in shock. He didn't seem to know what to say."

"I should've seen it sooner," Noah muttered. "It was Doug's office who refused to return my calls, not Knight directly."

"You were pretty deep in the reeds on this one," Crabtree said knowingly. "But Fulton didn't see it any faster than you did. I'd like to give you both credit for the arrest."

"All that matters is that this scumbag is going away forever."

"Now you can focus on laying your sister to rest. And you'll take some time off."

Noah closed his eyes. He needed to let Allison go. He knew that. And Crabtree was right. It was time. "Yes, sir."

The hospital was five minutes from the SPD. Despite the cold and the sleet that fell sideways, he walked there.

"Laura Colton," he said to the woman at the information desk.

"It's after visiting hours."

He dug into his pocket before placing his badge on the desk for her to see.

She frowned. "One moment," she said before tapping the screen in front of her. "Ms. Colton is in recovery. Room twenty-four."

"Thanks," he said before exiting the atrium and following the corridors to the Recovery ward. She wasn't in surgery, he consoled himself. Or the ER. Which meant she was going to be okay.

He'd heard her scream. As he'd followed Fulton across the pool area on the way to Bungalow Two, he'd heard her call for help. At first, he'd thought it had been coming from the pool cabana.

Like Allison, he'd thought, frantic. Then he'd discovered the couple grappling in the dark off the path behind it. He'd seen Doug on top of Laura, his hands around her throat, and he'd nearly screamed himself hoarse.

Noah passed the door to number twenty-four. He halted and backtracked, the soles of his boots squeaking on the clean linoleum.

Through the window, he could see her brothers, one on either side of her. Joshua was hunkered down beside her in bed. Her head nestled on his shoulder while Adam sat on the bed's edge, his arm across the top of her pillows, head low over hers.

Noah thought about walking away, leaving them alone. They were family. A proper one. And a proper family took care of their own.

He watched as his hand rose to knock.

Adam lifted his head as the others stirred. He motioned for them to stay where they were as he stood and crossed to the door. When it opened, he looked at Noah. More, he looked through him before blinking and seeming to come to his senses. "Oh," he said. "It's you."

"Can I come in?" Noah asked.

Adam ran a hand through his hair. It wasn't as neat as it usually was. "Are you here on police business?"

He should have said yes. What came out was "No."

Adam nodded and stepped aside.

Joshua sat up as Noah entered. Noah looked past him to Laura. She had raised herself up on her elbows. He could see the cut on her mouth, the red mark around the bridge of her nose, the fading bruise on her temple, and the shadows of hands on her throat that would soon fly their colors, too. She looked weary around the eyes, but clarity rang true in them.

Joshua rose and moved into Noah's path to the bed. When Noah only sized him up, Joshua offered him a hand.

"What's this?" Noah asked cautiously.

"I'd like to shake hands with Allison's brother," Joshua said.

The others must have told baby brother everything, Noah realized. He reached out and took Joshua's hand.

The man squeezed his. "If you hadn't gotten to her in time…"

Noah had thought along the same lines. If he and Fulton had been a minute behind… If he'd spent any longer on the phone tracking Doug's victims…

"You lost your sister," Joshua said, "and saved mine. I won't forget that."

"Nor will I," Adam added. "We owe you an immense debt of gratitude."

He didn't want their gratitude. He didn't want Joshua's idea of a truce. He'd spent the better part of the evening chiding himself for working after hours. If he'd been with Laura at the party, she wouldn't have felt compelled to run off into the night and…

He saw Doug's hands around her throat again. He heard her choking. His hands balled into fists and he felt the quaver go straight through as fear lanced him.

"May I speak with her?" he asked. "Alone."

"She's tired," Joshua began.

"It's all right, Josh," came the small, hoarse sound of her voice.

Joshua reached up to scrub his temples. Then he turned and went back to the bed. "A few minutes," he allowed, leaning down for a hug. "Then we all need to get some sleep."

"You don't have to sleep here," she told him. "Either of you."

"You don't have to talk," Adam replied as he, too, came forward. Joshua stepped back and Adam lowered a kiss to the top of her head. "Rest your throat. We'll be right outside the door."

"Definitely not listening," Joshua said with a half-hearted, ironic twist of his mouth.

Noah waited until they'd both left. When the latch clicked shut behind them, he approached the bed. Then he halted, conflicted. "I have a couple of questions."

She sat up a bit more. Wincing, she lay back on the pillows.

It nearly broke him to see her struggle.

She spoke haltingly, fighting the rawness of her throat. "You *are* here on police business."

"Your brother's right," he said. "Don't try to talk."

She tilted her head. "Questions require answers."

"Just nod," he told her. "Or shake your head. That's all the answer I need."

She sighed and, slowly, subsided into a nod.

"Ariana Fitzgibbons has been located. It seems Doug was just yanking your chain when he claimed he'd done something to her. She left Mariposa for Sedona after lunch with a friend she made during yesterday's trail ride. They spent the afternoon shopping and caught dinner after."

Laura's lips folded as she spun the hospital band on her wrist. She tried clearing her throat and closed her eyes. When she opened them again, there was a pained, wet sheen over them. "I'm glad she's all right."

It was a miracle Laura was, he thought. Digging in his pocket, he pulled out Allison's bracelet and held it up. She watched it swing from his hand.

"Did you find this in Doug DeGraw's bungalow?"

She hesitated. Then she inclined her head.

"You went to his bungalow?" When she nodded, he wanted to stop. He didn't want to know—didn't want to have to replay it in his head repeatedly. "Did you go there alone?"

Laura's eyes were heavy-lidded with fatigue and swimming in regret as she nodded again.

"Did you find anything else in Doug's bungalow?" At her nod, he said, "Drugs?" She nodded once more. He wanted to raise his voice as the storm inside him built. Desperate, scared, angry storm clouds he couldn't lasso. He had to work to keep his next question cool and flat. "Do you remember last night?"

Tears came into her eyes again. For the first time, she turned them away from him.

He gripped the bottom rail of the bed. "I need your answer."

She nodded.

"You remember promising me you wouldn't put yourself at risk?" he asked. "You remember looking me in the eye and giving me your word before you took me home with you and made love with me for the rest of the night?"

Lips taut together, she nodded. A tear slipped down her cheek.

His heart twisted. And it hurt. It hurt so much, he couldn't breathe. "I trusted you," he said in a whisper.

"I'm sorry," she whispered back. "I thought… I thought he hurt her. Like Allison."

He wanted to go to her. He wanted to slip inside the bed with her and hold her all night—until the storm quieted. Until he could breathe right again.

The early bruising on her throat glared at him. She'd made a promise. He'd needed her to keep it. He'd relied on her word. She'd broken it and nearly died before he could get to her.

He turned away.

"Where are you going?" she asked as he made a break for the door.

He wrapped his hand around the handle. Christ, he couldn't breathe. It was exactly as it had been in the autopsy room when he'd viewed Allison's lifeless body for the first time. He felt a part of his mind detach, float away. He wanted to follow it. But his body anchored him. His lungs strained, his chest felt tight and his head spun. Panic sank in. "I need some time."

"I'm okay."

He looked back and felt the quaver go to his knees. He heard the pounding of his heart in his ears. "You're not," he argued. "I can still see him choking you and hear you fighting for air. And I can't do this. Not until that gets quieter. I need time."

"How much time?" she asked.

"I don't know," he replied. He looked away from the tears falling freely down her face now. He had to get out of there before he split in two. "I don't know," he said again, at a loss. He snatched the door open.

"Noah," she called.

"Get some rest," he replied. Then he was out the door. He bypassed Adam and Joshua and their questions, needing to walk until he could no longer feel fear locking up the muscles around his lungs.

Chapter Nineteen

Laura had never seen so many orchids in her life. Most were rooted in pretty pots. The colors ranged from warm to cool. Some clashed, like the one with blue petals and pink centers.

Allison would have loved the symbolism. Laura tried to remember what each color meant. Red for strength. Purple for dignity. Orange for boldness. Yellow for friendship and new beginnings. Being surrounded by them would have made her friend happy.

Laura held that certainty in her chest as the memorial service came to a close. The setting of nature's cathedral—cloudless, open blue sky above, the carpet of earth beneath—brought to mind Allison's teachings of mindfulness and inner strength. *Sky above us. Earth below us. Fire within us.*

Allison's fire had been extinguished. And those who loved her, who came to pay their respects, had to learn to live without her—to move on. It was as simple and as hard as that.

Laura waited in line with her brothers to lay a rose on Allison's coffin. Over a hundred people had come to pay their respects from Sedona, Mariposa and across the country—yoga and meditation students, her friends and, of course, her brother, who had sat alone in the first row.

Alexis met Laura on the green. "It was nice, wasn't it?"

"Yes," Laura said. "Funerals are never easy, but this one made the last few weeks better somehow."

"It reminds me she's at peace," Alexis explained.

"She is," Laura murmured.

Alexis searched the crowd. "If you're looking for a tall, dark and handsome detective, he's doing well to avoid people over there."

She saw Noah's lone figure and her heart gave a squeeze.

"You know you could have let me in on your secret," Alexis told her.

Alexis wasn't accusing or unhappy with her. Still, the guilt came for Laura. "I know. I never thought for a second you would give me or Noah away. And I wasn't thinking clearly enough to realize how the lies would hurt others." She found Joshua mingling, grave-faced, with some former Mariposa guests. "I regret that now."

"Tell me one thing," Alexis said. "That conversation we had at Annabeth—next to those poor shrimp?"

Laura thought about it, then closed her eyes. "Oh. The shrimp."

"You talked about you and Noah spending the night together. Was that part of the act?"

Laura shook her head silently.

"So the two of you really..." Alexis trailed off when Laura nodded. "But he's over there. And you're over here."

"Precisely," Laura said with a weary sigh.

"What happened?" Alexis asked.

Laura felt relieved she was free to tell Alexis everything. Still, she found it hard to explain what had gone wrong the night Doug was arrested. "I broke a promise to him."

"What kind of promise?"

Laura shifted her feet. Her heels poked through the bed of grass, making her reposition them for balance. "He lost Allison in the worst way possible. And before that, he lost his mother similarly. He doesn't get close to people because he's afraid of losing them."

Alexis's eyes strayed to the marks on Laura's neck that were visible above her knotted black scarf. "He almost lost you, like he lost them."

"I promised him the night before I wouldn't confront Doug like I did Roger and Dayton Ferraday," Laura admitted.

"Why did you?" Alexis asked.

"I thought he was going to hurt someone else or already had. It was the same way when Tallulah told me that Bella had been hurt. I didn't think."

"You went into mama-bear mode." Alexis nodded. "I get it."

"Those men brought terror, rape and murder into my home," Laura said. "They brought it into a place where those things were never meant to exist."

"Have you told the man this?" Alexis asked.

"We haven't spoken since the hospital. He said he needed time."

"Allison would take this moment to remind us that time is fleeting," Alexis said, "and there's no time like the present."

"She would," Laura admitted.

"Is that Bella?" Alexis pointed her out in the crowd.

Laura shaded her eyes with her hand and waved when she spotted the young woman standing close at Tallulah's side. "Yes."

"Is it true she's coming back to Mariposa?" Alexis asked.

"Not yet," Laura said. "She still needs to heal. But I think she will, eventually. Tallulah won't be happy unless she has her under her wing. And I think Bella's learning how strong she really is."

"We'll all take care of her," Alexis asserted. "Not just Tallulah."

Laura couldn't agree more. "Are we still on for Taco Tuesday?"

"Absolutely," Alexis confirmed. "The Tipsy Tacos' owner

called to say they're planting a tree in Allison's name in the courtyard where they're opening up the space for outdoor dining."

"I love that," Laura declared.

Adam and Joshua walked to them. "We're going to pay our respects to Noah," Joshua told Laura. "Want to come?"

She took Adam's arm when he offered it. "Of course." To Alexis, she said, "We'll talk later."

"You know it," Alexis returned.

As the three Coltons ventured closer to the tree line, Laura watched Noah. She knew the moment he spotted them. He didn't so much stiffen as still—like a deer in the headlights. Laura felt her stomach flutter with nerves.

Sensing her agitation, Adam whispered, "Steady on, Lou," and curled his hand around hers.

She fought the inclination to lean on his solid form, especially as the distance to Noah shrank to inches and, suddenly, they were face-to-face.

"It was a beautiful service," Joshua told him.

"You did well," Adam pointed out.

Noah looked past them to where the coffin stood. "Thanks," he replied. Sliding his hands into the pockets of his black suit jacket, he shrugged. "I'm not sure what I'm going to do with all the orchids."

"You could take some home and donate the others to the hospital or nursing homes," Joshua suggested. He glanced at Laura and Adam in question. "Didn't we do that when Mom...?"

"That's right." Laura smiled at him softly. "We did."

Noah cleared his throat. "You guys reached out to help, and I refused it. I just want you to know I appreciate the offer."

"We're going to miss her," Joshua said. "Allison was the kind of light the world needs."

Noah lowered his head and nodded. "She was."

Laura could hardly stand to watch his shoulders rise and fall over a series of hard breaths.

"We're dedicating the plaque to her in the meditation garden tomorrow evening at six," Adam said quietly. "You should come. The plan is to light a paper lantern and let it fly. Laura and Alexis will light it. We'd like you to be the one who releases it."

Noah kept his head down. He bobbed it in a solitary nod. "I can do that."

Joshua reached out. He grabbed Noah's shoulder. "You need anything, Detective, call me. Penny's available whenever you need a long country drive. I can accompany you as a guide...or as a friend."

Noah looked at him with the light of surprise. "Thank you."

Adam reached out to shake his hand. "I'm holding on to Allison's fund. I don't care if it's now or thirty years from now. If you think of something you'd like to do in her name, all you need to do is let me know."

"I'll remember," Noah pledged.

Adam looked at Laura. "You need a minute?"

She nodded. "Please."

"We'll wait by the car," Joshua told her before he and Adam strolled off.

Noah ran his eyes over her. He pulled a long breath in through the nose, his chest inflating. "You look stunning," he said on the exhalation.

She lifted a hand to the neck of her dress. "That's sweet of you."

He glanced around at the lingering mourners, unsure what to say or do.

Laura reached out, then stopped. "Are you all right?" she asked.

"No."

He didn't dress it up or deflect. That was something.

"What can I do?" she asked. He hadn't accepted help with the service. He would hardly lean on her now, she knew. Still, she had to ask.

"You're here," he replied simply.

"Of course I am," she murmured.

"Let me look at you a minute," he requested after some thought. "Would that be okay?"

She nodded. "More than okay."

He took a step back. His eyes didn't dapple over her. They reached. The yearning in them, the necessity, made her heart stutter. They started at her feet before winding up the path of her skirt to her waist, her navel, her bodice, before landing on the bruising that hadn't yet faded from her neck. He blinked several times, lingering there, before circling her face.

She saw so many things in him, and they matched what was inside her—regret, need, longing, hesitation... There was so much she wanted to say to him. *I miss you. I love you. Please, lean on me. Just...lean.*

Her breath rushed out. "Noah."

He muttered a curse. "Part of me wants to chase these people off so I can have a single moment alone with you."

A match touched the dry tinder inside her. Hope flared as the fire caught.

"What would you do with that moment?"

His tungsten-green eyes spanned her face. They landed on her mouth as he answered quietly. "Beg."

Her breath caught. "No."

"Yes," he argued. "I told you I needed time. But I should've called. I should've checked on you."

She smiled knowingly. "Adam told me you called him to check on me. Every day."

"I should've grown a pair and called you," he grumbled.

"Why didn't you?" she asked. The distance had convinced her he didn't want this—whatever they'd made between them. And it had hurt—more than the bruises on her throat.

"Because I'm a goddamn coward," he said plainly. He paused, considering. Then he closed the distance to her. "You still want to know my secrets, Laura?"

She could smell the light touch of cologne he'd put on his skin. The flame popped, lighting little fires everywhere else inside her to catch and grow, too. "Yes," she breathed.

"I'm hands down, one hundred percent, head over heels in love with you," he said.

She closed her eyes. "You don't have to—"

"I do," he asserted. "I didn't call. Not because I couldn't move past what happened the night of the arrest. I didn't call because I've been grappling with the fact that you are the only woman in this world that I want. You're the only person I want next to me. And I don't deserve you, because what kind of man walks away from Laura Colton? What kind of man runs from the chance to be yours?"

"It's okay—"

"No, it's not."

"But it is," she said, bringing her hands up to his lapels. She traced them with her palms, caressing him as his lungs rose and fell under them. "We're both here now. You're saying these things. And you won't walk out again. Will you?"

He gripped her wrist. He didn't pull her away. Instead, he touched his brow to hers. "No." He ground out the word. "I won't walk out again."

They stood together as a strong breeze swept across the cemetery, lifting flowers and hats into the air. Laura felt the skirt of her maxidress flapping around them like wings, but she didn't move.

As the wind died down in increments, she said, "Tell me another secret."

He made a noise. After a moment, he answered. "I used to braid her hair when she was too little to do it herself."

She smiled at the image. "Softy."

"Yeah," he admitted. "She was the only person who knew that side of me—until you."

"Say more things," she requested.

He thought about it for a second. Then he lifted his wrist, pulling back the cuff of his jacket sleeve. Here, she'd noticed he carried a solitary feather on the inside of his arm. "This was my first tattoo. It's my favorite."

"You *do* have a favorite," she mused, touching it.

He nodded, his head low over hers as she traced the feather's shaft. She heard his slow inhalation and knew he was smelling her hair. "It's for my mother."

"Oh, Noah," she sighed.

"Every Christmas, I drive up to Washington and retrace my steps with her there. I go to the coast and hole up in a cabin we used to rent in the summer. I don't have anything of hers. We didn't have much. And everything that was hers got lost after she was killed. I only have memories. Every year, I'm afraid I lose more. I go to the cabin to remember, because if I don't, did she really even exist?"

"Yes," Laura assured him. "You're proof of that. Not just because you're here. Because you are the man you are—the kind that would take care of a little girl who had no one. The kind who puts bad guys behind bars and who does your sister and your mother proud every day."

He turned his lips to her cheek and kissed her softly. Lingering.

"I want this," she told him, her hands grabbing his lapels. "I want you. And if you try to tell me again that someone like you doesn't deserve me, I've got some ideas how my brothers can alter that line of thinking."

"Coyotes?"

"There's a gorge, too," she added. "What do you say, Detective?"

He scanned her, and his eyes were so tender they made all those little fires inside her hum. "I'm going to keep calling you Pearl," he warned.

"I'm used to it."

He nudged the pearl drop on the end of the gold necklace she hadn't taken off since he'd put it there. "My pearl."

When he said it like that, she shuddered and understood. "Do you want me? Do you want this?"

"Yes," he said, finite. "I want you. *All* of you."

She brought her hands up to his face. "Then you should know," she said, "I'm hands down…" She canted her head at an angle. "One hundred percent…" She skimmed a kiss across his mouth. "Head over heels in love with you, too."

His hands caught in the belt of her dress. "Come home with me," he said, whispering the words across her mouth.

"What about Sebastian?"

"Bring him."

"You don't like pets."

"I said I've never had one."

"You do now. I'm going to need my own drawer."

"Baby, you can take the whole damn closet. I'll have a key made for you. Just stay with me. Please."

She heard the plea and melted. "We both know my answer."

"I need to hear it," he told her. "Say yes."

"Yes," she told him. "I'm coming home with you, Noah. And I'm staying."

When he kissed her, his intensity brought her up to her

toes. Incapable of letting go, she wrapped him in her arms as his banded around her waist.

Laura knew he would be the fire her heart would warm itself by for a long time to come.

* * * * *

COMING SOON!

We really hope you enjoyed reading this book.
If you're looking for more romance
be sure to head to the shops when
new books are available on

Thursday 27th February

To see which titles are coming soon, please visit
millsandboon.co.uk/nextmonth

MILLS & BOON

LET'S TALK
Romance

For exclusive extracts, competitions and special offers, find us online:

- **f** MillsandBoon
- **X** @MillsandBoon
- **⊙** @MillsandBoonUK
- **♪** @MillsandBoonUK

Get in touch on 01413 063 232

afterglow BOOKS

Afterglow Books is a trend-led, trope-filled list of books with diverse, authentic and relatable characters, a wide array of voices and representations, plus real world trials and tribulations. Featuring all the tropes you could possibly want (think small-town settings, fake relationships, grumpy vs sunshine, enemies to lovers) and all with a generous dose of spice in every story.

♪ @millsandboonuk
◎ @millsandboonuk
afterglowbooks.co.uk

#AfterglowBooks

For all the latest book news, exclusive content and giveaways scan the QR code below to sign up to the Afterglow newsletter:

SCAN ME

afterglow BOOKS

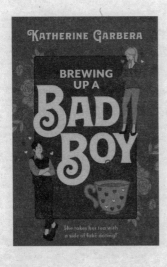

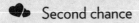